Barry Litherland

THE C⟨

Published by New Generation Publishing in 2014

www.newgeneration-publishing.com

 New Generation **Publishing**

Chapter 1

The body was that of a man of about fifty years of age. He was heavily bearded and lay, as if resting, with his back against a solitary boulder which lay to the rear of the cave. His hair, shoulder length, had the colour and appearance of calcified rock and clung to his face as if scared it might be parted from it. Water trickled from roof to walls and over the body. The face glistened in the flickering light that penetrated, briefly, into the darkness. One knee was raised, the other leg lying stretched out along the damp ground. His arms hung loosely at his side, his palms and fingers buried in the mud that covered the floor. His narrow, hostile eyes were unflinching and stared malevolently towards the entrance. In that dead face, they had an uncanny and unnerving sharpness, as if they alone were alive and had continued to watch suspiciously long after the final breath had left the body. The body was entirely naked, obscured only here and there by tiny rags that hung incongruously across his torso as if cast there by a long-vanished breeze.

For a moment Garth remained motionless, conscious only of the monotonous dripping of water, measuring the passing of years in the calcite growths that fell and rose like reaching fingers. He shuddered from a chill that ran deep, as if the air in that place was capable of reaching beneath his skin and bone to something deeper. He stared at the figure and, hideously, their eyes met. Unwillingly, through them, as if telephone lines connected them, the dead man asked him questions to which there could be no answer.

The line snapped; the link was broken. Garth stepped back and back again and stumbled out of the cave into the late afternoon April light.

His trek to the cave had begun early that morning. The route he had chosen, when planning the lengthy approach, could not be described as pleasant. The few guide books that deigned to make any reference to it described it as involving an uncomfortable slog over a vast, barren tract of unedifying land where the effort invested to cross it was out of all proportion to the return it could offer. Most guide books simply ignored it and very few people ever ventured there. A shorter route existed from beyond the village of Laurimore, some eight miles distant, but it too was rarely used and it was Garth's particular desire to begin the expedition to find the cave right from his own door.

He was not even certain that the cave actually existed. The only convincing reference to it was in a book he had found which was written in the early part of a previous century. Even then, it was mentioned only in two brief paragraphs and a cursory footnote. It appeared to have stimulated little interest and to have evoked nothing in the prosaic mind of the writer. He merely noted a low entrance, almost completely hidden and easily overlooked, a main chamber sufficient for a man to stand upright in, an unpleasant and sickly smell and a number of animal bones, probably from some poor creature that had taken its final refuge there during one of the spells of appalling weather that engulfed those hills. He had made a prompt exit and had moved on.

However, intriguingly, the writer also noted, '*I was drawn, however unwillingly, to peer into the uncertainty beyond the light cast from its narrow entrance, an action whose consequences none could have foretold. I was grateful that wiser minds than my own drew me back and reminded me that there are depths into which the human mind must not delve.*'

It concluded by saying, *'We covered and sealed the entrance so that no future traveller should be similarly tempted, nor waste his time on a futile search,'* a statement which was as curious as it was perfunctory.

Even if the existence of the cave could be assumed, its precise location seemed to have remained a matter of consequence to no-one. It was not indicated on any map of any scale that Garth could find. The information in his one source book was irritatingly sparse. It was only by a process of triangulation – in this case the referents being the topography, the rock strata and the one or two dejected looking clues from the book, - that he had managed to convince himself of the place where it might potentially be found.

When he awoke that morning and saw through his bedroom window how the cloudy skies gathered and wrinkled like a frown, it took no effort of imagination to picture a face, hidden there, displaying no encouragement to his foolish venture. He felt little inclination to move and was sorely tempted to remain in bed and enjoy a day at home, completing the many tasks that were required of him.   To make matters worse, the sky, which had been merely grey, was growing steadily more overcast and threw a sombre mood over the whole landscape.

However, he had persuaded himself that the adventure would be worthy of the effort and, since his rucksack was packed and his plans laid, it seemed ungrateful not to make best use of the day in the way he intended, so he clambered from his bed and, soon afterwards, headed out of the house. The almost pathless way began across a field not many metres from his new home and headed away from the familiar, enticing and attractive routes, - the mountains, the rivers and the lanes, - to ascend over grey heather towards distant, rounded hills.

After an hour, the few sparsely scattered houses in the valley were lost beyond a low, gradual slope and the road sank silently into the obscurity of a light mist. Unalleviated by any sense of movement, the whole landscape was enclosed, captured and imprisoned beneath a ceiling of cloud and within walls of bleak, unvarying moorland. It seemed that the only movement discernible for miles around was his heavy progress. Each step he took forced its way against the passive resistance of rock, heather and grass. He felt like he was intruding in a hostile land.

The first few miles followed an indistinct, rocky path, probably created by the passage of deer seemed to make its progress down the narrowing valley in a joyful and excited fashion, as if hurrying from the grey hills to join some colourful festival in the valley towards which it felt a natural bond and an immediate affinity. Occasionally the water lingered in deep pools which mirrored the pools of lemon primroses which grew along its banks.

Garth's pack, well stocked with provisions and emergency equipment, leaned oppressively against his back and jutting stones caused him to stumble occasionally. He was obliged to maintain a focus which rarely shifted from the ground before his feet. In the humid air perspiration trickled, stinging his eyes and attaching his clothing to his skin in a most unwelcomed fashion. Periodically, the path, - soon quite indistinct, - vanished for fifty metres at a time, giving way to wet peat or stretches of bog only to emerge smaller and weaker at the other side, as if its strength had been sapped by its transit. Soon it gave up and vanished altogether.

Garth began to wonder why he had chosen to undertake this journey in the first place. Was it merely that he was bored with the routine of renovation, repair

and decoration that had occupied him for several
weeks? Was he growing resentful of the seemingly
endless delays and problems that separated him from
Alice and Euan who had to remain in the town?
Perhaps his temporary isolation had permitted this
elusive and nondescript cave to flourish unnaturally in
his imagination and to fill with thoughts the unhealthy
void that was in his mind. He was increasingly aware
that the decision answered a need, which had been
growing in him for some days, to escape the confines of
the house and to experiences the empty wilderness of
the hills.

He stopped by a stream to splash his face and the
cold freshness of the water reinvigorated him. He was
gradually gaining height and, here and there, creased
and aged faces of rock peered from the hillsides. Above
him ravens curled, twisted and dived and in the
distance deer barked and barked again. By the early
afternoon he recognised clear indications of a change in
the rock strata. Lateral lines of limestone, fissured and
scarred, rose before a narrowing gorge through which
the stream, now bubbling and jovial, rolled across
white beds. Above him, even the clouds seemed to have
momentarily relented and, as if by way of an apology,
the sun smiled coyly from a brightening sky.

After another hour, as he approached the watershed,
he saw the limestone cliffs he had been searching for,
away to his left. He headed towards them to begin his
quest. In reality his search was of a remarkably short
duration. By what acts of nature the cave entrance came
to be cleared to a height of two feet he could not
imagine, but it lay at the foot of an escarpment and was
surrounded by a space free of vegetation and packed
loosely with black, wet peat.

It was with some difficulty that he found a route
along the foot of the escarpment where, by hugging

close to the rock, he could avoid sinking to his knees in the foul, dark pools. It was not, however, without mishap that he finally rolled into the cave mouth and rose from the musty floor to view the cavern he had sought. He grappled for the torch with his wet hands and its beams slowly penetrated and illumined by patches the depths of the cave.

When he recalled the events shortly afterwards, Garth had no clear recollection of what he expected to find in the cave. He tried to explain that he had given it very little thought. What he could assert, quite forcefully, was that he was completely unprepared for the scene that met his gaze.

Chapter Two

Detective Inspector Jack Munro liked brevity. He was brief himself, conveying an impression of angles and sudden shifts. As a young man he would have been described as wiry but now, in later middle age, his wiriness had tarnished somewhat and had lost something of its rigidity and form. He put to one side the statement of the previous day's events that Garth had just signed. He scratched an unshaven cheek with one finely chiselled hand and drummed the table with the other. He leaned back and sighed.

'Very detailed,' he said, 'and very thorough. Thank you.' He leaned forward and frowned.

Garth looked at him irritably. Only a day had passed since his exploits on the moorland and he was conscious of being fractious and ill tempered. He was still tired. He had spent most of the previous evening scribbling notes, just as Jack had asked him, and another hour had passed this morning completing his statement and answering seemingly endless questions.

'Jot down some notes. Do it as soon as you can; tonight, if possible,' Jack had said. 'I'll see you tomorrow early for a formal statement. Be detailed. Include anything and everything.'

He had done just as he was asked. If Jack was dissatisfied why then ………

'Well,' said Jack slowly, 'you can't be expected to notice everything - the floor of the cave, for example? Were there any marks, footprints perhaps, before yours? What about in the entrance? Did you see any signs that another person might have been there before you?'

Garth shrugged and shook his head. 'I didn't see anything on my way in,' he said, 'and afterwards I was too busy getting out. I had no intention of going back inside to check, not after ......'

'Quite! Quite!' Jack interrupted, turning back to the document and flicking through to the last page. He looked at it and then at Garth.

Soft, hazel eyes looked towards Jack and then flickered uncertainly. Jack's eyes were wires and sparks.

'No, it's very good,' he said, 'very detailed. It's the last paragraph, that's all. Are you sure you want to include it?' He shrugged. 'A little melodramatic?' he suggested.

'You weren't there. There was nothing melodramatic about it. Call it a trick of the light or whatever you want but, for a brief moment, there was a light in his eyes and it felt as if he was looking directly at me. It was unnerving. They weren't the most pleasant eyes either.'

'It's enough to unnerve anybody, finding a body like that,' Jack murmured, thoughtfully.

Garth shook his head. 'It wasn't that,' he said, 'though it was somewhat unexpected. It was as if ....' He paused to collect his thoughts and to frame them into something meaningful, something that could communicate the sheer terror of the moment. 'It's hard to explain. In that split second I saw my whole life – not in detail, not even anything specific, but a terrible awareness of missed opportunities. It was futility and death, futility and death. It couldn't have lasted more than a second or two but my whole life seemed encapsulated there. Do you understand?'

'A shock like that can do strange things to a person,' Jack said aloud. He looked quickly at the figure opposite him. 'Too much imagination, too much time spent thinking about things,' he thought silently. He looked at the document again. 'From a purely professional perspective I'll probably ignore the last few words. They don't really add much.'

He looked thoughtfully towards the window.

'Why?' he asked suddenly, indicating with a wide sweep of his arm towards the more impressive neighbouring peaks. 'You have so much to choose from! Why would you venture up there? Even the sheep avoid it! Nobody goes up there unless they have to. The occasional group of stalkers might be led that way once every few years; a farmer might let his sheep roam the higher slopes in summer. Those who have to go there have the sense to cross from the west on quad bikes or drive up in Land Rovers until it's impossible to go further due to the wet ground. Nobody goes up there simply for the pleasure of it. So what inspired you to head up there?'

Garth shrugged and a lock of greying hair fell forward over his eyes. He brushed it back. There remained something in the inspector's manner which reminded him that he was still not excused or forgiven for locating a body in a distant and remote place to which, despite his protestations, the detective inspector too was forced to ascend.

Jack reminded Garth of nothing so much as a twisted wire frame over which an ill assorted collection of clothing had been hastily flung. He seemed to possess a degree of nervous energy which made a condition of rest or equilibrium difficult to maintain. His eyes would flit from object to object as if unwilling to rest anywhere for any length of time. Then, disconcertingly, they would suddenly focus sharply and fix their subject with a penetrating stare. It felt as if his mind was stripped naked before him.

'Why?' he repeated, fixing Garth with just such a stare, like a butterfly with a pin.

Garth glanced at the book which had furnished him with the motivation for the journey and which lay on the scarred surface of the mahogany table by his side. The words which related to the cave he could recite by heart. Those words had been seeds which germinated unexpectedly and, once having taken root, proved impossible to remove.

Why indeed. He wished he knew and could explain. The house from which he had departed that morning and which he had purchased some months earlier, lay in a narrow valley surrounded by mountains which seemed to rise precipitously on three sides. In the first few weeks of his residence, when he awoke, his eyes were drawn to the cliffs and summits of those precipitous mountains. He watched the shadows of misty ghosts pass over them. He saw them hide from him in white shrouds. He waited with delightful expectation for those sunny breaks which would reveal them with accentuated boldness and grandeur. One day soon he would begin to explore them and to find his way to the peaks and ridges and trace routes that would lead him to know and understand them. To look at them made him feel vital and alive.

It was against that background that he would undertake his great task and prove himself for once and for all. Having recently inherited a sum of money sufficient for his purposes he had bought Aultmore and would fund himself for a year or two whilst he attempted to break through the glass ceiling that had so far restricted him. He would study and he would write and he would embrace the inspiring landscape and immerse himself in it.

Yet it was not onto those mountains that he had ventured that day. Instead, he had set of in the fourth direction over an expanse of damp moorland, gradually gaining height towards distant, rounded hills with a few

rocky outcrops. It was a challenge he had to accept.
Why? His frustrated isolation and his acute boredom
with the seemingly endless list of renovations had
merely provided a pretext for a journey that had been
taking shape, as if in mist, for some weeks.

Now, at home again, he had time to reconsider the
whim – he could call it nothing less – that drew him out
there.

It was difficult to explain this decision to Detective
Inspector Munro.

'An officer and a small team of unfortunates have
gone back up today,' Jack said, with a note of
admonishment in his voice. 'I declined,' he added, 'on
the grounds of age and seniority. Besides,' he added.
'I'm sure we got as much as we needed. One journey
up that track in a Land Rover was enough. To follow it
with a two hour trudge was significantly more than
enough.'

'I seem to have caused rather a lot of trouble,' Garth
mumbled, risking a half smile. He withdrew the gesture
rapidly. Sharp needles of eyes noted and evaluated his
words and looks, as if screening them for any trace of
irony. The eyes relaxed.

'At least I didn't have to carry him down,' D.I.
Munro said. 'That too fell to younger arms and backs
and the significant expense of a helicopter. However, I
would avoid my uniformed colleagues for a few days,
if I were you. Drive nowhere and keep your car
garaged. They're a spiteful lot.'

Garth had first spoken to Jack Munro on the moorland
the evening of his dramatic discovery in the cave. He
had hurriedly gathered his belongings and descended to
a point on his route where a mobile phone signal was
briefly available. He had then lingered into the late
evening until he saw a group of police officers slowly

moving over the moor towards him. He had grown cold and weary, walking up and down to keep warm or sitting huddled on the heather in his emergency bag, but one look at their approaching faces was sufficient to warn him that he would receive little in the way of sympathy.

His first impression on meeting Jack Munro was of a man disturbed from prolonged rest and annoyed at the prospect of a troublesome level of involvement with the requirements of his office. He walked disconsolately at the rear of his team and breathed heavily. He grunted a brief greeting, declining to remove his hands from either pockets or gloves for the requirements of formality, and glowered from under greying eyebrows.

'Where is he?' he asked curtly, his shortage of breath precluding a lengthier conversation.

'About a mile and a half up there,' Garth gestured towards the route of the stream.

'Shit!' Jack muttered.

He gestured to Garth to lead the party on and fell to the rear with a singular lack of motivation or curiosity.

Now, in the comfort of his own living room, Garth had time to re-evaluate his original assessment of the Detective Inspector.

'When are your family joining you?' Jack asked, sitting in the relative comfort of the new home and sampling some shortbread biscuits Garth had made available to him. He sipped a cup of tea noisily.

'Next week if I can get the place habitable by then,' Garth glanced apologetically round the room in which they now sat. 'I've got a busy few days ahead but it should be sufficient for us to move in properly. I suppose that's why I took a day off. I needed a break before the final surge!'

Jack's eyes flitted sharply around the room. They did not linger on any particular piece of furniture or photograph for long but Garth was uncomfortably aware that he missed nothing. Those eyes gave an ominous warning that perhaps there lurked within this angular frame a rather sharper mind that he had anticipated.

He risked another smile. It took no great acuity to draw certain conclusions from the sparse collection of furnishings with which his home was currently graced. Jack nodded towards a matching pair of church pews which stood facing each other at right angles to a large, open fireplace. A large log crackled.

'St. Biddulph's at Inverstrach?'

Garth nodded, 'For a small donation to the church restoration fund,' he explained. 'They drive a hard bargain.'

'It's hard to haggle with the servants of God,' Jack agreed.

There was little else for him to note. Two firm, blue, upholstered chairs, on which they were currently seated, loitered uncomfortably beside a mahogany table. A number of variously coloured rugs covered, rather than graced, the stone floor. A pine dresser stood with its back to the wall, as if aware of its incongruity, and embarrassed to find itself adjacent to an unpainted door.

'Mock Persian,' Jack's attention was drawn by one particular rug. 'I'm almost certain that one used to grace the floor at the Inverstrach manse.'

'It ended up in the salesroom with some others,' Garth informed him, as he saw Jack's eyes fall upon each in their turn, 'and the pine dresser. The books, the laptop and the photos are my own.'

'So this is the book where you read about the cave?' Jack said, picking up the bedraggled and worn book from the table. 'He turned it over and then glanced inside. 'It must be even older than me,' he said. 'Marius

Dorling – never heard of him. It's not a local name. Still, I'll ask.'

'It's a reprint. It was first published well over a hundred years ago. Even this copy is fifty or sixty years old. I doubt you could find it now.'

Garth indicated the footnote which had drawn him to the cave and then the two further references within the pages which he had carefully marked.

'That's not much to go on,' Jack said. He put the book down and looked directly at Garth. 'It's not much of a reason to go traipsing around the hills, is it?' Without waiting for an answer he continued. 'The trouble with my job is the waiting,' he complained. 'I'm always waiting; waiting for the autopsy, waiting for the scenes of crime report, waiting for forensics, waiting for this, for that .... There's nothing to do; at least nothing I want to do.' He seemed inclined to conversation.

'You've got the structure looking sound now,' he said, looking round the room again. 'I see you've finished the roof and the guttering and pointing the stonework; very nice.'

'Another day should see the outside finished and, in the meantime, I'm making progress with the kitchen and the bathroom. They're nearly done.'

Jack nodded his approval.

Aultmore stood in four acres of ground, much of which was separated from the garden by a wire fence and was under rough grass. An agreement, begun by the previous occupant, whereby a neighbour grazed a number of sheep there, was to be continued under his ownership. It was an arrangement that suited both parties. A gravel drive carved a straight line to the house from the narrow lane which joined the village of Inverstrach to the village of Laurimore and then wound onwards in either direction to similar villages with similar names all of which shared the quality of being a completely forgettable and indistinguishable scattering of houses sketched unwillingly along the sides of a narrow road. Both villages sported the luxury of a small shop and a church and Inverstrach was further graced by the presence of a hotel and bar and a small primary school.

The drive leading to the house passed briefly through a sheltering copse of spindly birch trees before emerging between a field and rough garden. It finally halted in front of the main house, next to a detached, ruined building which was set at a right angle to the main structure. This ruin now had the character of an outhouse but it had once formed a small cottage and attached stedding. The roof of the cottage itself was supported by large, wooden beams, visible here and there where large slate tiles had slipped. It retained all its walls, a single wooden door and a pair of rotting window frames. It was still sufficiently intact to be used to store sundry items left by the previous owner. To these oddments Garth had added his paint, plaster and tools.

The stedding had fallen into a greater state of disrepair. Slates and timbers had succumbed to the joint influences of neglect and time. They had stumbled and then fallen inwards leaving a jagged framework of walls and torn timbers which only rose to their full height and provided cover at the gable adjoining the cottage. A tangled knot of grasses, ferns and brambles, were gathering slowly around the ruined edifice and were unrelentingly claiming it as their own. Jackdaws, in the early spring weather, had already staked their claim as sitting tenants and were shouting their rights from the rooftop.

'What about the ruin?' Jack asked.

'I'm not inclined to do anything with it yet,' Garth said. 'Perhaps when Alice and Euan arrive and we've had a few months here we'll start to think about it.'

His mind slipped back to the figure in the cave. 'Do you think it was suicide or was he murdered?'

'We don't know anything for sure,' Jack said, 'so we're waiting, waiting. There was a healed scar on the neck. It looked like a knife wound. Nasty too; it couldn't have missed the main artery by much. But it couldn't have killed him. It was an old wound. There were bruises too on the arms and legs.'

'Why would he have taken his clothes off like that?' Garth asked, 'Not the warmest of places for naked rambling!'

'Ah yes, the clothes – now those we do know a little bit about. He didn't take them off. They weren't his. According to my forensic friend they were a child's clothes.' D.I. Munro looked down at the threadbare rug by his feet. 'Waiting for this, waiting for that,' he said, 'I hate waiting!'

'So where were his clothes?' Garth asked, 'and what happened to the child?'

Jack didn't answer. A mobile phone rang. He sprang to his feet with an alacrity Garth had not anticipated. He had taken the phone from his pocket and raised it to his ear before it had time to ring a third time.

'Yes?' he snapped. 'Yes, Jack here.' He listened impatiently. 'What do you mean, you can't find it? It isn't going anywhere!' he exclaimed. 'How can it have gone? Don't be so bloody silly.' He listened intently for several minutes, only interrupting with occasional grunts. 'Okay, okay,' he muttered at last. 'The team must love you! The Grand Old Duke of York, they'll be calling you! You'll have to put it all in a report. I don't know how you're going to explain it. Keep searching for any sign of the missing clothing. It could have been deserted or buried close by. Then get back down here before you lose anything else. Let's hope the autopsy is more useful.'

He put the phone down. He sat down and resumed staring at the rug.

'Well?' Garth ventured.

Jack looked up.

'It's a good job I'm unconscionably efficient,' he laughed. 'That will teach them to question Jack Munro! If I hadn't taken the whole team up there right off, if I hadn't insisted, they'd have nothing! If it wasn't for Jack Munro..........'

He smiled triumphantly and his eyes gleamed.

'It's a puzzle though,' he said. 'I don't want to be the one who has to explain it.' He shook his head and sat back down. He reached for his cup. 'How do you put that in a report?'

Garth looked at him inquisitively.

'The cave,' he explained, 'he can't find it. He swears they are at the same place but there's no cave. There's no entrance, no footprints, nothing, - just a dirty great limestone cliff and a lot of mud.'

Chapter Three

Portskail, situated at the end of a sea loch where a natural harbour provided sanctuary from the vagaries of the weather, lay some twenty miles from Garth's new home. It was universally referred to by the inhabitant of the area within a radius of thirty miles as 'the town'. If he asked a neighbour where one would find a particular item needed for an emergency repair, they invariably replied 'the town'. There was little likelihood that he would be confused. Portskail was the only town within sixty miles. If an item could not be found in the town then one was obliged to sacrifice a day and head further afield to 'the city'. A similar monopoly precluded the requirement for any title more specific than that.

Jack Munro had ample time for reflection during his drive back to Portskail. Although the narrow lanes, almost empty of traffic, demanded a degree of vigilance in case a wayward vehicle approached at speed from the opposite direction, they did, nonetheless, allow the mind some latitude during which it could flit from subject to subject as it pleased.

He glanced out of the car windows. Since the previous day a period of calm, warm weather had settled lightly on the land. The mountains, still sporting occasional patches of snow in shady hollows, seemed increasingly benign and had the look of giants resting on their rocky elbows to enjoy the unexpected warmth. Having bathed briefly in the chill morning dew they were clean and relaxed and without menace. It was a scene that seemed to have existed forever.

'Long may it last,' Jack said to himself.

There were unwelcomed signs of change in the landscape. Nothing could escape the relentless march of modernity. A string of ugly pylons loped brazenly across the road, and, on a distant hillside, turbines

turned with relentless calm. A few new tracks had been
carved here and there, with the generous support of
government money, to facilitate easier access for
vehicles to the higher slopes, where red deer roamed.
There were houses too, newly built or converted from
old crofts. Bed and breakfast signs indicated the
inevitable encroachment of the summer tourist – a
mixed blessing indeed.

Nonetheless, Jack reflected, there were still days,
perhaps even weeks, when he could find solitude and
calm, touch base, so to speak. 'I hope it lasts as long as
I do,' he said then. 'I would hate to be here when it is
finally and irredeemably spoilt.' As it would be; as it
inevitably had to be.

Jack enjoyed these periods of reflection and, under
normal circumstances, he would have reflected first and
foremost on the good fortune that had brought him to
these parts twenty years before. He was, in those days,
a junior detective with a growing reputation for flair,
finely tuned analytical skills and intuition. Ahead of
him, his envious colleagues could see a spectacular rise
through the promotional ranks, with all the pecuniary
and social advantages that brought.

Jack, however, was not a man to accept his fate
without question. During one of those reflective periods
that beset him even then, he took a long, hard look at
the road that was so clearly mapped out before him,
decided he did not particularly relish the journey,
turned abruptly into a side road, and was never seen
again. He still considered it the best move he had ever
made.

Now, twenty years later, he was a detective
inspector, living in a small town and working for a
force which served a largely rural population. He still
found sufficient challenge in his professional life to
occasionally stimulate his mind, which remained as

sharp as ever. He thought about the body in the cave and felt a palpable surge of excitement. Who was the dead man? How long had he been in the cave? How did he get there? How did he die? Where were his clothes? What was the explanation for the presence of a child's clothes placed on and around him? Finding answers to those questions would occupy him for the next few days. Then the prosaic answers would emerge and the pieces would slot together to reveal the mundane and depressing details of a life that had come to such an untimely end in that lonely place.

He slowed down as the car passed through the long, sprawling village of Inverstrach. There was no-one on the street that morning. Even the dog walkers were shut inside their houses. There was a new timber framed house under construction on the outskirts. Roofers were busy fixing slates. Their van was parked in the drive.

There was scarcely a village in the area that had not been adopted by people from the south. New houses were springing up all over. Portskail itself had gradually spread out and its ancient centre was now ringed and overwhelmed by new housing estates full of unfamiliar faces. The city, a hundred and twenty miles away, was growing at an alarming rate. Weekend visitors emerged from its grey streets and filled the roads with their cars. The summer was worse.

'It's all changing,' Jack reflected. 'We are being sacrificed on the altar of growth and progress.' He shook away a momentary pang of anxiety and allowed his thoughts to return to the mystery of the missing cave.

'How does a cave disappear?' he muttered to himself. He frowned. 'What are the possibilities? Firstly: D.S. Philip Bentley may have simply led them to the wrong place – a harmless, if rather foolish mistake, made by a man more used to the streets of southern towns than to Highland wastes. Secondly: there may have been a small slip of peat and grass which obscured the entrance and which my unobservant colleagues have failed to distinguish. It was, after all, a relatively small entrance.'

He shook his head as he thought of Phil Bentley, scrambling around the heather and peat in search of a lost cave. He laughed.

'A rock slippage might have hidden the prints which were mainly within the immediate vicinity of the entrance. The land beyond the peaty pools was heather and dry grass. The entrance was itself quite small and would be hidden from sight by a relatively slight fall. The question remains whether my esteemed colleague is sufficiently unobservant to have failed to notice a fresh fall of earth. He reached a sudden conclusion and expressed it aloud to the steering wheel, the windscreen and himself.

'It is merely an embarrassing inconvenience,' he said. 'It will give our city colleagues something to laugh about and, no doubt, I will subjected to a certain amount of stick but, in terms of the case itself, we have sufficient evidence to work on - thanks to me!' he added brightly. 'Besides, we all know where this is going. Death by misadventure, a result no doubt of appalling weather, (although how we reconcile this to the question of missing clothes, I'm not sure), or, and in my view a more likely conclusion, suicide. Some poor, unfortunate, despairing of life, has taken himself off to die alone..........and naked ....and in a very inconvenient location.' He shook his head again. 'Bizarre!' he muttered.

'I'll probably have to go back up there myself,' he growled gloomily.

The car slowed as it met the junction with the main road. A single car sped northwards before Jack turned right and headed along the empty road in the opposite direction towards Portskail.

His thoughts returned to the body. Behind those silent eyes there lay a story. No doubt it would be a trivial story of a very ordinary life which ended in an unfortunate tragedy. A life, he thought, not unlike his own. Jack reflected on his own life. There were no major achievement behind him and he had no great ambitions for the future. He had no desire to be memorable, famous, infamous or renowned. He was happy that a memory of him would linger for a short time in the minds of family and a few friends. He would be happy if he had done little harm and some occasional good. It would be pleasant to be respected, though, he thought.

Garth Fielding from Aultmore, he imagined, was rather different. The modest achievements, which would mark his own successful passage through life, would not be enough for Garth. He burned with a fiercer flame.

Entertained by thoughts such as these his journey passed quickly and without incident. He decided to call by the mortuary to see if there were any preliminary findings. He was met at the entrance by his colleague of many years, the stocky, white bearded, plump faced eminence that was Dr. Alexander Finlay. At the shoulders of this renowned physician stood two laboratory assistants, several years the younger, and carrying subservience like a badge of honour. Jack was immediately struck by the uniformity of expression on their faces. So taken was he by the identical ashen whiteness, the same fearful expression and dishevelled appearance, and the same anxious look of people sharply awoken from a shared, distressing nightmare which they carried, momentarily, into their waking world, that he reached for the camera which he kept beside him in the car.

'That,' he said to himself, 'is a competition winner! Wait there!' he shouted. 'Don't move an inch!'

He quickly snapped a photograph from the car window.

'No time for that! Come along in! Come along in!' Alexander and his assistants, white coated, pale faced, turned with a synchronicity that could not fail to amuse and impress.

Jack followed rapidly through the double doors, across a wide and oddly magnificent entrance hall, through a second set of doors and along a corridor towards the clinical interior. After twenty years it still felt strange passing through these doors. The building had once served a more prosaic purpose as the administrative centre of a whaling industry that briefly flourished in the port in the early nineteenth century. The grand entrance and the impressively timbered reception hall still bore witness to the income that was generated by this industry. Stern faced captains and ship owners, administrators and financiers looked down in haughty disdain from the walls.

They had stared impassively down when the building was used variously as a wartime prison, a hospital and a girls' boarding school. They had seen hope and despair in equal measure and with the same disdain. When the hospital was in need of expansion, however, the building, lying quietly on its southern fringe, was an obvious choice.

Jack followed the trio along the corridor to the next double doors which led through to the autopsy laboratory. A door to their left led into an office where the mundane work of writing up reports was undertaken. The two young assistants, a young man and a young woman not long out of college, entered the office, shut the door and firmly resisted all attempts to cajole or to force them out. Alexander was left alone.

'What's this, mutiny at the morgue? It sounds like the title of a bad detective novel. What's happening?' Jack inquired. 'Use your authority, man!'

Alexander seemed strangely lacking in anything that could resemble authority. He mustered what power he could and exclaimed to his rebellious assistants. 'You are scientists, damn it! Stop acting like superstitious, old wives! There's a reasonable explanation for it!'

Jack's curiosity was raised. He assumed a more serious expression but he retained, on a temporary basis, his tone of jocularity.

'Come, come!' he said, cajolingly, to the two young people who firmly resisted any of Alexander's attempts at entry, 'Tell Uncle Jack all about it! What has he done? Is it another contribution to the Sandy Finlay book of bad humour? You know what he's like! Forgive and forget!'

'We're not going back in there!' the young woman shouted through the battened door. Her face was pale but her eyes flashed resistance.

Sandy was losing his temper. 'You are two of the most pathetic, weak, soft centred, unprofessional, cowardly, unscientific, scaredy fools it has ever been my great displeasure to work with!' He emphasised his words with pushes and kicks at the immovable door. 'Just wait!' he threatened.

He turned round. 'Of course, I will shortly repent of my coarse words and angry outburst,' he said quietly. 'I can fully understand their reluctance to re-enter.' He nodded towards the laboratory door but before opening it he turned back to the young assistants. His tone softened.

'Go home!' he said quietly. 'Get your things and go home! Come back tomorrow as usual. There's to be no gossiping, mind! This stays between us, in here! If there's any hint of a journalist at my door I'll provide you both with references that will keep you out of gainful employment until your retirement! Am I understood?'

There was a synchronicity of nods, a discarding of white lab coats and a gathering of more secular garments and the assistants, with evident relief, hurried towards the door, almost falling over each other in their haste.

'Come and see for yourself!' said Sandy. 'Prepare to have your limited supply of hair stand on end. Are you ready?'

'Get on with it!' said Jack.

'You have been warned!' said Sandy, 'Regard!'

There was a moment's hesitation before the doors; his hand shook very slightly as he pushed. There was a tremor in his eyes and a hint of fear, quickly brushed away. It was momentary but Jack noted it, just as he noted the resolve that was required to act. Sandy pushed the laboratory door open and motioned for Jack to enter.

The laboratory looked just as it had done on the other occasions Jack had been there. The tools of the pathologists craft were laid out in preparation for the task ahead. Gowns and masks were ready for use. The stainless steel table on which the body should be placed was in order. The room was impeccably prepared. The assistants had obviously done their job with their usual efficiency and attention to detail. The laboratory was notable, in fact, only for the complete absence of a body.

'Don't tell me you've lost him, my white bearded friend!' exclaimed Jack. 'Two losses in one day would be rather too much! My careless junior colleague has already lost a cave!'

'On the contrary, my dear fellow,' said Sandy. 'I can assure you that he is most certainly still with us.'

He flourished his hand with feigned indifference to the wall adjacent to the door. Jack, on turning, restrained with difficulty a cry of alarm. He was, however, unable to prevent himself taking one and then two steps backwards and holding firmly to the empty table. It took a moment to reassemble the shrapnel pieces that had once constituted the shell of his natural composure.

'I would welcome your opinion, - as a respected professional,' said Sandy, with an expression which indicated some relief that Jack's reaction had been no less dramatic than his own. 'How do you think we might explain this?'

Behind the door, assuming the precise position in which he had last been seen in the cave, lacking only the child's clothing that had previously hidden some of the finer details of his nakedness, the body of the dead man lay propped against the wall.

'Imagine the challenge posed to my young trainees to enter a place of science, a place of logical analysis, observation and analysis, and find this.'

Jack, having gained some semblance of self control, was kneeling before the body. 'I assume,' he said dryly, 'that I can exclude from my calculations another extract from the Alexander Finlay book of practical jokes. I am still receiving therapy from the corpse that opened its eyes and sat up as the knife descended.'

'Ah yes,' smiled Sandy, 'the one that then sang 'Happy Birthday to You,' in a deep, sonorous baritone. It was beautiful. It brought tears to my eyes. You were very unappreciative at the time, as I recall.'

'It was a moment that will linger in my memory forever,' said Jack. 'My consolation is that you will be retired before I reach my next major milestone.'

'Such ingratitude,' said Sandy slowly, 'but no, I am unable to claim this as one of my own, although it may be necessary to indulge in a little subterfuge and plagiarise this event in order to calm the troubled minds of my colleagues. We can also rule out any act of retribution on their part. Their reaction, as you noted, was that of genuine believers. If I pretend to have tricked them they may hate me forever but it will at least silence them. It's a small sacrifice to give them peace of mind.'

'Well, he couldn't have got here on his own,' said Jack. 'We can be pretty certain of that! Someone must have moved him. Could someone have been attempting to remove the body and have been disturbed?'

'We cannot eliminate the possibility,' Sandy noted calmly, 'otherwise .....' He shrugged his shoulder. 'I admit that, at this stage, I am dredging deeply for alternatives.'

'Someone must be taking the piss,' said Jack.

'Not a phraseology that would be recognised in the pathologists handbook,' said Sandy, 'but I concur. Three question now remains – who, why and how?'

Jack stood up and averted his eyes from the corpse. There was something about those dead eyes and the position of the body which was particularly unsettling. He shuddered as if iced water had slipped over his naked skin. He quickly frowned and shook away the feeling and forced himself to look more closely.

'He doesn't look long dead,' he said. 'In fact, but for the absence of pulse or breathing and the presence of a distinctly white-grey colouration, he barely looks dead at all.'

'The formal autopsy will be delayed until tomorrow,' Sandy confirmed, 'since I am bereft of assistants. However, I can assure you he is most certainly dead. I can also confirm a startlingly incongruous fact.'

He paused a moment before continuing.

'I need to do a full autopsy to confirm this and I will deny having said anything as preposterous as I am about to reveal, but, it is my firm belief that death should have occurred much earlier. Look at that wound to the neck. The carotid artery is completely severed. This man had cheated death previously, probably when he was a child. It is very difficult to imagine how. I am tempted to say it would have been impossible, but for the evidence of my own eyes.'

'So what do you think finally killed him?'

'Ah, therein lies our dilemma,' said Sandy. 'I can see absolutely no signs of foul play and there are no exterior clues to the cause of death. You will have to await the autopsy. He has, however, been dead for a number of days. At the moment we must loiter impatiently in the ante rooms between murder, suicide and death by misadventure.'

'Come on, Sandy. Give it your best shot. What do you think?'

Sandy smiled. 'In the absence of the results of a full autopsy and until I discover a reasonable and scientific explanation, which I am sure I shall in due course, I am thrown back on the evidence of the scene. The man had no clothing. It is possible but most unlikely that he set off that morning in such a condition. Therefore he must have disposed of them himself or they were disposed of by another. He had tattered remnants of children's clothing laid over him. He either did that himself or someone else did it for him.'

'I've had officers searching the area for the clothing,' Jack muttered. 'They found nothing. But it's a big area. They may never find anything.'

'It would seem, on the balance of things, that the evidence is starting to point in one particular direction,' Sandy said. 'Do you agree?'

Jack was annoyed to feel a chill draft suddenly traverse his skin. He shuddered involuntarily.

Chapter Four

Twenty years previously, soon after Jack's installation in his new post, Alexander Finlay, pathologist and forensic adviser to the region, had arrived at the Munro front door at seven o'clock on a cloudy Tuesday night in April. There had been no reason for his visit, nothing had been pre-arranged and no advisory phone call had been received. The two men had only met previously on a handful of occasions and even then only in a professional capacity. He was carrying four bottles of a renowned dark ale brewed locally and a left leaning national broadsheet. He was wearing, Jack recalled, a dust coloured jumper casually thrown over the top of a dark blue, open necked shirt, and a pair of grey trousers. His feet were incongruously encased in a pair of sports' shoes, the irony of which did not escape Jack's attention. Even on their brief acquaintance it was evident that Sandy was not a man prone to prolonged bursts of physical exertion.

'Every morning, I apply myself for twenty minutes to sporting activity,' he had once announced. 'I complete the crossword in my chosen broadsheet.'

It was hard to imagine Sandy as a young man, impossible to contemplate him as a child. He was of the breed of men who seemed to have emerged from the womb into middle age and to have lingered in that condition ever since. He resembled nothing more nearly than a large and rather bedraggled teddy bear, stuffed to perfection but then maltreated and abused until the stuffing, which remained there in its entirety, was misshapen and out of place. His broad chest was surmounted on a modest width of stomach which in turn was supported by a mass of leg whose width seemed to exceed their length.

'I was never of an athletic build,' he complained ruefully. 'Somehow, my proportions were all wrong – too much breadth and too little height, too much in the torso and not sufficient in the leg, too much loose material and insufficient muscle. My greatest achievement in the untidy and (in my view) completely spurious world of school sport was to evade selection for anything that even vaguely resembled a team for the entirety of my years there and to have acquired, at the age of 13, the position of scorer for school sports – a position which I retained until I left at the age of 18. It remains, I believe, a school record.

'Still, I've made up for it in other ways,' he beamed. 'I have been, in my day, a renowned champion at chess, general knowledge and spelling and have won awards for my scientific, artistic and creative endeavours. I was also the Portskail Academy's all comers' tiddlywinks champion for an unbroken sequence of five years. I am content that I have made my mark.'

Jack soon realised that a powerful intellect inhabited that unusual and self deprecating frame. There was no flab where that was concerned. He was a first class intellectual athlete. There were few subjects about which he had no knowledge (any kind of sport being the notable exception) and several in which he had achieved a high degree of mastery.

He had decided upon medicine as his career of choice, much to the surprise of his family and friends who had anticipated a career of a more academic and refined nature. When he had turned, as it were, into the macabre business of crime and death, they had thrown up their hands in horror and given him up for lost. Eventually a vacancy had occurred, which had given him the opportunity to return home to the area in which he had spent a happy if not remarkable childhood. That had been twenty five years ago. He had never left since and looked most unlikely to do so now.

'One day,' he said, 'I hope to grace this very slab,' he said, patting the stainless steel upon which the subjects of his investigations were required to lie. 'Were an autopsy deemed necessary on my demise, I would consider it an honour to be dissected in the place that I have spent so many hours. However, I will be even more grateful if the occasion for such a ceremony could be postponed, if not indefinitely, at least for a goodly number of years. However, my height weight ratio and body mass index would seem to speak against me.' He slapped his midriff affectionately.

Jack had been rather bemused, both at the unfamiliar appearance of a man generally suited or sporting a white laboratory coat and at his unexpected arrival at his door. He had admitted him to the lounge where, over the bottles of beer, Sandy had proceeded to engage in discussion and analysis of the day's news. He offered no explanation for his presence, merely occupying his seat by the fire as if it had been specially prepared for him. Jack's wife, Kate, having initially remained in the room to engage in the kind of small talk that Jack found unbearable, soon found her presence unnecessary, not to say unwanted, and excused herself on the basis of a prior engagement with various imaginary pies and pastries and returned to a soft, kitchen chair and a good book. At ten o'clock precisely, Sandy asked if they could watch the news headlines on television and then, shortly afterwards, took his leave.

The following Tuesday he appeared once more and the pattern of the previous week was repeated. The following week, Jack and Kate found themselves anticipating with pleasure the arrival of this new, self appointed friend and the evening's discussion. Within a very short period of time 'Tuesday Nights' became the fixed event around which their lives revolved. Only holidays, conferences and occasional unavoidable appointments were allowed to interfere. They became a sacred institution.

Over the twenty years little had varied. Occasionally, Jack had suggested a game of cards and periodically Sandy appeared with chess or backgammon. Jack found himself acquiring a newspaper each Tuesday especially to prepare for their joint perusal of events.

These two men, both of whom presented a confident and out-going character in their work environment, were in reality of an unsociable and private nature. Whilst their colleagues socialised and entertained, these two men returned to their homes and their quiet pursuits. Neither made friends easily but friendships, once forged, were enduring.

Sandy lived alone now. His colleagues presumed he was a confirmed bachelor, a man for whom the attractions of lasting relationships had no appeal. He was now passing the age where his singular failure to seek solace in female company would raise eyebrows and the occasional comment. In his earlier years at Portskail it had been noted that he seemed to shun any society which might expose him to the risks of intimacy. On a number of occasions, when particular females had demonstrated a willingness to know him better, he had shown a fleetness of foot which belied his portly and lethargic appearance and he had made a quick and embarrassed getaway. This left his professional colleagues entertained and bemused.

To Jack and Kate alone he had revealed the reasons. One Tuesday, as the evening drew towards its usual end, he began to speak of his early marriage and of Helen, the one and only love of his life.

'We were just teenagers, mere children,' he said, 'but I knew then that I would never want to be with anyone else. I think I'd always known it.'

'When did you meet?' Jack asked.

'Nelson Lane Primary School, aged five,' laughed Sandy. 'She was my childhood sweetheart. I adored her even then. We went on to the Academy where we drifted apart. We met again at University in the city. She was a geology graduate and I was just beginning to discover the attractions of studying the dead and the appeal of forensic science. She was not repelled. We returned to this area for weekends and holidays when work and study permitted. It was an unforgettable time.'

He stared for a few moments at the moving flames of the open fire.

'What happened?' Jack asked quietly, uncertain whether his words would intrude into regions that Sandy would prefer to remain closed.

'She died,' he said simply. His eyes did not move from the flickering flame but Jack could see the glistening of tears. After a moment he shrugged them away. 'Leukaemia,' he said. 'But I always knew after that there could be no-one else. I chose a life alone. I am the most confirmed or confirmed bachelors and I always will be.' He smiled with an effort at brightness. 'We had five years together. Some people don't even get that. We had considerably more if you count from aged five!'

Intimate exchanges like these were few but never insignificant. In time, Jack, Kate and Sandy grew to know and understand each other as well as such reserved and private people ever could.

However, rare as these personal conversations were, it was rarer still for Jack and Sandy to discuss their work. A cursory comment about the nature of the day, - the annoying, amusing, agonising, frustrating, saddening, sickening or entertaining – was sufficient for them to cleanse themselves. Then they moved on to other matters.

It was unusual therefore when Sandy arrived on a Monday evening at half past five, without beer, without broadsheet and carrying a half bottle of single malt whisky. He had obviously driven straight over from his laboratory.

'This is serious, Jack,' he said. 'We need to talk.'

He walked past them and into the living room.

'Come in! Come in!' he said, like a man inviting them into his own home. 'You too, Kate; we need you to provide a different way of thinking. This is beyond two unimaginative, rational beings like Jack and me.'

He sat down in his usual seat but such was his degree of agitation that he was soon on his feet again. He paced towards the window where he stood, looking forgetfully down the street. Jack and Kate looked on, smiling but bemused.

'Now,' he said finally, turning sharply back to them, 'to business!' He returned to the chair, discarding his coat over the back. 'Sit! Sit!' He motioned to them brusquely. 'Forgive my abrupt manners, my dear,' he said gently to Kate, 'but I am troubled, very troubled. I need to understand what is happening. I've applied my not inconsiderable skills to the problems but I can find no solution. No, no! Don't interrupt at the moment! Let me say what I need to say.'

Jack, who had been prompted to interrupt by a real and growing concern for his friend's evident agitation, turned instead to the whisky bottle. He poured three glasses to all of which of which he added a quantity of water. He listened attentively. Kate sat down and leaned forward, her elbows resting on her knees, her dark eyes watching, as if to focus her full attention on his words. Her brown hair swam in loose curls around her face and fell in dreamy waves below her shoulders. She was growing older but Jack, watching from beside the fire, could still see the young girl fleetingly present in the bright, exciting eyes. He was momentarily distracted.

'This, my dear, is a rich, single malt whisky,' Sandy's attention too was distracted momentarily, 'from one of the island distilleries. You can taste the peat in it. Go on! Taste! Taste!' Jack nodded appreciatively. Kate failed to control a shudder and a grimace.

'I have − I should say I had − a body in the mortuary,' said Sandy. 'It has gone, vanished, disappeared - but enough of that for the moment. I can't do anything about that. Let's stick to the facts.' He brushed aside the unfortunate loss of the body with characteristic flourish of his hand. He ignored the bewildered expressions on the faces of his listeners. 'I had a body in my mortuary until very recently − I will return to that unfortunate event in a moment - which undoubtedly should have died from the application of a sharp incision to the throat; I say should have, for it is equally apparent that he did not. Of that I am also quite certain. That coup-de-gras, if we can call it that, whether by accident or design (and I have no clear evidence as to which might be the case) was administered when the body was much younger, perhaps even when it was a child. I was looking forward to exploring this strange paradox today, after a string of most inconsiderately timed meetings. Unfortunately the body I examined which, I repeat, was settled comfortably in the mortuary at six in the evening and, and which was nearer forty years of age, had vanished by one this afternoon. Gone! Disappeared! No trace! Nothing!'

This was rather too much to take in at once. Jack stared intently and sipped his whisky. Kate leaned back on her chair.

'Bad enough, you might think, but there's more to come,' Sandy continued, before his listeners had time to respond. His hand trembled slightly and the glass shook as he placed it uncertainly on a small table beside his chair. 'The clothing which was found on the body in the cave, I can now confirm, could obviously not have belonged to the said body but, to add further confusion, was of a size and character eminently suited to children of around eight years of age but from many years ago. I say children because the nature of the items would suggest at least one boy and girl. It will take time and an expertise greater than mine to establish anything more precise.

'Once again, bad enough, you might think, but there's even worse to come; yes, even more! Due to the foresight of your good self,' he directed a glance and a flourish towards Jack, 'I had a number of samples of dust, bones and rocks from the cave floor. I have spent a good part of the day studying them more closely. The bones which, quite naturally we had assumed to be animal bones – deer, sheep, fox, - were not animal bones at all. They were tiny fragments of human bone,' He paused, 'Young human bones. Bones not untypical of.....

'.......the bones of children of about eight years of age,' Jack quietly completed his sentence.

'Yes ...... and no,' said Sandy triumphantly. They were the bones of a child or children of approximately six to nine years of age,' Sandy confirmed. He shook his head. 'I've sent away soil samples away for a fuller analysis but I suspect from what I saw that there may be fibres and fragments of bone that date back even further. That cave has all the appearance of a burial ground.

'I am, of course, speculating wildly, a habit to which I am not by nature predisposed. That may perhaps give some indication of the state of my nerves. Thank you, thank you,' he took up the whisky, which Jack had pushed towards him, and downed it at a draft. 'We will have a more accurate picture when the results return but, given the urgency with which any of our rural concerns are treated in the metropolis, I would doubt if we will see them in the next week.'

'I think I need to revisit each of these points in a more leisurely fashion,' Jack said slowly. 'You say the body has gone, disappeared?'

'It has vanished into the night........rather like a crime scene,' Sandy beamed. Jack smiled ruefully. 'You saw the body yourself, last evening, Jack. After you left I replaced it on the trolley and returned it to the morgue for the night. I then locked up and went home. This morning I arrived early. My two young colleagues generally arrive about 8.30 and I felt that, given the circumstances of their departure yesterday, they would welcome my presence at the beginning of the day. I pursued my usual course, meandering through the intricacies of political and financial meetings and eventually, having rid myself of these unnecessary evils, I visited our departed friend only to find that he really had! Departed, I mean. The trolley was empty; the sheet was on the floor. That was in the early afternoon.

'Of course, after a momentary frisson, I immediately assumed that my young colleagues had persuaded themselves that the events of the previous afternoon were an elaborate hoax perpetrated by myself. They had decided to exact a suitable revenge and had arrived early in order to get their own back. However, a careful pre-emptive search (it was my earnest desire to find and replace the body so as to thwart what I saw as their attempt to exact a suitable revenge), - after an exhaustive search, I say, - I failed to produce the body. A close observation of my timid colleagues, undertaken over the following half hour, made it more than apparent that the poor souls were still in shock and were no way capable of such a deception.

'I decided that the best course of action was to announce the postponement of the autopsy for some spurious reason that I forget and to hint that the events of the previous day were, in fact, a rather ill considered whimsy, of which I was now heartily ashamed. I beat a hasty retreat into my laboratory and worked for the rest of the day on the evidence I had at my disposal. You, of course, were inconveniently out of your office and out of range of a mobile signal. Hence, my untimely visit here this evening.'

'Tell me more about the bones and the clothes,' Jack sipped his drink and his eyes focussed closely on his friend. He picked up a notebook. 'An aide memoire,' he said. 'From what you say I assume the cave must have been used as a repository for the bodies of at least three children and of other sundry remains, adult or child, spread across a century or more. Is that what you are telling me?'

'It's a place of internment or a place of disposal or a place of sacrifice. I'm sure the possibilities have occurred to you.'

'But our lately departed departed who, but for a stroke of very good fortune and some prompt medical assistance, should have been interred here some twenty or thirty years ago as a younger man or as a child somehow escaped death and, however implausibly, lived on to die here years later, covered in a few items of children's clothing with which he appears at present to have no connection.' Jack whistled and then snorted with laughter. 'Are you really saying that?'

'Without access to the body, - a most unfortunate occurrence - I cannot be certain of the actual cause of death; nor can I be sure when it occurred. I am, however, keen to explore any suggestion that might explain the evidence I have in front of me at present. At the moment, I can think of no other explanation, no matter how implausible or foolish.'

'Tell me about the clothes.'

Sandy's eyes flickered uncertainly.

'They would appear to be of a style and condition that would indicate they are very old – maybe a century or more. Other than that I can say nothing,' he said. 'I await a more detailed analysis of the evidence, which I despatched to the city laboratories today.'

'Should they not have rotted away over so many years?' Jack wondered. 'The cave was very damp and cold, hardly a good environment for preserving clothing, I would have thought.'

Sandy nodded. 'I have no explanation,' he said. 'We must await further analysis.'

'Were there any scraps of clothing which would correspond to the earlier remains?'

'They would most certainly have decayed into dust. I have sent samples of the dust for analysis, along with the bones.'

'Waiting again!' mumbled Jack. 'I hate waiting!'

'There is little else we can do, I'm afraid. However, there are some rather more pressing, pragmatic concerns.'

'Yes,' said Jack. 'How much of this present fiasco do we reveal in our reports?'

'Indeed.' Sandy nodded and resumed his drink.

'We also have the question of the mislaid cave,' Jack continued, 'which, were it not for the unfortunate disappearance of your dead body I would have put down to the unfamiliarity of my colleague with the finer details of navigation. However, I am suspicious of coincidence. I distrust it.'

'How do we explain it?' asked Sandy. 'There are, alas, numerous forms that require numerous entries. No doubt you are similarly beset. I haven't checked closely but I very much doubt that there is a precedent for the words, 'lost in transit' or 'mislaid' with regard to bodies or the scenes of crimes.'

'I suggest the temporary application of a personalised gagging order,' said Jack. 'The officer who has mislaid the cave will be easily convinced. He is a young, sensitive soul and is already dreading the mockery to which he will inevitably be subject when this comes out. The rest of the office will be unaware whether the necessary actions have been taken or not – at least for a time. I think the new inhabitant at Aultmore Croft will be too busy with their new home to be surprised at a slight delay.'

'So you propose we sit on it and say nothing.'

'I do.'

'I agree. It won't buy us much time but we may be blessed with some helpful revelation in the meantime. My assistants will, no doubt, continue to curse my very name but they are at least convinced as to the cause of the moving body. We must wait and see what emerges from the more detailed analysis.'

'I wonder if you will find the answers you are looking for,' Kate pondered. 'Wouldn't it be delightful if there simply was no rational answer? It's strange, isn't it, that hundreds of years ago such events would have been explained quite simply by most ordinary people as the result of forces beyond their control? It would have been the result of witchcraft, the Gods, magic. Whilst thinking people searched for and found the causes of the sudden darkening of the sky in daytime, people in the villages and farms were simply frightened or in awe. They sought explanations elsewhere. Nowadays, we have eliminated any notion of forces beyond our control. For every consequence we presume a cause, - quite rightly. Now, suddenly, you two are faced with consequences for which the causes are not at all clear; in fact, at present, they defy logical explanation. It is quite invigorating to watch you struggle!' She laughed.

'I do hope you are not suggesting we resort to a visit to the white witch of Portskail?' laughed Sandy.

'I merely note with interest,' smiled Kate, 'that faced with matters that you cannot explain, you are actually in a worse position than the peasants tending their crops in the Dark Ages. They at least had explanations that satisfied them. I have no doubt that an explanation will soon be forthcoming. However, in the meantime, you two are drifting without an anchor.'

'I suggest we burn a witch,' suggested Jack, 'and wait for everything to go back to normal.'

They both glanced ominously towards Kate and laughed.

Chapter Five

Twice each day, except on Sundays, a substantial, red and white vehicle ferry, the Spirit of the North, could be seen docked at Portskail harbour. For some of its passengers its outward voyage marked the beginning of a holiday adventure and a chance to enjoy the cool, ocean air and the passing seabirds. It opened up views of inaccessible cliffs and stretches of remote and silent coastline. For others, on the return voyage, it marked the first stage of the transition from holiday to home. For local people it was part of the regular pattern of life, - the journey to and from the mainland. Whether for hospital appointments, extended shopping trips or long planned meetings of a professional or personal nature, the ferry provided the one lifeline for the islands. Lorries vied back and forth with essential goods and strangely incongruous vehicles of a generally agricultural appearance occasionally clattered down its shallow ramps.

A young man by the name of Jamie had disembarked from the ferry when it docked at Portskail some hours earlier. It was a journey which, being a native of the outer islands, he had undertaken at regular intervals since childhood. Despite this level of familiarity, Jamie was still sufficiently young to enjoy the journey. Being a good natured youth of a practical rather than intellectual nature, he could not easily have translated his feelings into words but he was aware that the restraining magnetic field produced by his home, family and community gradually diminished as the voyage progressed. By the time he arrived in port it had all but vanished. Jamie felt like a free man and he was ready to take advantage of his well earned liberty.

Unfortunately for Jamie, Portskail was no den of iniquity and he would have been hard pressed to give any clear indication of the precise use he would make of his freedom. Instead, he stood on the quayside and inhaled the cleansing air and simply *felt* free. He had dressed carefully for the occasion, blending the requirements of the season with the demands of fashion. Under a generously large over jacket he sported what he had been led to believe was the very latest in menswear.

The business that had brought him from the islands not requiring his attention until the following morning Jamie passed much of the afternoon walking the harbour front and admiring the various craft moored there. It was a subject in which he had a commendable level of expertise. He spent time in enjoyable, technical conversation with mechanics, engineers, fishermen, yachtsmen and lorry drivers of his acquaintance. His gaunt, stringy physique and tousled hair were familiar to a number of these fellow enthusiasts who gathered in fluctuating groups along the quay. The hum of conversation, punctuated by loud bursts of gruff laughter, attracted the momentary attention of the occasional tourist, who turned sharply as if summoned, became briefly aware of the huddle of locals amid the crates and lobster pots, and moved on.

By late afternoon, having exhausted the opportunities these meetings provided, he found himself alone, bored and with little to do. The port was not well equipped with attractions for this young, unrestrained escapee from the claustrophobic morality of the outer isles. Having considered his options he realised, as usual, that they were restricted to one. He headed directly to the public bar of the Portskail Hotel, where he was sure to meet some more acquaintances and could pass several hours in convivial and gradually more inebriated conversation.

He had booked a room in a small guest house further down the same road, so now he settled himself back for a long, pleasant evening of pool, darts and drink, from which he only emerged at a late hour pleasantly aware that he was faced with only a very short distance to negotiate to his bed.

It was, in fact, only just past eleven when he emerged somewhat unsteadily from the bar. Being of a practical rather than imaginative nature, he was not inclined to notice the stillness of the air nor the deep chill and the crisp and effortlessly multiplying stars, other than to consider whether to fasten his coat and don hat and gloves for the brief distance to his accommodation. He decided, after a moment, that the chill was sufficient to warrant such attention to detail and he prepared himself as quickly as his clumsy fingers and blurred eyes would permit. A couple of fellow drinkers emerged behind him and headed towards the harbour mumbling their farewells.

Jamie drew his collar higher and set off. He walked uncertainly, his legs splayed in the style of a mariner maintaining balance on the deck of a wave tossed vessel. The footpath, which represented the deck of Jamie's present craft, proving somewhat unsteady, he found himself rolling in a rather ungainly manner from the supportive garden walls to the wide ocean of road beyond the kerb edge.

He stopped for a moment to regain stability and concentrated his blurred vision on the route he must follow. He was rather surprised when there floated into sight a tiny figure sitting on the kerb ahead of him. He moved his head from side to side to obtain focus.

It was a child, a young boy, of perhaps five or six years old, with shoulder length hair and a ribbed jumper such as might be worn by a fisherman in an old advertisement. Jamie, who was naturally suspicious of children even in daylight and under the most sober of circumstances, approached with particular care. The little boy initially seemed unaware of him. It was only as Jamie achieved an unaccustomed proximity that the boy turned upon him a pair of wide, sad eyes. Tears had formed channels down his cheeks and his eyes glistened. His stare did not relax.

'What's the matter?' Jamie asked uncertainly. 'Are you lost?'

The boy did not answer. Jamie looked anxiously up and down for some form of support, preferably of a female, motherly character, but the street was empty and as silent as listening stars. A crisp packet, dislodged from a waste bin and captured momentarily in lazy drafts, span half heartedly and lay still.

'You can't stay here, you know,' Jamie murmured. 'Where do you live?'

The boy continued to watch with wide, unflinching eyes.

'Where are your mummy and daddy?' Jamie slurred.

The tears continued to flow down the boy's motionless face. He neither moved to wipe them away nor added even the slightest sound to the silent spectacle. He just stared.

'What do you want me to do?' Jamie was beginning to feel distinctly uncomfortable. It was cold, it was late and he was beginning to feel decidedly the worse for his evening's excesses. He looked around desperately for someone to help him with the child.

Suddenly the boy clambered to his feet. He slowly held out a tiny, pale hand.

'What do you want?' Jamie repeated. He was becoming increasingly alarmed. He wondered if he could just slip away and leave the boy where he was; but he knew that such a choice was impossible. 'Wait there!' he said suddenly, a sober thought emerging momentarily from the confused fog of his mind. 'I'll get someone. I'll knock on this door!' He indicated an adjacent house towards which he made a movement.

'No!' The boy's voice was alarmed and fearful. He turned towards the road as if he was about to run away.

'Wait! You can't just go!' called Jamie. 'I wish you could,' he muttered to himself, 'but you can't. I can't let you.'

The boy turned back and held out a tiny hand once more. Jamie focussed closely and gently reached out his own hand which suddenly seemed large and coarse. He held the boy's cold fingers as if they might snap like slender, fragile icicles.

'You want me to take you to the police station?' he suggested. 'The police will help find your parents. They'll help you. I'll phone them,' he suddenly said brightly, recalling the mobile phone in his inner pocket and delighted at his perspicacity.

'No!' The boy's voice, more scream than shout, more cry than scream stopped him. His grip tightened and he pulled away in a direction quite the opposite to Jamie's intended route towards the comfort and the welcoming warmth of his Guest House.

'You want to go that way?' he slurred. 'You want to take me somewhere? Where do you want to go? Is it to your house? Is something the matter?'

The boy stopped. His hand dropped. He looked up slowly. Jamie shuddered. He felt cold. A fragmentary chill seemed to spread like splinters from his fingers to his arms and torso. In the flimsy glow of a streetlight Jamie was suddenly aware of the strange blueness of the boy's eyes.

'Like ice,' he thought. He shivered again. 'It's cold,' he muttered, 'too cold to be standing around here all night. What do you want? You show me!'

The boy held him briefly in an unflinching, blue stare and then turned and ran away down the street. He paused at a corner, as if waiting, and then turned aside and was lost to sight. For reasons he could never quite explain – curiosity, conscience, fear – Jamie felt impelled to initiate a stumbling pursuit. Each step was accompanied by a medley of oaths suitable to the occasion. The sudden acceleration did nothing to improve his level of discomfort and a wave of post alcoholic nausea was gathering momentum behind his blurred eyes. As he walked, without any clarity of purpose, he struggled to text a hurried message to a friend in the town. Unfortunately, his clumsy fingers conspired with the lack of adequate illumination to thwart the requirements of coherence and he gave up.

He reached the corner; the boy was nowhere to be seen. A cold draft stung his eyes. A frost was forming rapidly. He cursed half heartedly. He caught sight of the tiny figure, briefly and darkly illuminated by a distant streetlight. The boy was hurrying along the roadside. He turned and disappeared into a side street.

'Shit!' Jamie swore again. He swayed into an upright position, focused on his last sighting of the boy and continued his ungainly pursuit.

The boy was heading away from the centre of the town towards the open shore, where a small footbridge led over a tributary stream towards some newer houses and the old church. He turned between some trees onto a quiet path, overwhelmed in late summer by the relentless growth of bramble, but currently untroubled and clear. Jamie hurried after him. An exposed root caught his foot and he stumbled, catching his hand on an exposed stone. In the absence of a moon and the reassurance of the now fading street lights, he stopped and looked nervously about.

'I never did like the dark,' he confessed, nervously, to the night, 'especially among trees.' The branches above him were black against the sky. Below, a deeper blackness gathered. Evil things could loiter in that dark undergrowth. He looked hurriedly up again. The stars grew clearer now, as the lights of the town diminished. 'If I was sober, I'd go home.' He snorted an abrupt laugh, amused at the irony.

His momentary reflection was disturbed by a sharp sound from some distance ahead of him. He heard the creaking of a gate and then a wooden click as it was pushed back into place.

'The gate to the footbridge,' he said. 'Where's he going?'

When Jamie reached the footbridge he could hear the boy ahead of him. He had not taken the wider path left towards the shore; nor had he taken the right hand path towards the small group of modern houses which had been developed like an annexe to the main town from which they were separated by the river. He was heading along the narrow path straight on towards the old church.

The boy's night vision was evidently superior to Jamie's. At each step now, since the street lights had long ceased to influence the darkness, branches scratched like cat's claws at his clothes, or pawed at his eyes. Slippery, protruding roots offered unexpected and unwelcomed obstacles to his feet and occasional hollows held a brew of unctuous, clinging mud under a thin crust of frost. He swore and stumbled to his knees. His hands grasped mud and leaves. He clambered to his feet and staggered on.

He emerged from the trees, panting from the exertion and pained by the consequences of his stumbling and approached the church wall and the tiny wicket gate which opened onto a gravel path which led towards the arched thirteenth century door. The tower and its clock were silhouetted against the sky. Jamie was aware suddenly of the misty wreaths his breath was making in the darkness. Around him, silent and undisturbed, gravestones and memorials to the dead seemed to be watching with cold indifference. They were unwelcoming and sullen, hunched and secretive. He had no place here, in the darkness at this time of night. They leaned forward resentfully; or so it seemed to Jamie's anxious mind.

Where was the boy? Jamie looked nervously around. No amount of alcohol was sufficient to numb his superstitious anxiety or to overcome the irrational dread of encountering he knew not what.

There was a movement in the corner of the graveyard. The boy was standing by a particular grave, close against the wall. An old headstone, now at a precarious angle, leaned towards him. He was looking down, as if reading the indistinct lettering carved on its surface. He slowly raised an arm and seemed to indicate something. His lips moved.

Jamie wound blindly around the graves. The boy seemed to have disappeared again but then Jamie made out a shape, sitting down, leaning against the stone. He stumbled forward.

'Is this gravestone what you've brought me to see?' he demanded. 'What do..........?'

He stopped. There certainly was a figure leaning against the gravestone but it was not the boy. Bleeding, eyeless sockets gaped in the dead man's head. A ghastly, livid wound had ripped open his chest.

Jamie stared. He shivered. He looked frantically around. Of the boy, there was no sign.

Chapter Six

Jack Munro was not a man who paused to reflect at any length on the choices, for good or ill, which he had made in his life. Once the choices had been made, the path chosen and the point reached beyond which it was futile to look back, he made the best of where he was. Sandy, he quickly observed, was rather different. In periods of solitude or reflection his general direction of focus was backwards. He saw the paths he might have taken and the choices he might have made and he regretted their loss. His was a melancholy world and one in which he saw little good. He wore his misanthropy like a mask.

Jack resisted darker moods. He preferred to focus on the present and on times ahead and matters over which he had some control. He liked to plan and to anticipate. He liked to evaluate and solve. He was never more elated than when confronted by a complex problem through which he could weave an intricate and assured path to a final conclusion.

He approached crime in a manner at once compassionate and professional. He felt the deepest sympathy for the victim and yet viewed the crime coldly as a problem to be solved. He was stunned by the brutality of crime, aghast at the senselessness of it, horrified by its mindless indifference to the feelings of its victims, but he remained firmly focused on the task he was employed to complete. He could see the investigative path ahead. He had power and the authority over it. This was his appointed task.

As a child he had been of a quiet reflective nature, sensitive to the nuances of meaning in every look or gesture. He was hurt by the most innocuous of casual or careless remarks and would dwell at painful length on subtleties of meaning that the speaker had never intended or had long forgotten. As a teenager he had been stung by the indifference some of his peers showed to the feelings of others and gathered around him a small number of close and loyal friends.

As a young man, increasingly self confident and comfortably self aware, he retained his insight into the emotions of those around him but was less frequently pained by what he saw and heard. His manner became more reserved and analytical.

Now, as an adult, in the hearty prime of life, when death was still sufficiently removed to discount and the pains of adolescence a distant memory, he basked in a sort of contentment that felt as if it would last forever. Occasional rippling currents from the future and murmurs of past voices sent transient tremors of dread and fear through him but they were fleeting and quickly subdued. At times he clung closely to Kate, as a ghastly spectre of loneliness struck him with the force of a storm. He rarely spoke of these feelings and only ever to her.

When obliged to reflect on past choices he proudly declared that on two memorable occasions in his life he had made truly faultless decisions. These decisions, he would proclaim, had together produced the longest and most enduring periods of sustained contentment in his life. He was, he maintained, still basking in their radiance.

The first was the choice he made, many years ago, to forgo the attractions of a glittering career in order to move to Portskail. The second was to propose marriage to the radiantly attractive Kate after only three months of acquaintance.

It was characteristic of Jack to quickly and decisively resolve questions which would occupy others in weeks and months of soul searching. Crucial matters like these presented themselves to Jack with a crystalline clarity which astonished his colleagues and friends but which to Jack illustrated nothing more than the simplicity of the choice he must make. It was equally characteristic that having made a decision he would implement it with single minded resolution.

The attractions of Kate were not of that unmistakable character which immediately turns heads and promotes jealousy. She was pretty rather than beautiful, reserved rather than confident, elegant in a restrained, tasteful way rather than flamboyant. Her conversation was thoughtful and her humour subtle. Jack immediately dismissed all others from his mind and made her acquaintance. It was an acquaintance that blossomed rapidly into love and was consecrated six months later by marriage. They were both then in their early twenties.

Now, twenty five years later, the passion having inevitably subsided, their two children having grown, matured and departed to universities, cities and careers, they remained a comfortable, contented couple whose affection had grown rather than diminished with the years.

It was Kate who had taken the call at two o'clock that morning. She had not long been asleep, having been engrossed in a recently acquired book about the inner workings of the psychotic mind of a well known serial killer. She had a passion, shared with Jack, for explorations of the criminal mind; but where Jack generally resorted to fiction in his leisure hours, Kate turned eagerly to the study of real cases. The book now lay on the floor by the bed, where it had fallen from her hands.

Jack, snoring deeply, was at first difficult to rouse.

'Jack!' she said urgently, shaking his shoulder, 'Jack! It's the office. There's a body in the graveyard!'

Jack sat up and rubbed his eyes.

'Are they phoning me up in the middle of the night to tell me that?' he muttered. 'Check the date. It's not April the first, is it?'

Suddenly conscious of her words, Kate giggled uncontrollably. She passed the phone over and buried her head in her pillow.

A moment later Jack reached over her to replace the receiver.

'Got to go,' he said. 'There really is a body in the graveyard and it's a fresh one, not even buried. You get back to sleep. I doubt if I'll be back before morning.'

Jack slipped quietly down the stairs and out into the empty street. Kate heard the car door open and then shut, the engine hum into life and its sound rise and fade as it was absorbed slowly into the night.

Half an hour later Jack arrived at the church yard which, by now, had acquired a number of lights and a small number of officers and specialists, some clad in plastic gowns and hats, whom Jack recognised. The portly figure of Alexander Finlay bestrode the neatly cropped grass between the graves. Jack smiled to note the presence of pyjamas protruding from beneath his trousers.

With customary acuity he quickly noted the salient features of the scene, the position and posture of the body, its location in the corner of the graveyard, the stone against which it lay. He noted the imprints on the frosty grass. One set of prints led between the stones to the body. Their owner had stood a moment and then staggered back. They belonged to the witness. This much was obvious. There seemed to be no other prints.

'Surprising,' he murmured. 'No prints from the victim, no prints from the killer and no sign of a struggle.'

He checked that an adequate cordon had been placed around the scene.

'Make yourself useful. See if there are any other prints,' he told the police constable who had been first on the scene, 'and don't add any more of your own.'

He walked across to the corner of the stone wall and checked the ground on either side. He studied the top stones.

'Nothing,' he said.

He walked the perimeter of the church with a flashlight, checking the ground on either side of the wall. He walked the gravel path round the church itself.

'Anyone been in the church?' he called. No-one had. 'Anyone called the minister?'

The minister had, in fact, been disturbed by the lights and movements around his church and had quickly donned a coat and hat and headed over to see what was causing the disturbance. He was standing now in the arched doorway of the church, a somewhat bewildered and forlorn looking individual.

'Nothing like this,' he began, 'nothing ever ....'

'Can we check the inside of the church?' Jack interrupted him. There was no time for a discussion of the moral implications of such events, especially with a minister of the church. He had work to do. 'Can you put the lights on? Just to check, you understand.'

'Of course, of course,' the minister, pleased to have something to do, bustled officiously. He lifted the latch and swung back the ancient, heavy oak door and vanished down the centre aisle. Jack heard his footsteps fading along the stone floor. A moment later the church was illuminated, section by section, as he pressed the switches. Jack walked slowly forward looking at the ground and to left and right.

The minister was standing at the crossing between the lines of pews when Jack had finished his inspection. His head was bowed.

'It's dreadful,' he began, 'and in a churchyard! Nothing like this has……'

'Could you have a quick look round and make sure nothing has been moved or damaged?' Jack interrupted. 'There may be something you would notice that might escape the rest of us.'

The minister looked carefully around him. He took a few paces in each direction. 'Nothing,' he said. 'The choice of gravestone is rather ironic, don't you think?' he ventured as he concluded his scrutiny.

'Ironic? Why?' asked Jack.

'That gravestone marks the final resting place of the only person in this graveyard who met his end by an act of murder. I heard a few of the details of the story from a parishioner who has an interest in these things. It was a long time ago, well beyond living memory.'

'I hate coincidences,' Jack muttered as he left the church.

He crossed to where Sandy was kneeling on the crisp grass and scrutinising the body. A layer of frost was gathering around them. Sandy was directing a photographer.

'Nasty,' he said, noting Jack's arrival at his side, 'especially gouging out the eyes, like that; not the act of an entirely balanced mind, I suspect.'

'Get me a couple of shots of that gravestone,' Jack directed the photographer. He called the police officer over to him. 'It's Julie, isn't it? I can barely see you for these damned lights. Well Julie, see if you can make out the writing for me. I'd like a transcript on my desk in your best handwriting before you go off shift.'

'I think we can rule out suicide,' Sandy murmured sardonically, 'and accidental death is looking increasingly unlikely. Well, my boys,' he said to the figures standing around, 'This is only a preliminary opinion and must not appear in the press tomorrow morning but I do believe we've got ourselves a murder and mutilation – not a regular occurrence in Portskail.'

'There seems to be a substantial quantity of blood but a notable shortage of eyes,' Jack noted. 'Has our perpetrator removed them and taken them with him, do you think?'

'A trophy?' Sandy murmured. 'It's possible. Of course, we haven't checked his pockets yet.'

Jack looked at him aghast. 'That isn't even funny,' he said. He turned to an officer. 'Check them anyway,' he said.

'You can rule nothing out in this business,' said Sandy, dryly, 'You know that. However, judging by the quantity of blood I think we can be quite certain that the crime took place here. I may be stretching it a little but I would also hazard a guess that the extensive wound in his chest may also have contributed to his death.'

'Given that there is no evidence of a struggle we might assume the victim was unconscious when the coup de gras was delivered,' Jack commented. 'You can check that for me, of course.'

'Indeed.'

'I'm curious to know what our witness was doing wandering around a graveyard at one o'clock in the morning.' Jack looked around for Jamie. 'Where have you buried my witness?' he called towards the tiny huddle of people.

'We took him to the station,' Julie called back. She walked across to explain. 'He wasn't in the best of condition. He'd had a fair few drinks last night and he needed some black coffee. We couldn't get a great deal of sense out of him.'

Jack nodded approval.

'Nothing much more for me to do here,' he said thoughtfully. 'I'm sure I can leave matters in your very capable hands,' he smiled. 'I think I could manage a coffee myself. I'll see you later on in the day, Sandy. Two bodies, one unfortunately mislaid, two autopsies, two lots of reports to write up – I'm almost sympathetic.'

'Yes, this is becoming something of a habit,' the inevitable response came. 'We must stop meeting like this. People will talk. What will Kate think?'

Jack eyed him up and down. 'Necrophilia', he suggested.

Back at the station Jack gathered a coffee and went into an interview room where Jamie sat, his head and arms resting on the table.

'You look worse than the corpse,' Jack muttered, without any notable degree of compassion.

Jamie raised a bleary head and focused with some difficulty a pair of bloodshot eyes. He experienced some difficulty raising a smile and when he did he was conscious that he exposed a rough coating on his teeth and tongue, rather like a fungal growth on a tree trunk. He closed his mouth hurriedly before he provoked any more of Jack's caustic wit.

'What were you doing in a graveyard at that time of night?' Jack asked. 'We're you lost?'

Jamie avoided an answer. He was in no condition to fend off sarcasm. 'Did you find the little boy?' he mumbled.

'What little boy?' Jack demanded. 'No-one told me about a little boy.'

'There was a little boy in the town, outside the pub. He led me to the body.'

Jamie did his best to explain but the restrictions his condition had placed on his tongue precluded lucidity or coherence. Jack probed patiently for as much information as he could and then withdrew and spent a few minutes in communication with a colleague outside the door.

When they both returned a moment later they found Jamie slumped forward on the table, snoring loudly. After a half hearted attempt to rouse him, Jack appeared to lose interest.

'Wake him up, get a description of this boy he thinks he's seen and then pack him off to his B and B,' he said. 'In the absence of blood and gouged out eyes on or around his person and granted that he is unlikely to have valiantly attempted to trample over incriminating evidence and then have called the police, I think we can comfortably assume he has nothing to do with the crime itself. Add to that the fact that he appears to be the single most desperately ineffectual person I have seen in several months and I think we can let everything else wait. Besides, we'll get no sense out of him tonight.

'When you've got a description of this boy, you'd better circulate it. This little boy may have seen something of importance, you never know. And go and wake up Davies McLean from the primary school. See if the description fits any of his pupils.'

'What, now?' asked the officer, 'It's four o'clock in the morning?'

'I'm very well aware of the time, I can assure you. If I can't sleep, why should he? Wake him up! And remind him to check for absences in the morning. I want to find this boy. I've a busy day ahead so I'm going home to get a couple of hours sleep. If the press get a hold of this you can tell them they'll get nothing from me until I've had a decent sleep so they can come back in full daylight and after breakfast. Tell them ten o'clock.'

With that, he departed.

Once home he sat for a while in thought and jotted notes in a small book. He made a couple of phone calls to check progress and then, as the first glimmer of light stirred the darkness he slipped into the warm bed beside Kate. She stirred and murmured softly in her sleep and turned over. Jack, still shivering slightly from the cold, felt the warmth of her body slowly drive the chill away. He was soon asleep.

It was after eight when he awoke. The telephone was ringing; Kate was murmuring. He reached a flailing arm and successfully located the phone before she was disturbed.

'Yes? Who? Oh, Julie, right. Give me a second, I'm barely awake.' He sat on the side of the bed. 'Okay, go on.' He nodded, interjected a few brief questions and then leaned over Kate to replace the phone.

No sooner had he done so than it rang again. This time Kate stirred and, without opening her eyes, passed the receiver over.

First of all,' Sandy's stentorian voice resonated. 'I am happy to inform you that the body of the deceased remains precisely where it was placed. I have instituted regular checks. Without the benefit of a full autopsy, to which event I cordially invite you, shall we say three pm, I can at least confirm that he was probably killed by the wound to his chest and that the eyes were, mercifully, removed after death. The time of death I would estimate to have been little more than an hour before he was found.'

Jack sat up sharply. 'Then the little boy is likely to have been a witness to the crime,' he said, largely to himself.

'To which little boy are we referring?' asked Sandy. Jack explained. 'In which case, I am doubly glad that I telephoned you this morning. If he proves to have been a witness to the crime and that information gets out before you find him, your little boy is in grave danger.......'

'......which makes it increasingly important that we locate him,' Jack muttered, 'not only for his own sake but because it would seem possible – probable – that he saw something that might help us. It's a pity we don't have much of a description to go on. Our one witness to the presence of the boy was in no fit condition to give anything more than a very cursory picture. He says he followed the boy to the graveyard. His footsteps are quite clear on the grass and on the path leading from the trees to the wicket gate. There weren't any signs of the boy's prints and so far we've drawn a blank in our efforts to locate him or identify him. His description didn't ring any bells with our esteemed local head teacher. He may not even be a local boy. Still, these are early days.

'A car certainly drew up beside the church some time that evening but the grass seems undisturbed between the car and the location of the body. There are no prints and the gravel seems equally undisturbed. Either the body was dropped from a helicopter or someone had taken incredible care to leave everything completely as they found it, a very brave or foolhardy undertaking considering the time it would have taken and the presence of a murdered corpse nearby. I think I'll take another trip out there this morning. I need to have a closer look in daylight. However, first I must repair to the office. I'll see you this afternoon.'

He replaced the receiver.

'Why was he killed at the church?' Jack muttered to himself. 'Was it planned or merely fortuitous? And why was he killed by that gravestone in particular? Was it chance or design? I hate coincidences,' he snapped. 'I don't trust them. I don't trust them at all.'

Chapter Seven

Jack returned to the graveyard that morning. It was not a mere matter of professional necessity; nor was it solely because he had lingering doubts and uncertainties about the evidence the scene had provided. He simply knew he had to be there. There was something in the setting, the context of the crime that he needed to absorb, to internalise and to breathe with the familiarity of a confidante. There was something appallingly incongruous in the perpetration of such a savage act in such a place. The event itself was deeply shocking. The setting, in the quiet of a churchyard at night, deepened and intensified that shock. The incongruity was rendered even more notable by the precise location of the body by that one grave and the violent nature of its inhabitant's demise.

'Either it was meant to shock us,' he murmured to himself, 'or the setting has some significance to the murderer or the act was entirely random.' He looked closely at the gravestone, now carefully beneath a protecting canopy to protect it from the weather. It was tilted at a slight angle to one side and had slipped and fallen forward and away from the wall. Grey lichen mottled it in patches and moss grew sparsely here and there. The name was obscured by the effects of erosion and the pious message beneath was also largely effaced.

He smiled ruefully. He had asked Julie, that young, enthusiastic detective constable, to provide him with a transcript. That would have been no easy matter, in the dark and by torchlight. He hoped she hadn't lingered long over such an impossible task.

He watched two members of the team at work, on hands and knees, patiently combing the graveyard, inch by inch, for clues. He dispatched another two to the area beyond the wall where there was a small field, hedged on three sides and with a boundary of stunted trees on the other. A five barred farm gate lay in the corner of two of the hedged sides and provided access to a narrow track which in turn led down to a narrow lane which ran parallel to the shore, a field's width distant.

'Check the area around that gate,' he directed the officers. 'With luck there'll be some soft mud and a print or two for us to examine. And then look along the lane.' He looked around. The church tower rose from the far end of the building. Its grey stone seemed to have grown from the landscape. It seemed to Jack, in a sudden flight of imagination, that it looked firmly downwards, not without compassion, towards the scene. Built as it was to reach to heaven it couldn't quite shift its gaze from the earth. He shrugged away the fancy. 'Is that lane closed off?' he called.

His colleague nodded assent. 'We've secured the perimeter of the church and its approaches and the path down to the footbridge. The whole section is cordoned off, just as you asked.'

Jack nodded approval.

'Found anything?' he asked.

'We started at first light but there's nothing new; any news of the boy?'

Jack shook his head. He turned back from the grave and walked across the wet grass towards the narrow path that led to the arched door of the church. He sat down on a small recessed seat set within the deep wall of the stone porch.

Something about the recent chain of events disturbed him deeply. It was not merely the matter of two bodies discovered in a matter of days, nor was it the untidiness of the whole business of disappearing evidence – he was confident that these things would be explained in due course. It was, in part, the loss of control that these events carried with them, that bothered him. He should have been concerned with the question of evidence, identity, timelines, patterns and the identification of cause and motive. Instead his mind continually returned to other matters. Where was the boy who may have witnessed such a brutal murder and mutilation? Why could they not find him? Had he not told his parents what had happened? Why were there no signs of his presence in the graveyard? How had the murderer performed his gruesome act and also departed leaving no trace? Where was the body from the mortuary? How had he died? Was it a natural death, suicide or murder? There was little as yet to suggest a violent crime. The wound on his neck, no matter how significant, could not have caused his death. That was merely, yes, another coincidence.

He distrusted coincidence and yet there was nothing at all to connect definitively the two events. They were separated by character and by space – twenty miles and 2500 feet to be precise; and despite his suspicions there was nothing conclusive yet to prove that the first body had been murdered at all. There was also something slightly unworldly about the body in the cave which he could not quite define. Garth Fielding had felt it, Sandy had made mention of it and those eyes had even had a startling effect on Jack himself. Was there any significance in that? - No, probably not. There was the coincidental presence of the boy at one scene and of children's clothing on the body at the other. There were the remains in the cave of children from a different time. There was evidence which suggested the presence of bodies stretching back a hundred years or more. The graveyard corpse was found by the last resting place of a historic murder victim, killed over a hundred years ago. Of course, the bones in the cave might not have been those of murdered people; they could have been buried there, or have died in the winter cold……..and yet……

'Coincidences!' muttered Jack.

All these things seemed to tie the two events so closely in his mind that he had difficulty separating them. One dead body located in such circumstances was unusual in Portskail. Two was unheard of.

He was disturbed by the opening of the oak door. It creaked heavily on its hinges and opened on the flagged interior. The minister emerged from its silent darkness, his steps resounding hollowly on the stone. He let the latch drop with a heavy clatter. He turned a pale, ashen face towards Jack and was visibly startled to see him in the shadows of the porch.

'I needed somewhere to think,' Jack explained apologetically.

'And I somewhere to reflect,' said the minister in a soft, barely audible voice. 'I've been here for some time. I was just coming to look for you. There is something inside here that you need to see.'

He led Jack down the narrow aisle between dark, bare pews. The walls were stark and bare yet the lofty roof and the curved stone arches still managed to convey feelings aspiration and muted celebration, rising despite the constraining influence of an austere interior. The plain, glass windows of the nave brightened the interior with light, but high above the pulpit and just below the arched roof stained glass illuminated and enriched the space within with colour. It mourned and it celebrated, it rejoiced and it grieved but mostly it just observed. It watched Jack now, as he progressed along the aisle. It heard him tell the minister about the missing child and it saw the cleric's face age with shock.

'You must find him,' he said. 'You must find him the poor child!'

Their footsteps were deadened by the floor but echoed ironically in the high ceiling, like a parody.

'I do believe that ceiling is laughing at our dismal, little steps,' Jack murmured. 'The more seriously we take ourselves the more it smiles at us. Perhaps it sighs too, at our foibles and follies.'

The minister glanced sharply towards him but did not respond. He directed Jack into a dark pew to the left of the aisle.

'Look over there,' he whispered, 'beyond the kneeling cushion on the floor. We couldn't see it last night in the electric light.'

Just beyond the cushion on the dark wood were two perfect footprints in rich, crimson blood. They were large, obviously not the prints of a child's feet. They could only have been left there by the murderer.

Jack bent down and then backed slowly along the pew. He studied the floor closely. He walked slowly back along the aisle then he clambered through another pew and studied the floor on either side.

'Nothing,' he said, 'no prints, no blood, nothing. How did he get in or out without leaving a mark? Was the blood on his shoes when he came in? Why are there no marks across the grass or stains in the porch and along the aisle? Why are there no bloodied footprints leading out? He was so careful; and then suddenly so careless.'

'Perhaps he took his shoes off when he saw the blood on them?' the minister suggested mildly. 'He may have carried them from the body and across to the church.' He spoke apologetically as if his words were an intrusion. 'Perhaps he merely put them down in a moment of forgetfulness and then carried them out.'

'And didn't think to clear up the stain after he'd been so careful with everything else? Possibly, possibly,' Jack murmured. 'But why did he come in here in the first place? What was he looking for? Absolution? Forgiveness? Why would a man, who has just committed an appalling act of savagery, meticulously tidy up after himself then enter the church and leave clear footprints? Perhaps he didn't care if he was caught or not. .... What happened here last night?' He turned and looked around the silent building. 'What did you see?' he murmured, but whether his words were addressed to the missing boy or the stone arches, was unclear.

'I'll have to seal the church off until my team has a chance to gather evidence, I'm afraid. In the meantime, is there anywhere we can go to talk? I've a few questions I need to ask.'

'Of course,' said the minister. 'My house is not far away.'

The Reverend Edward Grey had ministered to the good people of Portskail for twenty three years, after a number of years spent as an army chaplain in different parts of the world. Jack watched his hunched shoulders and clasped hands. He looked like the embodiment of meekness, not the sort of meek that inherits the earth, he thought, but the sort of meek who has the earth taken from them by the cruel, the greedy, the callous and the selfish. He looked like a man who, being sensitive, caring and gentle himself, found it impossible to believe that others were not the same. His life had been a constant challenge to this belief but he had emerged resolute.

The events of the previous night seemed to have shocked him deeply. Even as they approached the gaunt, squat house with its mullioned windows set deeply in grey stone, Jack could hear him muttering to himself and shaking his head slowly in private contemplation. Jack glanced along the narrow path towards the door. Two garrets protruded like closed eyes from above the upstairs windows.

'It's far too large a house for an old bachelor like me.' Edward said, turning towards Jack. He was suddenly conscious of his poor manners. He had been so lost in thought he had led the way in complete silence until they reached the door. 'However, it comes with the job so I have to manage somehow. I only use a small number of rooms unless I have visitors. I'm afraid you will find it a rather dull, uninteresting place.' He smiled apologetically.

Jack prepared himself for a very 'vicarly' interior, dark wood, floral carpet, very traditional. He was somewhat surprised when the door opened upon an interior that seemed to have more in common with an Aladdin's cave or, perhaps more accurately, a rather refined antique shop. Certainly the floors, walls and curtains were of a depressingly predictable sobriety but the array of items displayed on the walls and on every possible surface immediately attracted the attention.

Jack took it in quickly. His eyes moved rapidly from the pair of silver flintlock pistols on the mahogany table to the cutlasses on the wall above; from the pith helmet to the display case of medals, from the collection of coins to a wall covering of Middle Eastern origin.

On entering the expansive living room he became suddenly aware that he was surrounded by the souvenirs of Edward's military career and of his passion for collecting antique items in the different parts of the globe where he was stationed. He was drawn to some framed photographs on the wall.

'Did you take these?' he asked.

Edward nodded. 'It was my hobby,' he said. 'I spent many years taking them.'

Jack scrutinised them with admiration and not a little envy. They were monochrome prints, all taken during a time spent in the Middle East. Sandy coloured men were working on a sandy coloured vehicle, no doubt repairing the damage caused by that very substance to the fragile engine beneath their hands. The photograph had caught the intensity of their concentrated faces, their unity of purpose and their immersion in the task at hand. Others were taking in the NAAFI, the officers' mess tent, or on patrols in armoured vehicles. Another showed a group of men stripped to the waist, cleaning their weapons and smoking.

'These are really most impressive,' Jack said. 'These people are engaged in all sorts of activities but it isn't the activity that attracts your eye; it's the men themselves – or rather, it's the individuality and the group identity of the men. Even the arrangement of their bodies, separate and yet leaning inwards, sharing space .... I am truly envious. These prints reveal my own paltry efforts for just what they are – snaps.'

'Thank you,' Edward smiled appreciatively. 'It helped pass the time and provided a minor record of the events and I had a captive flock as my subject matter. You see the best and the worst in such settings, the best and the worst.....' His thoughts trailed off momentarily. 'I have some photographs of the worst but I don't display them. Perhaps one day you'd.....'

'Very much indeed,' Jack replied earnestly. He looked around the room. 'Are all these things souvenirs of your travels?'

Edward nodded shyly. 'I'm afraid I have always been a bit of a collector of useless things. As a child I used to gather all sorts of things from the beach and insist on displaying them in my bedroom, - strangely patterned pebbles, oddly shaped driftwood, crab carapaces, shells and old bottles, you know the sort of things. The habit never truly went away. When I went overseas I liked to collect a few items from each place I visited. They have proved to be something of an incongruous mixture. Look at these,' he said, turning to a small collection of books to the left of an extensive bookcase. 'These are children's books, telling the story of Jesus. They are from all over the world, the Far East, the Middle East, India, Ethiopia and the United States. Do you notice anything about them?'

Jack flicked through their colourful and familiar pages. He smiled. 'Each book portrays Jesus as native to that country. We have an oriental Jesus, an Indian Jesus, an Ethiopian Jesus... How touching!'

'Yes,' laughed Edward. 'What a lesson lies there. Every one of these writers imagined that Jesus was like them, understood them and was one of them. How wonderful it is!' His enthusiasm was childlike but utterly delightful.

'If we could all identify with others like the writer imagines Jesus does, then ......' His voice faded wistfully.

'Then events like last night's would never happen,' Jack concluded.

'Exactly, exactly; it is dreadful, truly dreadful, and to think of that little child out there, alone.' He suddenly bethought himself and replaced the books on the shelf, 'But please,' he said, 'do take a seat and tell me how I can help you.'

Jack was relieved the conversation went no further. It would be unwise for a committed member of the church to delve into Jack's views on religion. He quickly asked the obvious questions. Had there been any suspicious activity near the church? Had he seen anyone hanging about? Had he heard any vehicles near the church that evening? Had he any idea who the victim might be? Did the description of the boy mean anything to him? When had he first realised there was something wrong at the church? What had drawn his attention to it?

Edward's replies were reluctantly unhelpful. He had seen nothing, heard nothing, suspected nothing and knew nothing that could be of help.

'What can you tell me about the grave where the body was found?'

'Ah, I can be of a little more help there,' beamed the minister, grateful to have at least something to offer, no matter how modest. 'I remember being told something of it when I first arrived here, although that was many years ago now and, I'm afraid, my memory is not what it was. The deceased was, I believe, a writer and traveller and lived somewhere in the south. He was not a local man. He had written a book about a previous tour and was revisiting the area. It must have been about 150 years ago. I'm uncertain of the exact dates. He was set upon by a thief as he neared his accommodation and was robbed and beaten. The criminal was never apprehended. There's really not much more to it than that. It's bitterly ironic that chance placed this poor soul at the very stone mourning another victim of senseless violence.' The minister shook his head despondently. 'He was buried here, I assume, to avoid the expense and trouble of getting him back home,' he murmured, 'or perhaps the poor man had no immediate family.'

Jack expressed his thanks and then trudged a disconsolate path back to the graveyard. He had expected very little and had not been disappointed. But it was there again, chance, coincidence, fate, and he felt peculiarly disturbed by it. Was it indifferent, blind chance that had brought these disparate events together and merely his desperate search for pattern, shape or connection that stirred his imaginings?

'Put thirty random numbers on a whiteboard in a room full of half intelligent people,' he said to Kate that evening, 'and most of them will pass their time trying to establish relationships between them. They will sort, shift, link, filter, try this and try that until they come up with something that, however tenuously, links those numbers together. And yet, those numbers were just random and unconnected. There was no purpose behind them, no guiding intellect selecting them for particular connections, patterns or properties. It was just chance. It's like that for me. I have to be sure that I am not tempted to create a pattern, to link a cause and effect, to struggle to make sense where none exists. Awkward connections keep intruding where I have no desire to see them.'

'And yet,' Kate said, 'some connection might exist. You can't simply discard the possibility. It might not be immediately rational or logical but you can't rid yourself of it. You have to wait, I suppose, until the evidence provides some insight.'

'I think it's called keeping an open mind,' Jack grimaced. 'I hate waiting,' he muttered. 'I want to go out and search out the patterns.'

'With these murders I am looking at four realities at least. Something happened in the cave; something happened in the graveyard; something happened to the victim in the grave; something happened in Sandy's mortuary. The reality of these events is there to be discovered. Something incontrovertible happened.

'Now, you start to look at these events like the numbers on the blackboard and you start to look for patterns, for causes and effects and for links; but there may not be a pattern. Do you see? There is one truth out there but there may be many interpretations. What I am looking at may be nothing more than a reflection of my own prejudices or those of my society and time. I am looking at these events through a distorting filter. I am trained to ignore patterns and relationships until they are proven and yet I am trained to watch for them. Yet behind all this there lies reality.'

He was engrossed in his argument and he spoke with increasing urgency and thought.

'An old man sits on a bench in a park. He is watching the children play. Thirty years ago that would have raised no questions. Today, he may be eyed suspiciously. That's a social and cultural context. One parents looks at him suspiciously; another smiles. They bring their own perspective with them to the scene. An older woman may view matters differently from a younger woman. A child runs across to him and they speak. Do the people in the park feel anxious or pleased? Behind all these interpretations lies a single truth.'

'It's part of your job to sift through all these interpretations,' said Kate, 'because one of them may be true.'

'Or none of them,' Jack said. 'Unfortunately, I too suffer from a need to find connections and I too have a perspective from which I view events,' Jack mused. 'It's those numbers on the board again; I can't help myself. It is very annoying.' He laughed suddenly. 'All these coincidental links are the product of my pattern seeking mind! Perhaps I should learn to love them!'

Kate laughed. 'Perhaps I should immerse myself in your intuitions. I think I'll see what I can discover about your murdered writer. I love ferreting about in local history. I will delve into the deepest corners of your imaginings and look for links that don't exist. It will be exciting. I'll start at the library tomorrow.'

'I don't know what I'd do without you,' Jack said. 'I really don't.'

'Nor do I,' Kate said softly, 'nor do I.'

Chapter Eight

Jamie stood at the stern of the outward bound ferry and looked thoughtfully back at the distant shore. He had abandoned the business that had brought him to Portskail and was going home.

His face could have been displayed on a temperance poster. He had taken an oath of sobriety which had lasted forty eight hours and looked set for longer. The words, 'Never again!' which had struggled through his teeth on more than one occasion in his early adult life, had never before been uttered with such conviction or with such sincerity as it had recently. Jamie, at this present moment, had no intention of drinking ever again.

It was not merely the memory of his pitiful state which lingered long after the final effects of his alcoholic consumption had worn off. That was a painful, recurring memory indeed but it was not the worst feature of his suffering. He was not even particularly troubled by the pointedly sarcastic tone adopted by Detective Inspector Munro and his initially scathing remarks. He had rather deserved that. In fact, Jack Munro, he decided, had a bark much worse than his bite. Having survived his initial sarcasm Jamie had found the detective remarkably sympathetic and actually of a quite friendly nature. No, it was his sense of complete inadequacy that made him feel so bad. If he had only been sober he might have noticed something useful. He might have seen where the boy vanished to. He might have identified the important clue which led to the safe recovery of the child and the capture of the murderer. If he had been sober he might have acted differently. He might have given coherent evidence. He shuddered to think that he might even have saved a life.

Jamie possessed all the heedlessness of youth but at heart he was of a sensitive and romantic disposition. In addition to feelings of genuine regret, he was also painfully aware that this adventure might have provided him with the one opportunity in his life to be a hero, to receive the adulation of an awed and admiring public – a public which, in Jamie's fevered mind, largely consisted of attractive young women of a similar age to his own.

There were substantial gaps in his recollections of that night in the graveyard. He could, for example, barely recall the details of his walk from the town to the church; he seemed to have existed in a dream like state from which only the barest and most fleeting of details emerged. He could remember a particular branch which struck him forcibly across his right cheek and he could recall quite clearly the shape of a tree root which had snagged his foot. He could still feel the clasp of glue like mud on his hands as they broke through the skin of frost. He could also hear, quite distinctly, the light, almost insignificant creaking of the wicket gate. His progress from one of these benchmark moments to the next, however, was a mystery he could not penetrate.

There were, however, painful images that were so completely and finely engraved on his consciousness that he could recall them with a clarity that caused him to tremble with emotion even now. He saw the body, the gouged out eye sockets, the bloody wound and the gravestone; but foremost amongst these images was the little boy with the tousled hair, the ribbed jumper and the vividly blue eyes, - eyes which seemed to have grown more vivid on each occasion that they opened in Jamie's waking or sleeping mind. He just could not shift that sight.

He shook his head as if to drive away the flickering scenes that flashed and changed with unwelcomed rapidity through his mind. Even when he was successful and the picture faded he was left with lingering, poignant emotions. He could not yet break free from them. It was all too fresh, too raw and too painful.

He gripped the handrail tighter and stared at the restless wake of the ship. Further and further out the waves radiated. They would eventually wash on the distant shore of the mainland, stretching from Portskail and around the loch to the open sea. The child was somewhere on that mainland, and Jamie was sailing heartlessly away from him. There was a little boy in that vast space who had witnessed this most awful crime and who carried and would carry for ever and ever those images in his young mind. Perhaps he was alone still; perhaps he had told no-one; perhaps there was no-one to listen to him. Jamie knew he was becoming sentimental and foolish but he also knew that he was sailing away from the little boy. He was going the wrong way. He could not forget the lonely tear stained figure trotting ahead of him under the frosty sky. Where was he now? Was he safe?

'I want to stay here,' he had said to Jack, barely containing the emotions that showed annoyingly in his eyes. 'I want to help find the little boy. I want to do something.'

Jack had been reassuring but firm. There was no more that Jamie could do now. He had given as good an account of the events as he could have been expected to do, under the circumstances.

'It wasn't as if you went to the pub and got drunk with the sole intention of hindering our enquiries,' Jack smiled. 'You couldn't be expected to anticipate the events that followed.'

No, it was important now for Jamie to go home to his family. He had experienced a dreadful shock and it would take some time for him to fully recover. In the meantime, if he remembered anything new, anything at all, he could always contact Jack.

'I'll give you my personal number and the office number,' he said. 'But you must go home now, for your own good. I'll let you know if we find out anything, I promise.'

Now, a few hours later, Jamie was standing at the bow of the ferry which was taking him, with very mixed feelings, towards his home. He had never before been so pleased to anticipate the welcome he would receive and the comfort he would derive from his reunion with his family. Such were the emotions he still felt, writhing and un-subdued like a coiling snake, that he imagined himself burying his head in his pillow and crying like a child. He needed, he thought grimly, the relief of tears. Yet, his eyes were also drawn unwillingly along the wake of the ship and towards the mainland. He had unfinished business there. There was no closure. He felt strangely incomplete. He pictured himself flailing helplessly in the open water, drowning.

As he stood there, other unwelcomed images returned. The boy was sitting on the cold kerbstones by the road's edge and turning that fearful, unblinking look upon him. He was scurrying beneath the overhanging trees which, in their magnitude, rendered him even smaller and more vulnerable. He was standing by the gravestone as a slight breeze ruffled momentarily a wisp of hair. Then Jamie lost sight of him. He did not see him go. There was no movement across the grass, no tiny figure slipping over the wall. He had simply gone.

Jamie clenched his eyes shut and gripped the rail.

When he opened his eyes he was aware that he was no longer alone. Another passenger had emerged from the hatchway leading to the passenger lounge below. He was standing obliquely at the rail at the further, port side of the stern. He was a man in his later middle years with rather unkempt, brown hair which the breeze caught and tossed and left all the more untidy. He had a dark but closely trimmed beard which reminded Jamie of a picture of an old seaman. He raised his eyes towards Jamie and nodded. They exchanged the usual pleasantries about the weather and the voyage and then fell silent. Jamie was in no mood for conversation and the stranger seemed happy to lean casually against the rail and look at the sea. Jamie didn't recognise him. He was probably a tourist of a lorry driver.

After a few moments he pointed towards the sea, without altering his strangely angled position beside the lifebuoy attached to the corner rail.

'Puffins,' he said. 'They're back early. I don't expect to see so many before mid May.'

Jamie looked where he was pointing, half back over his shoulder.

'No, not there,' the man said. 'You're looking in the wrong place. Look further out. Look beyond the wake. There's a raft of them out there.'

Jamie raised his eyes and saw two small birds floating just beyond the wake and then, beyond them, a larger group rising and falling on the waves the ferry had generated. He smiled. There was something in the sight of those first few migrant birds that always lightened his mood and brought a smile to his face. The seas would soon be teeming with life. He looked back towards the man but he had already moved away from the rail and was descending back to the warmth of the lounge or the shops, perhaps to rejoin a companion waiting at the bar. Jamie was alone.

Further along the rail, nearer the bow, a family, obviously on holiday, watched the seas excitedly. They had seen other puffins, guillemots and razorbills. The children pointed and exclaimed in lively, unrestrained voices. A line of gannets, white against the distant shore, made stately progress on ceremonial wings.

Jamie turned away and looked over the sea. He raised his eyes towards the pair of puffins, focusing initially too close to the ship. He raised his eyes; but as he did so it was not the birds he saw, nor was it the white wake breaking or the rolling waves, nor the distant shore. It was a small child pointing in that same manner as the stranger by the rail, towards a bloody body slumped against a leaning, grey stone. Jamie, in raising his eyes, was looking not at the body but at the gravestone against which it was leaning. The boy's eyes were asking Jamie to look, not at the bloodied corpse, but at the words sculpted on the gravestone above.

Jamie emitted a half stifled cry. 'He was pointing at the words!' he said aloud.

He fumbled in his pocket for his phone. He needed to tell Jack at once. It might be important.

There was, of course, no signal.

There was nothing he could do until he reached the island. He reached his hands to his head and then turned and beat his fists against the rail. The family near the prow turned and looked at him and then moved away. He turned and stumbled down into the lounge. There was nothing to do but wait until the ferry docked in an hour or so. Until then he would just sit quietly at a table and try to relax. More than anything now, he wanted to be alone. Being a young man of intense passions his reaction, he knew, was disproportionate and melodramatic. He needed to calm himself. Yet, such was his desire to offer something, - some new evidence that might be of assistance, - that his heart beat excitedly. Perhaps, he thought, perhaps ....

He was, therefore, particularly aggrieved to see Simon Keller's lank, insinuating form sidling across the lounge in his direction. Simon lived with his mother and her family in a small croft just outside the main village. His father, from whom she was estranged, lived in Portskail, where he had been employed as a police constable until his retirement. Now he tended his garden and formulated simple solutions to the world's problems which he shared via the medium of radio talk shows, to which he was a regular contributor. Jamie had known Simon since his arrival on the island at the age of seven and had disliked him ever since. There was too much of the ferret in his narrow face and sharp eyes, too much of the snake in his cold watchfulness and altogether too much of the slug in his manner of insinuating himself into company. He approached now with his customary look of feigned humility and Jamie gloomily anticipated the sneering unpleasantness of what he would have to say.

Simon had adapted readily to the occupation of journalist on the Regional Newspaper where he had quickly learned to specialise in the mean, the cheap, the sordid, the salacious and the distasteful. His pathetic victims were minor officials, local government officers, teachers, doctors, solicitors, clerics of all denominations, public servants and elected officers whose minor indiscretions were elevated and exaggerated by his florid prose and presented with shock and disbelief to an appreciative public, hungry for the humiliation of others. Jamie's distaste for Simon's self satisfied and smug readership was only exceeded by his disgust for the journalist himself. He felt acutely sorry for his victims. Simon also contributed smaller, homely pieces to the local Portskail news sheet.

He had flourished in his chosen profession and in recent months had sold several lurid stories to national tabloids. He had clear expectations that his future would draw him away from this parochial backwater and into a national context where his abilities would be fully appreciated.

To make matters worse, Jamie could not help but admit that Simon was a very gifted writer. He could weave words into an embroidered pattern of colour and wit. He was also relentless in his pursuit of success and was fiercely single minded.

Without invitation Simon curled himself onto the chair opposite Jamie and in a casual and languid tone began with pleasantries and small talk which, in Jamie's jaundiced view, conveyed all the pleasure of being caressed by worms. Simon obviously wanted something and Jamie was immediately on his guard. He was aware that those ferret eyes were watching him, weighing his reactions, probing for a weakness.

'So,' Jamie interrupted him, 'What are you working on at the moment, anything interesting? Any heads I should expect to see rolling down Portskail Main Street?'

Simon laughed without mirth. He tapped the side of his nose with a stained forefinger. Then he feigned indifference.

'Well,' he said, 'I don't suppose it will do any harm to let you into my little secret.' He leaned over the table, far too close for Jamie's comfort. 'I'm taking a particularly close look at some of our local police officials,' he said, nodding knowingly, 'and one in particular. I think you know him.'

Jamie was immediately on his guard. He shrugged.

'I'm really not that familiar with our local police force,' he smiled. 'I try to keep away from them if I can.'

'If you can, yes,' Simon drawled, 'but it's not always possible though, is it?' he smiled. He seemed to change the subject. 'I listen and I watch. There's not much happens in Portskail that I don't hear about. Sometimes I get a whiff of something going on, some sudden flurry of activity, a sudden movement of people and vehicles. I have a circle of acquaintances too, who are quick to let me know of any unusual activity, - at night, let's say, in a churchyard perhaps. Then I ask a few official questions. I get fobbed off with the usual bullshit. I hang around outside the police station and watch who is coming in and out. You can learn a lot just watching.'

Jamie felt his stomach lurch. He felt himself breathing more rapidly and was more conscious that ever of those penetrating, rat-like eyes watching him. He succeeded in maintaining a calm that he did not feel. He laughed.

'You might have seen me then,' he said. 'I can trust you not to mention it on the island, can't I? I don't want my parents to find out I was drunk and incapable! You'd think I'd know better at my age!'

Simon's eyes did not flinch.

'So you can tell me nothing about what drew our illustrious detective inspector Jack Munro to the church yard in the early hours?' he sneered.

Jamie shook his head.

'They locked me in a cell for my own safety and I was out for the count. I didn't hear a thing all night. I got an official warning the next morning and they let me go. Sorry.'

Simon paused slightly longer than was necessary or comfortable.

'Ah well,' he said, 'It was worth a try. Where were you picked up?' he asked. 'It wasn't in a graveyard, was it?' He smiled unpleasantly. He uncurled himself from the chair and went back over to the bar.

Jamie waited for a moment and then slipped out of the lounge and sat on a bench by the stern rail. He decided he would rather be cold than risk further the companionship of the ferret. Much to his relief, Simon remained below. Jamie did not see him again until they disembarked and, much to his relief, set off in different directions. He watched Simon hurrying past the row of houses near the quayside as he headed to the bus stop.

From the port there was the short bus ride across the island. He could not avoid conversation on the journey. There were some familiar faces from the village, a neighbour from an adjacent croft and a family of incomers who had settled on the island to escape the relentless pace of urban life. They all chatted as the bus rumbled over the deteriorating road. He joined in half heartedly but was relieved when he could finally disembark and begin the walk up the hill towards his croft and the sanctity of home.

He stopped on the close cropped path when he was some distance from the house and breathed deeply. It was a sunny afternoon but the cold wind blew from the east and bit deeply. He sat down for a moment by the wall of an old sheep pen and gained what shelter he could. In the lull of the wind he felt the warmth of the sun trying to break through.

He looked across the moorland to the distant sea. Here and there he could see the ruins of old cottages and decaying stone buildings. Towards the coast a scattering of croft houses remained. Some had been converted into family homes. Others belonged to families who had lived there for generations. Little had changed since he was a child; yet everything had changed. It was as though he was looking at it for the first time. Years had passed in those last few days.

He felt tears pricking his eyes and then he wept and the relief brought by this release overwhelmed him. It was several minutes before he felt sufficiently revived to be capable of continuing his walk. By the time he reached the familiar gate and the doorway of his home he felt composed enough to withstand without emotion his mother's effusive hugs and his father's anxious looks. He fell back in a familiar soft armchair and, he was shocked to realise, felt safe for the first time in days.

Chapter Nine

Garth wiped his hands on a chequered cloth and smiled appreciatively at the newly tiled kitchen. He had returned to the task after a brief evening meal and had quickly completed the final touches. It looked perfect. The combinations of colours which he and Alice had discussed at such lengths, the browns and greys, the whites and creams, had suddenly emerged from their isolated corners and fragmented spaces and had joined together in one delightful whole. The result was as light and airy as he had hoped.

'Though I say so myself,' he murmured with satisfaction.

He was feeling particularly pleased with himself that day. The bathroom was tiled and painted and the kitchen was within a day of completion. Having laid the laminate floor and installed the electrical goods he had merely to complete the final touches on the cupboards in order to place a tick next to it on his diminishing list.

'Two weeks ahead of schedule,' he said to himself. 'That's the benefit of being here on my own with nothing else to do!'

There was something rewarding and soothing, he thought, about a practical task successfully completed. He would be able to sit back that evening with a pleasing sense of self satisfaction which his creative and professional work rarely gave him. He had been engrossed for hours, almost mindlessly and the outcome was almost perfect. It had consumed him entirely. He wished all his days could be like this.

Unfortunately, it was all a distraction. Tomorrow he would think about his writing again and he would be restless and anxious until he set something down on paper.

That was how the year would be spent; moments of serene forgetfulness would be interrupted by times when he would be beset by the savage desire to lay down some meagre token of his existence. He would spend the weeks oscillating between these two competing forces and it was between these extremes where his family would be expected to exist, hopefully with some degree of contentment.

He frowned, momentarily beset by anxiety. He had hoped to use his evenings to begin some preliminary sketches for his work but he had made little progress. The hours spent in repetitive tasks had certainly given his mind time to wander around the many ideas that had been simmering on a low heat. Occasionally ideas had bubbled and spurted and he had been stirred by their sudden warmth. He had been briefly excited by the emergence of an embryonic idea.

'Tonight,' he had murmured then, 'I will think more about this. Tonight I will make a start,'

Each day he had anticipated with excitement the commencement of his work. But the evenings arrived and he found himself beset by a series of minor tasks which he felt he could not sensibly postpone. By the time he was free of them it was too late to make a successful start.

'Tomorrow,' he said to himself, again and again, 'Tomorrow!'

But the next day he was preoccupied with final touches to his building and decorating and was soothed by the ease of activity.

'It'll be much easier to work once everything is done,' he thought, 'and when Alice and Euan are here.'

He consoled himself by reviewing and clarifying his ideas in preparation for that time.

'Only a few more days!' he said to himself.

The house was fit for family occupation at last. Only vanity had prevented him from informing Alice of his rapid progress. He had a childish desire to surprise her with his achievement. Now, Alice had left her job, said her final farewells to her colleagues and was busy packing their final possessions. Euan would bid farewell to his school friends at the end of the week and soon after that they would begin their new life in their new home.

'And what a new home it will be,' he said to himself with satisfaction, 'and what a wonderful quality of life we shall have. I can hardly wait!'

It was almost eight weeks since Alice and Euan had last seen the house. Since their brief holiday, the windows and doors had been replaced, the stone work pointed and the whole exterior repaired and refreshed. Some tiles had been replaced or re-bedded and guttering had been renewed. The kitchen and the living room were all but ready as were two of the three bedrooms. He had still to complete the entrance hall and reception rooms with flooring and paint and the final bedroom had scarcely been touched. However, he saw no reason now why it should not be sufficiently complete for their life to begin. Any few outstanding tasks could be left until they were happily together again.

'You're going to love it here,' he said aloud, just as if they were present before him. 'We're going to be happy. Can you imagine it? Happy! We can make a fresh start.'

The last year had not been a success. He knew he had not been easy to live with. He had felt under pressure at work; he had watched his academic dreams flicker and fade. He had been depressed and resentful. His moods had been at best unpredictable. At the worst times he had been depressed, anxious and impossibly selfish. It had been impossibly hard on Alice and their relationship had suffered. Were it not for Euan, he often thought, they might not have survived.

Life, he believed, now offered them new hope. He had a momentary vision of the years laid out ahead like a rolling landscape under a blue sky with scattered clouds and a gentle, warming breeze. They would walk the undulating path through green meadows and abundant flowers; they would hear the hum of insects and listen to the songs of birds. Metaphorically speaking, of course, he told himself, and smiled. But mountains or meadows, moorland or fields, breeze or wind and rain, he felt there was a freshness in the life that lay ahead which was only threatened by time.

He saw a far horizon and over it there loomed a sombre mist which gradually extended and seemed to bubble with low, ominous cloud. He imagined he saw it growing and billowing gradually towards him and gathering with implacable intent.

He shuddered as if the sun had slipped behind those distant clouds.

'I have to write my book,' he murmured, 'make my mark, show I was here. There's no time to waste.'

He felt a momentary qualm in his stomach and a familiar fear welled up. Perhaps the demons that had threatened their happiness over the last year would move here with them. Perhaps they would never be free of them. He thought involuntarily of the body in the cave. It lay before him in its nakedness and once again its eyes connected with his as if with a blue, jagged flame of ice.

'Perhaps you know something,' he found himself saying. 'You know ……but what do you know? And would I want to hear even if you could tell me?'

His mobile phone rang, breaking sharply into his reverie, and he was brought rapidly back to his house, his kitchen and the present moment.

'Yes?' he said. 'Oh, Jack, it's you. Yes, yes, of course. What time? Yes, I'll be here. Yes, I look forward to seeing you tomorrow. I .....' The line had gone dead.

'A busy man,' Garth muttered. Still, he was pleasantly excited at the thought of renewing his acquaintance with a local inhabitant. His days generally lacked variety and, although busy and rewarding, were devoid of human company. Only the postman or a craftsman broke the silence with an occasional visit. He was also pleased to think that he might learn a little more about the body in the cave.

As evening fell the hills gathered closely as if listening just outside his window. He particularly liked this time of day. He liked to delay turning on the lights or closing the curtains until the last, lingering glow of daylight was extinguished and stars had begun to appear clearly above the ridges. Even in the darkness the mountains were there, darker even than the darkest night. An alien, agnostic presence, they saw and they heard and they made their silent judgement. His little house seemed to shrink beneath them and became small and insignificant, a grey, stone cottage, snuggled beside a copse of trees, a narrow lane and a narrow stream passing by. Sheep grazed, pale and patient, or lay hunched and unheeded by the old, stone walls.

Strange, that as it shrank beneath their stare, to Garth the house grew warmer and safer and more completely one with the fragile world around it. He moved from the window and sat on his cushioned pew, beside the glowing logs on the fire. He added another and sparks momentarily flew before the fire grew more subdued and began the onerous task of chewing into flames the new bone he had thrown it. The thin wisps of smoke that had curled to the large chimney were supplemented by a sooty grey complement provided by the fresh timber.

He was settled and warm, if not entirely comfortable. The cracked timbers of Victorian church pews provided at best a limited aid to relaxation even with the addition of an array of cushions. Such woodwork, it seemed to him, was designed rather to keep the occupant awake and attentive than to promote comfort and rest. Beside him, he had a bottle of beer, the enjoyment of which (being one of a small number of carefully regulated vices) he had been anticipating for some hours.

Unwillingly, he crossed the room at last to close the thick curtains and to turn on the light.

The guilty book, which had been the unwitting initiator of his and Jack Munro's troubles, lay open on the pew. He picked it up and flicked through it to a page marked with a piece of card. He had found a brief reference to his own home, a discovery which prompted an inexplicable surge of pleasure.

'The small house of Aultmore' it said, *'is situated between the track which leads from the obscurity of Inverstrach to the inconsequential village of Laurimore and the Gednoch Burn. It extends to twenty acres of coarse grazing and fishing. The mean dwelling house is obscured by a protective copse of silver birch, rowan and pine, and offers no immediate welcome to the traveller. It has been held by the same family for several generations. Adjacent to the house is a sordid cottage adjoining a stedding, let by the owner to a poor family whose identity I did not discover but whose piteous condition I could not help but regret. Records contain no other names than Aultmore and indicate*

that the land has been handed in direct succession from father to son for at least two hundred years. The current owner, Jeremiah Aultmore, a surly, morose, single man of idle, solitary pursuits and misanthropic nature, is well suited to the isolated, desolate setting where his more generous forebears built a successful life through hard and relentless work. Being a confirmed bachelor by choice and nature, Jeremiah is likely to be the last in his line. The future of the land and house is, at the present time, uncertain.'

'Uncertain, no longer,' Garth mused contentedly. 'Aultmore has a future!'

He had read the passage a number of times and was intrigued by its tone. He imagined the writer calling upon old Jeremiah in the hope of refreshment or accommodation. His welcome had, perhaps, been less that convivial and he had left with a grim and uncomplimentary view of the old man's character. He tried to picture the scene, the old, surly man by the fire offering unwillingly the barest of cold offerings to his unwelcomed guest. The guest, having made every effort to engage the old man in conversation, is repulsed by the brevity and sharpness of his answers and eventually falls silent. He contemplates the bare, mean room, its dark corners into which the dim light of a single candle can barely reach. The very flame flickers nervously as if embarrassed at its own inadequacy. He is glad to escape to the coarse, uncomfortable bed and to a broken night's sleep. He is even happier to escape into daylight the next morning and to resume his journey. As he departs he sees a ragged family at the door of the meagre cottage which is now Garth's store room and feels sorry for them.

His comments no doubt reflected some such experience, Garth imagined. He smiled to himself. His eyes were feeling heavy. No doubt as a consequence of the warmth of the fire, the calming effects of the beer and the arduous labours of the day, he slipped into a light slumber from which he only woke in time to reflect, with some irony, that it was time he was thinking of bed.

Before then, however, he would try to phone Alice. They had agreed that they would keep in daily telephone contact, an agreement entered into without full knowledge of the complexities involved. There was no landline at Aultmore and the mobile phone signal was at best inconsistent and frequently nonexistent. There were some days when the signal could only be reliably obtained from the driveway just beyond the front door. Inevitably, such occasions were during the least hospitable conditions or at the worst part of the day. Tonight was to prove one of those occasions and, after several futile attempts from indoors, Garth donned a warm coat and resorted to the driveway.

The spring evening now carried with it a penetrating chill. Stars overwhelmed the shadows of sparse cloud which scurried by to leave the clearing sky. There was no moon and shy stars tumbled into view until the sky was rich with them. Such was the growth in their numbers that Garth could imagine the sky turning completely silver and as bright as day as more and more tumbled into view and filled each remaining gap.

'It's a beautiful night,' he told Alice. 'You'd love it. The atmosphere is so still and so clean I can see more stars than I've ever seen before. There'll be a frost by morning. I've almost finished the inside of the house now. It's ready for when you arrive.'

They spoke in greater detail of the renovations, the new kitchen, the bathroom, his temporary furniture and their excitement that they would soon be together.

'Euan is desperate to move,' Alice said. 'He asks every day. He's nervous about starting a new school and sorry to be leaving his friends but he's excited at the same time.'

Garth had made enquiries about schools and had already enrolled Euan at Inverstrach, which was the nearest village. He told Alice what he had found out about it. It was a small school with just two classes. It had a field and a playground and looked out across the village street towards a small playing field behind beside which was a tiny lochan surrounded by trees. Just along the road, perhaps a hundred yards away, stood the Inverstrach Mountain Hotel and a war memorial. There was little else.

'The teachers at the school seem really nice,' he said, 'and the children seem very friendly and gentle. Tell Euan there are red deer on the moor most mornings,' he continued. 'They come down to the river at night. By nine o'clock they have disappeared back into the hills. Tell him that today I saw a fox crossing the drive and that there are eagles that fly along the high ridges.'

He told her about the mercurial Jack Munro and the mystery of the missing cave and they laughed.

'Rural detectives,' she said. 'They don't just lose evidence they lose the scene of the crime! What will your detective do, do you think? Perhaps he'll call out tracker dogs to try and find where it's gone!'

'I like Jack, though,' Garth said, 'He's not at all what I had imagined. He took one look round this room and seemed to know all about me. It was quite disconcerting! He struck me as a man it would be difficult to get to know but perhaps well worth the effort.'

It was at that point that the mobile signal chose to cut out and to decline further co-operation. Several further attempts ended in failure. Discontented as he always was when a call ended without affectionate words of parting, he was obliged to accept the abrupt termination of their dialogue and to return inside. At least they had been able to speak for slightly longer on this occasion.

A light flurry of air caused the leaves to stir on the trees and thin filaments of cloud slipped past beyond their silhouetted branches. A sound, a hiss, a cry, rose in the breeze and vanished with it. Garth stopped for a moment to listen.

The breeze came again and, with it, the same sound only this time louder and clearer. The hiss was more of a gasp and the cry more of a wail, trailing and fading as the wind eased.

He waited. In the distance a deer barked. A moment later it barked again. It sounded closer; it had probably turned its head towards him. Branches were indistinctly silhouetted against the sky, their absence of foliage permitting cheeky stars to peep from secret places.

The renewed breeze moved the branches lightly and the stars flickered. The sounds came again. A gasp, quite clear now, came from the vicinity of the ruined cottage. The cry that followed it was subdued. It sounded so lonely, like the cry of a child lost in the darkness. It drew Garth back instantly to long distant, half forgotten childish terrors. It cried for comforting, reassuring arms and words that would drive away the echo of a nightmare.

He turned towards the cottage and followed the pathway round. He stumbled to the doorway and waited. Surely the sound would come again. It would be clearer and nearer; he would locate its precise position.

From close beside him, within the ruin and at the height of the eaves, there came a sudden hiss followed by a second, longer and more drawn out. There followed a strange, loud screech. He shuddered and then, 'Barn owls,' he thought with nervous delight. He had heard their eerie, nerve tingling calls once before, on a holiday in Wales. Then, as now, they sent a shiver along his spine which he was unable to repress. He moved slowly into the ruined doorway and waited in the darkness.

There was a screech, a silent movement of white, shadowy wings, a brief glimpse of a pale, disc-like face and it was gone. A small amount of mortar, dislodged from its ledge, tricked to the ground. The owl fled, a pale ghost, into the darkness outside. Fearing that even at this unusually early stage in the season there may be eggs or young Garth backed out of the ruin. His heart was beating foolishly, erratically. He could hear it in the silence.

It was only as he regained his composure and began to reflect on the delightful news he would share with Euan and Alice that his primitive fear subsided and he became calm once more. It was at that moment of excited serenity that a second sound arose. It emerged from the building with such speed and intensity that he was driven back, step upon stumbling step before he turned and fled into the house. He fumbled with the lock and stood, trembling, with his back pressed against the door.

A scream of such magnitude and fury, emanating from a point just beyond the wall by which he stood, carrying such despair, grief and terror, filled him with a dread that he could not subdue.

'Barn owls,' he repeated to himself, over and over, 'it was barn owls with young.'

Chapter Ten

Jack was in his office early that morning. The police station was an old building, full of angles, columns, arches and cornices, set back, smugly Victorian, from the narrow main street of Portskail. Jack's office on the first floor was a small room, barely sufficient to hold a modestly sized pine desk supporting a computer, a printer and a telephone. The remaining space available for work was much diminished by the presence of a number of papers and boxes which, whilst not untidy, created an impression of a man engaged in a perpetual search for order which he could not find. The room had two exterior windows which looked out over the street and two interior windows which looked out from either side of a door onto the space generally occupied by the small number of permanent staff under his command. One young officer was currently walking towards the door whilst hurriedly donning a coat. Julie, the only other figure in the room, was seated at her desk completing a report using two fingers on a computer keyboard.

Jack felt a pang of guilt at his recent treatment of the departing officer but the temptation had proved irresistible. Besides, he would have to get used to it. The police profession could be merciless.

'Now, think back, Phil! When did you last see the cave? Have you checked everywhere? Retrace your steps. Think of everywhere you've been until you find it!'

It worked well for keys, wallets, purses and the like. It might work for a crime scene.

'Have you checked all your pockets? What were you wearing? Think hard now!'

Phil was a short, stocky young officer who had all the appearance of having recently been freed from a rugby scrum. He had tried to smile but was only too pleased when he could escape to pursue his regular duties. Under normal circumstances he delighted in Jack's caustic wit but under normal circumstances he was not its target. He was more familiar with the role of entertained observer. His powers of repartee being somewhat restricted both by nature and pay grade he chose to suffer in grim silence and to stoically accept the inevitable consequences of his ill fated sojourn into the hills. He consoled himself with the thought that Jack would himself be subjected to more than a little sarcasm from his city colleagues.

Jack's returned to his office and the papers which littered his desk. They had obviously been recently scrutinised and temporarily laid aside. One was a meticulously composed report by Philip Bentley who had so carelessly mislaid the scene of the first crime. Even at a cursory glance it was evident that he was anxious to justify himself and to make it clear beyond doubt that he had been efficient, thorough and comprehensive in his search. His account was scrupulous and detailed and full of serious self justification.

'...... followed precisely the route of the previous day.....departed from the river at the point where the limestone bluff appeared and the ground levelled ....made my way to the foot of the cliff across the grass and peat ....traced a route round the cliff foot ....searched every possible location ....'

The words, 'The cave was no longer visible. It had completely disappeared, leaving not a single trace,' were typed in bold font and underlined.

Jack smiled. These keen, young police officers were far too serious. He laid the first report back on his desk and picked up a second one.

He slowly turned on his swivel chair and perused the second document which he held carefully between thumb and forefinger of his left hand. A brief smile flickered across his face as if he were struck by some irony in the document – which indeed he was. Then he frowned.

'Another coincidence,' he murmured, darkly, 'I hate coincidences.'

He jumped to his feet and tapped on the interior window. Julie looked towards him.

'Well done, Julie!' he called through the glass, pointing to the document. 'Well done indeed! Give yourself yet another gold star! I don't know how you managed to translate this but it is a remarkable piece of work.'

Julie smiled. Another young, serious police officer, he thought. Where do they find them? He felt old.

He stopped and turned and wagged an admonishing finger, 'Nonetheless, Julie, you have done me one great disservice. You know how much I hate coincidences.'

Julie looked up inquisitively.

'This murdered man – the one beneath the gravestone – I dare say you noted his name and the place of death?'

Julie nodded. 'Marius Dorling,' she said.

'I have recently encountered that very name whilst at Aultmore House.'

Aultmore House!' Julie laughed. 'But that's near where........'

'Precisely,' said Jack. 'It is remarkably close to the very place where the murder took place all those years ago. And Aultmore, Julie, is the new home of the gentleman who was so inexplicably drawn to locate the cave where our first body was found.'

He turned away, shaking his head and reading once again the transcription before him. 'The murder victim was the author of a book that I saw at his house,' he murmured, largely to himself. 'I don't trust coincidences. They make me itch.'

As if to emphasise the point he scratched his head energetically.

He turned to another document and his mood changed again. The eyeless body in the graveyard had not proved difficult to identify. He was Malcolm McColm, aged forty three, senior partner of Dunnett and McColm, Solicitors and Estate Agents. They had a new branch, recently opened right there in Portskail and he had, until recently, occupied a substantial dwelling house a few miles beyond the town. He was the son of Angus McColm, a renowned city barrister, who had recently retired after many years of successful practice. Malcolm had recently separated from his wife of fifteen years after a foolish mid life liaison with a young and indiscreet office clerk who had foolishly betrayed some of the more salacious details of her secret life to Simon Keller. The subsequent revelations of bondage and sado-masochism in the local paper had brought an untimely end to both his affair and his marriage. It had also brought a significant pecuniary reward to Simon who had sold the salacious details he had prised from the young woman to a national tabloid.

Jack left the office unwillingly that morning. He had to visit the wife of the dead man who, despite the breakdown of their marriage, was still deeply distraught at the events of that night and the brutality of her husband's death.

The detached, affluent house where they had lived seemed so incongruously safe, so neat and bright. It sat alone in an extensive garden with colourful, bordered lawns and trimmed shrubs and trees. Daffodils sprang from the lawns and nodded and bowed. The gravel driveway was so carefully groomed it had the appearance of a mosaic of individually laid stones. Its façade radiated Edwardian self satisfaction and opulence. The interior of the house too was warm and elegant. The ugly, brutal and chaotic scene in the graveyard seemed to belong to a different world and different time. It was hard to imagine that bloodied, eyeless corpse having any place in this secure and ordered house. Yet, just beyond that ordered world, another world existed and occasionally and catastrophically intruded.

'You don't lose all your feelings for someone,' Andrea McColm sobbed, as she led him to a comfortable lounge, now draped in sombre gloom behind drawn curtains, 'no matter what they've done. We were together for a long time. We were happy some of the time.'

She was engaged in a familiar, long and lonely process, reconstructing the past in a form that she could hold on to and celebrate. Reality is too harsh a bedfellow. Eventually she would create a mythology that might keep her warm at night.

'Everyone needs their illusion,' Jack thought. 'If you don't reconstruct the past you have to live with its grim, sordid truth. You can't reminisce and be comforted by the dark reality.'

'Do you have any family nearby?' Jack asked gently. She shook her head. 'We had no children,' she said, 'Malcolm's parents live in a house just outside the city. Mine are from further south.'

'Is there anyone we can contact for you?' he asked.

'You're very kind,' she sobbed, 'but no. My parents are on their way. They set off as soon as they heard. They'll be here very soon. I don't need anyone else.'

Jack asked his questions. He built a picture of the victim. He was a well respected, very ordinary man, a keen golfer and amateur painter, a man whose business involved little of consequence – the buying and selling of properties, the preparation of documents, wills, legal agreements. There was nothing questionable in his past, nothing controversial in his dealings. He had no enemies, was involved in no disputes and had been an exemplary husband and friend, failing only in this one, foolish extra marital affair. It was his rather extravagant mid life crisis. Mrs. McColm had been alone in the house that night but there was no reason to believe she was capable physically or emotionally of such a violent crime.

Jack was glad to finish his questions, to express his condolences and take his leave. He found such sadness hard to deal with. In a few months she would have created her new truth and she would be able to speak from the heart of her delusions. For now, there was nothing to say or do, no remedy he could prescribe. His task was, at best, to apply some soothing balm to a wound he could not heal. Finding the culprit and the motive would help her achieve closure and begin reconstitution.

As he pulled away he saw a car carrying an elderly couple draw up outside. Their pale, anxious faces caught his attention and, momentarily, a door opened on the private grief, the guilt and the regrets, the memories of good and ill, that would now accompany them all through the long days ahead. It was a door he quickly closed.

It looked increasingly as though the murder was merely opportunistic, a thought which disturbed Jack considerably. Crimes that had a clear motive were usually isolated and singular events. They had a profile, a contour of cause and effect and there were consequences for the killer. An investigation followed and almost invariably a conviction. Random acts of unprovoked violence, which were without apparent motive, were different. This particular crime had the additional complication. The attack was not merely one of brutal frenzy which might indicate a schizophrenic mind. It was sadistic. There was no reason to suppose that any psychological abnormality which had provoked the crime in the first place would necessarily have been assuaged by the death. On the contrary, there was a possibility that other crimes would follow.

It was a thought that Jack did not divulge at that time to anyone. He certainly had not divulged it at the hastily convened press conference outside his office, despite the insinuating probing of Simon Keller. He found himself selfishly hoping that if there was another murder it would occur elsewhere. There were few journalists present at such short notice which pleased Jack There was one representative of a national radio station, two camera crews, two regional reporters and the ghastly Simon Keller.

Jack loathed Simon Keller on sight. His worm like questioning seemed to hint at a far greater knowledge than he could possibly possess. He asked about witnesses and, alarmingly, about the ages of witnesses. He asked about the nature of the wounds, the cause of death; he wondered if there were any unusual features to the murder. He obliquely questioned whether a crime of passion had been considered and whether Jack had obtained any useful information from his visit to the bereaved widow. He asked if there was to be an appeal for anyone to come forward. Jack felt as if he was being probed and manipulated for purposes that were not completely clear. He knew that whatever the motivation was, it would not be to anyone's advantage, least of all his, to offer direct answers.

He firmly applied the cricketing principle of the flat bat and provided only the information which he wished to place in the public domain. For the moment he did not intend to reveal the existence of a possible witness and he would not elaborate on the precise nature of the victim's wounds.

He emerged from the meeting with competing desires. He wanted to wash away the film of slime with which Simon Keller had somehow seemed to coat him, and he wanted to land a blow of significant force squarely between those narrow, suspicious eyes.

'I'm going for a ride in the country.' He muttered angrily to Julie, as he grabbed his coat. 'If anyone wants me I'll be at Aultmore but I'll trust you to make sure that nobody does.'

An hour later he pulled in the drive of the house and drew up beside the ruined cottage. His mood had improved during the scenic journey. It was always like that. The lochs and mountains and ever changing clouds seemed to grant him a perspective that was easily lost in his working life.

Garth had heard him approach and met him at the door. Since he received few visitors he was keen to make the best of any opportunity for conversation and the coffee was ready before Jack had removed his coat. Garth felt rather foolish now as he thought back to the previous evening and wasted no time in a self deprecating account of his supernatural encounter and his unnatural fear.

'I couldn't get back in the house quickly enough!' he laughed. 'I felt as if I was being chased by demons. It quite unnerved me.'

'A barn owl screeching within inches of your ear is enough to send anyone running for safety,' Jack smiled. 'I believe there is a theory that a half glimpsed, silent barn owl, passing like a white mist in your peripheral vision, is the explanation for many a ghost sighting.'

'It sounded horribly human and yet unearthly,' Garth continued. 'It took me several minutes to convince myself that it was an owl. I turned the lights on and the radio just so that I could fill the house with life. I really wanted Alice to be there! Superstitions!' he laughed.

'Superstitions I can handle,' said Jack, 'it is coincidences that worry me.'

Since he did not seem inclined to elaborate, Garth turned to the reason for Jack's visit.

'I was wondering if I could borrow that book of yours,' Jack explained. 'Kate, my wife, has a keen interest in local history and her interest in this particular book has been aroused as a result of our recent mini crime wave. She is indulging me by doing a little research.'

Since Garth was inevitably unaware of recent events, Jack briefly summarised them as far as he felt able.

'It's not what you would expect in a little place like this,' he smiled, 'but don't worry. There have been very few murders hereabouts. It may surprise you to know that the author of that very book was one of that very small number of distinguished corpses.'

He saw with delight the expression on Garth's face change.

'He was murdered at no great distance from this house' he said, 'and is buried in the graveyard at Portskail.' He could not elaborate further. 'There can be no link, of course,' he smiled, 'but our curiosity has been aroused so Kate, my wife, is doing some detective work of her own.'

'The writer certainly had a poor opinion of the owner of Aultmore House,' Garth laughed. He brushed through the pages of the book to the section he had marked and handed it to Jack.

'Jeremiah, from this account, would appear to be the unsavoury sort of character that I often meet in my business,' Jack noted, 'but ugliness, as well as evil, (and for that matter goodness) are in the eye of the beholder. The writer would appear to have an ugly mind.'

'There are one or two other references to the house and land. Other places hereabouts are mentioned too. Some of them I recognise but others must relate to houses and crofts that have long since been deserted and have vanished from maps. He seems to have travelled quite extensively round here, almost obsessively in fact. I found some of the details quite tiresome and repetitive. At times he seems almost resentful at being here at all and yet he was here by choice. There are several references to the tiresome and uncomfortable nature of travel. He mentions at frequent intervals that he wants to go home.'

'Did he indicate where home was, at all?' Jack asked.

He didn't.

Jack was pleased to accept a guided tour of the property and to hear an account of the detailed renovations and alterations that had been undertaken. They finally emerged from the house and stood beside the old cottage. Jack scanned the ground and then clambered inside the ruin. He bent down below the ruined gable and picked something up carefully between thumb and forefinger.

'An owl pellet,' he said, 'there are several of them below this wall.' He held them out. 'From the skeletal remains,' he smiled, 'I would suggest that a mass murderer of field voles is present in this establishment. I have a friend who could probably tell you when the vole died, its gender and age and the approximate date of death. Unfortunately he usually saves himself for the human deceased.' He laughed. 'I wish all my crimes were as easy to solve as this one. The owl is guilty. It's an open and shut case.'

He clambered over the loose stone and the rubble from the collapsed roof.

'This seems quite well constructed,' he ventured, 'better than you would expect for some old cottage and stedding. The stones have been cut smooth on their outer faces. There are two well finished walls with rubble infill. It must have been reasonably solid in its day.'

'There was originally the one main house and this small cottage, which in Jeremiah's day was let to some impoverished family,' said Garth. 'They probably worked on the land or acted as unpaid servants in return for food and a meagre shelter. I can't imagine they would have been particularly well treated. Jeremiah doesn't sound the kindliest of landlords. The book doesn't say much but what it does say is far from flattering.'

'His predecessors were probably better disposed towards their tenants, if one can judge from the quality of the building,' said Jack. 'Maybe they had relatives staying there.' He turned and looked towards the house. 'So that would have been the home of old Jeremiah,' he said, 'and this housed some poor servant or labourer –

probably both. 'The men and boys would probably have worked on the land and the women and girls in the house and garden. That's an interesting discovery for you.'

He clambered back up the rubble and rooted further into the corner beneath the leaning timbers. The wall was taller there and held firmly to the adjoining storage area. 'Ah, I see it. The owls will be nesting in the gap beneath the top of the internal gable wall. Can you see?'

Garth looked closely until his eyes became accustomed to the half darkness. A stone had been dislodged leaving a narrow entrance into a cavity in the wall.

'That's the source of your screaming child,' laughed Jack. 'They couldn't have been more than ten feet away from where you were standing. They pretty much screamed in your ear!'

He stepped back away but, as he did so, he stumbled and leaned heavily against a half fallen roof timber. Where it was secured against the wall, in the rafters, it slipped with a sullen crack and some rubble cascaded around him. Loose masonry tumbled him and a single large, rectangular stone, dislodged from the wall, fell and landed on the rubble by his feet. He clambered quickly out.

'I think that building is best left to the owls,' he said, dusting himself down. 'I'm going to take that stone as a warning. Don't go meddling where you're not wanted. The next one might hit me!'

He laughed again as he made his way back to his car, aware that now, where there had been one cavity below the rafters there were now clearly two, symmetrically arranged either side of the apex.

He shook his head. 'What's the chance of that?' he laughed. 'Next year your owls might have neighbours!'

Chapter Eleven

Alice had grown tired of the town where she had lived with Garth since they married. She found the bustle of its streets and the eternal rumbling of traffic increasingly oppressive.

The town had grown. Like some giant caterpillar, it had begun by nibbling away at the available green spaces within its boundaries, chewing up the allotments, ingesting the waste ground, biting small enclosures and paddocks. Unsatisfied, it looked around for more food to maintain its interminable growth. It nibbled cautiously at the greenery of the surrounding countryside. It liked what it found and chewed voraciously.

When they first settled there Alice and Garth could walk from their house to the edge of the town. The University where Garth worked was still fringed with farmland; but the caterpillar, which had devoured a small woodland, hedgerows and fields to create his new faculty building, was relentless in its search for food. Soon the University itself was part of a sprawling suburb. Munch! Munch! It gnawed and chewed beyond the ring road, defoliating and destroying. Munch! Munch! It eyed greedily the neighbouring villages, once separated by belts of quiet greenery, by small fields and woodlands and streams, and it desired them. It chewed away at anything that could feed its appetite until the villages were part of the town and still it chewed. In one end went the rural scene Alice had known and loved and out of the other came roads, houses, industrial estates, offices and traffic, traffic. And still it went on. Soon it would join this town with the next and that to a further town and then another and another. One day, all the green spaces would be no more than a memory. Everywhere she turned was the roar of traffic, the stench of pollution, the ugliness of sprawling humanity. Only the parks were left, small, carefully protected pockets of artificial green; only the trees lining the roads; only patchwork gardens lining the streets.

She had to get out before it was too late. Already she felt the caterpillar inside herself beginning to gnaw. She would not allow it to transform her own nature. She did not want her life to become meaningless and without value. She did not want to give up hope, not yet, not while she was still young enough to change, not while Euan could be saved from the chaos of selfishness she saw gathering. It was time to make a move, before it was too late.

Garth wanted to achieve something memorable to mark his presence, to complete his research and conclude his book. Alice wanted only to find a home where they could settle for the rest of their lives. She wanted somewhere where she could watch Euan grow, mature and blossom unrestrained by the fear of traffic, fear of strangers, fear of bad influences, the internet, chat rooms, drugs and alcohol, and crowds, crowds of irritable, selfish, indifferent, bustling people rushing God knows where or God knows why. She wanted to have a home where the pace of life could be slowed sufficiently to allow him to develop slowly and naturally from childhood to maturity. She wanted them to live where the pressures of daily life would be of a different nature from those that beset her in the town.

'Every day, I feel as though I am being pushed along,' she complained to Garth, 'pushed and prodded, obliged to hurry, obliged to keep going forward. I feel as if there is always someone just behind me, annoyed at my slow pace. I don't know where I am going any more. I just have to go forward because there is absolutely nowhere else to go. There's a mad,

chattering crowd at my back shouting at me, all
pushing.'

Now, at last, she would be leaving the town behind
and she felt revitalised. She watched Euan emerge from
the crush at the double doors of the modern school
building and race across the playground. Together they
turned away from the regular cluster of parents and
children at the school gate and, for the last time, headed
through the streets towards the calmer refuge of the
public park.

The park and gardens had wide, meandering
pathways, large areas of open grass and avenues of
trees. Its flower beds, lake, bandstand and children's
play park offered Alice an interlude of comparative
peace and a chance to withdraw, however temporarily,
from the angry crowds. Here she had heard an echo of
her childhood and recalled in the perfume of the roses
and the honeysuckle on the botanical garden walls a
wistful memory of a distant past.

It was not long, however, before she was reminded
of the sordid present by the futility of gratuitous and
monotonous graffiti which scarred every vacant surface
around her.

'I can't wait to leave this place,' she thought. 'If I
don't get out of here, I think I will go mad. I can see the
future lumbering towards me. It picks me up like some
flotsam caught by a wave. If we don't leave I think it
will cast me on the desolate shores of some despairing
madness. Only the past seems to make any sense any
more.'

Garth, she knew, also wanted a new start. If he was
successful, he would never return to the town again.

Alice watched the people in the park and felt a
temporary calm radiate from the sun which emerged
with gratifying warmth from a bubbling, cumulous
cloud. An elderly man with a lugubrious look not

dissimilar to that worn by his ageing brown and white spaniel, made brief, smiling mention of the weather as he passed by.

A young woman, wearing a running top and pink leggings into which she seemed to have been unevenly poured, jogged heavily by. A couple lay under the expansive branches of a beech tree in the mottled shade. Further away, where the scattering of solitary trees ended, a group of young men were kicking a football on an open space of grass. She could hear the heavy thud of their feet against the ball. A family with two young children were feeding the ducks some distance away by the muddy border of the pond. She could look at them dispassionately, even sympathetically, now that she was leaving.

'The day after tomorrow,' she said contentedly, 'We shall be at Aultmore.'

She looked round for Euan. He was at the top of a slide. A number of other children were playing. Parents of the tiny ones sat on benches in the sunshine and watched. Alice watched and smiled. Euan saw her and waved. He slid rapidly down the slide, landed on his feet and ran across to her.

'I'm going on the roundabout,' he called.

A little girl, perhaps six or seven years old, was sitting alone on the roundabout. She swung her legs gently. Her fair hair hung half way down her back from below a wide brimmed sunhat of a soft, pastel shade with a floral design. A silk neckerchief of a similarly soft hue hung round her neck to protect her from the afternoon sun. She wore a long, pale, closely woven cambric dress. Its sleeves were of a full length and seemed gathered at the wrist. It was of sufficient length to cover her legs to below the calf. Her ankles and feet were bare. She held a pair of tiny shoes in her hands.

'Oh, how lovely she looks!' Alice thought. 'She's such a delicate, pretty, little girl. Speak to her, Euan. She looks rather lonely there on her own.'

Euan, fortunately, could not hear his mother's thoughts or he might never have run across to her. The suggestion that a girl could be pretty or worthy of singular scrutiny would have caused him sufficiently acute embarrassment to ensure he turned away. Instead, undisturbed by his mother's wishes, he spoke to her casually and soon the two of them were playing calmly on the roundabout and chatting.

'I wonder if he knows her from school,' Alice thought.

A rowdy group of older children ran towards them from the slide and climbing frame. Euan recognised one or two year six boys from his school. He didn't know their names. He didn't like them. They were rough and noisy. As they moved in her direction, the little girl slipped from her seat on the roundabout and ran across the grass. She knelt down by a flower bed and gently touched the flowers. She glanced occasionally and warily towards the roundabout and the children who were now spinning aggressively and screaming. Occasionally her eyes caught theirs and she watched them as they watched her.

'Beauty and the beasts,' Alice murmured. 'I wonder if her parents are sitting somewhere nearby?' She looked distractedly around. A mousy haired, harassed looking woman was sitting on a nearby bench. The woman was in her late twenties, Alice thought, but looked older. She had the narrow lipped, hard look of a woman prematurely aged by children and poverty. She had a pushchair beside her and was busy wiping the mouth of a toddler who had just finished an ice cream cone, with evident relish but a notable lack of skill. She called across to her older child, a five year old boy

who, to Alice, had the look of a future armed robber.
She saw Alice looking towards her and smiled, patting
the emerging bulge which would soon add to her
blessings and, Alice mused, to a potential rise in the
local crime rate. They exchanged a few words. There
were a few other adults around. A couple of men stood
beside push chairs and chatted whilst their toddlers
flitted from place to place. Some other parents stood or
sat in tiny groups. None of them looked as though they
might be the parents of the girl. Alice looked back
towards the flower beds.

The little girl stood up and half skipped a step or
two on the grass between the rows of flowers. She held
a yellow spring primrose in her hands, close to her
chest. She stopped and watched as Euan ran casually
towards her and stood at her side. He said something to
her and she raised her head momentarily and smiled.
They exchanged a few more words and then the little
girl hopped and half skipped a few more steps in a
distracted and dreamy manner. Euan walked beside her.
Alice saw them speaking and smiled.

She looked absent-mindedly across the park again.
When she looked back, Euan seemed to be speaking
more seriously and the girl was responding with an
enthusiastic flurry of words and was jumping up and
down excitedly. Euan turned and ran across the grass to
Alice.

'Mum?' he called breathlessly. 'Can I give her my
new address, please? She knows all about Portskail; she
even knows Inverstrach! Can you write it down for me,
please?'

Alice laughed. 'So that was it! No wonder they were
talking so enthusiastically! They were making plans!'
She took out a card from her bag and handed it to Euan.
'I had some of these made specially,' she smiled.

'Perhaps she can write to you. Our phone number is on there as well.'

Euan grabbed it from her hand and ran back to where the girl was waiting. She took the card and then ran around the flower bed and giggled. Euan followed. Then they sat on the grass and talked. After a few minutes they ran to the swings and then, as the bigger children gathered, they went back to the flowers and the grass. After another few minutes the girl ran across the grass towards the trees and then stopped and waited. Euan glanced back to where his mother was sitting. Alice gestured him to follow. She knew he would not venture further than he should. She watched as he followed the girl towards the trees and then out of sight.

'Perhaps she comes from one of the houses backing onto the park,' Alice pondered, 'or perhaps her parents are down by the lake. Perhaps Euan is going to meet them now. She looks like a little girl from an old monochrome photograph, like a little Edwardian girl at a garden party! Someone must have spent hours combing that hair!'

She had little time to reflect further. Euan had appeared from the trees on the far side of the park and was running towards her. Alice was disappointed to see he was alone. She met him on the path that would take them home. He was breathing hard and was rather pale.

'What's the matter? Did she not want to play?' she asked.

'She had to go home,' he said. His voice was subdued and anxious. He glanced back towards the trees. 'She didn't want to play. Can we go now?'

'What's the matter?'

'Nothing, I just want to go home, that's all. Can we go?'

He pulled at her sleeve. He was nervous and fearful and his face was pale and almost tearful. He kept looking anxiously across the park towards the trees and the path where he had followed the little girl. It was as if he needed to get away before she came back.

'Are you sure there's nothing the matter? What's happened?'

'Nothing; I don't like it here. I want to go home.'

'But.......?'

'Please!'

He took her hand tightly in his and remained close by her side until the park was a long way behind them. Every few minutes he would look back along the path as if they might be followed. When they reached home he ran upstairs and closed his bedroom door behind him. A moment later, Alice heard the familiar sound of his favourite computer game.

'How very strange!' she thought.

Chapter Twelve

The following evening Alice spoke to Garth on the phone. She spoke about the afternoon at the park and about Euan's strange behaviour.

'It started last night when we got back from the park. We saw a delightful little girl there. You should have seen her, Garth. She was so quaint and pretty. She was dressed in such an old fashioned way and yet it was altogether lovely – very tasteful. Euan ran across to the roundabout where she was sitting on her own. Most of the other children seemed rough and noisy and uncouth beside her. Anyway, soon they were playing nicely together and chatting away, as if they were old friends. It may be fanciful of me but I thought they looked like kindred, gentle spirits in a rather noisy and coarse world. Well, after about fifteen or twenty minutes she ran off towards the path and Euan went after her. I lost sight of them. When he came back a few minutes later he was in a dreadful mood. He just wanted to go home. He kept saying he didn't like it there any more. He seemed quite upset.

'I wondered if perhaps she said something unpleasant to him, told him she didn't want to play with him. Perhaps she had told him to go away. Children, even elegant, sweet little children, can be rather blunt at times.

'Whatever it was, it certainly seemed that she had hurt his feelings. He was strange all evening, very quiet. Before dinner, he just sat at his computer playing that interminable game, shooting monsters. When he came down to eat he barely spoke and then he vanished upstairs again straight afterwards. When I went to see him, about half an hour later, he had stopped playing on his computer. He was sitting cross-legged in the middle of his bed. The curtains pulled tightly shut and he had both his room light and his bedside light on.

'What really upset me was that he had taken all his soft toys – you know how fond he is of all those toy animals and characters he has collected – and he had rammed them into drawers and cupboards. There wasn't a single furry head to be seen!'

To enter Euan's bedroom was like lifting the lid on a treasure chest. From an early age he had loved to collect things. His eye was drawn to unusually shaped pieces of wood or pleasingly coloured pebbles, to shells, fossils, boxes, tins and bottles, to any number of pieces of junk which in some way attracted him. He loved to forage amongst antique or second hand material to emerge with some unusual item that had caught his attention, a horse brass, an unusual figurine, some strange (and often broken) toy.

On holiday one summer he went exploring and found an old bottle in the corner of a woodland glade, just beyond the campsite where they were staying. Its neck contained a small glass marble which, under pressure from the gassy liquid that once lay beneath it, must have formed a tight seal. He washed it out and cleaned it and set it carefully by his sleeping bag. He spent every spare minute of that holiday, when they weren't elsewhere, excavating his site and unearthing a variety of other bottles, including one which was strikingly blue and had contained an indigestion remedy, another of a generally cuboidal nature with a narrow neck which carried the word 'Poison' marked ominously on its side, another that looked like an old ink bottle with a fractured rim and two or three others of a less distinctive nature. They were now carefully set out on his window sill with a few of his favourite cowries, top shells and whelks and some fossil shells in limestone.

His bookcase which stood against the wall to the left of his window, next to an old wicker work chair, was beginning to find itself overwhelmed by the number of books he had collected. Until he had recently been distracted, much to the concern of his parents, by the attractions of computer games, where he fought (with much shedding of blood) against the forces of darkness, he was rarely without a book. When he was not out with friends or cycling round the block of houses where they lived or escaping to the park, he was curled up reading the novels of Alan Garner, Susan Price, Leon Garfield, Nina Bawden, Terry Pratchett and Susan Cooper. Books of an adventurous, supernatural, mysterious or historical nature predominated at different times.

On a small table adjacent to the bookcase and in the corner furthest from the window lay his scrapbooks, souvenirs of family holidays, with neatly written accounts of days spent in castles, on mountains, by lakes, in villages and by streams, with postcards, tickets, menus and photographs to accompany and illustrate them. Each daily account had been meticulously scribed in the evening before going to bed.

Pride of place, however, had always gone to the multitude of soft toys which he had acquired from various sources over his entire eight and a half long years of childhood. Some were set out on the low pine dresser, which occupied the corner of the wall opposite the bookcase. Others sat in the corner of the room where he could see them as he drifted to sleep. The remainder were carefully positioned around his pillow and accompanied him into his dreams at night. This favoured position was subject to a strict rotation so that each toy had its turn. Just the previous night the long limbed monkey and the sleek polar bear, which had lain on his pillow, had given way to a pair of small, furry puppies with pink tongues.

Since his eighth birthday he had shown some fleeting inclination to remove these toys from sight, especially when friends came to call. However, he had been temporarily reassured by, at worst, the indifference of his friends to his furry companions or, more frequently, their positive endorsement, and their future seemed rather more secure. It would have caused him some pain and guilt to have hidden from sight a family of toys who had developed distinct personalities and who depended on him just as much as he depended on his parents.

Now they had been banished from sight without ceremony and, it seemed, without regret.

'I hardly saw him for the rest of the evening,' Alice continued. 'I managed to cajole him down to watch some television with me for an hour. He just snuggled up and held me really tight. He was almost terrified when I told him it was time for bed. He insisted on keeping his light on, like he did when he was younger and the door had to be left slightly ajar.'

In fact, Euan had lain awake for a long time after retiring to his bed. He read for some time and then cast the book aside and lay on his back. He stared at the ceiling and saw its painted surface dissolve into mist. He saw movements in the mist, taking gradual, unpleasant shape. He rolled on his side and looked past his bedside light, past the wicker chair in the corner to the bookcase and the wall. He imagined faint cracks in the wall paper, like wrinkles. There was a blue, velvet cushion on the wicker chair. Set at an angle against the back it bore a shape that his imagination turned into an aged head with a crooked nose and deep set eyes. He slipped out of bed and rammed it into a drawer. He scurried back to his bed and he stared again at the wall. The intertwined wands that made up the chair back were like creases in an old face.

'I won't sleep,' he said. 'I won't sleep. I won't close my eyes. I won't grow old and die.'

He turned over and faced the chest of drawers and the pictures on the other wall. In the half gloom the pictures seemed to move and change. As he stared at them they became indistinct and lost their shape and form, absorbed into a soup of changing colours from which new shapes and new forms emerged. They were like figures moving in and out of shadows, of mist. He could hear his heart beating heavily in his chest.

The shapes frightened him. Some of them were grotesque monsters such as he might find in his computer games; others were distorted faces which changed like moulded clay or like shapes in clouds. The eyes were the worst. They were rarely clear but they were old and they were darkly indifferent to him. Some were cruel. They did not seem to have seen him or to know he was there. He didn't want them to see him. He buried his head under the covers, slowly. He wanted it to be daytime again; he wanted the room to be full of light, clearing the dark corners and smoothing out the folds and creases. The bedside lamp wasn't enough to dispel the shadows. He wanted to open the door wider and put on the outside light but he lacked the courage to climb out of bed. He curled up his knees and wished his mother would come up to see him.

'I mustn't fall asleep. I mustn't close my eyes. If I fall asleep, they'll see me and they'll creep over to my bed and when I open my eyes they'll be there, staring at me and .... '

'It was about ten o'clock,' Alice continued, 'I had just listened to the news headlines and was getting ready for bed. I heard him sobbing. I opened his door quietly and he was lying on his side, buried under the covers, curled up in a ball and crying. He seemed so tiny and so lonely. I was really worried by now and I went across the room and sat down beside him.'

Euan sat up and grabbed his mother and buried his head against her. He was shaking and sobbing as if a whole world of cares and fears had suddenly descended upon him.

'What's the matter, darling?' she asked. She stroked his head. 'Have you had a bad dream? Don't worry, my love, I'm here now. Mum's here. You'll be alright now.'

She suggested a hot, milky drink but he shook his head fiercely and clung tighter to her, digging his fingers into her side until it hurt.

'There now,' she said in a soft voice. 'Tell me all about it and I will make everything right again. What's the matter?'

'The room is full of monsters and horrible faces,' he said through his tears. 'They live in the shadows. They're everywhere. They're watching me and waiting till I go to sleep.'

'Where are they?' asked Alice. 'Tell me where they are and I'll chase them away.'

It was what they said when he was younger and had been convinced that a monster lurked in his cupboard or under his bed. She had laughed with Garth as they remembered themselves, creeping around his bedroom saying, 'Shoo!' under the bed and 'Shoo!' through the cupboard doors, chasing monsters down the stairs and out into the street. It had worked in those days and Euan had always slipped back to sleep.

'It won't work! They won't go away! They're not frightened of you any more! They're waiting! There's nothing you can do to get rid of them! I've seen them!'

'Come on!' said Alice. She stroked his head soothingly. 'Come to my bed. We can snuggle up and go to sleep. You'll be safe there. I'll look after you. There are no monsters in my bedroom.'

Euan nodded and they slipped through to the main bedroom, his bare feet padding on the wooden floor. He sniffed and rubbed his tired eyes with his hand. Sometimes it was easy to forget just how little he still was, Alice thought. He snuggled down, his head sunk into the soft pillow.

'Can we keep the light on, please?' he asked quietly.

'Of course we can,' she whispered and hugged him close. She was worried. It was difficult dealing with problems when you were on your own. She wished Garth were there with her and she felt a momentary loneliness overwhelm her.

'Tomorrow,' she thought with relief, 'Tomorrow all the bad things will be over and we will start afresh.'

'Why have the monsters come back?' Euan yawned.

'I don't know, my love, but they'll go away now.' She was quiet for a moment, allowing sleep to make its stealthy approach. 'When did they come back?' she asked quietly. She didn't want to make too much of a childish fear but it was two years since he had last experienced these night terrors. She thought they had gone forever.

'Just tonight,' he said quietly. He yawned and lay on his side and rubbed his eyes. 'I don't want to die,' he said, and the tears burst from his eyes and he sobbed. 'I don't want you to die or dad. I'm frightened of dying. The monsters will make us die.'

Alice forced back the tears that were pricking the corners of her own eyes and held him close. He was so small and vulnerable. She was angry at the terrors of life that beset him. This was the worst rite of passage of all, the realisation that the endless summer of infancy was not part of an eternal dream state but would end abruptly, finally and horribly. The passage of time, the inevitability of loss and grief and the awful finality of death were suddenly revealed in all their ugliness.

Alice could not speak. 'It's cruel!' She told herself. She cried silently, furious at she knew not what. 'It's vicious and sadistic! How could you do such a thing?'

She wanted someone to blame; but there was no-one. There was nothing. The dark, bleak emptiness of eternal night gathered around them, just beyond the window. Only that brief, flickering light separated them from the darkness and it was very, very fragile. She shuddered and held Euan as if she would never let him go again. She would protect him from everything, even death.

'You mustn't worry,' she said soothingly. 'People die when they are very, very old. It's a long, long way off. It's nothing to worry about.'

'I don't want to get very old and die,' he said.

'You're just a little boy,' she sighed. 'You've got so many years ahead and so many things to do. You don't need to think about getting old. Think of all the good things. If you think about good things, all the darkness goes away.'

'Hideous platitudes,' she thought, 'why don't we just say that death is hateful and that life is unjust and cruel? We age and decay like a piece of rotting fruit. There is only the darkness and the monsters.'

She knew why. You have to protect and reassure the young; they find out the truth soon enough. You have to temper them in preparation for their immersion in harsh reality. You want them to stay forever the same but that cannot be. It is the duty of parents to desensitise the young that they may face and endure the future. God, Heaven, Santa Claus, the inevitable power of good over evil, the magnificence of human achievement, heroism, selfless sacrifice, even love perhaps, were myths of childhood that would not be dispelled without pain.

'Only the love of a parent for a child is real,' Alice thought. Then she thought of the selfish cruelty of some parents to helpless children and tears came to her own eyes. She held Euan tight.

'People aren't always very old when they die,' he whispered. 'Sometimes children die. And sometimes ....'

'Nothing is going to happen to you, I promise,' Alice interrupted to soothe and caress. 'Mum and dad are here to protect you.'

Her tears rolled silently. It was so unjust, so arbitrary. One child was born and lived, another died. One was born to affluence, another to want. One was born to nurture another to neglect. After an arbitrary birth only chance, fate, malice, the concern or indifference of others lay ahead. Her heart reached out in that moment to all the children in need or want, the neglected, abused, despised, bullied and all those whose night fears would not be soothed away.

It was a prayer offered to emptiness. There was no answer. There was nothing there.

'I liked that little girl in the park.' Euan spoke so quietly his mother could barely hear him. 'We played by the flowers. I told her about Aultmore. She goes up there on holiday. She stops near Portskail. Then she ran across the grass. She waved to me. She wanted me to run after her. She went to the trees and then the path. Then she ....'

Alice waited. He would begin again in a moment.

'She was sitting on a bench. She looked just the same. She was facing away, looking towards the lake. She was leaning forward and looking at the ducks. I ran across and spoke to her. Then she turned round.'

His whole body convulsed and he turned round and buried his head against her and clung so tight she could barely breathe or move.

Alice was crying unrelentingly as she spoke to Garth on the telephone. Her words came in short bursts interrupted by sobs.

'It must have been so frightening for him. He must have been terrified. …… It wasn't the girl at all…..he had lost sight of her. She must have gone to play somewhere else or she had met her parents. She was probably waiting for him. …… When that head turned he expected to see a bright, round little face…..a child's face, a little girl. …… But it wasn't. It was a shrivelled, old, wrinkled face in a tiny, frail body. …. It was an old woman, smiling from a toothless mouth. The poor boy had mistaken her for the girl. It scared him dreadfully. He ran straight back to me and said nothing.

'No wonder he was looking behind us all the way home. No wonder he suffered such night terrors. His new little friend had suddenly grown old before his eyes and was slowly dying.'

Chapter Thirteen

Euan was not the only person to have difficulty sleeping that night. Across the Island Sound, in his remote croft, Jamie too lay awake, staring at the ceiling of his bedroom. He was listening to the restless sounds of the sea on the shore. His thoughts were jumbled and distorted like waves, stirred by the changing gusts and breaking relentlessly on the rocks. They refused to take any coherent shape but came and went in a disturbingly haphazard fashion. Each time he closed his eyes confused images stumbled forward and surrounded him and half familiar yet incoherent sounds beset his ears.

The angular shape of the body in the graveyard approached, faded and reappeared and became the man at the ferry rail who, in turn, transmuted into the narrow, mean figure of Simon Keller. The little boy came and went, growing and fading, at one moment alive and the next lying dead by a gravestone. Then there were eyes which emerged from his dreams, eyes without faces, always watching him, always staring at him, unflinching eyes, questioning eyes, terrified eyes. Each time they appeared he gasped for air and sat up, sweating and fearful and the images and sounds slowly faded; but it was impossible to sleep until he was so acutely tired his mind had no choice but to succumb.

The solicitations of his mother and the support of his father had enabled him to talk through the events on the mainland, to give temporary shape and form to them. He had been able to purge to some degree and for some of the time the emotions that had been his constant companions since the night of the murder. In the daytime, with the sun shining through the windows of the croft and the pale grasses bending before the constant breeze, he could forget for some length of time the things that had happened. He busied himself with spring tasks, repairing fences damaged during the winter storms, clearing debris and preparing the garden for its season of growth. He cleaned the windows, cleared the gutters, weeded the garden path and made minor repairs to the small number of outbuildings and animal sheds.

When he had no household tasks he went for long walks along the varied shoreline. He watched for otters feeding on crabs and fish in the weedy pools. He disturbed oystercatchers which were taking up residence on the shingle shore and which rose indignantly with angry, warning calls. He stirred the tiny flocks of sanderlings as they rose and fell with the waves, running up the sandy beach and back again to the rhythms of the sea, as if they were on tiny wheels. It was peaceful, normal and cleansing. Turnstones and migrating purple sandpipers foraged in the seaweed as they had throughout the centuries. The chill breeze seemed to disperse the shadows around him. It seemed a lifetime away from the horrors of that night at Portskail.

And yet those events in the graveyard had happened. They were part of the same world as the otters, the oystercatchers, the sanderling, the flying sand, the sea and the sky, even though they happened so far away. He felt at times as if he had brought these things with him like a virus. It had spread from the cities and the towns and had reached Portskail. Now it might be here. How long would it be before the islanders themselves were infected?

His mother and father looked on with a mixture of anxiety and relief. They didn't know how to feel. It was good to see him busying himself about the place. He seemed to be taking a new interest in the mundane routines of island life and to be finding some satisfaction in them. But he was restless and, once still, was brooding and pensive. They hoped that the inevitable passage of time would free him of the traumatic effects of his experience.

'Soon,' they told themselves, whenever a shroud of doubt fell on them, 'he'll be busy again with seasonal in-shore fishing. He'll find temporary work in the island's hotel bar and will work a few afternoons in the garage. Life will gradually return to normal. He will be at peace with himself. It will just take time.'

A day passed and then another and another. He was still restless. He could not remain still and rarely took a moment's break from activity of one form or another. It was as if he didn't dare stop, as if he needed to be occupied every moment of the day. Even in the evenings he found it difficult to sit with them in the tiny living room. Television programmes, films and music, which had been his main source of entertainment, no longer seemed to hold his attention.

Night time was the worst. They could hear him moving in his room until the early hours of the morning. Sometimes he called out in his sleep. They heard stifled moans and cries. Occasionally he would shout. In the morning, when he awoke, his eyes looked dark with lack of sleep.

His mother and father felt helpless. All they could do was to allow time to pass and hope that the civilised normality of their quiet world would act as a balm to his wounds.

Jamie knew how hard they were trying to help but their anxiety made him feel worse. No matter how they tried they could never rid him of those unwelcomed and ugly visions that assailed his sleeping and half waking mind. Every night the ritual was the same and he knew it would be several hours before sleep would eventually overtake his exhausted mind.

He was not a young man whose life had been affected much by death or tragedy. His early years and teens had been spent within a protective blanket which his mother and father had thrown around him and which had been secured in place by the environment and community within which he lived. People here were born, grew old and died and the natural order of life repeated itself like a rhythm in music, like the tides on the shore. Life occurred as it was meant to occur. It rose and fell, grew and faded like the seasons. It rolled back into history and prehistory, creating a landscape of life just as the sea and the winds carved the landscape of the islands.

The islands were not without their tragedies, of course. Nowhere could avoid the pointing finger of fate or the sudden glance of random choice. There were accidents and sudden, unexpected deaths and there were younger people struck occasionally by disease and death; but these were uncommon. They were dreadful, numbing events and shocked the community for a while. Then, gradually, a natural process of reflection and grieving seemed to absorb their impact like the mossy ground absorbed the shock of a footfall. It was absorbed into the spirit of the island like water into sand.

This death on the mainland was different. It was unnatural. It had been imposed violently by a malicious will; it was not a natural death, nor an accidental one. It was an act of brutality. It extinguished a precious spark of life with the casual barbarism of someone extinguishing a candle with a hammer. It was an act undertaken by design, with anger and - he shuddered to think of it, - perhaps even with pleasure.

Even more hideous and unnatural was the exposure of a tiny child to the sight and sound of such a ghastly event. This was not an image for a child to view, not a

burden for a child to carry, not a memory for a little
boy to experience over and over again. The horror of
death, particularly of abrupt, unexpected and brutal
death, was something from which a child should be
protected.

Jamie groaned and held his head. He thought of
himself in the graveyard and groaned again. He could
not tell his mother and father how deeply he regretted
his lack of sobriety. He could not describe how
disgusted he felt. He was ashamed that he could be of
so little help to the police.

His mother and father were typical of a generation
on those islands to which excess was defined in very
restricted parameters and was usually part of the lives
of other people, who deserved both their pity and their
disdain. Whilst not denying themselves the pleasure of
an occasional drink, they were saddened and confused
by the incidents of public or private drunkenness,
which were not altogether uncommon amongst their
community. To learn that their son was actually drunk
would have caused them a level of distress that Jamie
was unwilling to inflict.

He had gone to some lengths to overcome the
impression he had given the detectives on that first
night. He had revisited the police station the following
morning, having taken some trouble to dress fittingly
and to present a demeanour which revealed him in a
better light. He was clean shaven, well groomed and
smartly dressed. D.I. Munro had seemed to re-evaluate
him when they met which offered him some relief. He
had managed to offer little more information, however,
and still smarted at his inadequacy.

He felt relieved therefore when he eventually spoke
to Jack by telephone from the island and described
what he now believed he had seen. He described how
the revelation had come about. Jack was appreciative.

'Thank you,' he said, 'Thank you. It is only a small piece in a large jigsaw but sometimes details like this can be important. If you think of anything else, no matter how trivial or insignificant, make sure you let me know.'

Jamie, not for the first time, mumbled incoherent apologies.

'Forget it,' Jack told him. 'There's a big difference between enjoying a drink and being a drunk. You're not a drunk.'

'Have you found the boy?' Jamie enquired.

No, he hadn't been found.

'Do you know who the victim was?'

'Yes,' Jack told him. It hadn't taken long to find out. He was a local man.' He told him what he could. It would be on the television and in the news. He hadn't mentioned the little boy to the press. He didn't want the press involved for at least another day. He was concerned that the boy might be a witness. If anyone asks him – not that it was likely anyone would – say nothing.

Jamie promised he would remain silent. 'Can you let me know if you find him?' He had just sufficient courage to ask, 'and if there's anything I can do, please, call me? ……..I feel…..I feel…..'

'I know,' said Jack. 'I understand. Yes, of course.'

It was eleven o'clock in the morning. Jamie had slept late and long. His mother, both compassionate and indulgent, had resisted his father's entreaties to rouse him early and give him some occupation to take his mind off things. She was convinced that only a few days after his return to the safety and reassurance of home, more than anything he needed rest. Whilst his father had been loudly snoring, she told him, not without a note of reprimand, she had lain awake listening to Jamie turning and groaning into the early hours of the morning.

'Sleep will do him good,' she said. 'It will help heal his mind.'

His father nodded. 'When he wakes up we'll find him some more things to do so he won't be moping about. He needs to be kept busy. We'll send him to some of the neighbours with deliveries of eggs. He needs to meet people again.' With that, he made his departure and his wife turned, donned her own outdoor clothes and wellington boots and went out to collect the eggs.

Jamie had been beset by dreams which had roused him several times during the night but as the day moved towards lunchtime he sank into a deeper and more restful repose. It was only as he became gradually aware of the light penetrating his curtain and the sound of the hens and the lambs beyond his window that his deeper dream approached the surface of his consciousness.

He could see the boy once more. He could see the gravestone and he could see the slouching, blinded, disfigured body. It seemed as bright as daylight now and the boy was pointing towards the stone. There was something different in his demeanour from Jamie's previous recollections. It was evident now, in the light that shone full upon him, that the boy's lips were moving. He was mouthing, quite clearly, one word. He said it once and then again. He stared all the while at Jamie.

Jamie awoke suddenly. He sat up in bed and his face was beaded with sweat.

In the moment of half awakening, when his conscious and subconscious minds were vying for supremacy, he screamed, so loudly that from the yard his mother heard and hurried indoors, the one word, 'Daddy!'

He sat up in bed and swung his legs over the side. He heard his mother entering through the kitchen.

'It's alright! It's alright!' he called. 'It was just a nightmare. I'm fine now. I'll be down in a minute.'

He stumbled to the bathroom and rinsed his eyes. What did it mean? He looked at his face in the mirror and shook his head grimly.

'This is doing no good,' he muttered. 'I can't go on like this.'

It was clear now what he had to do. But first of all he would phone Detective Munro at Portskail. He was sure the boy had been trying to tell him something; but what did it mean? He got through to Jack straight away.

'It may mean nothing,' he said, 'just a scared little boy calling for his daddy. But you said to phone if I remembered anything, no matter how trivial.'

As he put the phone down he heard the kitchen door open behind him. His mother was entering from the garden. 'I'm going back to the mainland,' he said, 'Don't try and talk me out of it. I've got unfinished business there. I know that now.'

'I'm glad to hear it,' a dry voice sneered.

Chapter Fourteen

Jamie span around. Simon Keller was standing at the
door, leaning against the door frame. He was being
directed into the kitchen by his smiling mother.

'Go straight in, Simon. Don't stand on ceremony.'
She beamed at Jamie. 'Here's a friend come to see how
you are,' she said. She turned back to Simon. 'It's just
what he needs,' she said. 'I'll leave you two boys
alone.' She bustled back into the garden having
performed what she felt was a pleasing, therapeutic
duty.

Jamie tried and failed to hide his irritation at this
unwanted intrusion at such an inopportune moment. He
had resolved on immediate action and had plans to
make. Now those plans would have to wait and he
would be required to parry a few more thrusts from this
unwelcomed visitor. He hoped his mother hadn't said
anything to arouse Simon suspicions as they came in
from the garden. Simon was either unaware of Jamie's
feelings or chose to ignore them. Either way, he was
probably indifferent to them. He had a job to do.

'As you know, I'm running a couple of pieces on
your detective friend, Jack Munro.' Simon sat down
astride a kitchen chair. 'A national tabloid has bought
the first one. I'm in the serious money again.' He
grinned. ''Inept Cop Loses Crime Scene'. I can see it
already. It'll be a banner headline. What do you think?'

Jamie shrugged.

'I don't know what you're talking about,' he said.
'What crime scene?'

Simon ignored him. 'For the second piece I was
going with 'Drunk Stumbles on Graveyard Corpse'. I
thought it served you right for being so uncooperative
when we were on the ferry. I nearly missed this story
because of you. That was very naughty, especially to a

friend. This story could make me! It's my ticket out of here! Still, I got the story without you, so no hard feelings!'

He laughed and wagged his finger like a scolding teacher. Jamie struggled hard to resist the urge to punch his smug face.

'Lucky for you my source came through. I'm suggesting the second headline reads, 'Now Where Did I Put My Witness?' I've got a photographer waiting for a suitably bewildered pose. I'm sure he'll find something. He usually does.'

'Where did you hear all this?' Jamie's heart was pumping hard and his breathing came in short gasps. Simon was enjoying himself.

'A source or sources close to the police,' he grinned. 'I think that's the correct formula. They are reliable sources, though. I don't think there'll be any complaints about the accuracy of my story. Can you tell me anything more about the boy?' he suddenly asked, his small eyes trapping Jamie in their cold stare. 'The police are being very evasive. What about the murder? Can you give me your point of view, or even a few gruesome details? If you are helpful I can go easy on you, make you out to be a hero even. What do you say?'

Jamie told him what he had to say.

'You shouldn't be so hard on me,' Simon said. 'I've got a job to do. I'll find out everything I need whether you tell me or not.' He leaned forward suddenly angry. 'You make me sick,' he snapped. 'You think I'm being cruel and unkind to these people? Ha! What kindness do you owe to corrupt officials? Why should you leap to the defence of public figures who pretend to be oh so virtuous whilst leading sordid, secret lives? What makes people in authority deserve your pity, who spend their lives telling other people how to behave when their own behaviour is contemptible? I search out hypocrites in every field of society. That's what I do best! Your detective held back information about a crime in order to protect his own reputation! Wake up! These people deserve to be exposed!'

'Perhaps he wanted to protect the witness,' Jamie said. 'Have you thought of that? Your story might put him at risk.'

Simon spat contemptuously.

'You are so naïve,' he snarled, 'so small minded, so hemmed in by your little island mentality, so noble and altruistic, so very ...... community spirited! Haven't you learned yet? Look around you! Open your eyes! There's nothing but hypocrisy and self interest out there! People will be nice to you if it's in their interests; but they'll turn on you once that interest is threatened. There's no such thing as altruism or selflessness. Even the church is full of self interest. It's riddled from top to bottom by greed. Look at the Vatican! There is more corruption at the top of the church than there is in the Mafia! Look at the Government! They play their little Westminster games, scoring points here and there, patting each other on the back for a clever remark, a headline. It has nothing to do with the truth or with compassion or with any more of those values you hold so dear! Look at them! Snorting hogs! Look at your council! Look at your schools! Look anywhere! Then tell me that what I do is any worse than the things you see around you! You need me! I don't let them get away with it! Wake up, Jamie! Wake up and grow up!'

He stood up. 'I'm on my way out of this dead end place and if I have to clamber on a few deserving corpses to do that, I'll not be stopped. I'm not going to end up like my father, stuck in some grubby little house in Portskail after years of dead end work. No wife, no money, no friends. P.C. Bob Keller, pathetic constable

Keller, cock-up Keller, your local, useless, village plod, famed for his honesty and incorruptibility. Much good it did him! Watch out for the headlines!'

He turned and stormed towards the door. Then he stopped and turned back. He relaxed and tried to smile. 'Don't worry. I'll go easy on you,' he sneered. 'You're a small fish. I'm after the big boys.'

Then he was gone.

Chapter Fifteen

'Have you seen this?' Jack flung the local newspaper on the desk in front of Julie. 'Inept! He calls me inept! Just wait till I meet that little runt! Where does he live? What's his car number plate? Where does he drink? Has he any outstanding parking tickets? Is he cruel to animals? Does he have any overdue library books? Does he hang out his underwear on a Sunday? Get me something! Anything! I want him arrested! I want a car outside his house! I want an excuse to take a blood sample, a DNA sample, a urine sample, a semen sample! No, scratch that! No semen unless it's extracted by Dynarod. And that blood sample – I want a pint!'

Julie knew better than to contradict him. She nodded and pretended to take notes.

'And you!' He turned to the unfortunate Detective Sergeant who had just that moment entered the office. 'This is your fault, Phil! Have you seen this? I'm in a national tabloid! Have you seen this picture of me? I'm scratching my head. I look like Stan Laurel! Where did they get that? He makes me sound like a bloody fool! You're the bloody fool! You lost the cave, not me! Get on the phone and tell him! No, don't! Turn round! Go out again! Come back in when I've gone!'

Phil dutifully turned on his heels with the barest of grins and made a hurried escape. Julie looked towards the floor and pretended not to have noticed. Only the most acute of observers would have noticed the flickering hint of subdued laughter on her face.

Jack was in no better mood when he got home. Even when Sandy arrived at eight o'clock, he was still pacing the room. Kate, having offered what support she could, had retired to the kitchen to complete some fictitious tasks.

Sandy entered with a broad smile.

Ah!' he said, 'Our man in the local headlines! A celebrity, albeit a minor one! Never mind; be generous! Think altruistically! Whilst he's picking on you he's leaving some other poor sod alone.'

'You seem to be taking my misfortune very much in your stride,' Jack noted.

'It could be worse. He might have written about my missing body. The town would have been awash with zombie hunters. And it would have been me in the headlines.'

'I'm glad to have done you a service,' Jack threw himself on his chair and laughed sardonically.

'Ah,' Sandy muttered, 'you may want to hold back on that laugh. I have it on good authority that you are about to be serialised in one of the National Tabloids. And rather worse....'

'There's worse? Is that possible?'

'Our ferrety little journalist friend seems to have got wind of your missing witness. That, too, will be going national although, in the interests of maximum journalistic impact, it had to be held back until after the first headline. It features as part two of his 'inept detective' series. First he loses this and then he loses that. That, I believe, is his general drift.'

'Bastard,' Jack leaned forward. 'Shit faced, slimy, self satisfied, arrogant, muck raking, self-seeking bastard!'

'Elegantly expressed, my dear friend,' laughed Sandy, 'but I have to concur. What he lacks in integrity he more than complements with a lack of charm, personality, humanity and sensitivity – the true qualifications of an out and out bastard. But, you must confess, he really is a very thorough and quite talented bastard.'

'How is he getting this information?'

'Ah, I fear you must consider the presence of a mole in your establishment. Someone, somewhere, has been less than discreet. Could it be someone on your staff earning a few extra pounds to supplement their meagre salary?'

Jack shook his head. 'That's unlikely,' he said. 'They might not be the sharpest chisels in the toolbox but they are very loyal to each other. If anyone let slip a piece of information it would have been accidental rather than planned.'

'Who else could it be? Who knew about the lost crime scene or the boy? It could be the minister, I suppose? Men of the cloth have been known to be overcome by the workings of conscience. I should know. I was brought up a good catholic. I had a post graduate degree in guilt by the time I was eighteen.'

'Jack shook his head. 'He knew about the boy, of course, but I don't think he had any knowledge of our crime scene. In fact, outside my office and our good selves I don't think there was anyone else who knew.'

'Well,' said Sandy, 'I think we can rule you out and I hope you will do me a similar courtesy. Whilst I would not be averse to a significant donation to my retirement pot, I would profess myself unwilling to do so if it involved a face to face encounter with that ghastly little reporter. Besides, I would not come cheap.'

'Of course, it could be more than one person,' Jack remarked. 'Simon Keller is more than capable of worming tiny snippets of information from different sources. If he knows about our foray into the wilds he might approach our friend at Aultmore, for example. He might eavesdrop at the hotel or listen in on our police channels. It wouldn't surprise me to find he'd tapped a phone or two. Then he could draw some information from our witness at the graveyard or from the minister. As far as the little boy is concerned, we couldn't hope to keep the secret for long. We've been in contact with every primary school and nursery between here and the city. We've circulated his description to every police station. We've contacted social services. It's all been done with a request for confidentiality but there is bound to be chatter.'

'The boy could have been taken by the murderer already,' Sandy suggested quietly. 'Have you thought of that?'

'I've thought of little else. However, we don't know that the murderer was even aware of him. I think, on balance, we would have put him at greater risk if we had issued a description any earlier. After all, we can't be entirely certain that he didn't know the killer. Why else would he be in the graveyard if he hadn't followed someone? And what child of that age would play a game of 'follow the stranger' on a cold, dark night, long after his bedtime?'

'Then the newspaper headline could put him in grave danger.'

Jack nodded. 'Our best chance now is to flood the news with it, make this boy so visible that no-one will dare hurt him. It's our best chance.'

'I suspect my missing corpse will not remain secret for long,' Sandy said gloomily. 'I will be joining you in the hall of shame. It wouldn't be so bad if we could have featured in a reputable broadsheet but to be a tabloid headline, oh the ignominy!'

'I think you are safe for a little while yet, certainly long enough to find something as substantial as a body! No, he's been distracted by the cave and the missing boy and has managed to contrive himself a couple of good headlines. He'll pursue those a little further yet. But he'll come back to the cave soon enough. He'll want to know what we found there. Once he knows there was a body he'll pursue that and then .... I think we need to give some serious consideration to establishing what sort of an idiot is capable of playing this sort of joke on you and where they might hide a corpse. It's not something you would want in your garden shed.

'I think I'll quiz your two assistants. It may be a revenge attack on you that has got rather out of hand. They could have drawn in one or two other people who have suffered from your macabre humour over the years.'

'Ah, I was so much younger then and foolhardy. To be fair to myself, though, I never tampered with the truly dead. All of my pranks were played using fictitious corpses. I did not enter my profession to offend the bereaved or act disrespectfully towards the departed. However, not everyone saw the distinction. They 'bid me take life easy, as the grass grows on the weirs; but I was young and foolish and now am full of tears.'

'W.B. Yeats.'

'Indeed.'

'I didn't know you were brought up in the faith?' Jack smiled, recalling Sandy's earlier confession 'I had you down as a dyed in the wold atheist.'

'A Catholic childhood is a prophylactic to atheism,' Sandy said. 'You can only ever be a lapsed catholic. You can give it up but you can never get rid of it – rather like a Facebook Page.' He laughed. 'Six years at Saint Theresa's Primary School ensured a thorough indoctrination. From that point on, I was doomed to a life of regret. My secondary years were spent at Saint Saccharine the Sweet, so named because of the bitter aftertaste of truth that underlay its sweetness. There I learned to secretly doubt. University drove the last vestiges of belief from me. But ....'

'But...?' Jack asked.

'But it left me with a lifelong feeling of sadness and regret; sadness that it could not be so and regret that it was not so. That's a catholic education for you. It indoctrinates you to a point where you are inevitably damned. The tower of cards they so carefully help you construct collapses and you are left with despair; and despair, of course, is a sin above all other sins. The inevitable product of my education was damnation.'

Kate had chosen to quietly enter the room as Sandy was speaking. She stood thoughtfully by the door before sitting beside Jack. He enfolded her in a strong arm.

'The damned are a mighty big army,' she said quietly, 'if despair is the criterion.'

''I had not thought death had undone so many' - T.S. Eliot this time,' said Sandy.

'Every Christmas I get the decorations out,' Kate continued. 'We set out our little manger and stable with all the animals; we've done it every year since the children were tiny.' She laughed a little nervously. 'We play Christmas CD's and Jack dredges up his old clarinet and plays carols very badly. I go to church too, not out of any belief – that vanished long ago, - but out of longing.'

'Wishing it might be so,' said Sandy quietly. 'The illusions of childhood are brutal betrayals. I find it difficult to stay sober at Christmas. It is one of my two periods of complete self pity.' He laughed. 'I think of my Helen and I want to see her again. I so, so want to see her again.'

They were quiet for a while.

'But I never will.' His voice was barely audible. 'That is my final damnation.'

It was some time before normal conversation returned over coffee and cake.

'How did you hear about the forthcoming headline about the boy?' Jack asked.

'Ah, now that relates directly to my membership of the Portskail Chess Club. Among its members are several notable local dignitaries, teachers, professional classes, the academic, the hatefully precocious young and the editor of our local newspaper. Between games we sometimes escape to a neighbouring room and chat. It is a sad indictment of the paucity of our experiences that we inevitably chat about our work. It is a form of discussion where I can contribute little, given the rather macabre nature of my work, but I listen and I ask questions. Our editor is a loquacious man and needs little encouragement. He is quite fond of listening to his own voice, you might say.'

'It must be a wonderful place for hearing gossip,' Jack laughed, 'perhaps only bettered by the golf club bar.'

'I fear nothing could compete with that particular establishment but I am afraid my sporting prowess rather goes no further than the very occasional attendance at the nineteenth hole for dreadfully boring social occasions. I am not one of the initiates.'

Their conversation followed its normal course. They spoke of the books they were reading and the news headlines. They spoke of music and poetry, television drama and film, art and photography. The evening ended just as it always did, immediately after the ten o'clock news headlines.

As they lay in bed that night Kate lay quietly, unable to sleep. She lay still and stared into the darkness. All that talk of lost dreams and broken promises, of false hopes and cold realities had subdued her spirits. Jack rolled over.

'What's the matter?' he mumbled, 'Can't you sleep?'

'Hold me,' she said, 'I feel sad. Sometimes the world out there seems a big place and not a particularly nice one. I feel as if all our happiness is balanced on the head of a pin.' She snuggled close against Jack and his arm closed round her. 'I felt so sorry for Sandy,' she said. 'He was happy with Helen, you can tell that; he must have thought the future was bright and full of promise. Then, it was suddenly gone. Nothing has been the same for him since. You can tell he misses her dreadfully, even after all these years.'

'He's not a man who shows what he feels,' said Jack. 'We've known him for years but what do we really know? I've never even seen a photograph of Helen. There are none in his house, or at least there are none on display. He told me once that he couldn't bear to look at them, not casually, not day in day out. He said they would become something that merely accompanied his day like cornflakes for breakfast. He wanted them to be special, always. He keeps them in a drawer in his bureau and looks at them at a set time each evening, just before bed. We know nothing about the life they lived together, apart from occasional references to holidays or special occasions. If you ask questions he tends to divert you away from them. He's very private and yet .....' Alice felt him shrug his shoulders.

'You think you have learned all there is to learn about him and then you are given a tantalising glimpse of a new door, partially opened,' she said quietly, 'like tonight when he spoke about his catholic upbringing. After all these years I had no idea.'

'He has built a pretty effective defensive barrier over the years.' Jack said. 'He is witty, bitingly sarcastic and hugely intelligent. He's used all these talents to create a public face. He hides behind that face and feels secure from anything that could cause him any more hurt. He has mastered the art of ironic detachment,' smiled Jack. 'It's his protection. It keeps him from getting to close to anyone or anything. I think these recent events have temporarily cracked his armour. It will, no doubt, be fully repaired by the next time we see him.'

It saddens me to think of him like that.' Alice murmured. 'He's always alone, even when he's with other people. No-one can approach too closely. He will never find anyone else.'

'He doesn't want anyone else. He married Helen in life and death. He might have lost his faith; he might be the most thorough going atheist of our acquaintance; but he cannot break the stranglehold those early values had on him. Nor does he want to. They are the only things that are holding him together, I think.'

'I think you are the closest thing he has to a true friend,' said Kate, 'and I'm very pleased. He has made a very good choice.'

They were quiet for a moment.

'Hold me,' Kate said quietly, 'I feel lonely.' She shivered. 'It's all this talk of death. I feel terribly small tonight. I'm glad you are here. I'm glad we have each other. I don't want to be on my own, ever.'

Jack bent forward and kissed her head.

'I love you,' he said and he held her fast until she fell asleep.

It took somewhat longer for him to close his eyes.

Chapter Sixteen

The interior and exterior of Aultmore House had been struck by a wreck of packing cases. The furniture from their old home was now beginning to arrange itself in some sort of order, having been carefully directed to the appropriate rooms during the lengthy process of removal. The packing cases were another matter. Each one had been carefully labelled with a black marker pen with the name of its destination - kitchen, lounge, main bedroom, Euan's room, spare room, bathroom and, optimistically, garage. Thus far things had not gone as well as they might have done and the process of opening and disposing of the contents of the boxes had just reached that point where it seemed impossible to believe that it would ever be concluded. Alice had taken a break, having been engaged in the process since before six that morning. Feeling her zeal waning she decided to drive down to Inverstrach with Euan to visit the tiny shop and have a look at the school where Euan would be going after the holiday.

Garth had removed his temporary furniture from the house. He had crushed it into the roofed cottage and wedged the door tightly shut. He had not long returned to the house when there was a knock at the door. It was repeated a moment later rather more loudly. Garth was sitting by the kitchen table looking out from the side of the house towards the lane and the grey moorland. He opened the door to find a smartly dressed, slightly built youngish man standing on the gravel path. He was cleanly shaven and had a slightly polished look like a pair of new shoes. Garth immediately imagined he must be a member of some Christian sect bent on missionary work. He adopted the cautious stance of a native, agnostic warrior prepared to resist encroachment. He was suddenly impatient to continue unpacking the crates that surrounded him and eyed the intruder with resentment.

'Ah,' the stranger began and his narrow lips widened into a friendly smile. He looked appreciatively at the exterior of the house, its new windows and roof. 'It's hard to remember now just how desolate and neglected this building looked before you came here. You've done a remarkable job of restoration and improvement. I think our editor is quite correct. It really does deserve a write up in our local newspaper.'

Garth retained a cautious, distrustful air and made a guarded reply. The young man seemed to suddenly realise that Garth had no idea who he was and laughed.

O, I'm sorry, how silly of me, I haven't introduced myself, have I? My name is Simon Keller. You might have heard of me?'

Garth shook his head and regretted he hadn't. He remained cautious. Was this sleek young man selling something? Simon looked mildly surprised.

'Ah, you are obviously not a subscriber to our local news sheet. You could hardly have missed my name if you were. You'll have to remedy that if you want to know anything about anything in the area. It isn't exactly at the cutting edge of journalism but if you want to know about school events, galas, sheep or cattle, the successes of local citizens or special deals at the Portskail shops and restaurants then it isn't to be missed.' Simon laughed slowly as if rinsing his mouth. 'For me it is something of a hobby and my tiny contribution to the good of the local community. My more serious work is in the Regional Newspaper. I freelance for Nationals as well. Do you know?' he continued smoothly, 'There are old people in the area who buy the Portskail and District Times simply to look at the births, marriages and deaths, - particularly the deaths? I'm sure they take a strange sort of delight in seeing the names of contemporaries they have outlived.' He rolled another laugh around his teeth like a mouthwash. 'Schadenfreude,' he said knowingly.

Garth relaxed. He had been bracing himself for a long and pointless discussion with a mild mannered bigot with a complex; or perhaps to fight off the enthusiastic advances of an over eager double glazing salesman. 'Come in,' he said with some relief, 'If you can fight your way past the packing cases. Our furniture arrived yesterday. I've got the coffee on. You've caught me at a second breakfast. We were moving furniture and unpacking till after eleven last night and started again around six this morning. I'm just taking a well earned break.'

'Well, if I'm not intruding, that would be most welcome.' Simon insinuated himself around the door and sloped into the kitchen. 'I'm not usually a morning person myself but my editor thought a short piece on our new neighbour and his renovations would be quite nice for the paper and I had some time to spare today. He drove past here the other evening and was attracted by the work you'd done. Looking around, I can see what he means, despite all the crates.'

He cast a practised, authoritative glance around him. Garth was flattered. 'It's been hard work,' he said, 'but it's starting to feel like a home now. My wife and son have joined me and by the end of the day much of this will be in order. It'll take a while to get completely straight, though.'

'Ah, it must be nice for you to have your family here. I'm a bachelor myself – far too young to settle down just yet - and I still find going home to an empty flat rather disappointing. I can imagine what it has been like for you for the last few weeks. I was brought up on the outer isles and I can't remember ever going home to an empty house. I still go back there as often as I can. Where are your wife and son at present?'

His words slipped from his lips with the smoothness of grease. He asked Garth questions about the house and about his family with an ease of manner which made him seem genuinely interested. Garth was only too pleased to answer him and quickly appreciated Simon as a genuine and sincere young man.

'Have you any photographs of the house when you first arrived?' Simon asked. 'It would be good to include before and after photographs for comparison. It would show people just how much you have achieved.'

Garth rooted in a drawer and took out a photograph of the house. It was recognisably the same structure with the front door placed somewhat to the left of the centre, the small gables, the sash windows and the twin chimneys. But there the similarity ended. The windows were obviously rotting and several tiles had slipped from the roof or were broken. Lichens and mosses were growing from the tiles and the walls. One gutter had fallen. The paths were overgrown and some plaster had fallen from the gable end and above the doors and windows. It had suffered the inevitable fate of a house left empty and neglected for some considerable time.

'You've done a lot of work in a remarkably short time! You must give me a guided tour, if you can spare the time.' Simon held the picture between finger and thumb and cast a disinterested glance at it as Garth poured the coffee. 'I don't suppose all this work has given you much time to meet your neighbours.'

'A number of them have dropped by over the weeks I have been here, no doubt driven by the twin motivations of friendliness and curiosity.'

'Perhaps more by the latter than the former in many cases,' laughed Simon. 'I hear you've met my friend Jack Munro as well. He's very much a local character, very caustic until you get to know him, but a fine man and a good detective.'

Simon looked around the room and changed the subject. It was better not to seem too keen. He asked a few desultory questions about the house, feigning interest. He would feed out a bit of line before reeling him in again. 'You must be glad to have your own furniture up here,' he commented. 'It's always good to be surrounded by your own possessions.'

'Yes, but I think we'd better restrict any photographs to the outside at present.' Garth looked around with a rueful smile. 'I don't think the inside would make good copy. Still, it is better than it was. For the last few weeks it has been furnished with random items gleaned from various sales. The only criterion was the price.'

'Jack said you worked in a university but that you were taking time out to complete some writing?' No-one could accuse Simon Keller of not being prepared, not doing his homework. He had found out enough about Garth to maintain his lies.

'Yes,' Garth said, rather defensively. He didn't want to talk about his work. 'But we'll need to get properly settled in first. It's hard to concentrate on academic work until everything is in place. There's plenty of time. I have a twelve month sabbatical.'

A few harmless enquiries followed. There was nothing in Simon's manner to suggest an ulterior motive. He was a local journalist on a parochial little newspaper doing a piece on the renovations undertaken by a family who were newcomers to the area – very homely, very warm and cosy, a good news story with a pleasant link to the crofting past. There was nothing threatening about Simon Keller.

It would have taken someone with far greater experience to draw attention to the sharp eyes that weighed Garth's reaction to each sentence, to point out the precise way in which his casual, harmless questions moved and swam around those of more significance, hiding them from naïve scrutiny. It would have taken Jack or Sandy or even Jamie to mark the motion of his long fingers coiling and uncoiling involuntarily as lies slipped from his tongue. Only someone who had encountered Simon frequently would recognise the insincere laughter, the calculated dialogue and the manipulation; but that was his skill and his genius.

Now he came to the point.

'Jack was telling me about your adventure in the hills,' he laughed. 'I'm sure that wasn't the welcome you expected.'

It was a shot in the dark but it was well aimed. Garth was visibly startled.

'He told you about that?' he inquired.

'Oh yes,' Simon smiled and coolly lied. 'He's known my family for years. My father was a police constable for many years before he retired. They still go fishing together occasionally. Jack is like an uncle to me and my sister.'

Fictitious sister, he thought; fictitious fish. Be careful now; don't lay it on too thick. Keep it conversational, relaxed.

'It must have been quite something, finding that!'

'Yes indeed,' said Garth. 'I don't even know why I went up there in the first place; I was searching for some lost cave I read about in a book. I think I just wanted to go somewhere alone. When you have spent years in the city it is nice to find silence.'

'Well, at least you found your cave.' Simon was drawing on the line now. 'Slowly, slowly, he's almost in the net,' he thought.

'I almost wish I hadn't!' laughed Garth. 'It seemed harmless enough at the time. I just wanted to find the cave that was all. I was quite thrilled when it was there in front of me at the foot of the bluff. It seemed an ordinary enough place, a low narrow entrance leading into a small cavern and a narrowing tunnel beyond. I certainly wasn't expecting to find.....well, you know.'

'Yes, it must have been quite a surprise!' Simon felt his heart rate quicken. This was what he liked about the job. This was what he was good at. He was winding him in fast now.

'It scared me half to death, I can tell you. Imagine how you would have felt if you had crawled into a cave to find the naked body of a man staring at you. His eyes were terrifying.'

'Got him,' Simon thought, with a sly, inward smile. 'He's in the net, thrashing about. He's mine.'

Once his trust had been gained it took Garth little time to tell Simon everything he knew. Simon could hardly believe his luck. Over coffee and biscuits Garth described every detail of his adventure and the removal of the body to the mortuary.

'...which is precisely where my next stop will be,' Simon thought. There's nothing to be gained from staying here any longer. 'Well,' he said aloud. 'I think I've got enough to make a decent article. I'll get a photographer out later in the week. I'll get him to give you a ring first.'

'Do you not want that guided tour?'

'Oh yes, of course,' Simon smiled. He finished his drink and biscuit and stoically faced the prospect of a celebratory tour in which he had not the slightest interest. Ten minutes later, as he drove away, he met

Alice and Euan entering the long driveway. He stopped
and wound down his window to introduce himself and
to briefly explain his purpose. He overflowed with
good humour as he exchanged pleasantries. You never
know when it might be useful, he told himself.

Back in the house, Garth was happy to think he had
made another good natured, local acquaintance.

'What a pleasant young man!' Alice was thinking.
She was feeling particularly pleased. She had met a
couple of local villagers in Portskail. One old lady had
particularly welcomed and even invited her for a cup of
tea. Now, this young man had taken the trouble to stop
and speak to her. 'Everyone is so friendly. It's going to
be wonderful living here,' she thought. 'It's so different
from the town.'

It was only later in the day, as darkness gathered
once again, that Garth wondered if he had, perhaps said
rather too much to the young journalist. Jack had asked
him to say nothing, after all. But then Jack had already
spoken to Simon about the cave so there couldn't be
any harm done, even if Simon was a journalist. Could
there?

Garth felt a sudden spasm of doubt. He drove it
away quickly but it reverberated in his thoughts and left
a residual tremor that he could not shift.

Chapter Seventeen

Later in the evening, after Euan had gone to bed, he
stood, as he often did, at the front door to allow the
cool night air to clear his thoughts. The sun was
slipping below the hill behind the house and the first
stars were blinking tiny eyes of light. It was remarkably
still. The newly born leaves which had recently
emerged on the trees were motionless, trapped as in a
photograph. There was scarcely a sound. Garth
breathed in the chill air and relaxed. Alice joined him
and he put his arm round her. This was their new world,
far from the rush of city traffic, the noise and the
pollution. There were no street lights here, nothing to
diminish the depth of the sky. From their door they
couldn't even see the nearest house. The silence and the
darkness were absolute.

From within the ruin came the unmistakable hissing
and scratching of his barn owls. He smiled. 'Listen!' he
said. 'Those are our barn owls!' It was wonderful how
the sound rose and fell. It was like a rose photographed
against a black curtain. It came from darkness and it
vanished into darkness. It grew like a bloom of sound.

A sudden screech clawed the silence and vanished.
Their eyes glistened and they listened and watched like
intruders. The shriek came again, louder. It had a
primeval quality that tapped at the windows of rational
thought and warned of something beyond. Alice was
aware of a quickening, strange, involuntary fear. It was
a primitive fear of the unknown, a fear of a sudden
sound in the silence, of a cold touch in the darkness, a
fear of a strange otherness of which she could have no
comprehension. It spoke to her of the fear of being
alone, of being lost.

She held close to Garth and resisted the sudden
desire to hurry inside and close the door. He smiled

because he too had felt that same primitive response and had suppressed his desire to flee from it. It was like a threatening monster in the darkness of childhood. His mind slipped momentarily to Euan's night terrors and he was how easy and how wrong it was to simply dismiss such fears. Poor Euan, childhood was such a hard place to live.

Then, once again, there gradually arose another cry, a wail that gripped them both with a cocktail of fear and pity, compassion and dread. It was the same cry he had heard before but closer and more insistent. It was like the cry of a child in the lonely darkness, lost and fearful. There was terror and anguish in that cry. It was both a human sound and the cry of a wild animal. Alice gripped his arm tightly.

A shadow of white ghost fanning silent wings drifted from the ruin. It slipped across their path and vanished into the darkness. The barn owl was hunting.

They turned back into the house and closed the door. Primitive though it was, the fear had been all too real.

The next morning Garth decided to look more closely in the ruin. He took Euan to show him precisely where the barn owl nest was situated so that they could leave it entirely undisturbed. Tonight, he thought, we can let Euan stay up late to hear and perhaps see the owls. He also wanted to check the wall where Jack had dislodged the stone. It was the wall adjoining the roofed end of the cottage, which he had imagined to be secure.

With Euan's help he pulled away some of the fallen timbers that lay over a pile of rubble by the adjoining wall. They worked steadily and quietly and the barn owls remained in their nest, undisturbed. Together they carried each timber out and laid it on the garden to be sawn and burnt at a later date. Then they turned and clambered over the rubble.

Garth could see quite clearly now where the barn owl nest must be and pointed it out to Euan. He could also see the neat space where Jack's stone had become dislodged. It was a rectangular space, perhaps eight inches wide and five inches high. The stone itself lay at his feet. It was about ten inches long and each face was regularly cut.

Garth picked up the stone clambered to the top of the pile of rubble beneath the hole but it was sufficiently high to be at too sharp an angle for him to reach up and replace it.

'We need the ladder,' he whispered. 'Come on!'

He left the stone on the ground and they went to fetch a small ladder which they had left leaning against the gable wall of the main house, beneath the kitchen window. They carried it carefully back and raised it against the wall. Its feet slipped momentarily in the rubble and then held firm. Garth clambered up, holding the heavy stone between his hands and using his elbows to balance against the ladder. He lifted the stone into position and glanced into the hole. He stopped. He carefully stepped back down the ladder and set the stone securely on the ground before re-ascending. He reached into the space. It was deep, far deeper than the length of the stone. Garth half expected his hand to emerge inside the other room but it did not. His fingers instead closed down upon a dusty item concealed there. He drew it out carefully and dropped it down to Euan. Then he clambered down the ladder and they hurried into the kitchen where Euan laid the item on the table. It was a musty, wooden box with a tightly fitting lid. It was roughly made and very simple but it had obviously been made with care and no little skill.

Euan's enthusiastic fingers had little difficulty prising the lid off the box. He removed the contents, item by item, and placed them on the table. They stood back for a moment and looked curiously at what they had found. There was a child's rag doll, a small, musty notebook or diary and a long thin bladed knife about six inches long. There was something hideously incongruous about finding such items hidden together.

Euan picked up the doll and looked at it closely. Strands of wool protruded as hair from a round face with black, button eyes and a hand sewn mouth and nose. Its arms and legs were set on parallel trajectories from its flattened body and the coloured rags from which it was made had lost much of their colour. He tried to imagine its owner. He saw a little girl running along the garden paths trailing the doll by its arm. He saw her again sitting outside the cottage, holding it close and talking to it – her baby.

Garth took it and turned it over in his hands. 'It looks old,' he said. 'Imagine, Euan! A little girl must have played with this doll once, long ago.'

It made him feel rather melancholy to hold it. The girl had long ago grown up, grown old and died. Yet here her doll had remained, forgotten, no longer wanted, betrayed to the loneliness of neglect; and yet within it there still lingered a fragile memory of its owner. 'Like life,' he thought gloomily. Humanity too had been discarded like a forgotten toy, hidden for eternity in a ruined wall until it rotted to nothingness.

He put it down and teased open the flimsy pages of the diary. Their edges were darkened, the pages stained with damp and mildew and the writing had paled to the very edge of legibility. Here and there he could make out a child's writing. The letters and words were carefully formed and were shaped with the practised care of a child rehearsing a new skill. On the first page he could discern the words of a prayer, evidently written from memory as a lesson. He put it aside to read later but Euan picked it up.

'Can I keep this?' he asked.

'Yes, but look after it. I'd like to read it later.'

The knife was old. The narrow wooden handle was finely shaped to accommodate a hand. It was strangely carved with a grotesque face at the haft, the sort of face one might expect to see on an old church. It looked as if it had been hand carved as an amusement during long winter evenings. Someone had enjoyed making it. Garth had a distinct impression that the likeness had been taken from life and grossly exaggerated and caricatured. He showed Euan. A mean, shrivelled little man with greedy eyes and grasping hands peered over a bulbous nose. It was really remarkably fine. The blade was tarnished and carried a dark stain along the sharpened edge and on parts of the blade. Garth scratched the stain curiously. Then he put it down and stood back.

'I may be mistaken,' he muttered, 'but I think that might be blood.'

Chapter Eighteen

'Mum? Can I keep the rag doll?' Euan asked. 'I want her to sit with my other toys on the window sill.'

'I'll need to wash her first. Let me have a look!' Alice inspected the doll. 'It's a bit fragile, Euan; it may not survive a good wash. I'll try washing it by hand in the sink.'

'Can you do it now?'

When Euan started to unpack the toys and books that would soon grace his bedroom, Alice had been concerned to see how he would treat his army of soft toys. Would they be restored to pride of place or would they be hidden from sight in drawers and cupboards for fear they would absorb some evil from the darkness? She was relieved to see them gradually filling their regular spaces on cupboards and chairs. He hesitated when he held the rag doll.

'I don't know whether to put her with my bottles because she's is old or with my soft toys because she is a doll,' he said.

'Let's see how she cleans up first,' Alice suggested and they went into the kitchen and filled a bowl with warm, gently soaped water. She carefully immersed the doll. The water soon became discoloured and then too dirty for further use but the doll, upon inspection, had remained gratifyingly intact. Alice emptied the bowl and then refilled it and began again. Once more the water grew misty and then grey and then so discoloured that it was hardly possible to see the doll through it. Once again, however, the doll seemed to have withstood the treatment without sustaining too much damage.

'So far so good!' she smiled at Euan. 'She'll need a stitch or two here and there but I can do that when she's dried. Shall we try one more soak?'

Euan nodded and they began again. This time, although the water became murky and grey it was definitely clearer than it had been. When the doll emerged he could see the colours of her patchwork body and head much more clearly. The colours had faded but they were still clear. There were pink patches and yellow patches. Her eyes were small, black buttons and her hair pale strands of wool. Her body was covered in a mixture of various hues, all neatly stitched together.

'She's called Daisy,' Euan said.

'How do you know?' Alice asked.

'It's in the diary. The little girl wrote that she took Daisy down to the burn to look for fish. Then she says that Daisy was playing with her in the field with the cattle. She says Daisy climbed up trees and chased butterflies with her and that Daisy slept with her.'

'That's nice,' smiled Alice. 'Daisy must have been a well cared for little doll.'

'The little girl had a brother too,' said Euan. 'He was called Tom. The girl was Hannah. Tom was a year older than Hannah. Hannah says that Tom and Daisy are her best friends.'

'Where is the diary now?' Alice asked. 'I'd like to read it.'

'I'll show you later,' said Euan. 'I'm going to read some more soon.' After a moment he said, 'Their mum had died. She had been very ill. She had coughed a lot. Hannah and Tom lived with their dad. They had lived in the town but then their dad was ill too. They had a nice house in the town and their dad was a blacksmith but when he was ill their dad couldn't work any more and they had to leave. They came here because their dad's brother lived here. Their dad did lots of work here but their uncle wasn't very nice to him.'

'My goodness, you've found out a lot about them,' laughed Alice. 'Oh look! That last wash has got all the dirt out. I'll hang her up to dry and this evening I'll try and stitch the bits that have come undone.'

'I think I'll put her with the toys,' Euan said thoughtfully. 'I think Hannah would like that!'

'I'm sure she would,' laughed Alice. 'She'd be really pleased to think Daisy had found a new home after all these years. Now, run along and play – unless you want to help me with more unpacking!'

Euan didn't want to do any more unpacking EVER and quickly vanished. A moment later, Alice heard him call to her.

'I'm going to play in the garden and the field. I'm going to explore!'

'Don't go far!' she shouted back. 'Stay in sight of the house!'

She heard the door click shut.

Garth emerged from the study, holding his back. 'Books! Books! Books!' he moaned. How many more can there possibly be?'

'Look out there!' Alice nodded towards the window. Euan was heading across the gravel paths towards the fence. A number of sheep had gathered on the other side. They quickly ran as he approached. 'Isn't that lovely to see? There is our little boy enjoying a new life free of ugliness and endless noise.' Garth put his arm around her shoulder and squeezed her affectionately.

'Look!' she said, 'The doll is cleaning up really well. I do hope I can repair her. Euan really likes her. She's called Daisy, you know. He found that out from the diary.' She laughed and quickly repeated the information Euan had told her.

'I wonder why there was a knife hidden in the wall?' Garth said. 'It seems a strange thing to keep with a doll and a little girl's diary. It's hardly a child's toy.'

'It probably belonged to her father,' Alice said. She hung the doll above a radiator where it could dry slowly. 'Come on!' she said, 'Let's tackle another box or two before dinner!' Garth groaned.

Euan spent a few minutes watching the sheep in the field and then decided to climb the fence and run over to where the narrow burn wound beneath rowan and birches. He clambered on the rocks which protruded here and there and searched for tiny fish which occasionally darted from beneath stones or under the bank. He dipped his hands in the stream to try and hold them but he was too impatient to wait and invariably scared them away. Another day he would return with a jar and he would wait patiently for them to swim into his cupped hand.

'Hannah and Tom caught fish in the burn,' he said to himself. 'They played right here, just like me.'

He followed the stream upstream as it curved round the trees and passed under a tiny bridge just along the road from the entrance to his new home. He leaned on the bridge and looked down at the water in the tiny burn as it splashed over the rocks, falling slightly as it flowed downstream through the field he had just left. He clambered down a slight banking to rejoin the stream on the other side. He knew that if he followed the burn upstream it would curl away from the road and pass between two large rocks. There he would find a waterfall falling through a tiny gorge, at the bottom of which it would form a deep pool.

'Hannah used to play by that pool sometimes,' he told himself. 'Sometimes she played with Tom. Tom used to make boats with twigs and leaves and push them over the waterfall and Hannah would watch them as they tumbled down to the pool. I bet I could swim in that pool in the summer,' he thought. 'This was Hannah's favourite place.'

Having clambered up to the pool and jumped from rock to rock beside it he sat for a while on a small stone ledge just above the water. From here he could look down into the water and dangle his legs whilst beside him the tiny waterfall splashed and rumbled on its path down the slippery rocks. It was strange to think that Tom and Hannah had probably sat here, all those years ago.

Later that evening he read some more of the diary.

'Uncle Jeremiah was a very nasty man,' he said at breakfast the next morning. 'He was a horrible bully. He used to hit Tom and he shouted at Hannah. He was really unkind to their dad too.'

'Oh?' asked Garth, 'Have you read more of the diary?'

'I finished it last night,' Euan said. 'I wish there was another diary. I want to know what happened next.'

Garth and Alice laughed. 'It's not a story book!' Alice said, 'It's someone's real life!'

'Yes, but Old Jeremiah and their dad had just had a massive row. Hannah was really scared. Jeremiah was going to throw them out but their dad said he couldn't. He said he had no right to throw them out. He said that one day soon it would be Jeremiah who would have to leave.'

'My goodness!' said Alice, 'It sounds even more interesting than a novel!'

'Hannah said it was a big secret but her dad had found some papers. Jeremiah had hidden them but her dad found them. He was very angry. They had a big row and then the diary ended. It just said, 'Tomorrow dad is going to Portskail. Tom and I must stay here until he gets back. When he comes home we will not have to worry any more. Everything will be better and we will live together in the big house.'

'It sounds like their father had been cheated out of his inheritance by Jeremiah,' Garth suggested, 'and then he found the papers which proved he was the real owner. He probably suspected they were hidden away somewhere and waited until Jeremiah was out in order to search for them.'

'Oh, how wonderfully exciting!' said Alice, 'But what a shame there isn't another diary! We may never know what happened next. I wonder if they got rid of nasty, old Jeremiah and lived happily ever after. I do hope they did!'

Euan thought so too. In fact, the next morning shortly after breakfast, he decided to do a little further exploring of his own. When he was sure that Alice and Garth were safely tucked away with the few remaining packing cases he donned a coat and made his way to where the aluminium ladder had been left the previous day. It was quite a difficult item for an eight year old boy to move but Euan managed, by a mixture of lifting and dragging, and with frequent rests, to manhandle it towards the ruined stedding. It took even more effort and one or two unfortunate slips before he could raise it against the wall adjacent to the gap where the original treasures had been found.

He ran back to the house and slipped quietly through the door, returning a few moments later with Daisy in one hand, now refreshed and dry and ready for a new life after so many dormant years, and a small torch in the other. Euan picked up a short branch from the ground in front of the building.

'I can use this to get things from the hole,' he whispered to Daisy. 'You can sit down here by the doorway and be my look out!' He set her down against the outside wall. 'Let me know if you see anyone!' he said, in a conspiratorial voice.

He slowly clambered up the ladder and, once at the top, reached his arm deep into the space. He felt carefully from side to side, his fingers scratching at the dust. He pulled his arm back and shone the torch. The space widened at one point; he could feel a space and four sharp edges. Another stone had been removed leaving a secret hiding place He peered deep into the recess. Once more his arm delved deep until his shoulder was pressed firmly against the wall. He stood on his toes and held tight with one hand on the top step. There was definitely something else in that space but he couldn't get his hand far enough around the corner.

He clambered down the ladder and looked thoughtfully at the stick he had collected. He broke it in half and then clambered back again. He carefully contrived to turn the stick around the tight corner and into the secret space and dragged at the invisible item within. It took several attempts and more patience than Euan generally possessed before he could dispense with the stick and carefully remove from its hiding place the item secreted within. He drew it carefully out. It was a soft, leather wallet about twenty centimetres by ten and, Euan noticed with increasing excitement, was not empty. It bulged gently with hidden secrets.

'Treasure!' he whispered, and his hands trembled. 'There may even be another diary!'

Before he had an opportunity to investigate or even to take his first step backwards down the ladder, he was distracted by a strange, soft sound coming from just beyond the doorway. It sounded like someone singing in a hushed, low voice.

'Mum?' he called out. 'Is that you?'

There was no answer; and now he noticed that the singing, although indistinct, was very childlike. It sounded like a little girl singing a lullaby.

He clambered down the steps as quickly as he could and stumbled over the rubble and out of the door. There was no-one there. However, Daisy, who had been sitting with her back against the door frame, had grown restless. She had struggled to her feet and had set off to walk towards the house. Unfortunately, her limbs, although clean, had not regained their former strength and lacked the muscular and skeletal support they needed to make the journey. She had fallen and was lying on her back midway between the outhouse and the front door. Euan looked around. He could hear the radio in the kitchen. Perhaps that was the sound he heard.

'Sorry I took so long,' he apologised to Daisy. He picked her up by one arm and hurried into the house. In his other hand he carried the leather wallet.

'Mum! Dad!' he shouted. 'I've found something in the wall!' Mum and dad were busy unpacking boxes and did not hear. 'Come and see what I've found!' They emerged for a moment from a back room. 'I found these!' he laughed excitedly.

'Perhaps those are the papers that proved who owned the croft!' Garth exclaimed. 'I'd really like to take a look.' He was moving towards the kitchen when he saw the look Alice directed at him. 'Perhaps I'll wait until this evening,' he said. He grimaced. 'We've got the unpacking to do.'

'I'll take them to my room!' Euan was already closing the door behind him.

The papers contained in the wallet were very old, which was exciting, and they were written in a very neat but very old fashioned hand which was even better. The paper was thick and coarse. They looked as

if they might have been written with a quill pen.
Unfortunately, although Euan could decipher a small
number of words, when they were placed together in a
sequence they made no sense. The sentences were very
grown up, he decided. What were of even more interest
to him, however, were the maps. There were three
maps which Euan, having been engaged in some
mapping work at his school the previous term, could
see were of the same area but to different scales.

He laid them out on his bed. They showed
Aultmore. One placed the house in its wider
surroundings and showed the river and an old track
which must have preceded the road to Laurimore and
Inverstrach. The house was set in the middle of the map
and the adjacent fields, the edges of the moorland and
the bridge were all clearly drawn. The second map
showed just the house, the cottage and stedding, some
fields and the river. It was outlined in black and
obviously delineated the extent of the entire holding.
The third was a particularly close view which sketched
the layout of the main house and the cottage and
stedding.

'Look, Daisy,' said Euan. 'This is where you used to
live; and this is the house where nasty, old uncle
Jeremiah lived!'

He looked through the other papers. 'No diary!' he
frowned.

He stood by the gable window and looked out. From
his room, which was at the front of the house, he could
see the ruin. He was also shocked to realise that he
could also see a child sitting by the ruined doorway and
playing casually amongst the grasses and the stones.
She looked as if she were talking or singing to herself.
He looked down to see if a car had pulled up while he
was playing. Perhaps a neighbour had called while he
was looking at the maps and was, even now, sitting in

the kitchen with his mum and dad. There was no car, however. The little girl looked up at him but did not wave or call. Maybe she was from the nearest croft and had walked down with her parents. He hurried down the stairs and into the kitchen; there was no-one there. He ran outside but there was no girl either.

'Where's she gone?' he wondered.

He looked around and then checked inside the ruin. There was no sign of her. He ran back to his front door and then looked back down the drive. Under the trees, just at the point where the drive curved right towards the road he saw her again. She was a little girl of about seven years of age and had long, fair hair. She wore a long, floral dress which fell to below her knees but her arms were bare. She wore a straw hat with a red ribbon. When she saw him she jumped up and down and waved.

'Mum!' Euan called. Then he shouted louder, 'MUM!!'

Alice came running from the house just in time to see the little girl skipping towards them down the path. Behind her a man and a woman were calling her back. 'Bethany! Come back here!' Bethany had obviously chosen not to hear them. They strode after her as quickly as they could whilst striving to retain a degree of dignity.

'I'm so sorry,' the woman called to Alice. 'Bethany, I am not at all pleased with you!' The couple hurried forward to make their introductions but in one respect, at least, there was no need. Euan beamed and then his mouth widened into a huge grin. He ran towards the little girl as if towards a good friend. It was the little girl he had met in the park.

'I knew you'd come!' he cried.

Some time later, seated around the kitchen table and refreshed and relaxed by the combined influences of tea and cakes, apologies having been made, the situation was explained. When Bethany ran and met her mother on the path in the park she was very disappointed that her new friend had not followed her. She didn't understand where he had gone. She told her mother all about Euan and showed her the card that Euan had given her. She explained that he was moving to a new house called Aultmore. She remembered it especially because he said it was near Portskail. Every year they went to Portskail on holiday. She was very insistent that Euan had told her to come and see him but they had not intended to disturb Alice and Garth. They had hoped that merely to see Euan's new house from the road would have been enough to satisfy Bethany. Once they were outside the house she had insisted on walking down the drive so that she could see the house. Then she had seen Euan and, well, that was that.

Alice had liked Bethany on sight and was already predisposed towards her mother and father. How could they be anything but delightful when they had such a lovely, little girl? They were soon in relaxed and comfortable conversation. Garth was initially more hesitant but it took little time for him to discover that he shared a passion for mountains and literature with Marcus, Bethany's father. The conversation continued in a relaxed and comfortable manner until Marcus and Meg decided it really was time for them to leave. Before they departed it was agreed that they would all meet at Aultmore the next day and perhaps to go for a walk together.

While their parents were talking Euan and Bethany had escaped to his room and he introduced her shyly to his toys. He was pleased that she shared his delight in them.

'Of course you've already met Daisy,' he laughed. 'Daisy is very old. I found her in a secret place in the old stedding. She belonged to a girl called Hannah, hundreds of years ago.'

Bethany looked puzzled. 'She's lovely,' she said, 'I've never seen her before, though.'

'I heard you singing to her,' Euan said, 'when I was in the ruin.' Then he remembered that the sound he heard might have been the radio and checked himself. 'Anyway, I definitely saw you playing outside the cottage. I was watching from my window.'

Bethany shook her head. 'I haven't been near the cottage,' she said.

Chapter Nineteen

Unfortunately, due to a strange set of circumstances, the two families were unable to meet the next day until lunch time. The road through Inverstrach had been closed and Bethany and her parents were obliged to detour several miles north and then west before approaching Aultmore from the Laurimore direction. Instead of the longer walk they had intended, Garth and Alice took them as far as the lower crags from where they could look down on the valley, the road and the house.

It was only in the evening as they listened to the radio that Alice and Garth heard something of the events that had left the road closed to traffic for several hours. It was strange news but few details were given. It was some time before the full picture emerged.

The tiny village of Inverstrach looked as if it had been planted by accident in the mountainous landscape. Its long, narrow street consisted largely of cottages, separated by small, enclosed fields which stretched down towards a tree lined burn. Some of the fields had been developed in recent times as a new period of growth had seen the arrival of incomers from overcrowded towns and the cities. Many had retired there in search of the peace and quiet of village life. Their house names expressed their hopes, 'Rainbow's End', 'My Retreat' and 'Rivendell'. Several had improved their rural idyll by surrounding their homes with hens, ducks and, occasionally, goats. Signs on gates offering free range eggs for sale were as common as signs offering bed and breakfast.

Two or three houses bore the gaudy signs of estate agents. These people were going back home, driven away by loneliness, isolation, boredom, the weather, a lack of facilities, or by their own insatiable restlessness. For them the dream had burst like a soap bubble.

At one end of the village street stood a tiny primary school and a stern looking chapel built from grey granite. Inverstrach Mountain Hotel stood at the opposite end. The windows of its bedrooms, restaurant and bar looked out, grimly optimistic, on the street and car park. The sign at the roadside swung patiently. The summer seasons were short and, when they were over, the owners depended on the restaurant, the bar and the tiny village shop at the rear of the building to sustain them. Gavin Lord, polishing glasses and brasses behind the bar, looked as immovable as the building itself. Equally stoical was the weathered war memorial which stood opposite the hotel at the top of four stone steps. It was surrounded by a small area of grass and, in summer, narrow beds of bright flowers.

The tiny village was currently basking in a radiance of spring growth. Pale green leaves sprung from the branches of the birches; primroses and daffodils illuminated the roadsides and the banks of the burn. Viewed from the high pastures, against the backdrop of inspiring peaks, Inverstach was modest and proportionate. It looked as though the natural world had stepped aside momentarily to permit its development but had not retreated far and would, one day, reassert its ownership. In spite of its ramshackle design the village seemed to belong to the landscape and to have acquired a temporary leasehold there.

Jean Sanderson had lived in a small house just beyond the centre of the village since her marriage in 1951. Her children had grown up and, one by one, departed to the city for employment. When her husband died in 1998 she remained in the house alone.

'Where else would I go?' she asked. 'Everything I know is here.'

When she reached her eightieth year, her children suggested that she move into sheltered accommodation in Portskail but she was resolute. Inverstrach was her home. She knew people there. She could look out of her window and watch people passing outside. There was a tiny shop that met most of her needs and neighbours who would help her. There was even a bus service to Portskail. Her children could not persuade her to move. They organised what help they could and Jean now had a meal delivered daily and received some home help. They resigned themselves to her decision.

'Stubborn, that's what you are!' They shook their heads. They gave up trying to convince her but they did not give up worrying. They visited her as often as their busy lives permitted. In recent times their anxiety had grown. She was having greater difficulty walking and often only managed her daily visit to the shop with the support of a frame. She was forgetting things too.

Garth had met Jean and spoken to her on his first visit to the shop at Inverstrach and Alice had already been invited in for coffee. Now they would call to see her whenever they passed that way. They liked Jean. She was full of tales about the families who lived in the village when she was a child. Despite her failing memory of more recent events she could name every inhabitant and their subsequent movements. She could recall the workers in the fields, their annual round of seasonal tasks, their tools, their food, their homes and the trivial details of their daily lives. She had no difficulty recalling times when the lochs froze and the streets were full of snow to the window sills or describing the hillsides before they were planted with the trees that now rose to forty feet or more. She remembered the old shepherd who lived in an old house

out on the moor in the summer months. She could
describe the inside of her childhood home more clearly
than she could her current house and remembered lying
awake, unable to sleep for the sound of corncrakes in
the meadows. She could recall the toys she had played
with as a child. She had just yesterday told Alice, just
as she had previously told Garth, all about the children
she had grown up with and how time, wars and tragedy
had stolen them away, one by one. Now she was the
only one remaining. She was never entirely sure which
of the stories she had already told and repeated them
over and over. It was a small price to pay for the
pleasure of her company. Now grey haired and frail,
she had until not long ago played the violin in the local
ceilidh band. She loved reels and jigs with a passion.
She had a sharp eye and even now a ready laugh. It was
easy imagine her in a regular corner of the Inverstrach
Mountain Hotel with her friends.

Whilst her grasp of the details of girlhood scenes
had grown in sharpness poor Jean was gradually losing
her grasp of life in the present. Even her flimsy hold on
the hours of the day was fading fast. It came as no real
surprise to Gavin Lord, looking out of his bedroom
widow at seven o'clock that morning, to see Jean
pushing her walking frame ahead of her through his car
park.

'She'll be coming fore her paper,' he said to
himself, 'the poor old soul.' He hurried downstairs and
opened the shop door for her.

'You're far too early for your paper, Jean, my dear,'
he laughed. 'You're up before the birds this morning.
Come on in. I've just put the kettle on. You'll join me
for a cup, won't you?'

'Aye, aye, I will' she said and gave him a shrewd look. 'But HE won't.' She nodded her head in the direction of the war memorial.

'Who won't?' Gavin enquired.

'Him!' She nodded towards the memorial rather more impatiently.

Gavin thought he understood. She was referring to a familiar name she had seen on the monument, perhaps someone she knew as a child before the war. He felt rather sorry for her. The past was where she lived nowadays, he thought. 'No,' he said, 'none of them will be coming back. It's a tragedy.'

Jean looked at him sharply. 'Sometimes I think you're not all there,' she said. She turned her frame round laboriously and made her slow progress towards the door again.

'What about your tea?' Gavin laughed. 'You're in a hurry this morning, aren't you?'

'Come with me,' she said. 'We can have tea while we wait for them to come.'

'Who are we waiting f....?' Gavin began. He gave up. There was no point in trying to make sense of this. He followed her out and chatted idly as they crossed the road. 'There must be some familiar names on there,' he said, indicating the memorial, 'old friends.'

She nodded. 'Dead and gone,' she said. 'But I don't know him.' She stopped and waved a hand towards something at the top of the steps.

Behind the memorial, leaning against the stone as if in rest, lay the body of a man of about forty. His legs were stretched out before him and his hands lay palm upwards at his sides. His eyes were wide open and he stared ahead into vacancy. A pool of blood which flowed from an open gash in his chest had soaked into his shirt and trousers and spread across the stone steps.

It had dripped over the step before it stopped. Staring upwards from each of his open palms was a dead eye.

For a moment Gavin simply stared. Then he felt Jean's hand gripping his arm.

'Come on,' she said, 'I think we'll have that cup of tea now while we wait for the police. Best be quick before anyone else comes along here.'

Gavin, thus spurred into action, led her painfully slowly back to his kitchen. He called through to his wife, Jennie. After as brief explanation he left her with Jean whilst he called the police and then positioned himself by the memorial. Thankfully the body was at the back and largely out of sight from the road. But it wouldn't be long before children would be gathering just along the road to wait for the secondary school bus to Portskail. It wouldn't do for them to see this. There would be the morning dog walkers too.

He needn't have worried. In less than half an hour the road was closed in both directions and the scene of crime was protected from intrusion. Screens and a tent like structure had been hurriedly erected around the monument. The school bus was cancelled and some delighted children were granted an unexpected holiday. Officers were placed at each end of the village and the whole area was cordoned off. Julie was busy talking to Jean and taking notes. Gavin too was called upon to explain the events of the morning. A number of curious villagers had gathered at their gates. They spoke in hushed voices with shocked looks. Things like this didn't happen in Inverstrach. Phil Bentley was busy speaking to a group of them. Had anyone seen anything? Had they heard anything, any sounds in the night, any cars in the early hours? They shook their heads. No-one had seen or heard anything. One or two faces flinched with disappointment and annoyance. They lived close by. Why could they not have heard something? It was tragic event, a terrible thing, but it was exciting too.

Jack took the call to inform him of the unpleasant news as he was preparing to leave his house that morning. It did not improve his mood. Struggling as he already was with the fourfold issues of the press, the first murder, the lost boy and the missing body he felt particularly aggrieved that someone should have the affront to add to his woes. He was also desperately aware that this was now rapidly moving beyond his pay grade. He left a message for senior colleagues in the city and, optimistically, asked for help to support his investigation. He knew it was unlikely to remain his investigation for long. They would descend upon him with the sole purpose of causing him irritation, aggravation and hair loss.

That, however, was not his primary concern at present. He reached the scene an hour later, a short time after Sandy who was already kneeling by the body. They stood together, grim faced, and looked at the scene.

'I know you are the detective,' Sandy said at last, 'and I don't want to intrude on your preserve, but those eyes look a pretty good fit for a pair of empty sockets we've seen recently.'

Jack knelt down and looked closely. He called the photographer. 'I want a shot of these eyes and hands from here,' he said, 'and here.' He turned back to Sandy. 'He's been particularly carefully positioned, it seems to me. What's this?' The lips on the corpse were slightly parted. 'Jack stepped back. He looked pale. 'You take a look, Sandy. You're more used to these things than me.'

'His tongue has been cut out,' Sandy confirmed quietly. 'I'll tell you more when I get him back to the mortuary but the chest wound, I would hazard, was caused by the same implement and by the same person as in the graveyard. I think you've got a problem, Jack.'

Jack looked around. 'Why here?' he said. 'Why would he be placed by a war memorial, of all places? Is it simply an opportune place or is it significant?' He looked from the body to the memorial and then up and down the lane. 'It has all the appearance of some sort of ghastly ceremony,' he murmured. 'It looks staged in just the same way that the murder by the grave looked staged. I'm sure it has some significance, either symbolic or specific and individual.'

'Where's the woman who found him?' Jack called across to his colleagues. They indicated the hotel. Jack strode across the lane and found Jean in the kitchen still drinking tea and eating biscuits with Jennie. Jennie had a solid and reassuring look; her natural colour, like her natural appearance, had long since been lost to memory. Nowadays, she was precisely what you saw. It was unwise to wonder what she might have been. Whatever had once been had gone forever. But she was a good natured, cheerful soul who breezed through her daily role in life with blousy goodwill.

'Here she is, detective,' she said with a wide gesture towards the old lady.

'Jean?' Jack smiled broadly. 'I should have known it was you! How are you, my dear? It must have been quite a shock for you!'

'It was a bigger shock for him,' she replied dryly and munched her biscuit.

'What were you doing out at that time of the morning?' Jack asked. 'You should be more careful!'

'I was taking my pretend dog for a walk.' Jean roared with laughter. 'I know people think I'm going daft but I still see what I look at and I still remember a bit of what I see. And I'm not frightened wandering about my own village.'

'So, you tell me what you saw,' Jack smiled.

'Him!' said Jean with practised obscurity. 'I saw the dead man! He was dead when I got there, honest, officer! It must have been the other one what done it!' She laughed again.

'Come on, Jean, enough of the teasing! You are my favourite girl but I might still arrest you.'

'I'll make a run for it,' said Jean. 'You'd never catch me!' She sipped her tea and picked another biscuit from the tin which lay open in front of her. 'I can't resist a chocolate biscuit, especially if it has cream in it. These are minty. Now,' she said, 'do you want to know about then or earlier?'

Jack looked at her sharply. 'Tell me about earlier,' he said.

'I don't sleep as well as I used to,' Jean explained. 'I wake up and I can't get back to sleep. Sometimes I have to get up and walk about a bit. I ache, you know. My back and my legs ache. That's when I heard the car.'

'What time was it, Jean? Did you look at your clock?'

Jean shook her head. 'It was dark, though. I'm still nosey, you know. I still peep out from behind my curtains. I like to know what's going on. There are a lot of new people in this village now, you know. There are too many new names. I forget them. People aren't as friendly as they used to be but there are enough of the nice ones. I'm having trouble keeping up with their names but I still like to meet them.'

'Did you look out this morning?'

'Oh yes. I heard a car, you see.'

'What did you see?'

Jean leaned forward and whispered. 'I saw a car,' she said and laughed as if at a joke. Jack smiled patiently. 'I couldn't see who was in it. There were no lights. But I know there was someone in it.'

'How do you know, Jean?'

'I know because he got out of the car, silly! He went to the back and opened it up. It was one of those big, square-looking things, like a posh person's Land Rover.'

'What happened then?'

'I don't know. I needed the toilet. When you are getting as slow as me, you don't hang about. When I came back, the car had gone. It was very disappointing.'

'What did the driver look like?'

Jean shrugged. 'It was a man, - quite a big man.'

'What about the car, Jean did you see its colour?'

'Dark,' said Jean in a whisper, 'Just like the man. He was dark.'

'Do you mean he had a dark skin?'

'No, he was just dark. Well, he would be, wouldn't he? It was pitch black out there!'

Jack laughed. 'You are incorrigible!' he said. 'I'm tempted to place you under arrest but I don't think the police station could cope with you! You'd have them all tied up in knots.'

There was little to be gained from further questions. Jack marvelled at the incongruous mixture of lucidity and confusion.

'I'm going to send one of my young officers across to take a statement,' he said. 'Now you be nice to her and don't go teaching her any bad habits! I'll pop in and see you in a day or two.'

'I'm your star witness, aren't I?'

'You're always my star, Jean. Take care, now.'

He spent some time directing his staff around the crime scene and arranging door to door interviews. He gave Julie the task of patiently coaxing from Jean all she had seen. Then he left Sandy to arrange the removal of the body and returned to his office.

'I need some time to get a grip on this,' he muttered. 'I've been running around like a fool, looking for this, losing that. I need to think. I need to get this under some sort of control.'

Control, however, was proving difficult to achieve.

Chapter Twenty

'It seems that the murder near Aultmore was rather more gruesome and mysterious than our minister has been led to believe. It is really quite an intriguing story!'

Kate had a triumphant gleam in her eye. Her hours of research had obviously produced pleasing results.

It was evening and Sandy, at Kate's insistence, had joined them for dinner.

'He will need company this week,' she said. 'We can't have him moping about in that house of his, not this week of all weeks.'

Their conversation had been fragmentary and uninteresting. Both men seemed preoccupied with their own thoughts and concerns. Jack's mind was now so engrossed in his investigation that he was scarcely aware that he was poor company. Sandy was approaching the anniversary of Helen's death and his mind slipped constantly back despite his efforts to maintain conversation.

Fortunately there had been food and wine and they were sufficiently comfortable in each others company to tolerate silence without anxiety.

It was into one of these long lapses that Kate decided to inject her own stimulating subject. She had suppressed it with difficulty all evening.

'Ah, you have been ferreting away at our local archives, I suspect,' smiled Sandy, rousing himself. 'You have the smug look of someone who has discovered a truth that has escaped the rest of us. What do you say, Jack? Shall we indulge her or shall we turn away and feign a lack of interest?'

'I suspect that we will hear the story whether we choose to listen or not,' Jack suggested.

'Now, admit that you want to hear my story,' Kate insisted, 'or I will remain silent. You will be in a state of torment all evening. Go on, admit it!'

'Oh, I dare say we can indulge you,' Sandy said dryly.

'Not good enough! Confess you want to know!'

Jack confessed on their behalf. They sat back on their chairs without moving from the table as Kate spoke.

'I have been visiting our library for an hour or two each day,' she said, 'usually in the morning as soon as it opens. It took some time to search out the records of the death and they were no more illuminating than the account we have heard already. They merely recorded the death of a man at Aultmore and gave his age and the date of his death. By a strange irony that date is at the end of this week, Friday in fact.

Sandy's face paled and he looked down. It did not go unnoticed by his friends. Kate, aware of the mistake she had made and shocked at her lack of sensitivity, blushed deeply. She chose to move the subject on to give poor Sandy time to recover.

'I then searched for what I could find about the man himself. Since we know that he wrote one book it was always possible that he wrote others and that there would be some information about his life from various literary sources. It transpires that he was far from prolific. He wrote two books, both of which concerned this particular area. We have encountered one, which was a personal account of his travels around the region, his encounters with various inhabitants and his reflections on the history, geography, flora and fauna of the place.

'The second was a book of stories about the area; some were old folk tales that he either collected from various books and journals or heard from local people. Others were stories of real events, which were all gathered from the local community. Some concerned events which were still within living memory; others had been handed down by previous generations and related to local families and their properties. A very small number were about contemporary events and people still living.'

'I imagine that might have made him a few enemies,' Jack said. 'It isn't everyone who wants to have their family or personal laundry washed so publically.'

'Most people prefer to leave their skeletons well buried,' agreed Sandy. 'If some writer came along with a shovel and started digging it would not meet with universal approbation. I am beginning to see a plot unwinding in this narrative.'

Kate grinned. 'Don't be too hasty in your judgements,' she teased. 'You will have to wait and see.

'Our librarian is a dear soul. She is fascinated by all things local and when she heard what I was doing she was terribly keen to help. I don't think they get very many people under the age of sixty in there nowadays and very few seem to access the archives. She vanished for some length of time, into a musty cellar deep below the library I assume, and then returned with a dusty little book in one hand and a rather tattered, tired looking volume in the other. Actually, I am exaggerating merely to add drama to my story. The first book wasn't dusty at all. It was old and the pages were thin and curling at the edges, but it was remarkably free of dust.' She looked up excitedly. 'It was the book of stories written by our murdered friend.'

Both men had ceased eating and were sitting back. They both held glasses of red wine. Jack swilled his casually around the glass. Sandy was still. He leaned forward.

'Continue, my dear,' he said. 'I will admit now that you have my full attention. Did the stories give any indication of the possible identity of the murderer or the motivation for it? That would be rather more than we could hope for but it would be the most stimulating outcome of your researches.'

'Oh, there were several possibilities. The writer seemed unconcerned about the effect his stories might have on people living in the area at that time. He rather resembled a modern tabloid journalist in that respect. In fact he made me think of a certain nasty little hack of our acquaintance. Some of his stories were sensationalist, certainly libellous if not true, and revelatory in the extreme.'

'You said she brought you another book,' Jack asked. 'What was that about?'

'Ah, my husband the detective,' Kate laughed, 'has noticed the clue I laid. Yes, that book was particularly important. You see.......' She paused momentarily to savour the effect of her words, 'that book was written some years later by a completely different author and contained an account of the murder of Marius Dorling.'

She sat back and laughed, delighted with the reaction of her listeners.

'Now, where would you like me to go next? Shall I indulge in a little eighteenth century gossip and tell you about the misdeeds of some of the local population or shall I go straight on to the story of the murder?'

'Oh, I think we should proceed in as direct a line as possible,' Sandy suggested. 'We can return to the salacious gossip and the eventual revelation of the list of suspects at a later time. What do you think, Jack? Shall we hear about the bloody deed while we drink our blood red wine?'

'I think a tale of murder as the evening light fades and night approaches would be most appropriate. Shall we leave the dishes and adjourn to the living room?'

'Well,' Kate began, when they were settled, 'Marius Dorling was in his mid forties at the time of his death. He was from a reasonably well to do family of merchants from a mill town in the south and made a more than adequate living from investments and by working for a publishing company, an income which he supplemented by writing occasional articles and pamphlets. He was writing, we must remember, at a time when interest in the wilder, rugged beauty of our area was becoming more fashionable. Wealthy people came from the south to absorb its sublimity and to wallow in its romantic associations. Our own regional centre, where he settled for a few years, was benefitting at that time from an influx of wealthy visitors. Our author, it would seem, capitalised on that development. Not only did he pen details of particular walks, he also acted as an occasional guide to the very rich.

'From his writings it would appear that he held his patrons in as little esteem as he did some of the poor inhabitants of this area. Both were reviled in his texts. He was, to say the least, a man of misanthropic tendencies.'

'Ah, a man after my own heart,' said Sandy, 'I raise my glass to him!'

'There is little in his first book – the volume about his travels - to suggest anything more than his incapacity to flatter or praise where no virtue is seen. The example you read about the owner of Aultmore is a fair example. There are others in a similar vein but they are occasionally balanced by praise for acts of generosity and kindness. Unfortunately such examples are not frequent and the book does not paint a particularly flattering picture of local inhabitants.

'In the second book – and I must confess to having read more of that one; the first was a rather heavy, tedious affair, - he seems to have gone out of his way to select tales which reflect a range of human attitudes, from the selfish, the cruel and the ignominious to the kindly and the caring. There are stories of savagery and betrayal and homely tales of virtue and selflessness.

'There is one story, however, which has a direct bearing on what we have been discussing. It would appear that a cottage, adjacent to Aultmore, had been occupied by a dependent of old Jeremiah Aultmore. You will remember the none-too-flattering account of our writer's encounter with that particular gentleman. This dependent was an older brother of Jeremiah's who had fallen on hard times. His wife had died, probably of tuberculosis and he was left with a young daughter and a son. The girl was about eight years old at the time of the events in the story and the boy perhaps a year older. This impoverished family had had been living in the cottage for about four years.

'There was a dispute. Inevitably it was about money. In crime stories, it appears to me, the great motivator is either sexual or financial. In this case there was some talk of an inheritance which was to come to the older brother but which was stolen by the younger.

'Not long after the argument the older brother was seen hurrying along the streets of the city. He was carrying a number of papers and was seen to vanish into the office of a notary of some importance. Three days later he had packed up his belongings, taken his little boy and girl and vanished into the night. Jeremiah said they had argued about rent and work. Jeremiah described his older brother in less than flattering terms. He called him a wastrel and a scrounger and said he was glad he had gone and taken the children with him. He suggested they try the slums in the city of some seaport if they wanted to find him. Old Jeremiah retained the land, the property and the money until his death. No-one came forward to inherit and the land, I presume, passed out of the family.

'Rumours abounded, of course. There were enough people who thought little of Jeremiah and a good number who thought well of his brother. There were some particularly touching anecdotes about how well the older brother cared for the children. He worked hard, when there was work to be had, and whatever he earned he used for them. Some said he spoilt them but most saw no evidence that his love and attention did anything but enhance the striking qualities the little children showed. Other people said he had simply given up believing he would ever be fairly treated by the miserly Jeremiah.

'The story penned by our late writer went a little further. He all but suggested that the brother was murdered in the cottage and that the little boy and his sister, being witness to the whole thing, were similarly disposed of.'

'There would seem to me to be circumstantial grounds then for suspecting old Jeremiah of the murder of Marius Dorling,' said Sandy, thoughtfully. 'It could have been revenge for the accusations he had made or perhaps even a pre-emptive strike against someone who might reveal more about the disappearance of the brother and niece and nephew. Just imagine how our little, rat faced hack would ferret away at a story like that!'

'I suspect – and I speak now as a detective – that the story Marius wrote provided a very clear motive for murder,' said Jack. 'But I also suggest that Jeremiah, being a cunning as well as devious gent, would have carefully provided himself with an alibi or would have a cast iron explanation for the presence of the author near the house. Have you discovered any evidence of an explanation?'

'I have indeed,' Kate said with satisfaction, 'Jeremiah declared that he wasn't in the house that night, He was at an inn some distance away. It was a place where he wasn't personally known but he brought forward five witnesses to his presence there that night. He also hinted that the author might have been visiting his home for some nefarious purpose, perhaps to add blackmail to slander.'

'So he got away with it?' Sandy leaned forward and picked up his glass. 'Is that another nail I hear being driven into the coffin of a just and righteous God?'

'Well,' said Jack, 'that certainly is some story but I suspect, from the look on your face that you have another revelation to make.'

'Marius did not undertake all of his journeys alone. His son, a boy of about eight years of age, travelled with him. The boy whose name was Joshua was with him when he was murdered and he was never found. No body was ever found. He was never seen again. His mother died without ever knowing what happened to him.'

Jack was visibly startled. He stood up and paced towards the window. He pulled back the curtain just sufficiently to stare out onto the dark street. He saw the reassuring lights in his neighbours' houses, the familiar cars, the reassuring landmarks of his daily existence. He fought back the primeval terror that had momentarily gripped him.

When he turned round he saw that Sandy had not moved. He still stared towards the fire. His face seemed drained of colour and his eyes were unnaturally bright.

'There is no reason to assume any connection between the clothes in the cave or the bones we found and this tale,' he said, aware that the same threads were weaving their dangerous pattern in his friend's mind, 'and the coincidental appearance of a child at the scene of this murder and of the one in the graveyard is just that – a coincidence.'

Sandy's voice trembled. 'The boy was by the grave of Marius Dorling. He was looking at the grave. Your witness says he heard him say the word, 'daddy'. And the boy has vanished.' He looked up. 'You don't think.....?'

'What? You think that we'll find him in the cave?' Jack tried to smile. 'No, of course we won't! Behave yourself! It's that Catholic upbringing of yours allowing you to make strange supernatural connections. You are socially programmed towards superstition.' Now he forced a laugh. He allowed space for Sandy to regain some degree of composure. His friend's discomfiture leant him strength to subdue his own emotions.

'Well,' said Kate, 'I anticipated that my story would have a certain impact but you have exceeded my expectations.' She laughed nervously. 'I have solved a two hundred year old murder, perhaps. I should have been a detective.'

Jack had regained his usual calm. 'You have certainly proposed a very worthy hypothesis and if I were enquiring into that particular case it would be a direction I would pursue vigorously. With today's forensics and my own genius I have no doubt we would nail the culprit. Unfortunately he has escaped earthly justice and his victims will have no retribution.'

'I have often wondered why there is no room in the justice system for a little honest revenge.' Sandy, having allowed himself to escape momentarily from his sardonic, protective shell, now re-established himself firmly within it. He looked at them sheepishly for an instant before his head was thoroughly withdrawn and his detached, ironic manner reasserted itself.

'Perhaps justice could be served by allowing victims and their families, or their appointed champions, a certain amount of time in a closed room with the offenders. The sentence could then be measured in minutes and, in the case of more serious offences, a sliding scale of weapons.

'You are hereby sentenced to five minutes and one leather strap whose dimensions shall not exceed fifty centimetres by five centimetres. You are sentenced to ten minutes and one baseball bat. However, five of those minutes and the baseball bat are suspended for one year.'

'Do you think the penalties meted out would fit the crime?' asked Kate, allowing herself to enjoy the absurdity of Sandy's proposal. 'Would it not depend on the background of the victim, their perceptions of what constitutes a suitable balance of hurt and forgiveness?'

'I suspect that on balance the punishment would match the crime. No-one would wish to bring an average burglar to the edge of death; they might receive a modest beating. A child molester, however, might, even with the same sentence, find themselves more savagely treated. Some people, it has to be said, might be mutilated, crippled or even killed, but that would only be in situations where the crime was sufficiently unpalatable and tempers ran particularly high and the sentence was of sufficient duration. Of course there would be miscarriages of justices. That can hardly be avoided.'

'I think you should pen a letter to your Member of Parliament without further delay,' Jack contributed. 'We should set up an online petition. There are enough people out there who are sufficiently barking mad to sign it. This could gain widespread support. Sandy Finlay – the great reformer – might go down in history!'

'The Angel of Death and Retribution!' said Sandy, smiling darkly. 'I am not a man to be trusted with the destiny of others. I was taught to believe in damnation, remember! And I too am one of the damned. I have despaired.'

'You don't believe any of it, though!' laughed Kate. 'You are an unbeliever.'

'Certainly,' Sandy looked at them both sharply. 'When I die, the switch will simply be thrown to 'off.' I will be no more. That is the moment when my damnation ends!'

Chapter Twenty One

'William McPhee, surveyor, aged 42, living with Rosalind Carthy, aged 37, no children but proud parents of a large, overly intimate Labrador and a small nondescript terrier rather too fond of the sound of its own voice.' Jack shook his head. 'Apart from the rates these surveyors charge to spend half an hour in your home in order to find fault with it before sale, I can see no reason for him to be murdered. Ms. Carthy can see no reason for it, his colleagues and friends can see no reason; even his dogs can see no reason. But a reason there must be!'

'Well, at least we've got one connection with Malcolm McColm,' Phil Bentley turned on his chair, smiling optimistically. 'There was no reason for either of them to be murdered.'

'I'm not sure that connection is going to get us very far,' Jack noted, 'and it hardly narrows down the list of potential future victims. No, either there is a connection we haven't found or, more worrying, these are random acts whose motivation is in the mind of the perpetrator rather than in the identity of the victims. Our clues in that case would be in the method and the locations.'

'How was the bereaved coping?' Julie asked.

'Not well,' Jack sighed. 'I hate interviews like that. 'Apparently Mr. McPhee had an appointment late the previous afternoon to look at some ruined croft with a prospective buyer who contacted him directly through his office. It was arranged by phone and the name was fictitious. The croft was several miles from Inverstrach. Ms. Carthy received a text late in the evening to say he was remaining at Inverstrach for the evening and would be back very late or even the next morning. She assumed business had adjourned and he was having a meal at the hotel. When he didn't return she grew concerned and phoned his mobile and his office, both to no avail; when she heard about our murder her anxiety became panic and she contacted her local police at Strathnarn.'

Strathnarn was a small seaside town, not dissimilar in size to Portskail, forty miles to the south. It shared the popularity of Portskail with summer visitors from the south but had the disadvantage of long, sandy beaches and numerous caravan parks.

'I'm afraid she was in a dreadful state.'

There was a knock at the door. Three heads turned to see a fourth head, rather tousled and ill balanced appear round the door. Jamie had arrived on the mainland the previous afternoon and had decided to consult Jack before he began his mission. He looked nervously at the three officers and was momentarily bereft of words. Jack took pity on his and led him through to the inner office.

'Come in, come in,' he said. 'How can I help you?'

'I know you told me to stay on the island,' Jamie blurted out. He felt uncomfortable now and wished for a moment he had made a different decision and had simply gone about his business. His plan seemed foolish and childish. But he had made his choice and he had to continue. 'I know there's nothing I can do that you can't do; but I just have to be here. I can't sit there looking out to sea, carrying on as normal, when ...... well, when I could be doing something. I'll walk the streets; I'll ask questions; I'll do anything.'

Jack immediately knew better than to challenge him. He saw at once that beneath his naivety and his embarrassment his resolve was firm. Besides, his intentions were good and there was little harm he could do and Jack liked him. He was a kind hearted, sensitive lad and he cared – he actually cared. He would wander round until he got bored or saw the futility of his quest and then he would go home. He would feel that he had at least made an effort. Jack did not expect him to find the boy.

But, a few days later, that is precisely what he did.

He started his search on the streets near the harbour and then worked systematically outwards. He had spent many hours planning his strategy and came armed with a detailed map. If that little boy was within the area, he intended to search exhaustively till he found him. He spoke to people in the streets, especially old people and parents with young children. He scrutinised children and parents in the park. He spoke to parents at the school gate and by the nursery entrance. He chatted with shopkeepers and hotel proprietors. He visited the camping site and the caravan park. Each day he widened the arc of his search, penetrating deeper into the outer areas of the town. With some misgivings he trod the same path along which he had followed the boy to the church.

Soon his search had moved beyond the church to the new housing estate and the large, detached houses beyond. Still without any success he wandered out along the small number of lanes and the two main roads that led away from the town. Gradually the houses thinned out and then there were single, isolated farms and lonely houses. Still he found nothing.

In the evening he sat alone in his room at the Portskail Hotel and scrutinised and updated his list. Line after line had been crossed through. There was little left. He had visited the bar of the Portskail Hotel only once and had restricted himself to a single drink. There too he made his enquiries. Tomorrow he would visit the minister and he would speak to some of his friends and acquaintances by the harbour. Then he would make a final foray out into the countryside beyond the furthest boundaries. But what could he do then?

It was hard for him to describe his feelings when he phoned home each evening.

His father, aware of the disappointment that lay ahead if his search proved fruitless, warned him to be prepared for the worst.

'The police have been door to door. They've had dogs out and teams of policemen combing the area. They've been on television. If *they* can't find him, it isn't likely you will.'

His mother was proud of him. He seemed to have grown up almost overnight. His efforts on behalf of this little boy, of whom everyone was now aware after television and newspaper coverage, were seen and appreciated by all her neighbours. She was anxious, though, about his reaction were the boy to be found murdered and lying in a ditch somewhere, as seemed increasingly likely as they days went by.

Jamie listened to them both but refused to be discouraged. The police, he told them, must have missed something. They might have missed someone or perhaps people might be afraid to speak to them; not everyone wanted to speak to the police. He looked upon his days of failure not with growing despair but as a gradual but successful narrowing of his search. He was convinced that each day brought him closer to the solution. Tomorrow would confirm this implicit belief or it would merely prove that he had been insufficiently thorough the first time round. In that circumstance he would begin again but with renewed vigour and even greater concentration. Nothing would shake his conviction that the boy remained alive.

His mother was correct. Were the boy to be found dead, the impact on Jamie would have been considerable.

'When are you coming home?' she asked him. 'You've done all you can.'

'I'll come home when I find him,' Jamie said firmly, 'but not before.'

Each evening he phoned Jack to let him know the progress he was making. This was an important part of his day's ritual. He could describe his systematic procedure and explain how he had eliminated certain areas from his search. On the final evening he was quite excited.

'I've covered nearly everywhere now,' he said. 'I'll find him any day now, I'm sure of it.'

Jack, although he was scarcely inclined to say so, was growing increasingly impressed by Jamie. He could not help admire the young man's tenacity nor could he doubt the compassion that drove it.

'That young man is not without intelligence and ability,' he said to Kate. 'I think I may have misjudged him.'

'Have you ever thought of joining the police force?' he asked Jamie, much to the amusement of the latter who was momentarily lost for words. When he put the phone down he felt some small stirrings of pride. He shook them away at once.

'There'll be time for feeling like that when I've found the boy, but not before,' he warned himself.

One evening, Jack called at the hotel to see him. They sat in the lounge, nearly empty at this stage of the season. The bar and optics shone in expectation of the business to come and the tables, polished, deep mahogany, were matched in their brilliance by the thick carpet, red velvet and brown leather sofas and heavy curtains. They sat by a log fire, still necessary on these cool spring nights. Jack looked at the soft drink in front of Jamie and at his own golden pint.

'Abstinence is no substitute for moderation,' he said. 'Self denial is all very well but the harder choice is to make wise decisions.' He laughed. 'I've chosen a glorious pint of real ale. I suggest next time you reconsider and simply exercise caution.'

Jamie was impatient to discuss the implications of what he had remembered.

'He was pointing at the writing on the stone and he said, 'Daddy' or 'dad'', he explained to Jack. 'What does it mean?'

Jack had given it some consideration. 'There are two obvious interpretations,' he said. 'No doubt there are others but these seem to me to be the most interesting. Firstly, he is simply looking at what he has seen and is crying for his father. 'I want my daddy!' Secondly, he is looking not at the stone but at the body and is saying, 'Daddy did that!' Of course, he might have been saying, 'This dead man is my daddy!' but we know that the victim had no children.'

There was a newspaper on a chair beside the fire. Jack saw his own face look up at them from a photograph with an amusingly puzzled expression. 'You'll have seen this?' he said. 'Simon Keller!' He spat the name contemptuously. 'He's a most unpleasant little man, a contemptible, spiteful, weasel of a man. He's annoyingly talented too – a most annoying combination.'

Jamie nodded emphatic agreement.

'We will not let ourselves be distracted,' Jack picked up the paper and tore out the offending page. He rolled it into a ball and threw it onto the fire. 'There,' he said, 'that's disposed of. Now, think for a moment of what you have told me. The boy was looking at the stone. In fact he was indicating the writing on the stone.

He said the one word, 'Dad' or 'Daddy'. That's what you told me, isn't it?'

Jamie nodded.

'So the illogical logic could be that the boy was saying, this is my daddy buried here in this grave. This man, murdered about two hundred years ago, is my daddy. That is what might follow from what you have described. That, we know, is impossible. The boy was six or thereabouts. The corpse was a hundred and forty'ish. Nonetheless, there are people, quite a number of them, who would love to turn their back on the rational and to dive headlong into a mire of superstition and supernatural conclusions. It would feed into their mythology. We are obliged to see things differently. We look for sensible, logical solutions. We are required to reject that analysis. For example, the boy may have been saying, 'This is like my daddy; my daddy is dead like this and is buried in a graveyard.'

'What does it mean for the boy?'

'Well,' said Jack, 'that leads us onto more treacherous ground. If he ran home and told his parents what he had seen we must wonder why they haven't come forward. Is it fear? Do they have something to hide? Are they examples of those people nowadays who are described as distrustful of the police? If his father was the perpetrator then the boy will have been spirited away or worse. If the father is dead then the boy may have told someone else who is equally unwilling to come forward or he has remained silent about what he saw. He is likely to be traumatised if he saw the actual murder.'

It had taken some time after he left Jack for these thoughts to marinate in Jamie's mind but, by the time he spoke to Edward Grey the next morning they were ready to be served. At eleven a.m. precisely he walked down the gravel drive towards the Edwardian edifice and knocked loudly on the door. The sound echoed through the entrance hall and faded as the sound of footsteps on the wooden floor approached him. The heavy door swung open and Edward Grey welcomed him and led him into the strange interior.

'I don't know that I will be able to offer you much help,' he said as they sat down over tea and biscuits, 'but I'm sure it would be of some value to you to be able to talk about your dreadful experience that night. Is that why you are here? I must confess the whole thing was a dreadful shock to me too. It is hard to imagine the effect it must have had upon you and upon that poor child.'

'No,' Jamie explained hurriedly. 'It's the boy I want to talk about. I don't matter. I'm fine.'

'Ah, I've spoken to D.I. Munro, you know. I'm afraid that much as I would like to be of help I am unable to do so. I racked my brains without success. The school and nursery children are, I believe, all accounted for. No child of that description was on holiday at that time and no child of his description has been reported missing. I think,' he paused for a moment and looked at Jamie. He patted his hand, 'I think we have to expect the worst. I think….'

'No,' said Jamie, sharply interrupting. 'He's alive, I know he is. I'm going to find him.' For a moment he saw the child again and heard his tiny voice.

'Daddy,' he said or 'dad.'

'Have any children gone away – on holiday, perhaps, or to stay with relatives?'

Edward shook his head. 'Jack asked me the same thing,' he said. 'He also checked the hospitals. He looked anxiously at Jamie. 'Your search is very commendable, it really is but I doubt there remains a single question that has not been asked nor a possibility that has not been pursued.'

'No-one has asked the right question,' Jamie said firmly.

He looked around the room. He was thinking hard. His attention was drawn to one photograph on the wall. It was a monochrome print of a group of refugees on a dry, dusty Middle Eastern dirt track. It was a family of five and they carried their belongings on a hand cart. The sundry items that protruded from it seemed anachronous and random, as if they had been flung on the cart with little time and little careful thought.

The adults had the wide eyed, frenzied look of the displaced. The certainties of the life from which they had been expelled had been replaced by the terrifying enormity of an uncertain future. The woman carried a baby inside a shawl. The two children, a boy and a girl, were dark eyed and thin and walked barefoot in the heat.

The family were part of a long, meandering line of dispossessed people on a desperate journey to find safety.

Edward saw him looking at it. 'They are the real victims of war,' he said. 'Most of them, if you took time to ask them, wanted nothing more than to be left alone to bring up their families. They were guilty of nothing. Yet they were hated and persecuted and driven from their homes. They would be no more welcome in the lands to which they fled. Somehow, the plight of people like these is well under the radar when fighting starts. 'One death is a tragedy, a million is a statistic.' Wasn't that what Stalin said? I wanted to take photographs that showed that each one of that million is a tragedy. Too many people and races have been stripped of their humanity by hatred and persecution.'

Jamie's mind, stirred by compassion for this anonymous family and the multitude of the betrayed around them, thought of minorities closer to home.

He was struck by a sudden thought.

Have there been any travellers around here?' he asked, suddenly excited. 'Gypsies, whatever you want to call them?'

Edward was thoughtful.

'We do get them occasionally,' he said, 'but they rarely stay more than a day or two. You hardly notice them'

'They are under the radar,' said Jamie.

Edward looked up suddenly. 'There is a caravan down by the shore about a mile away,' he said. 'I saw it from the church tower this morning. There was a van parked beside it and I could see a dog. It was there some days ago but it had gone so I thought nothing of it. It only arrived back last night.'

'Was it there on the night of the murder?'

'It certainly wasn't there on the following day. Of that I am sure. But ...... yes, it may well have been there the day before. Fancy me not thinking of that before!'

'Were there any children?' Jamie almost shouted. 'Think hard!'

'I don't know. I really don't know,' cried Edward, 'but ......'

'But ....?'

'But there were clothes on a line. There were quite a lot of clothes. I think, perhaps ......' Edward shrugged. 'No, it was a long way off. I can't be sure.'

'It doesn't matter!' Jamie cried. '*I'm* sure! *I'm* sure! Can I use your phone?'

'Jack,' he laughed, almost overwhelmed by his own emotions, 'I think I've done it!' He would not believe after all these days that he had not achieved his goal. 'I

think I've found him. No, I'm sure I've found him!'
and he explained with varying degrees of lucidity, his
discovery. Jack spoke firmly at the other end of the
phone, asking questions, issuing instructions pulling
gently but decisively on emotional brakes to prevent his
young friend from precipitous action.

'I'm going down there now. I've got to,' Jamie was
saying. 'No, don't worry! I'll not approach the caravan
before you get there. You're where? Oh, about an hour?
Okay, okay, I'll just go for a walk along the shore, just
nearby. I'll just look. Yes, I understand…….. No, I
have to go……… I have to.'

He was oblivious to warnings of potential danger or
potential disappointment. Edward could hear Jack's
patient voice attempting to instil a degree of calm to the
surging waters of Jamie's emotions. Yes, the father
may, after all, be the killer. Yes, he understood that the
boy may already be dead. Yes, he might simply be
mistaken or the family may have nothing to do with the
missing boy. Yes, he understood, he understood.

In reality Edward saw that he waved aside anything
that could challenge his conviction that he had found,
perhaps even saved, that young child.

Jamie put down the phone, He turned and hurriedly
shook hands with Edward and, his eyes glistening,
headed for the door.

'Wait a minute!' Edward called after him. 'If you
are heading out where angels fear to tread, you'd better
have some clerical support. I'm coming with you.'

Shortly afterwards they set off across the field
behind the graveyard. They turned left along the lane
and then down a track and across a field towards the
shore. Jamie strode impatiently forward.

Chapter Twenty Two

Jamie's pace slowed as he neared the shoreline. The sky was clouding over and the distant horizon threatened rain towards late afternoon. A breeze was stirring the surface of the water and ripples were growing into waves and rising fretfully up the shingle and seaweed shore. From where he stood the shoreline curved away, past the travellers' caravan and onwards until it was released from the shackles of an opposing headland and stared out towards the open sea and the distant shadows of the outer islands. Two small, brightly coloured boats rose and fell in the shallow waters below isolated houses on the far shore.

The pungent smell of rotting seaweed surrounded him but he breathed deeply and beyond it smelt the tang of sea salt. A faint aroma of burning driftwood also slipped towards him. He looked along the shore to see a thin wisp of fine smoke rising from the travellers' camp. A dog barked. A man's voice called out.

Edward, breathing heavily, caught him up and was relieved to stop and rest.

'We shouldn't look in so much of a hurry,' he panted. 'We're just out for a stroll along the shore, remember. It's Jack Munro who is looking for a witness and a possible murderer, not us.'

Jamie nodded. 'I just want to know that I'm right,' he said. 'I want to see the boy for myself.'

'Well,' said Edward, 'let's pause for a moment and look around and then carry on with our walk; but let's go slowly. The path leads along the edge of the shore by the field where they have their caravan. We'll be within thirty metres or so at the closest. We can stand there again for a moment or two looking out to sea. But we mustn't hurry and we mustn't do anything to raise any concern before Jack arrives. If needs be we must move on beyond the field and then return ten minutes later. We are two people out for a walk, nothing more. If that man is a killer or has any involvement in this ghastly business he will be constantly on the look out and constantly anxious. Now, are you sure you can do this?'

Jamie nodded.

They progressed more slowly now, partly by design and partly because the shoreline path was increasingly muddy or stony. It appeared to have sustained itself well on its route from Portskail to this point but was now gradually losing purpose and concentration. It meandered at one moment onto the stony beach from which it only rescued itself by passing over slippery rocks. The next moment it clambered forgetfully up a sandy banking to find itself pressed tight against a barbed wire fence from where it had to drop quickly back to the shore.

There were fewer footprints now. Most people walked as far as the edge of the burn and then retreated rather than face the long trek to the open sea. The scenery changed little and walkers were granted little reward to compensate for their efforts.

Nonetheless, it was only a matter of a further fifteen minutes before Edward and Jamie reached the end of the enclosed field where the travellers were pitched. The caravan was situated close to a low, stone wall on the far side of the field. A number of stunted rowan trees had struggled to grow above it but had been twisted and deformed by the prevailing wind which blew in from the sea. They leaned away, beaten back by years of adversity. The field itself had been used to pasture sheep but at present it was empty and the grass was ankle deep and uneven.

The caravan looked little different from the caravans that arrived in their hundreds in the summer season. It was quite a large van with twin axles and looked relatively new, certainly no more than a few years old. Parked in front of it but at a distance of several metres, was a large, blue van, whose origins pre-dated the caravan by many years. Within the angle created by the two was a small fire and beside the fire a man was sawing driftwood into small pieces, occasionally casting pieces into the flames. Every few minutes he stopped and wiped his forehead with a grimy, chequered cloth. A dog watched them curiously from the front of the caravan steps, its mongrel ears twitching in their direction and its bright eyes following their movements. It took a few hesitant steps towards them but seemed to decide that the journey was not worth undertaking and returned to the caravan where it lay down and curled round.

Its movement drew the attention of the man to their presence. He stood up and rested the saw. Edward raised a hand and waved and the man responded.

Edward and Jamie moved forward, rounding the edge of the field and, in the process, approached rather closer to the man. He was a tall, stocky figure, unshaven and sporting a head of wavy, brown hair. His movements gave the impression of restrained strength and his clothing covered a strong, muscular frame. His arms hung wide of his sides, as if driven outwards by the bulk of his upper arms. He wore old, blue jeans and a black jumper whose sleeves were rolled up to his elbows. He smiled and revealed a full mouth of teeth whose whiteness was accentuated by the swarthy colouring of his face.

'It looks like rain is coming,' Edward called.

The man looked at the sky. 'There'll be a storm tonight, I think,' he said.

Having exchanged these pleasantries Edward and Jamie were about to move on when the door of the caravan opened. The dog looked up expectantly and its tail flicked a welcome. Curious to know, no doubt, to whom the new and unfamiliar voices belonged to, a little girl stood and watched them. She was probably about five or six years old and had long, fair hair which fell halfway down her back. She wore a long, pale dress which fell from her shoulders to below her knees in one elegant sweep. She sat on the bottom step and fussed the dog and, all the time, watched them curiously.

'What a delightful, little girl,' Edward called, at ease now in his ministerial role, his dog collar clearly indicating his function. He leaned against a fence post as if ready to engage in some further conversation. The man seemed inclined to accommodate him.

'Aye, she is,' the man called back, with obvious pride, 'and she knows it!'

It was Jamie now who seemed inclined to move on. He shuffled nervously as the man lay down his saw and strolled across. The little girl ran across and held her father's hand. When he stopped some distance from the strangers she hid shyly behind his legs but not before the two men had noticed her extraordinarily blue eyes.

'What lovely eyes you have!' said Edward, smiling towards the girl who made every effort to hide herself from the strangers.

'She takes after her mother,' the man called, drawing attention to his own deep hazel eyes. 'Her brother is just the same. They're twins.'

Jamie looked sharply up. He was about to speak but he felt Edward's hand restraining him. It was fortunate for Jamie at that moment that their attention was drawn to three cars making their inelegant progress down the rough track towards the field. The man turned angrily back.

'What the hell do they want?' he muttered. Jamie saw two police cars, preceded by Jack's own car, hobble to a stop just beyond the caravan at a field gate. The man strode back across the field towards them. 'They never give you a minute's peace,' he snarled. 'Get inside the van and don't come out till they've gone,' he said to the girl. 'Tell your mum we've got company.' As she scurried towards the van, the door opened again and Jamie caught a brief glimpse of a young, fair haired woman and, by her side, a tiny, blue eyed boy. The girl fled into the van and the door was closed behind her.

'That was him!' whispered Jamie, grasping Edward's arm in his excitement. 'That was the boy in the graveyard! He's alive! I've found him! I've found him!' He was suddenly aware that tears were rolling embarrassingly and uncontrollably down his cheeks and he was barely restraining his laughter.

'Thank God he's safe!' murmured Edward. 'Thank God!'

Jack, followed by four uniformed officers, approached the man. There ensued a few moments of angry conversation then Jack moved deliberately towards the van. The man stepped forward to prevent him but was restrained with some difficulty by the policemen. A few moments later the fair haired woman and the two children emerged from the van and were accompanied by Jack and one of the police officers to the cars. The man was dragged with difficulty, still struggling, and forced into the rear seat of one vehicle, his hands now cuffed behind him. An officer climbed in beside him and another climbed into the driver's seat.

Jack looked across towards Jamie and briefly nodded to acknowledge both their presence and the success of Jamie's search. Moments later the three cars moved away up the track towards the road and towards the Police Station at Portskail. The dog was left, barking and running backwards and forwards along the field edge.

Edward took Jamie by the arm. He turned him gently round and led him back towards the distant church and home.

In the meantime, Jack returned to the station. Having wisely left his colleagues to suffer (in the case of one car) extended verbal abuse wishing all forms of pain and catastrophe upon their families and (in the case of the second car), tears, distress and outrage, he reflected with some satisfaction on his judgement of Jamie. The young man had proved himself and his self belief had been rewarded. He would find time to visit him at the hotel later, assuming Jamie didn't pre-empt matters by arriving even sooner at the station. As he parked his car and entered the building beneath its grey Victorian portico he prepared himself for the interviews to follow.

'Let's have him in one room and the woman and children in another,' he directed the struggling group that entered behind him, 'and phone Children's and Families Social Work. I need a social worker down here as soon as possible. Julie!' he called across to where his startled junior had turned on her seat to see what the noise was about. 'You go and sit in with the woman and children. See if you can calm them down. Try and explain that I gave up eating babies some years ago. Tell her I'm a vegetarian. Tell her I breed puppies and make cuddly toys. Tell her what you like but stop that infernal din! And you!' he turned to where the man was resisting every effort to force him into the interview room. He raised his voice with sudden severity. 'You've got five seconds to get in that room before I charge you with resisting arrest, actual bodily harm, upsetting my officers and not having a TV license! NOW GET IN THERE AND SIT DOWN!'

With a final outburst of abuse the man kicked at the door and then flung himself resentfully into a seat behind a table which, wisely, was bolted to the floor and resisted all attempts to remove it. The officers followed him into the room and stood silently and menacingly beside the door, their natural bulk enhanced by the body protection they were wearing.

The doors closed and a degree of quiet settled on the office.

'I think I'll give them ten minutes and get myself a coffee,' Jack said, with a look of feigned shock. 'Such profanities, such obscenities, such a range of foul language – who would have though a humble traveller would be blessed with such a vocabulary? I hope you covered your ears, young lady!' He tutted loudly and shook his head before vanishing into his office to refresh himself with coffee. After a few moments the door opened and he summoned Phil Bentley, who had returned to his work at a desk in the corner.

'I want you to talk to the woman. See where they've been recently. Ask her how the children have been. Offer what reassurance you can. Get them some food and something to drink. Let her think we just need to clear up a few things and then we'll let them go. We need her co-operation before we speak to the children so go very easy. Don't mention anything about the murders. Keep Julie in there with you; she's better at being womanly than you are. It might be useful. In the meantime, I'll tackle Godzilla in there.'

The man looked up angrily as Jack entered and sat at the table facing him. He clenched his fists on the table top. Jack stared at him with humourless eyes and placed a folder silently before him. For a moment he said nothing at all; he simply stared at the man as if waiting for him to speak. Then he moved suddenly and opened the folder to remove a piece of paper.

'What's your name?' Jack asked.

The man seemed inclined to refuse an answer but thought better of it. He sat back.

'Samuel Letheren,' he said. 'Aged thirty six, odd job man, part time forester, occasional labourer, buyer, seller, trader and, according to you lot, thief, wastrel, fraudster, poacher and tinker.'

'You left out murderer and mutilator of corpses,' Jack said.

Samuel laughed without humour. Jack watched him impassively until the laughter died away.

'Describe your movements over the last week or two,' he said, icily calm.

Samuel thought for a moment.

Now you mention it,' he said. He leaned forward over the table and whispered, 'they were very loose on Monday. I think it was the rabbit I ate the previous evening. They're back to normal today, though. Thanks for asking.'

Jack didn't smile. He waited. The man fidgeted and then spoke.

'Okay,' he said. 'We were here for a few days last week. I was working in the forest above the town. Then I was given some work over near Inverstrach so we moved on. We were camped down by the river just outside the village. It's a regular spot. Someone will have seen us. We came back here – work again – yesterday. You can check at the forestry office. I often get casual work at this time of the year.'

'You have a blue van, I see?'

Samuel nodded.

'Did you ever park it in Inverstrach?'

The man thought for a moment then shook his head. 'It never left the field. I walked up to the road and got a lift to the forest. Rachel doesn't drive.'

'So it wasn't in Inverstrach in the early hours of last Thursday morning?'

Samuel shook his head. 'What's this about?' he asked.

Jack opened the folder. He took out a photograph of the second murdered man and turned it towards Samuel. He watched his reaction carefully. He noted the widening of the eyes, the tightening of the lips. He noticed the way his body tensed in an involuntary spasm and then relaxed. He noticed the fists clench tighter and a slight flush come to his cheeks. He saw him work to control his reaction and to appear disinterested, unconcerned and unaffected. He watched as he turned the photograph round and pushed it back to Jack.

'Do you know this man?' Jack asked.

'I'd recognise him if I saw him,' Samuel smiled. 'That hole in his chest is a dead giveaway.'

Jack showed no reaction.

'He was killed at Inverstrach when you were camped in the field below the village. I'm surprised you haven't heard about it.'

He took out a photograph of the first victim and pushed it towards Samuel.

'This one was killed in Portskail churchyard when you were camping in the field by the shore.'

'You're not suggesting I had anything to do with this, are you?' Samuel grasped the table and leaned forward. 'I've never seen these men before in my life!'

Jack did not move or blink. He stared icily at Samuel. 'Sit back,' he said. 'It's time to tell everything you know. If you don't tell me, I'm sure your wife and children will.'

Samuel was on his feet. 'You leave them alone!' he shouted. 'They don't know anything! There's nothing for them to know! I don't know these men! I've never seen them before! I heard the forestry men talking about some murder in Portskail but I didn't listen much. It was nothing to do with me.'

'Well, we'll see,' said Jack, gathering his papers together. 'I'll go and have a chat with your family now.'

'No!' Samuel shouted. Then he fell back in his chair and groaned. 'Ben isn't well. He's not been well for days. We're worried sick about him. He's barely said a word for days now and he won't leave his mother's side.' He sank back and Jack noted the unwelcomed presence of tears in his eyes. Samuel angrily forced them back. 'Please! They don't know anything; none of us do. We keep ourselves to ourselves. We don't get involved in things that don't concern us.'

'Did you overhear the foresters talk about a witness?' Jack asked, 'A missing witness?'

Samuel shook his head.   Then he looked up and stared directly at Jack. 'I had nothing to do with these murders,' he said. 'We know nothing about them. I give you my word.'

Under different circumstances Jack might have laughed but there was something about Samuel that rang true. He was tempted to believe him. He did believe him.

'Does Ben ever wander off on his own?' he asked. 'Mine did at that age. If I turned my back for a minute they were off down the garden, along the back lane, in a neighbour's house. Are your two like that?'

'We look after our children.'

'I'm sure you do.' Said Jack, 'I just wondered if he wandered off, worried you to death, like mine did.'

'Sometimes,' Samuel admitted, guardedly. 'You know what boys are like.'

'Could he have wandered off at night without you knowing?'

'What? Are you trying to say he did the murders? He's a six year old psycho, is he?' His laughter was defensive. Beneath the aggressive posturing, Jack could see an anxious and worried man.

Jack allowed a flicker of a smile to slip briefly across his face like a light between shadows. Then he stared once more at the man before him.

'No,' he said, 'but he might have been a witness. We need to talk to him.'

He saw an incredulous look give way to shock and then to fear. Samuel's defences had fallen away completely. Jack could see both his strength and his weakness laid bare before him. He loved his family. He trusted no-one else to look after them. The world beyond this tiny nucleus shared different values; they were unfriendly, even hostile. They could not be trusted. They were not like his people. He looked at Jack and saw what his father and mother had seen and their parents too, and theirs back into time. He did not trust him. He saw the other police men and women and he did not trust them.

'He won't speak to you,' he said. 'None of us will. We know nothing of your murders.'

'You may need our help to protect Ben,' Jack warned, as he put the photographs back in the folder and moved towards the door. 'There is a murderer out there and he knows Ben might be a witness. He'll be looking for him.'

'We can look after him,' Samuel responded. 'No-one will hurt Ben.' He folded his arms and said not one more word.

Jack left the room.

Chapter Twenty Three

Phil and Julie had met with a singular lack of co-operation in the other interview room. Rachel had remained obstinately quiet and, whilst the little girl had responded quickly to the presence of crayons and paper at one end of the table, Ben had not moved from his mother's side at the other. Julie had managed to engage the little girl in harmless chatter but had steered carefully away from any mention of the reason for their presence in the Police Station. She asked her about the picture she was drawing, about her dog, about her dress. Ben was unwilling even to volunteer his name.

Rachel looked at Phil suspiciously and her eyes constantly darted to where Heather was busy with her drawing.

'You must be very proud of them,' Julie said. 'They are beautiful children.' She could not help but notice how beautifully Heather's hair was brushed, how clean their clothes were, how spotless their faces and hands. Their eyes were wide and of a blue that was almost transparent. When she looked at them it was as if she was staring into their souls.

Their mother, Rachel, shared their fair hair and blue eyes and had obviously been an attractive young woman. She was not particularly old now, perhaps in her mid thirties, but years of distrust had narrowed her eyes and given them a sullen look. There was no transparency here.

'They are well looked after, if that's what you mean,' she muttered, defensively. She held Ben close and a sharp look warned Heather to be careful with her words.

Phil asked about where they had been staying and what they had been doing. The answers were guarded but were essentially the same as those of her husband. He asked about Samuel's work. He asked where they had been for the previous week or two. The answers were the same.

The door opened and Jack ushered in a dark haired young woman, casually clad, and with a relaxed, confident air.

'Hello, Rachel,' she said, with the familiarity of a regular acquaintance. 'I didn't know you were back in these parts.' Her voice was a city voice but it was tempered and softened and carried no note of threat or judgement. It was the voice of someone who was showing she would offer support but would not intrude. It was a voice that was designed to elicit trust. 'I'm June Whalley, you remember me?'

Rachel's half smile acknowledged unwelcomed acquaintance. She was not deceived by that friendly tone. It was a cultivated artifice, the voice a professional used when dealing with the likes of her. These were the people who took away your children just because they lived a different life from other children. They had tried to take her away when she was a girl but her father was too clever for them. By the time they came to get her they had gone. Samuel hadn't been so lucky. It had taken him a year to get back to his people.

June had moved over to Heather and was praising her picture. Heather glanced at her mother and then proffered the picture to June.

'For me?' said June. 'Oh how nice! I'll pin this on my office wall when I get back.' Everyone will admire it. Are you going to draw another picture for the police lady?'

Heather nodded and set to work on another piece of paper.

'Hello, Ben,' June smiled at the boy but he buried his head deeper in his mothers shoulder. She glanced at Julie and Phil. 'This isn't like you! You're usually such a lively little chatterbox!' She spoke to Rachel. 'What's the matter with Ben?'

Rachel shrugged and stroked the boy's arm. 'He probably doesn't like getting dragged off to a police station for no reason.' She glared at Phil. 'He's been a bit clingy for a few days,' she said, 'ever since we were here before. It's just a phase. He'll be alright again soon.'

'Has he told you if anything upset him?' Phil now asked, 'When he was at Portskail before?'

Rachel shrugged. She didn't know. 'I thought he'd been told off by someone,' she said, 'or someone had been nasty to him. It happens. But he's been like this for days now.'

'Did you hear about the unpleasant events hereabouts?' Jack asked from the doorway. He didn't want to speak in front of the children but he had little choice. He spoke quietly, directly to Rachel.

'Sam told me about something that had happened at Inverstrach. He heard about it at work.'

'There was another unpleasant event at Portskail. It was the day before you left to go to Inverstrach. We think a little boy was in the graveyard at the time. He might even have seen what happened. He was probably so scared he ran away the only direction he could. He ended up in the town towards midnight. He found a young man there and led him back to the body. Then he vanished. He probably saw that he could get home now and didn't want to get into trouble. We think Ben might be that boy.'

'We want to go home,' Rachel's eyes registered shock and fear. She hugged Ben close. They were being drawn into matters that did not concern them. They could end up in all sorts of trouble if they got involved with these people. When they were on their own, amongst their own sort, they were safe. They minded their own business. She could feel the walls of an alien world pressing in on her.

'We don't know anything,' she said. 'We haven't seen anything. There's nothing for us to tell.'

'Can we ask Ben?' Phil asked gently.

'You can ask if you want,' Rachel said, 'but he won't answer you. He won't even tell us what's worrying him. We've tried.'

She was correct. Ben's eyes were clenched shut and he gripped her more and more tightly. He was shutting out the questions. He was trying not to listen. He didn't want to hear or to think or to remember. Rachel's eyes betrayed an anxiety that she could not suppress. She brushed a tear from her eyes.

'We need to take him home,' she cried. 'He'll get better when we're at home. Where's Samuel? He needs his father.'

'How has he been sleeping?' June asked.

'He has bad dreams,' said Rachel, sobbing now. 'He wakes up in the night and he cries. Sometimes he screams.'

'Does he ever wet the bed?' June inquired delicately. 'I know he was sleeping through when we last met.'

'He's started wetting the bed again,' Rachel cried, 'just in the last few days, ever since ....' She did not finish what she was saying. She stood up. 'I want to take them home. You've no right to keep us here. It's cruel.'

Julie turned from Heather and looked towards Jack. She was suppressing some powerful emotion. 'Have you seen the lovely picture that Heather has drawn?'

she said. 'You really should see it.' Her eyes conveyed a meaning that her words disguised.

'It's a story,' said Heather, 'a scary story,' and she giggled.

Jack picked up the picture. He showed it to Phil. 'That's a very scary picture!' Jack said, 'Don't you think so, Phil?'

Phil definitely thought so. A faint flush suffused his cheeks. 'Shall we see if it scares mummy?' he said. Jack put the picture on the table, turned it round and pushed it towards Rachel. He leaned on the table. The picture showed a scrawled stone that could have been a grave. A child's drawing of a man was beside it and from his centre there flowed scribbles of red crayon which could only be blood. A large figure comprised of two circles stood at one side and at the other side stood a smaller figure, as if watching. For a moment or two, Jack did not take his eyes off Rachel. Then he picked up the picture and turned back to Heather. He kneeled by her side.

'Who is this?' he asked, pointing at the small figure.

'Ben,' she said.

'Who told you this scary story?' he asked.

'Ben did,' she said.

Ben had his arms round his mother's neck

Jack took the picture and went towards the door. 'I'm going to show daddy this scary picture,' he said, 'and then we'll see if we can get some biscuits and drinks, maybe even some ice cream or a milkshake and we'll all sit down together and talk.'

A moment later he set the picture on the table in front of Samuel.

'Heather drew this. The little boy is Ben. He's watching a murder taking place in a graveyard at eleven o'clock at night. My guess is he woke up in the late evening and slipped out of the window. It was probably still reasonably light. You probably didn't even know he was gone. In the gathering darkness he found himself up by the church and he saw something pretty horrible. He waited, hidden no doubt by the gravestones, and when it was safe to do so he ran in the only direction possible, away from the things he had seen and towards the town. There he had the good fortune to meet a young man who came back with him to the graveyard. Perhaps he wanted to show the young man what he had found. More likely he wanted him to be there to make sure the monsters had gone and that he was safe to run home, which he did as soon as he could. Does that sound about right?'

'He's only done it once before,' Samuel looked up. 'He thinks it's a joke. He has a bed in one end of the van and he's learnt how to open the window. He slips out and wanders down by the shore. Last time, I saw him and brought him back. I guess we laughed as well as telling him he shouldn't go off on his own. This time we didn't see him. Until this moment, I had no idea he'd been out again. He must have climbed back through the window. He could reach it if he stood on the gas cylinder just beneath.'

'And the next morning you all woke up to find a little boy who was deep in shock, only you didn't know it.'

'How could we know it? He wasn't eating as much as usual so we just thought he was a bit under the weather. He stayed with his mum like he does when he's sick. He didn't go out of the van much except to play near the steps with Heather. He was quiet, very quiet, but we weren't to know what had happened to him.' He stared at Jack defiantly. 'Do you think we wouldn't have looked after him if we'd known? We're good parents!'

'I'm sure you are,' Jack said quietly, 'but Ben needs help. He needs the sort of help that you can't give him on your own. You need to speak to a psychologist and to get advice as to how to help him; and he needs our protection. Someone out there knows he was a witness to a murder. That same murderer has now committed two horrible crimes. Do you think another death would bother him? You've got to let us help you!'

Samuel stood up.

'Are you going to arrest me?' he demanded. 'If you're not, we're going home now. We don't need your protection and we don't need your help. We'll look after ourselves, same as always. By the end of the day we'll be gone. Your murderer won't find us; neither will you or your psychologist. No-one will. Disappearing is easy.'

'You'll have to tell us where you are heading,' Jack said. 'Ben is a witness to a murder.'

'Stick a pin in a map; we might be there.' snapped Samuel. 'Ben could end up murdered. I'm not staying around to find out what happens next.' He walked towards the door and opened it. Jack motioned to his colleagues not to stop him. 'Rachel! Heather! We're going!' he called. 'Ben!'

Rachel emerged from the interview room with the children but just as they did so, Jamie entered the swing doors at the front of the building and ran up the stairs, two at a time. He opened the door just as the traveller family were reaching it on the other side. Ben stopped. He stared at Jamie for a moment. Jamie smiled and bent down.

'Hello,' he said. 'It's nice to see you again.'

Ben hesitated but only for a moment. He released hold of his mother's hand and went across to Jamie who held out his hand to receive him. Ben grasped the hand and leaned forward.

'Tell Daddy,' he whispered. 'Tell mummy. Say it wasn't my fault.'

'Of course it wasn't your fault,' Jamie squeezed the tiny hand between his. 'Mummy and daddy know it wasn't your fault. Shall we tell them all about it?'

Ben nodded.

'What do you say to you doing all the talking and we'll just listen in,' Jack suggested quietly to Samuel.

Samuel shook his head. 'I don't want any of you involved. We look after our own.' He looked at Jamie and he looked at Ben by his side. Ben was whispering to him. His face had brightened into a half smile. Rachel was sobbing. Heather was observing the unfolding drama as if intent on creating another picture.

'We're going back to the van,' Samuel said. 'Come on!'

'You come too!' Ben whispered to Jamie, 'Tell mummy and daddy it wasn't my fault the man got hurt.'

Jamie looked up. Samuel glanced at Rachel and at Ben.

'If you want to,' he conceded, 'you can come too; but no police, no social worker and no psychologists!'

Jack nodded to the police officers who had taken a brief opportunity to head for the kitchen and the coffee motioned them to take the family and Jamie back to the caravan. He exchanged a look with Jamie that said plainly, 'Find out what you can and come to see me.' Jamie nodded.

'That young man never ceases to amaze me,' he said, turning to Phil and Julie.

When he re-entered his office, in search of a period of peace, rest and reflection, he found Sandy waiting for him. He had taken Jack's seat and was resting, sprawled out with his head on the chair back and his feet on the table, half asleep.

'Ah, here you are at last. I thought better than to disturb you in the midst of your interviews. It sounded rather rowdy for my delicate constitution. I prefer the companionship of the dead – they are so much quieter and less disruptive, unless they move around a room or disappear on you, of course. However, in addition to bringing you these reports,' he indicated some papers on the desk, 'I have come to announce progress on that front.' He paused a moment, as if for dramatic effect. 'I have found our missing body and I believe, although I will never be able to prove it, that I also know the identity, or identities, of those responsible.' He glanced towards the door. 'From my poor viewpoint here I did notice a young boy just departing, a boy not dissimilar to the one described by your inebriated witness. Perhaps we are making progress on two fronts.'

'Tell me about the body first! Where was it?'

'Ah,' said Sandy. 'I blame myself entirely for a quite unwarranted oversight. You see, in their wisdom, those city officials who designed the mortuary twenty years ago included facilities that a scattered community like ours was unlikely ever to need. I closed down several of these useless facilities including two compartments where, to avoid technical jargon, we keep our dearly departed on ice pending their final farewells. Both compartments have been switched off and locked for many years. There was no reason to check them. However, by pure chance I noticed that the thermostat on one of them was registering a particularly low temperature whilst the other was at room temperature. I gathered the only key from my office, unlocked the padlock, slid back the bolts, opened the door, drew out the trolley and, to cut a long story short, found our missing corpse. I have sealed him back in place, complete with lock, to avoid any further disappearing tricks.' He waved a key. 'This, my dear friend, will not leave my possession until the autopsy is completed.'

'And whom do you suspect?'

'I'm afraid that my two young apprentices bit off rather more than they could chew. Having moved the body in revenge for what they perceived as my grotesque practical joke, of which crime I continue to maintain my innocence, they found themselves overtaken by events. It was impossible for them to repair the damage they had done and they decided that discretion was the better part etcetera. No doubt they have been waiting with growing anxiety for me to find the body. No doubt they are now dreading my response. They fear that their futures may rest on a single word from me. I will let them sweat. I intend to overlook the matter entirely but I will not let them know that they are free of suspicion. I will let them suffer for a few weeks until time and distance gradually restore their inner harmony. It will be a long, slow process.'

'Cruel,' was all Jack could say.

'How are your enquiries progressing?' Sandy asked. Jack showed him the picture that Heather had drawn. 'Ah, so you were right. You do have a witness.'

'A silent witness,' Jack told him, 'who refuses to divulge his secret; and parents who refuse to co-operate. They will be gone by morning and there is little I can do to stop them.'

'Ah,' said Sandy.

'However, I have one chance. I am placing all my hopes on a young man from the outer isles.' He smiled with an air of mystery. 'I am hoping he will surprise me just one more time.'

'Otherwise,' Sandy replied, turning Heather's picture in his hand, 'You are looking for a rather large, stocky man whose head is the same size as his torso and who has but a single ear and a very small, round nose. I suggest you give the identikit picture to our journalist friend. He was hoping for a story about an incompetent police officer, a useless pathologist and a missing body. This picture may compensate in some small way. He will be most disappointed.'

'For that blessing may we be truly thankful,' said Jack.

'Amen,' Sandy replied.

Chapter Twenty Four

Simon Keller was feeling particularly pleased with himself. His recent articles on the bumbling rural detective who first of all lost a crime scene and subsequently mislaid a witness had done well. When a second murder quickly followed on the first he had been the first person his national tabloid had thought to contact and he had managed to provide them with an account of the crime graphically enhanced by a number of salacious details available to no-one else. A few words with the loquacious landlord at the Inverstrach Mountain Hotel had provided more than enough. All that was then required was a cynical twisting, bending and knotting of the true facts to enable him to present his subsequent article as the third in his series on the incompetent Jack Munro. 'Don't Lose This One, Jack!' the headline ran.

He reflected with some satisfaction, that his writing had made an impact. Things were happening. A number of offices at the Town Hall were now occupied by senior detectives from the city. Jack Munro would be smarting.

Simon Keller now had some time on his hands. He had returned to another line of enquiry and was hot on the scent. As was his normal practice he approached the question of the body in the cave by a circuitous route. A direct approach would at best give him answers to questions he asked. Simon considered himself a master of a darker art; he wanted answers to the questions he hadn't asked, perhaps hadn't even thought of. He stood by a lamp post opposite the old Fishermen's Hall where the pathology laboratories were now situated on the fringe of the main hospital site. From there he kept a close eye on the stately building where Sandy and his assistants were housed until he saw Sandy emerge between its sturdy, granite columns and head down the road. Simon had made the unfortunate decision to pit his wits against the pathologist several times before and he had never emerged victorious. Neither his cunning nor his cajoling, nor his subterfuge nor his threats had any effect whatever. Sandy, secure behind his defensive wall of words, was immovable. This time, he thought, he would look for a weaker link.

He strode into the building with the look of a man who was expected. He knocked on the door of the office.

'Mr. Finlay!' he called to no-one in particular. 'It's me! Simon!' He smiled and a set of teeth as narrow as his face gleamed momentarily white. The smile did not improve him, applied as it was to acknowledge the excitement of beginning his deception, rather than to indicate any good feeling towards the wider world. As he heard the door behind him open the manipulator's smile changed to one of false friendliness, a smile designed to set others at their ease, well applied and effective upon those, like the two assistants, with whom he was not directly acquainted.

'Sandy, - I mean Mr. Finlay, - is expecting me,' he said brightly. 'I'm doing a piece about him for the local paper. People have a strange view of your profession. I think they imagine you permanently up to your elbows in blood and constantly smell of death.' His laughter had a loud, hollow ring and his eyes were mirthless, but his casual and relaxed manner, well honed and rehearsed, was sufficient to put people at their ease. 'I'm planning a piece which will put that right and show Sandy as he really is, at home and at work.'

Duncan Marchbank, assistant number one, white coated, anxious and with a pallor matched only by that of his clients, allowed a momentary nervous smile to cross his face. Then he withdrew it as if it had escaped without his permission. He couldn't be sure whether Simon's words were serious or if they had an ironic cast. They may hide a trap for an unwary apprentice. Alexander Finlay as he really was? What did that mean? He selected a look of non commitment from his limited arsenal of expressions.

'He's not here. He just went out. I don't know when he'll be back. I'll ask Rebecca. She might know.'

He shuffled backwards through the double doors as if uncertain whether he could leave Simon or not. He returned a moment later. Simon heard the hurried patter of feet taking small, urgent steps towards him. The door swung open and Duncan returned, preceded by a tiny figure with a halo of closely cropped brown hair surrounding a small round head.

'Mr. Finlay's not here. He's just gone out,' she said. Duncan nodded agreement and reinforcement.

Simon smiled pleasantly. 'And......?' he asked.

'And he's gone out. He's not here,' said Rebecca, eying him with some caution. 'I don't know when he'll be back; might not be back today at all; I can't say.'

'We can't be sure if he'll come back,' Duncan nodded, as if translating her words. 'Sometimes he does, sometimes he doesn't.'

'Ah, isn't that just typical of Sandy,' Simon laughed, with the smoothness of a slug.

Duncan and Rebecca looked uncertain as to whether it was typical of their mentor or not.

'He makes an appointment for me to interview him and then he forgets all about it!' Simon laughed a relaxed and good humoured laugh. 'Never mind,' he smiled, 'I'll catch up with him another time.' He turned as if to go and then turned back as if a pleasant thought had just occurred to him. 'I say,' he said, 'I'm sure Mr. Finlay wouldn't mind me getting a few comments about him from his trusted assistants. He speaks very highly of you. Could you perhaps say a few words about how nice he is to work for or about his sense of humour? He is rather famous for his sense of humour, isn't he?'

Rebecca and Duncan weren't sure whether Sandy would mind or not, nor were they sure whether it was their place to express an opinion about working with him. They weren't sure they should comment about his sense of humour. They shuffled and glanced at each other and said nothing.

Simon took out his notebook. 'Would you say he was an efficient, hardworking professional from whom you have learned a great deal?' he asked sweetly.

Rebecca and Duncan weren't sure what they'd say so they said nothing.

'How long have you worked with him?' Simon asked patiently.

Not long; a few months, just since they came out of college.

Had they heard some of the great stories about Sandy's practical jokes?

They were not sure whether they'd heard anything about them or not.

'What can you tell me about the body from the cave then?'

If it were possible for two faces devoid of colour to achieve an even more deathly pallor it happened then to Rebecca and Duncan. Simon found himself glancing towards their feet as if he expected to see the entire content of their veins and arteries forming a pool there.

'We didn't move it!' said Rebecca. 'We found it like that! We don't know.'

She didn't elaborate on what it was that she didn't know. Simon's journalistic nose twitched. The scent was strengthening.

'It wasn't us who moved it, anyway.........if it moved at all, which it might not have done, because we don't know anything,' said Duncan mysteriously. He didn't want to give anything away.

'It was a great practical joke, wasn't it?' Simon laughed, as if oblivious to their state of anxiety. He followed his hunch. 'It was typical of Sandy to think of a trick like that! Where's the body now? Back where it should be, I'm sure?'

Duncan and Rebecca weren't sure what they sure about but they were certain they didn't know who or what. They had no idea when or why either! As for if and whether, the answers to such questions were a mystery to them and well above their pay grade. They were quite sure that they had no time to talk now, though. That was certain. They were quite sure that they had pressing business behind closed doors, out of sight. They were positive that they had to go.

'He might be here tomorrow,' Duncan said as he followed Rebecca back through the double doors. 'Come back tomorrow. First thing in the morning is usually best. He'll be able to answer all your questions about missing bodies and such things.'

'Where did he move the body to?' Simon called but it was pointless. They were gone. The smile which had played about his mouth for the last few minutes left Simon's face and was replaced by a look of contempt. He turned and walked out of the building. Once outside he stood on the steps and pondered his next move. He did not ponder for long.

He headed purposefully across the town, a matter of ten or fifteen minutes walk, to the Police Station. Sandy was just emerging. Jack spoke to him at the door and then vanished back inside. Simon grimaced. Those two were up to something. Always quick to suspect conspiracies he was particularly vulnerable when he smelt a story. He looked suspiciously round. No-one could be trusted. Those two had probably spent the last hour collaborating on some fiction to ensure there was nothing for him to find. It was a plot to subvert his enquiries. He watched as Sandy strolled in his general direction. He saw his expression change when their eyes met and he was aware that the thoughts that sped to the pathologists mind were not of the kindest. However, Sandy smiled a professional smile and made as if to pass without further conversation. Simon turned and walked beside him.

'Do you have any comment to make about the body that was found in the cave?'

Sandy had no comment to make and was, indeed, surprised that a journalist of Simon's vast experience should quiz him on a matter which, even if there had been a body in a cave somewhere within his jurisdiction, which he really couldn't comment on, was quite obviously a matter for others not himself.

'Where is the body now?' Simon called.

Were there to be a body, which Sandy had neither confirmed nor denied, then this body would undoubtedly be handled in the same way as any other body and would be kept on ice pending decisions as to how to proceed, which decision, as Simon, a man of vast experience, would know came from the coroner. Sandy could recommend a good book on the nature of pathology but he felt it might be rather challenging for someone who was not from a medical background.

'Who moved the body then? Was it a practical joke?'

Sandy was shocked to imagine that he or any of his staff could be considered capable of levity of an inappropriate nature at an inappropriate time with a body that might or might not even exist.

'Where is the body now?' Simon shouted after the departing figure.

'Ah, a philosophical question,' Sandy waved over his shoulder. 'What happens after death to a life that may or may not have existed? Let me know if you find an answer!'

He stopped momentarily and turned round. 'I would even break the habit of a lifetime and buy one of your filthy tabloids if you could answer that question.'

He smiled, waved, turned and strolled away. 'That's another victory to me, I believe,' he murmured to himself with satisfaction.

Simon was angry and humiliated.

'You patronising, arrogant, sanctimonious pratt!' he snarled, smarting from defeat. He turned and walked angrily away, his mind already considering a list of victims upon whom he could take his revenge and whose decline at his hands would restore his self esteem and self worth.

At that precise moment he saw Kate Munro run up the grey steps and enter the police station. The sight of poor Kate, who would probably not even have recognised Simon Keller, immediately filled the journalist with loathing. He hated them all, Jack, Sandy, all those establishment people who looked down on him from their cosy, comfortable heights.

A plan had been slowly taking form in the cauldron of his calculating mind. But that was for tomorrow. For now he had little to do. He decided to wait. Feeling rather conspicuous in the street he slipped inside the door of a Hospice Charity Shop which was conveniently placed almost opposite the Police Station. He picked up a book and idly flicked through its pages. Two elderly volunteers were the only people present in the shop, one manning the till whilst the other scurried from a store room at the rear to the different displays, redistributing items recently acquired. Simon glanced up as they talked across the width of the shop. The woman by the till, timid, elderly and grey, spoke into the void as if uncertain to whom she was speaking or where they might be. Her head twitched from side to side, mouse like. For a moment, nervous eyes, ringed by thin framed spectacles, glanced at Simon. Their owner ventured a fragile smile which he reciprocated unwillingly. She had the frightened look of a round eyed lemur.

Her bustling colleague spoke from across the floor, her head emerging momentarily above the rail of ladies clothing before dropping again beside an array of kitchen utensils and crockery.

'It was Jean who found him, you know,' she called. 'I heard that from one of her neighbours. You know Jean, don't you?'

Jean Sanderson? Oh yes, she knew Jean, poor, old soul. Her mind was drifting a bit now, they said. Her health wasn't good. A shock like that wouldn't help her. Something like this could kill her.

Simon listened more carefully.

'Goodness knows why she was wandering about at that time of the morning!' the bustling lady continued. 'She actually saw the murderer, you know, saw him drive up! She even saw him get out of his car!'

Miss Timid was shocked. She trembled. Did poor Jean really see that? How dreadful it must have been for her!'

Their conversation was interrupted by the opening of the door. Simon's eyes gleamed and a thin smile broke through his narrow lips. An old lady who witnesses a brutal crime and was left unsupported by callous local services held a lot of promise. He sensed another headline. Tomorrow was going to be a busy day.

He glanced out of the window as Kate emerged and headed down the street. Having little to occupy himself for the next hour or two he decided to follow her. He was obliged to complete a perfunctory task in the afternoon and complete a most uninteresting piece about Aultmore. It was the price he had to pay for information but he resented it nonetheless.

He walked casually out of the door and followed Kate round a corner to a new, single storey building which housed the library. For Portskail it was a proud statement of modernity, only matched by the Health Centre and the new leisure complex. All three buildings boasted a length of window, broken by flat, perpendicular columns of unostentatious pale grey stone and all three shared a tone of bland, characterless functionality only alleviated by the good nature of those who worked within.

Simon looked at his watch. There was little to be gained from following Kate any further and yet he found the impulse impossible to resist. There was something about pursuing a victim, unseen, that he found very satisfying, almost as satisfying as appearing at their shoulder in a manner that made them feel that they had been observed in some skulduggery for which he would make them pay.

'I can spare an hour,' he thought and strolled through the glass doors and into the library where a covering of deep carpet muffled the sound of his feet and enabled him to take a seat a few metres behind Kate from where he could, with some difficulty, make out a few details of the computer searches she was engaged with. He picked up a daily newspaper and positioned himself with care so that his prying could not to be seen.

It was frustrating work. He was sufficiently close to see Kate accessing census materials but not to see the names she was researching nor the location. He saw her looking through newspaper archives but, once again, his observations produced no detail. He knew she was probably researching her own family or perhaps Jack's but the more time he spent just beyond range the greater grew his sense of conspiracy and the more wildly his imagination ranged.

There came a moment, however, when he had an opportunity to move rather closer and to cast a practised eye over the screen. Kate stood up and went over to the reception desk, which was conveniently out of sight near the entrance. He strolled casually across to the computer and, standing for a moment to glance at an adjacent shelf, scanned the monitor.

He smiled unpleasantly. 'Well,' he said, 'how very curious! How very, very strange! I wonder what she is looking for?'

It was another half hour before Kate logged off the computer, gathered her papers and coat and headed for the door. Simon soon found himself over an adjacent computer and quickly accessed the one web address he had managed to identify and the one newspaper of which he had taken particular note. One clue led to another and Simon moved enthusiastically through the pages. Another hour passed. He looked at his watch impatiently. He really would have to go. A deadline loomed.

It didn't matter though; he had discovered what he needed. It was pure chance that had led him to follow Kate Munro. He had a spare hour; he felt inclined to play a little game of spies, expecting nothing of interest. What he had discovered had filled him with surprise and delight. This would be the best story of them all. This would teach them not to underestimate Simon Keller. This would wipe the smile off the face of that sanctimonious, arrogant Mr. Alexander Finlay.

'Tomorrow,' he murmured, as he hurried from the library and headed for the newspaper office, 'is going to be a very busy day.' He laughed. 'Who would have thought.......?' He shook his head and laughed again. It was not a pleasant sound.

Chapter Twenty Five

Jamie was trying to keep a firm hold on a reality which seemed to be constantly slipping away from him. Just a few weeks earlier he was a carefree, easy going kind of person, rather selfish and not really much concerned with the lives of others. He would have described himself as a pleasant sort of young man but not particularly ambitious, perhaps a little short on drive and motivation, but friendly to his neighbours and friends, popular in an average sort of way, tolerant. He couldn't claim to have any particularly noteworthy features. He would have liked to have been blessed with a strong physique, good looks, a ready wit and a natural charm. Like most people of his age he was gradually resigning himself to what he actually was; pretty ordinary, really.

He wasn't even sure he liked himself that much. 'If I wasn't me and didn't know myself as well as I do, would I want to be friends with me?' he had mused. The answer came back, 'Well, maybe,' or 'Probably not,' depending on his frame of mind at that particular moment. Now, a few short weeks later, he reflected with satisfaction that the answer was, 'Yes, most certainly'. He had achieved something; he had proved himself. He was worth knowing.

Now, and he still wasn't sure how it happened, he found himself in the caravan of the Simpson family and his relationship with them was rapidly improving. At the outset he had only begrudgingly been permitted to accompany them back to their pitch. It was largely at Ben's insistence and because both Samuel and Rachel were mightily relieved to hear their son speak again, even if it was to this stranger. They were acutely aware, and rather resentful, that it was this quiet, unassuming young man who had made it possible and not them. Ben seemed willing to talk about the events that had so distressed him and of which they had been completely unaware but he needed Jamie to help him. In that case and if Ben trusted him then maybe they should give him a chance.

Jamie was invited into the caravan, therefore, with no great warmth and with evident mistrust but without resentment. Rachel and Samuel did not want this stranger in their home any longer than necessary, casting a critical eye over their belongings, finding fault with how they lived, criticising how they brought up their children or earned their living. This was how it always began with outsiders. You should only trust your own. They would tolerate him for Ben's sake and that was all.

Jamie stopped at the doorway and removed his shoes. It was impossible to walk in the countryside without picking up a tread full of mud and leaves, - or worse. He sat where he was placed by Ben who leapt on the seat beside him. Samuel watched him carefully.

'Tell them!' Ben said. 'Say it wasn't my fault.'

'Do you want tea or coffee?' Samuel asked, rather less brusquely than he had initially intended. Jamie wasn't like the others. He hadn't asked banal questions about their life or passed stupid comments about the difficulties of living in a caravan. He hadn't engaged in the patronising pleasantries that hid deeper motives. In fact, Jamie had said nothing that he didn't need to say. It was quickly apparent that he had no intention of judging them and no desire to do so. With Ben safe on one side of him and the precocious Heather on the other side he looked completely contented. In fact, he spoke only to the children until they were all seated with coffee and a plate of scones.

He noticed the arrangement of the caravan, though. He saw two small rooms at end, one of which was just sufficient to hold the children in bunk beds and the other accommodating their parents. The sleeping area was separated from a small galley kitchen by a modest living area. There was a tiny bathroom and shower of sparkling white which he could just discern through a door half ajar facing the kitchen. He took it all in as he might have taken in the décor of a friend's living room in an island croft.

'Shall we tell mummy and daddy about how we met?' he asked Ben in a smiling, conspiratorial voice. 'Shall we tell them about our adventure?'

Ben nodded and Jamie began the tale from where he met Ben in the streets of the town, how Ben wanted him to come with him and gradually allowed the story to unfold before Rachel and Samuel. Every now and then Ben interrupted with a word or phrase of his own but he was mainly silent.

'….. and eventually I found myself in the graveyard and there was Ben,' Jamie concluded, 'pointing to where the man's body lay against the gravestone.'

Ben sprang to his feet. He adopted the position he had assumed by the grave and he pointed seriously. 'Dead!' he said.

So that was it! He said, 'dead!' not 'dad' or 'daddy!' It was 'dead!' that he was saying. Jamie smiled to himself. It would amuse Jack to hear that.

'Now, Ben,' said Jamie. 'Do you want to tell mummy and daddy what happened before I saw you in the town?'

'Will they be cross?' Ben whispered in his ear.

'Of course not,' Samuel said.

'It wasn't your fault,' Rachel told him. She moved across the van and sat down beside him. 'You tell us what happened.' Jamie felt momentarily proud. A barrier seemed to have been drawn away. Even Samuel leaned forward and smiled.

'Did the man die because I sneaked out?' Ben asked quietly. 'It was bad to sneak out, wasn't it?'

'It wasn't your fault,' Rachel said firmly back. 'None of this is your fault. You ask Jamie!'

Ben looked up tearfully. Jamie shook his head and squeezed the little boy's hand. 'It's not your fault at all,' he said.

'You didn't make him dead,' Heather contributed. 'That was the bad man! He did it!'

Slowly, with much prompting and questioning, Ben told them how he had been lying awake in bed and had remembered a special stone he had found by the shore. It was green and shiny and very hard. He was going to bring it to put with his treasures in his magic box but he had forgotten it when he came in for tea. He wanted to get his stone before the sea washed it away so he sneaked out of the window without waking Heather and ran across the wet grass to the shore. He couldn't see his stone so he wandered along to see if it had been moved by the tide. Then he noticed the church tower above the trees and he forgot about the stone. He thought he would have an adventure and go up to the church. He could see a path. When he got to the church he saw a graveyard and he was scared.

'Ghosts!' he whispered. 'They come out at night! They run round the graveyard and they dance and there are bones and skeletons and things and they all dance and go Rrrrrrrr!' He raised his hands like cat's claws. Jamie looked frightened and then smiled.

He was standing on the path which led to the church porch when he heard a car stop beyond the wall. It was a big car, as big as the van daddy drove, but not a van. It wasn't daddy so he hid behind a gravestone and watched. The man was big and a bit fat. He looked old.

He had a big long coat on and a hat. Ben didn't see his face. The man pulled a wheelbarrow out of the back of his car. Then he pulled something heavy and it flopped into the barrow. It was half covered in black plastic, like you put in bins, he said. The thing was very heavy because the man was panting as he dragged the barrow. Its wheels crunched on the gravel. He stopped at the end of the path and wiped his forehead. He pulled the black plastic and the heavy thing dropped on the ground. Then Ben saw it was another person but he wasn't moving. The fat man pulled the body off the plastic and then leaned it against the stone. Ben didn't see anything else. The big man had his back to Ben and was doing something to the body. He couldn't see what. He was getting scared. He didn't like the fat man and the body and it was dark. The ghosts would come soon. He wanted to go home but the man was in the way. He ran away, as quiet as a mouse, and went through a gate. Then he ran and ran and ran. He was very upset and scared. Then he was in the town, but there was no-one there. It was dark and cold and he was frightened and he started to cry even more. He sat down by the road. Then he saw Jamie and he felt safe, even though Jamie smelt funny and spoke in a silly voice and wobbled when he walked. He thought Jamie was nice. He helped him. He followed after him through the trees and up to the graveyard.

When they got back to the graveyard he didn't feel frightened any more but he didn't like the body. It had horrible eyes. He showed Jamie why he had fetched him. That dead man, he tried to tell him, that's why I couldn't go home. Then he climbed over the wall, followed it round to the fence and followed the path down to the shore. He climbed in his window and clambered into bed.

'Will the bad man come for Ben now?' Heather asked helpfully.

'No,' said Jamie firmly, 'Ben is safe with mummy and daddy and you. You wouldn't let anything happen to Ben, would you?'

Heather assured Ben forcefully that she would squish and squash the bad man and stamp on him like a fat jelly baby.

The police will catch the bad man and lock him away,' Jamie said, 'and they'll not let him out ever!'

Samuel picked Ben up and sat him on his knee. 'We are going to drive a long, long way from here. No-one will find us. Mummy and daddy will look after you. Our friends will look after you. No-one will ever hurt you.'

He looked across at Jamie.

'Thank you,' he said, and Jamie knew he was sincere. 'I hope you'll come and see us when we come back.'

'Yes, please come and see us,' said Rachel. The children nodded.

The next half an hour passed quickly. Jamie spoke about the croft where he lived, about his mother and father and the animals they kept. He found a common interest with Samuel in machinery and engineering and told them about his seasonal work on the fishing boats. Samuel, in turn, spoke of his own work in forestry and on roads, at markets and sales where he bought and sold items, often of machinery, with a shrewd eye for a profit.

'I buy something for fifty pounds, do it up and sell it for a hundred,' he said and then, with a gleam in his eye and a sly wink, added humorously, 'all those ten per cents add up, you know!'

Jamie did no think he had ever felt as good as he did at that moment. The young man who had emerged from that bar only a matter of days ago seemed as if he belonged to a different world and a different time. He had grown immeasurably and in so many ways.

It was time to go. Jamie parted from the family and headed down to the shore. Ben walked with him. At one point, he suddenly stopped and bent down.

'My stone,' he cried delightedly, 'it was here all the time!' He held the hard, green crystal for Jamie to see then he turned and ran back to the caravan, turning to shout goodbye as he stumbled up the steps.

Jamie headed directly to the Police Station where he found Jack and his two colleagues in the outer office. They were seated around a table and were obviously taking a break from their investigations.

'Pull up a chair,' Jack called to him, 'and come and join the team. Tell us what you've got! I'm just having an extended rant about my city colleagues but I'll stop now.'

Julie and Phil were obviously relieved by the interruption and moved to allow Jamie to sit down.

As Jamie spoke, Jack became more and more serious and thoughtful. When he concluded he said quietly, 'Thank you, Jamie. That's a most impressive account and very helpful. Now, I am going to ask you all to give me the rest of the afternoon to myself. There are a few things I need to check and I need to think. I really need to think. We'll meet tomorrow at nine. I think we are getting closer to the end of this thing.'

Chapter Twenty Six

The storm, which had threatened all day, eventually broke over Portskail in the late afternoon. Having dismissed his colleagues, Jack was alone in the office. His mind was concentrated and focused. He felt sharp and incisive and a frisson of excitement stirred his surface like a breeze on a still lake. He was ready. He would wrestle this problem and overpower it. He would struggle to get a firm grip; he would wrench it, twist it and turn it until it fell and submitted to him. It was time to begin.

Jamie had hurried back to his hotel, escaping the first deluge with a sudden acceleration that saw him entering the lounge just as the rain began to fall. He sped upstairs to his room, discarded his coat and fell back on his bed, feeling a sense of elation and self satisfaction that he wished could last forever. He would go home soon, perhaps tomorrow or the next day. He had plans to make for his future.

An hour later he decided to stroll down to the public bar.

'I'll have a pint of that local free ale, John' he said to the landlord, pointing at the relevant pump. He looked around the bar and nodded to a couple of familiar faces. 'Abstention is no substitute for discretion,' he said to himself, and smiled a wise smile.

The field, where Samuel and Rachel had parked their caravan, was empty. The ashes from the fire, glued to the earth by the falling rain, formed a dark circle on the grass. Other circles were forming in hollows as they slowly filled with rain water. The wind curled the sedges and whistled through the fence. The sea splashed on the rocks. It was as if they had never been there. As soon as Jamie had left them they decided not to wait until the next morning. They would head

towards the outskirts of the city where they knew some
of their people would be settled for the spring. They
would stay there until it was safe to move on. The car
and caravan pulled out of the field and up the track as
the rain began to fall.

At Aultmore, the new friends beat a hurried,
laughing retreat from the mountain slopes as the clouds
gathered and the rain fell. They dropped out of the mist
and splashed their way uncomfortably for the last mile
to the house. Once indoors they changed from of their
wet outer clothes and sat by the fire, their faces glowing
from the application of sudden heat. Bethany's wet
outer garments had been replaced by an ill fitting
tracksuit of Euan's which was too small for him but in
which she was enclosed like a dormouse in a nest. She
was curled on a chair beside her new friend and was
growing drowsy. Much to her annoyance, her eyes
were refusing their orders to remain open. She would
soon be asleep. Euan had already succumbed and was
leaning against her breathing gently. The soft murmur
of adult voices wrapped round her like a blanket and
she drifted into a warm sleep.

Kate was alone her living room. It would be some
time before Jack would be home and she was looking
impatiently from the front window. Pools of water had
gathered in the street and lights were on in
neighbouring houses. She was restless and troubled and
strangely anxious. The fruits of her labours in the
library lay about her. There were a few sheets of paper
scattered in a seemingly random fashion on the chair
and table, as if she had cast them there in annoyance,
irritation or despair. They were annotated in lines of her
small, neat handwriting. She turned away from the
window and walked over to the chair and picked one up
and looked at it.

'Why?' she asked. 'Why didn't you explain? You shouldn't have been alone with such a burden. We could have helped.'

She threw the paper down. 'Please don't work late tonight, Jack,' she begged her absent husband, 'not tonight! I want you to be near me.'

The room was growing dark as though night was falling but she didn't put on the light. She sat in the half darkness to wait, and watched the lightning tear the sky like a murderer's blade. The darkness poured through the open wound and filled every corner with black blood. It was impossible to hide from it.

In his large echoing house Edward Grey was looking through some monochrome photographs of mutilated bodies, crying children, angry adults and weeping mothers, who stared up at him as if pleading for his intercession. What could he have done? What could anyone do when there was such hatred and anger? People in those places no longer saw others as human beings. It was how they coped, how they killed, how they performed their brutal acts. It had always been like that, through time, through history. Perhaps it would always be like that, if there were no God, no belief. He was testing his faith and he would emerge victorious. He had to. If his faith were taken away he would be left to face the desolation of eternal darkness and he would be alone.

Sandy was alone. A flash of lightning and a wild crack of thunder reverberated overhead. He sat beside an old roll top bureau which he had opened. He too was looking at some photographs. Although these photographs were of a happier nature he was overwhelmed by sadness and despair. His faith had been challenged and had failed.

'It will soon be our anniversary, my love, very soon,' he whispered to the eternally young face in the picture. He kissed it tenderly and took a sip from the whisky glass beside him. 'I love you,' he said, and a half smile broke through the gloom; a rainbow of grief. 'What would you think of me now?' he asked. 'I'm old and without hope. I am finished. I cannot carry on without you.'

He threw back his head and wept into the emptiness.

Simon Keller was alone with his laptop. He was busy composing. He was taking each sentence and twisting it like razor wire until all its barbs and sharp edges were perfectly positioned to cause the maximum harm and the maximum entertainment. This was what he enjoyed. He had an appointment the next evening. He would attend a meeting which would provide the finishing touches to his work. He was looking forward to that. He was armed with enough knowledge now to prise out the information he needed and revenge himself upon a primary foe. It was going to be good. He savoured it with a snake like tongue and imagined venom dribbling over the words. He looked at his watch. He had plenty of time to finish his writing. Let the wind howl outside, let the rain fall. Tomorrow he would unleash a storm of his own.

'At eight o'clock,' he smiled nastily and spoke to an imagined adversary standing before him. 'I'm going to twist the knife so slowly it will coil your intestines.'

Jack stared at the whiteboard, which he had dragged into a prominent position in the outer office. It was not enough. That one board implied connection. It suggested he could deal with three murders as if they were in some way one. He must study each separately. He was impatient to begin. He crossed the room to a storage area and dragged another board into place beside the first and then returned for a third. Then he sat down again. For twenty minutes he did nothing. Then he started to speak slowly to himself. There was no-one in the office. He could risk the embarrassment of discovery. He would take control.

'No superstition,' he muttered, 'and no coincidences.' He stood up and paced up and down. 'Let's look at what we've got.' He wrote 'Death One' on the board and underlined it: No mystery, just a corpse. Cause of death unknown but NOT the wound to the neck. Murder, suicide or accidental death, we don't know which or how because we didn't have a body. Sandy thinks it was probably murder. The post mortem will prove him right or wrong. A dead body doesn't vanish of its own volition; so some one moved it. Who, I wonder, and why? Is Sandy correct in his assumption? Let's say he is. Let's say he isn't.' He was writing quickly now. 'There are children's bones in the cave and children's clothes were on the body. Was the cave a resting place for the dead, all those years ago, or were murders committed here? Were bodies dumped here, where they would never be found? Who did the clothes belong to? Is it possible that they belonged to the man? Were they taken there by him and, if so, why? Where are his clothes? Why is he naked? Is he naked by choice or by force? Is there any evidence of force? Did he die in the cave or elsewhere? Who were the children whose remains we know were there? Was one of them the son of Marius Dorling, our travel writer with a vitriolic streak? What happened in that cave?'

He paced up and down the room, his hands pressed against the sides of his head. Once again he stopped and spoke. Everything was a fog of darkness but his thoughts were a beacon which would shine a penetrating light into its obscure corners and reveal the monsters who lingered there.

'There are too many questions that cannot be answered,' he muttered. 'Some we cannot answer until the autopsy on the body; others are speculative or impossible.' He began to circle and underline, to filter and categorise the questions according to criteria that were becoming clearer to him. When he had finished he stood back and looked closely. 'What if the body was removed to prevent us answering these questions?' he mused. He worked on the board again and then sat down and studied it closely.

A few more lines and circles followed before he was satisfied with the results. Then he wrote 'Death Two' on the second board and began again. Why had the man been killed? What was the motive? Why had he been taken to the church graveyard? It was not accidental. The location of the second body proved that. Why had the eyes been removed? That was not mere brutality, awful as it was. Their presence by the second corpse proved that. Had he seen something? Had he refused to see something? Was it a warning to someone else? What did the blood in the church signify? He had taken off his shoes and walked from the body, along the gravel path, and into the church. Had he sat down in a pew and placed the bloodied shoes on the floor, then picked them up and left the church? Why did he do that? He did not replace his shoes to go outside; there was no blood on the aisle or in the porch or on the path. He must have walked to the car over the gravel and stone. Why would he do that? Was it out of some perverse sort of respect? Jack thought of repentant, flagellant pilgrims crawling to a holy shrine.

Once again he paused and reflected before circling, underlining, drawing connecting lines and arrows and adding scribbles here and there. He erased some questions and added others.

'There were no footprints.' He murmured. 'Someone took great care to remove them. There were no track marks from the wheelbarrow. He raked over the stones before he left. He's either super cool or he didn't care if he was seen. What sort of person could have done that, after stabbing someone to death and gouging out his eyes?'

A few moments later he turned to the third board and the third death and began again. This time arrows flew from one board to another, indicating connections, suggesting potential links and establishing clear patterns. There was nothing to connect the two men and yet the murderer certainly connected them in some way. The similar nature of the crime showed that. The eyes which had been gouged from the first body had been left by the second; that connected them. What was the common factor that linked those two men and motivated the killer?

He collected some papers from his desk and rooted through them. He placed two of them side by side and studied them. The victims had been at the same university at the same time. They may even have known each other. They had both been born and lived within the wider geographical area but would not have known each other before they went to further education in the city. It was hardly a significant link; half the pupils in the area gravitated to that particular university. It was, however, the only evident connection. There seemed to have been no contact between them subsequent to University. What did it mean?

Jack sat back. He frowned. He was motionless for some time before a flash of lightning followed quickly by rumbling of thunder outside the window stirred him into motion. There was something in the weather that reflected his mood at that moment. The storm was immediately overhead now and the street outside was dark. Rain which fell across the road in diagonal lines was blasted horizontal by sudden gusts which howled angrily at the window. The wind wanted to come in, to smash the glass, rip the furniture and smash it against the walls. In its fury it wanted to destroy, destroy. It wanted to tear down the blinds, scatter and ruin papers, smash the computers, overturn tables and chairs. It hated the bright room, the cosy warmth of the office. It growled and rampaged and swore. It beat on the roof with thudding fists and drove hail like bullets to wound everything it saw.

He stood at the window and looked out at the empty street. No-one was out there now. Anyone who had been caught in the deluge would have taken shelter in one of the few shops still open. They would wait now until the worst of it was past or until there was a lull in the storm and would then dash for home. Flood water was flowing like a stream down the street, past overflowing drains where it gathered in widening pools before tumbling on.

What ghastly motivation drove the murderer to *his* frenzy? What fury drove *him* on?

He returned to the boards and attacked them with a ruthlessness that mirrored the passion of the weather. He wiped out phrases and questions and sentences until he was left with skeletal remains. He sat and stared and, for the first time, he saw a pattern forming from the indistinct and confusing mass before him. He had grown pale with the effort and breathed quickly, as if in some discomfort.

Outside, the lightning flashed in the distance over the sea and the thunder had moved on. The storm, having vented its fury on the town, saw that its work was complete and now rampaged over the sea. There would be no ferry leaving the harbour that evening.

Jack moved slowly now. He picked up his coat as if it was a great weight and headed towards the door. He was perspiring heavily so he loosened his collar and mopped his brow with a large handkerchief. The storm had left the air close and solid. It held the town in a suffocating grip, like a fire blanket over flames.

Jack headed for his car and went home. He had a lot to think about and a dark path to tread the next day. By the time he reached his front door he felt distinctly unwell. Kate took one look at him and directed him to bed before she telephoned the doctor. It was well after hours but she was quickly put through to a duty doctor at the hospital. Having listened as Kate described the symptoms she decided that a visit would be necessary and arrived an hour later. She found Jack in a light sleep from which he awoke abruptly, as if from a dream.

'I know!' he shouted. It took a moment for him to realise where he was and to recognise Kate by his bedside and a serious, dark haired, bespectacled young woman, who could only be a doctor. 'I'm fine,' he said, 'I'm fine, really. I just got overtired. There's no need to fuss.'

The doctor routinely checked his pulse and his blood pressure and his temperature. She asked several questions. 'Have you any pains here? Any pains there? Any pains anywhere?'

'No,' said Jack, 'No, no, no. I'm fine.'

He did not say how he really felt. 'Yes, doctor, I've got pains everywhere. My head hurts, my chest hurts and my stomach hurts. Even my jaw aches. My feet are sore, my back aches; I've got a stiff neck and a mild groin strain. I also feel as if something inside my head is going to burst out at any moment. I want to go to sleep.'

'You're as fine as a man can be whose blood pressure is reaching take off velocity,' the doctor told him, peering seriously above her spectacles as if to add to the gravity of her pronouncement. 'Have you been under any stress lately?'

Jack couldn't help but laugh.

'You must take a few days off,' the doctor told him firmly. 'Make an appointment for next week and we'll see if your blood pressure has fallen.'

'I will, doctor,' Jack lied. To himself he said, 'As soon as this is over, I'll take a couple of days. 'Till then ....'

The doctor prescribed a sedative and left.

'I'm afraid I'm not a very good patient,' Jack said to Kate, 'but I will take this sedative and try to sleep through till morning. Now, sit by me and let's talk awhile. I'm sorry to have worried you. I've been doing a lot of thinking; you know it's not good for me,' he smiled.

'I've been doing some finding out of my own,' Kate said. 'Oh, Jack, I know I shouldn't have done it and I'm really sorry. I feel awful. I feel as if I've been spying on a neighbour only this is worse because I've been spying on a friend. But I didn't do it because I was nosey; it was only because I cared and I wanted to help. Do you understand?'

'Not one single, blessed word!' Jack laughed. 'Slow down and start again.'

'Promise you won't be annoyed!'

'I'm too tired to be annoyed and, besides, I know you would have meant well.'

'That's what people always say when they think you are an interfering old busybody,' Kate said glumly, 'but it's too late now. I'll have to explain.'

She sat on the bed. 'It was after we were talking the other night, the evening after Sandy was here. I felt so sorry that he couldn't talk to us about Helen. I wanted to find out more about her.' She paused for a moment and then blurted out her confession. 'I've been on the computer and in the library and I've found out about her. Oh, Jack, I wish I hadn't. It was awful.'

'Go on,' said Jack quietly. He sat up and put his arm around her.

'Sandy and Helen were never married,' she said. 'Helen died before their wedding could take place. She was a geology student, studying for a doctorate in the city. She didn't die of leukaemia. She was killed in a traffic accident. She had just come down from the hills after doing some field work and was walking back along the road when a car struck her. It knocked her down and dragged her along the road and then somehow ran over her. Her body was found in a ditch at the side of the road the next morning. That was the day before her wedding was to take place.'

Jack sat up. 'O God,' he cried. He remembered his own feelings on the days before his wedding. He imagined he heard the knock at the door that Sandy must have heard and he knew how it felt to open it and find police officers standing there. He felt the same surge of dread and the same sure knowledge that something was hideously amiss. He heard their words and felt the disbelief Sandy must have felt; he knew the torment that followed. He looked at Kate and thought of losing her and he knew just what it would have meant to Sandy all those years ago and ever since.

'Did they find the driver?' he asked. He suddenly felt very old and very tired.

Kate shook her head. 'It was just a dreadful accident,' she said. 'Someone telephoned the police the next morning to say they had hit a deer and that it had fallen into the side of the road. It was getting dark and it was foggy, they said. They didn't stop. They didn't know they had hit Helen.'

'Where did she die?' Jack asked. He closed his eyes and lay back on the bed and felt a weight of sadness fall on him. It was as if all the casual and indiscriminate cruelty that saw a life wasted and a life destroyed was there before him.

'She was studying unusual rock formations somewhere in the higher reaches of the hills,' Alice said. 'She had just come back down; it was dark and she was walking along the lane towards Inverstrach. She was a mile or two from Aultmore.'

Jack held his head and moaned. 'Don't say any more.' He put his fingers against her lips. Don't speak. Not this evening. I think I'll take that sedative now,' he said. 'I need to sleep.'

Chapter Twenty Seven

Bethany was sitting on the step just outside the front door of Aultmore. She was singing softly to herself and held Daisy on her lap. Everyone else was indoors. The storm which had rudely interrupted their mountain walk had also prevented her family from returning to their apartment in Portskail. Garth and Alice were concerned that the road may be blocked by flood water or fallen branches and insisted they should stay. To be driving along narrow lanes in the murky darkness, they insisted, even after the storm had subsided would have been unnecessarily perilous. It was an offer that was gratefully accepted.

It was a wise choice. Their own gentle burn had risen with astonishing speed and had created small pools in the adjacent meadow. Towards Portskail water had overflowed from the fields and filled a dip in the road and branches had fallen. Late in the evening the wind still growled menacingly outside the windows and the curtains moved uneasily as drafts penetrated the sash windows and stirred them.

The spare room had not yet achieved the status of guest bedroom, being cluttered with half opened boxes and unarranged furniture. However, it was blessed with a bed and offered a degree of primitive comfort which outweighed the potential hazards of a difficult journey on a dark, damp night. Spaces were cleared to give the impression of functionality and a camp bed was erected to accommodate Bethany.

In the end, the camp bed proved unnecessary. Having fallen into a rosy sleep on a comfortable armchair next to Euan, Bethany had been carried through and laid on her parents' bed where she spent the rest of the night, warmly sleeping, tucked between

her mother and father. Her golden hair encircled her
flushed face like an aurora round the sun.

Euan woke as his parents attempted a similar
manoeuvre to transfer him to his bed. He stumbled
drowsily up the stairs. Before clambering into bed and
drifting to a deep sleep he stood for a moment before
his window. Behind the curtain he could hear the
tapping of hail stones against the glass. It was the final
flurry of the storm. The wind rose and fell half
heartedly. He opened the curtain and looked out
towards the cottage and its ruined stedding. It was dark
and hunched against the cold. The walls shone as the
light from his window obliquely struck their wet
surface.

'Goodnight, Hannah. Goodnight Tom.' he said. He
pulled the curtain quickly across as if fearful to hear a
response. 'Goodnight Euan. Goodnight Euan.'

The children slept late the next morning and then
played by the stream. After lunch, they played for a
while on Euan's computer before Bethany slipped
away. Now she was alone by the front door. She
hummed a tuneless melody and looked dreamily
around. The storm had cleared. The weather was
brighter again and the water had subsided. The spring
sun was drying the ground. As she hummed, her hand
scraped lazily and distractedly at the gravel path beside
the step. It was a moment, therefore, before she realised
that her humming had been taken up by another voice.
She looked round, expecting to see her mother. She was
being teased. She stood up and looked in the door,
ready to pretend to be cross. Her mother, however, was
far away, deep inside the house. The humming ceased.

Bethany turned back to her play. She cupped Daisy
in her arms and hummed her little tune again. A
moment later, the sound was taken up once more by
another soft voice similar to hers. For a moment she

imagined they sang a little duet, full of gentle melancholy. The second voice seemed to come from over near the cottage. Bethany wandered hesitantly towards the ruin holding tightly to Daisy. The singing stopped but it was immediately replaced by a soft giggle and then smothered laughter.

'Let's play!' a girl's voice seemed to call from the ruin.

''Come and play with us!' called a boy's voice.

She wondered if anyone else, standing on the path at that moment, would have heard the voices singing and talking softly. Would adults have heard them or only children or were they perhaps speaking just for her? Would anyone else have heard two children turn and scurry across the pile of stones and rubble inside the ruin? Would they have heard a sound like animals struggling in the undergrowth and breaking through the dripping fronds of grass, the sedges and branches behind it? Would they then, like Bethany, have heard the slow movement of freshly sprung leaves and woven branches creaking in a light breeze? But there was no-one else on the path and no-one to hear Beth as she clambered through the ruin, crossed the adjacent lane and ran out onto the moorland beyond.

Euan was standing at his window. He saw Bethany emerge from behind the ruin and skip happily away. He watched as she crossed the narrow road onto the moorland. He saw her grow smaller and smaller and eventually disappear over the rising ground and into a hollow beyond. He quickly forgot his computer game and ran out to follow her. He grabbed his coat from the hook behind the door and then returned and grabbed Bethany's. He stopped for a moment. His mother was in the garden describing to Meg her plans for a vegetable plot and herb garden. His father and Marcus were in the living room poring over the documents Ben had found in the stedding. He decided not to disturb them. He headed for the kitchen where he scribbled a hurried note. He knew how his parents would worry if they didn't know where he was. 'Gone onto the moor to follow Bethany,' it said. 'I won't be long.' He grabbed a couple of bars of chocolate and some biscuits stuffed them in his pockets. He opened the fridge and removed a couple of sandwiches left over from the previous evening. Better to be prepared, he thought.

The sun was high and was breaking fitfully through the lingering remnants of the storm. Clouds, torn and bedraggled, had the look of refugees fleeing after an attack. They seemed hurried, anxious, scattered. They were unconnected and uncoordinated except in one thing. They were fleeing before further harm could come to them. The sun burnt them a strange dark purple-red which contrasted starkly with the darkness of their interiors and the flailing white whisps of their edges.

Fifteen minutes later, had anyone been watching, they would have seen a second, tiny figure head purposefully over the vast expanse of grass and heather moorland. They would have wondered what purpose that tiny speck of life could have to cross such a barren waste. They would have feared for his slender hold on a frail thread that guided him and kept him safe. His hand might slip; the thread might break. When he clambered over the first rise and dropped into the hollow beyond, it would have seemed to an observer that he had vanished from the earth, so complete was his disappearance. But there he was, and there Bethany was, and they followed the fragile, slender, silver thread that connected them to the future and they followed it alone. Euan was gone. Bethany was gone. The empty moor showed no sign that they had passed. Their tiny footprints barely bent the grass.

It was some time later before the adults in the house realised they were not playing in the house or garden. Alice found the note and quickly reassured everyone that they would not be far away. Nonetheless, she walked to the road and looked out over the moorland. She could see no sign of them. An hour passed and then another. They grew more anxious.

'It's not like Euan to go for so long,' Garth said. 'He knew we might be going out this afternoon. Where can they be?'

'He says he was following Bethany,' Meg said anxiously. 'I wish they'd gone off together. Why would Bethany have gone off by herself? Oh, she can be such a silly, scatter brained, day dreaming little girl!'

'Euan was playing on his computer earlier. Bethany doesn't really like computer games,' said Marcus. 'Perhaps she set off on her own? She can be very impatient if she gets an idea in her head. Maybe Euan saw her and followed her.'

'I'm going to have another look,' Alice decided. She took binoculars and walked quickly through the ruin to obtain a view. With increasing anxiety she scanned the distance. She moved slowly, backwards and forwards, sweeping gradually, scanning for a different fleck of colour, a movement or tiny silhouettes against sky or rock. There was nothing. She began again, slowly checking the moor until her arms ached with the effort.

Suddenly she stopped. Two tiny figures emerged from the hollow and stood on the low crest looking down towards her. They were close together, one figure slightly larger than the other, a boy and a girl. It could be Euan and Bethany. Alice focussed closely and held as still as she could. She groaned and let the binoculars fall. She knew, even at that distance, that it was not them. It must be some other children from a neighbouring cottage.

She hurried back to the house. A decision was quickly made; Marcus and Garth would get themselves ready and set out to follow the children. They would set off towards that low crest. No matter how unlikely it was, Euan and Beth may have seen those other children and have chosen to follow them. They might be playing, even now, with new friends from a nearby cottage, in which case they may well have lost all track of time. Alice and Meg would remain at the house in case the children returned from a different direction. They had phones. They could keep in touch as long as the signal held.

The two women had an increasingly anxious wait. They walked repeatedly to the door and along the drive and looked down the road and across the moor. Alice wandered down by the stream just in case they had doubled back along the burn. Eventually the phone rang.

Garth spoke. They had seen no sign of the children. They had reached the crest and had called the children's names. They had spent some time searching the hollow beyond where they came across a tiny burn, no doubt a tiny tributary of their own. There was an obvious route uphill beside the burn which they were going to follow. He would phone later if they had any news.

Another two hours passed and the men on the hillside and the women in the house were growing more and more alarmed. Surely they would have returned by now no matter how distracted by play; their hunger alone would have nipped at their heels like a sheep dog and driven them down. Something must be wrong. Why had they heard nothing?

Eventually the phone rang once more and Marcus's voice spoke, crackling and intermittent; 'Seen a boy ….. Euan probably …….heading up ……..hurrying,

.........didn't see Bethany .... maybe ahead of him ......or maybe still chasing after her......follow them up....signal bad.......'

The phone went dead. Alice and Meg stared desperately out of the window. It would not be more than an hour or two before the sun would sink and the valley would fade into darkness.

Hours seemed to have passed before the phone range again. Marcus's voice was almost inaudible. His final words, before the signal failed, were stark and clear and sent an icy shiver through the two women, 'getting   late.........mists   closing in.....rain........police.......tell   them,....towards the..........'

The signal had gone. Unfortunately, when Alice tried to use the phone she too had no signal. They made a quick decision.

'You stay here in case they come back!' Meg said. 'Keep phoning to see if you can get through. In the meantime, I'll drive towards Portskail until I get a signal or I'll call at a cottage on the road to see if I can use their phone. Anything is better than just sitting and waiting.'

A few moments later, Alice listened to the drone of the engine as it rumbled down the drive and then folded into the silence. She turned the lights on and waited.

Up on the hill, Garth and Marcus had been heading steadily upwards. They crossed the stream where it joined a larger stream which they followed between increasingly steep and narrow slopes. They rose onto the more even ground above and glimpsed waterfalls tumbling, one after another, as the stream tumbled out of the thickening mist and darkness and fell steeply past them.

The minutes moved relentlessly past them and merged into hours. The mist which had slowly rolled over the higher slopes lumbered relentlessly lower. The wider slopes to left and right had become indistinct and then disappeared completely. Only the steep slope leading by the stream was faintly visible and the stream itself was heard more often than seen.

'We have to follow the stream,' Garth called, and it was as if the fog grabbed his words, wrapped them and buried them as soon as they were spoken. 'I know where it leads. I've been here before. If Euan is up here, he knows to stay by the stream. He will keep Bethany safe until morning and then make his way down, even if we don't find them.'

His words echoed as hollow as his hopes. The children weren't dressed for a night in the hills. It looked increasingly like rain and the breeze, which had been light, was now strengthening. The children may not have been able to follow the steep ascent by the stream.

'We have to find them soon,' Marcus said grimly. Garth nodded. They did not speak again and headed gradually towards the top of the rise. It was not long before the rain arrived, light at first then gradually increasing in intensity. At first they were protected from its full force by the slope up which they clambered but as the slope eased and they reached the crest it became harder and harder to make progress. The ground levelled off and the stream was slower and more sluggish. They walked close to its edge now and their feet sank in the peaty hollows. They breathed painfully and their progress became slower and slower. It took increasing effort simply to keep each other in sight and to stay close together. Every few minutes they rested for a few seconds before forcing themselves onwards. Even with the head torch that Garth had taken from his rucksack they could see little.

They stopped for a while beneath the steep bank of a peat hag and allowed the worst of the rain blast to fade. The fog now coupled itself to darkness and held a lock on the landscape so complete that they dared not venture from the stream.

'We've gone too far,' Garth cried through the wind. He held a compass and a map but without significant landmarks and with no specific idea where safety lay he dared not venture any further. 'We'll have to go back over the crest and take shelter near the stream. There's nothing else we can do. The police will be on their way and mountain rescue. We'll have to wait for them.'

Marcus nodded weakly and the two men retreated to find shelter until the bad weather should pass and they could search again. Night had fallen heavily all around. The sun had long since given up for the day. No point lingering with all that fog. If only the fog would lift, the rain stop, the day come.

They took it in turns to blow blasts on the emergency whistle. One, two, three, four, five, six, then a rest then one, two, three, four, five, six, rest again, patiently signalling through the fog to distant, attentive ears. Garth studied the map in the beam of his head torch. The ground had levelled to what felt like a watershed. Not far ahead, had they continued on their route, they would have reached a small lochan. The crag, the bluff and the limestone outcrop lay away to their left. He tried to establish a bearing but the map was difficult to see, the wind ruffled and tore it and the rain was gradually penetrating it and wearing the edges.

They had been crouching for some time as the rain slowly penetrated their waterproofs and dampened their skin. They were becoming dangerously cold and weak. Of the food they had brought, - a few biscuits, some fruit and chocolate bars, - they ate little. The children would need the rest – if they could find them. Garth put the map back in his wide front pocket and looked closely at Marcus, who looked up and wiped away the raindrops from his face with a wet sleeve. He would not be able to go much further.

'If they haven't found shelter we won't find them alive,' Marcus whispered hoarsely.

Garth felt strangely calm. Perhaps it was fatigue or perhaps he was succumbing slowly to the conditions. He shook his head. 'They'll be safe,' he shouted. 'I know this will sound strange but I think I know where they might be.' He stood up.

He looked up the shallow bank which was providing them with a slender degree of shelter. Marcus followed his eyes and saw, through the mist, a shadow, a shape appearing. It was caught momentarily in the beam of Garth's head torch. 'What was that?' he called, his voice struggling against the shouting of a sudden gust of wind that swung over the stream and beat against them. 'There! Focus the beam there!' By the time Garth had focused the beam the apparition had gone.

'What was it?' he shouted.

Marcus shrugged. 'It was probably a red deer,' he laughed, almost hysterically, 'or a sheep.' His laughter sank awkwardly like a fatuous joke.

The two men looked at each other for a moment but the decision, they knew, had already been made.

'Come on!' said Garth. 'Anything is better than sitting here.' He shone the beam onto his compass and set a rough bearing which would lead them to the limestone outcrop and, if he could locate it and if it hadn't been buried in a landslip, the cave.

They scrambled up the bank and stumbled over the boggy ground, tripping over deep tussocks of grass and scrambling through peat hags as the rain penetrated their clothing and the wind blew in restless gusts. The mist swirled and deepened relentlessly.

'What's that?' Marcus shouted.

'Where?'

'I thought I saw a light, a red glow! Yes, there! Look! There! Get the whistle!'

Garth fumbled for the whistle and then blew. They waited and listened and then blew again. By now they were making progress only by staggering forward or crawling slowly on hands and knees. They were suddenly exhausted in a way neither of the men had known before. They were aware that a dark shape was emerging from the mist. There was a brief flicker of a torch. Ahead of them, Garth recognised the unmistakable, low opening of the cave.

Chapter Twenty Eight

When Bethany set out across the moor late that
morning, with no coat and no hat, her head was full of
imaginings. Euan had shown her the diary, which she
had read eagerly, and he had told her about how he had
found the doll and the knife with it in the wall of the
ruin. She had thought about Hannah and Tom each
evening and they had accompanied her into her sleep
and filled her dreams. She had awoken to find herself
thinking about them. She had already built a firm
picture in her mind of how Hannah would look and
what Tom would be like. They were a composite of
characters she had encountered in numerous reading
books and on screen in her favourite films. She knew
that she would have been friends with Hannah and that
Tom would have been a big brother to her. They would
have played together and have had adventures just like
in her books. Hannah would have told her everything.
She would have explained why horrible old Jeremiah
hated them so much and why her father had fallen out
with him. Bethany would have comforted her and made
her feel better. She would have told her that Jeremiah
was a nasty man and that they should tell the police
about him. Hannah would also have whispered to her,
in secret, a secret they would share for ever and ever.
Hannah would have told her what had happened to her
and Tom and where they had gone to after they had left
the cottage. They had run away from Jeremiah who had
threatened their lives and they had changed their names
and lived on a croft of their own with sheep and pigs.
Bethany liked pigs so Hannah would too.

That morning, when Bethany heard someone
singing quietly along with her, she knew it must be
Hannah. She knew that Hannah would be with Tom
and that they would be somewhere round the ruin.

When she scrambled into the building and heard
something moving in the leaves and bushes she
understood immediately that it was the children and
that they wanted her to follow them, to come and play,
to be their friend. She had scrambled through the
undergrowth after them. Once over the road and on the
moorland edge she had stopped for a moment to watch
a fox, no doubt disturbed by the children, make its
leisurely progress away to the east and vanish into a
copse of trees above the stream. Then she looked across
the moor and heard the children calling to her and
laughing. She knew where they were and headed
happily away on her adventure. She thought wistfully,
for a moment, about Euan. She wanted to go back and
find him and tell him to hurry, hurry, that Hannah and
Tom were waiting to play and that they would have a
wonderful adventure together. She looked at Daisy and
asked her what to do and Daisy told her to go and play
with her new friends. If she stood on the top of that
slope over there (Daisy pointed with her raggedy cloth
hand) Bethany could wave her arms and Euan would
see her and come after her. That was how it always
happened.

Bethany agreed and trotted out over the moorland
and over the rise and into the hollow beyond. She knew
that Hannah and Tom were by the tiny stream and
followed them up and up and up. Every now and then
she heard them laughing and calling. Occasionally she
caught a brief glimpse of one or the other of them,
playing high up by the stream, sitting on a distant rock,
rising as a dark silhouette against the sky. Sometimes
they waved to her and she waved back.

Sometimes it was as if they played together.
Bethany hopped over the stream and Hannah followed
her. Tom was higher up, showing off. He jumped from
one side of the stream to the other from high up on the

banking. Sometimes he rolled fiercely down the slope on his side and Hannah and Bethany, rather more cautiously, copied him. He was older than them and he was more daring.

'I wish Euan was here to play with us!' Bethany murmured wistfully. She felt rather guilty. Euan was her newest and best friend and she had left him behind and gone on an adventure on her own. She had made new friends and she knew that Euan would be sad. Euan was probably the same age as Tom. They would have leapt across the stream and rolled down the bank together.

Bethany realised she had forgotten to wave when she was on top of the rise. She hugged Daisy tightly. 'Do you think he'll be sad?' she asked. Daisy thought he would be very sad but that he would forgive her because he was her best friend. Besides, she would find something to take back for him, some treasure perhaps or a special stone.

Nonetheless she looked back over the moor and wished he was there. But, 'Come on, Bethany!' Tom shouted. 'See if you can get across this mud by balancing on stones!' and 'Let's follow the stream to the very top!' said Hannah.

When they reached the larger stream they followed it uphill past a sequence of rocky waterfalls in a narrow gorge. They had lost sight now of the distant valley. The stream curled upwards and away towards the distant watershed but a vague and intermittent track led onwards. It looked like the track made by a quad bike. Bethany could hear voices, now very distant and faint. She followed the track until the sound of the water had slipped away and only the breeze, her own footsteps and her rapid breathing remained. She could no longer hear Tom and Hannah. It was only then that Bethany realised just how far she had gone.

'Hannah? Tom?' she called anxiously.

No-one answered.

'I want to go home now. Can you show me the way back?'

Suddenly she felt terribly alone and frightened. She clambered further up the hill to find her friends. She wondered if they had gone further on and had forgotten her. Perhaps they thought she was following them or maybe they were waiting just ahead. Perhaps it was a new game and they were hiding, ready to jump out and surprise her. She wasn't sure any more. Her progress was slower now and she looked back more frequently. She felt lonely and tiny and alone. She wanted to see Euan or her mummy and daddy coming up the hillside towards her but there was no-one. She sat down and sobbed quietly.

That was how Euan found her half an hour later. He had hurried over the moorland and over the rise, only to find she had gone further on. He caught occasional glimpses of her in the distance and shouted her name. She did not hear him. The breeze was blowing towards him and carrying his words back towards the valley. He hurried on, taking a direct line up the hillside but as fast as he travelled he did not seem to make much impression on the distance between them. He lost sight of her for long periods of time but that was because she was following the stream and he was pursuing a line that would, if only the surface would ease underfoot, allow him to intercept her.

Occasionally he heard her voice carried towards him but it was faint and distant, like the cry of a bird. It sounded like she was playing. Euan was feeling cross. Why didn't she wait for him? She must have known he would follow her. It wasn't fair that she should have adventures on her own. They were friends. They didn't have many more days before Beth would have to go home and then there would be no more chance for ages. For a moment he wanted to go back down to the valley. It would serve her right. If she didn't want to wait for him and play with him, why should he chase after her? Each time he stumbled on a snag of grass or twisted and nearly fell on a projecting rock, or felt his foot sink sickeningly into a mossy hollow, he felt more and more exasperated.

Then he saw her again and he was sure she wasn't alone. She was playing high up on the stream with other children. He could hear them quite clearly now. So that was it! She had met someone else and was playing with them instead of him! Jealousy was added to exasperation and annoyance. But he was getting closer. He drove himself on and on. He came to a larger, tumbling stream and some waterfalls.

Further on, he came to a faint track and saw two small footprints leading away from the stream and he followed their direction. When the track became indistinct and then vanished he followed a direct line onwards. His feet were sore and he was tired and cross and afraid. He had been walking for hours. Then he saw Beth, sitting alone and sobbing, and all his anger fell from him and he was, once again, her best friend and she was his. Nothing else mattered. They would look after each other now. Everything would be alright.

'Where are your friends?' he asked.

'They've gone off without me,' she cried, 'and I don't know how to get back. I'm lost.' Her voice cracked and tears would down her cheeks in narrow channels. 'I don't like it here on my own.'

'You're not alone now,' Euan said. 'Now *we* are alone! We're alone together!'

'Is that good?'

Euan thought for a moment. Maybe it wasn't exactly good but it was definitely better.

He sat down beside her. 'Who were you playing with?' he asked.

'Hannah and Tom,' Beth said simply. 'They led me up here from the cottage. They played with me by the stream. Then they came up here and I lost them. I think they've forgotten me.'

'It couldn't be them,' Euan cried. 'They've been dead for ages.'

'If they're dead then I couldn't have played with them, could I, silly? But I did play with them so they're not dead!' She brushed some chocolate crumbs from her jumper complacently. Euan could think of nothing to say. That was what his father called female logic. His father had advised him never to argue with it. 'It defies all the normal rules of argument,' his father had said. 'You can't win so it's better to give up gracefully.' Until now, Euan had never quite understood what his father meant.

They had walked a long, long way up the hill. The valley was out of sight and ahead of them the ground rose through bog and peat towards the watershed. The stream, silent now and distant, could just be seen as it emerged momentarily on the crest before it vanished from sight.

'We're almost at the top of the hill,' he said. 'You can see cliffs over there.' He pointed away to his left. Some distance ahead the unmistakeable outline of pale cliffs could be seen, just emerging from heather and peat and curling round and away to a wide col. A moment later they could no longer see them at all. A dark mist was lumbering menacingly over the crest and down towards the valley. It was like a huge tide, a tsunami of cloud, and it would overwhelm and bury everything in its path.

Euan felt a surge of panic. The sun had gone and a chill ran over them. Beth shivered. He gave her the coat and hat he had carried up the hill for her and they shared the few items of food he had hastily stuffed in his pocket. They could not stay still for long. They would need to get out of the mist by dropping down towards the valley, but the valley was a long way from where they had unwittingly found themselves and the mist was moving ominously fast.

'We can follow the stream,' Beth suggested, doubtfully. Euan agreed but they had barely struggled to their feet before the mist reached round them and pointed in all directions at once and whispered to them, 'This way! That way! Up! Down! All ways are the same now! Follow!' The mist laughed and threatened, pushed and hurried, led them this way then that. They could not find the river. They tried to walk downhill but always, after a few minutes, they found themselves once more dragging themselves through peaty pools and grassy bogs of sphagnum moss heading at first level and then uphill. All the while, the mist thickened. It clung to them and gradually penetrated their clothes.

They were lost; they were scared and they were shivering with cold. They were both sobbing.

'Stop!' Beth called. Then she shouted, 'Help! Help! We're lost!' as loud as she could. She listened for a moment to see if there was any reply and then she shouted again. 'Please help us! Help! We're lost!'

'There's no-one here to help us!' Euan said miserably. 'We're on our own. We're lost.'

But they were lost together, like Hansel and Gretel. Beth seemed to have momentarily re-entered the world of her story books. 'Come on, Euan!' she cried. 'Shout with me!'

They shouted. 'Help us! We're lost! Help!'

Their voices, swallowed by the fog, seemed to reach no further than they would from a locked cell, deep underground. They listened, but there was nothing to hear. Only the wind slipped round them like a puppy in play, and leapt up and licked their faces and pushed them. They heard a distant rumble like a small engine.

'Is that thunder?'

They were shivering fiercely now.

'Hannah!' Beth shouted suddenly, 'Tom!'

She listened intently for a moment and then, as if she had heard some distant response, no louder than a bird cry carried by the breeze from beyond the fog, she grabbed Euan's arm. 'Come on!' she said urgently. 'It's this way! Hurry!'

She pulled him directly up the slope and, despite his protestations, would not stop. She didn't care if she was going the wrong way. Euan knew that they had to head downhill; it was their only chance. If they went downhill they might get out of the fog and see where they were. Then they might be able to head for home. If they went up hill they would just be going further and deeper into the mist. He tried to stop her. He struggled free and stood still and refused to move; but the fear of being alone or of losing Bethany was much worse than following some strange whim of hers. When she stopped and waited and called to him, he had no choice but to follow.

Every now and then she stopped and shouted. 'Hannah! Tom!' and then she listened intently for some answering call on the breeze. Then, as if in response to some faint sound, some cry, some call that Euan could not hear, she adjusted her direction and set off once again.

A light rain was falling when she stopped. There was rock under her feet and ahead of her a small, pale crag rose from the grass and heather. It loomed unnaturally large in the mist like a brooding giant. She almost expected it to raise a rocky head and begin to move. She stopped and listened. This time she had no need to call out. There came towards them, carried on the breeze, a faint wail, almost like that of an animal. Euan heard it too.

'What was that?' he asked in a hushed and anxious voice. He imagined wolves hunting out there in the wilderness.

'That was Tom,' Beth laughed. 'That is his secret call. He uses it to tell Hannah where he is when he is hiding from nasty Uncle Jeremiah. Sometimes, if Jeremiah sees him, he gives him a beating with a stick. Tom is scared of Jeremiah but he won't run away and leave Hannah. Sometimes he hides in the hills for days but he always comes back. That's their special call. Hannah makes a call like this.' She cupped her hands round her mouth and made a single, piercing scream which ended so abruptly it seemed to fly from her lips with a sharpened point that could pierce even the fog. 'Hannah showed me!' she said. 'Hannah said I could be her pretend sister and Tom would be my pretend brother.' Then she looked at Euan. 'But you'll be my best friend,' she said, 'for ever.'

The wail came again and Beth turned towards it. She followed the slope at the bottom of the crag until she reached another and then another. Soon they had to drop steeply down, scrambling on their elbows and heels to reach the bottom of a third crag. This one was much more substantial. It stretched away from them and above them until it formed a steep, fissured cliff, as wrinkled as an ancient face. They were walking on peat now, broken occasionally by grassy or stony patches. Here and there the peat was wet and sucked at their ankles and they had to clamber round the very edge of the cliff to avoid its dark pools.

Suddenly the rock along which they were edging slowly changed. Their hands were still scratched by the sharp edges of rock but from their chests to the ground the stone had disappeared. They were standing on freshly fallen rubble next to the opening of what seemed to be a small cave with a long, narrow entrance about three metres wide. Euan shuddered; he remembered the story his father had told them about the body in the cave. Only the previous evening he had spoken of it to Beth.

'This must be the cave!' he whispered.

'I know!' Beth answered. 'Come on!'

She bent down on her hands and knees and clambered through into a darkness that became impenetrable within a few yards. She touched the edge of the rock inside the entrance and felt round and up. Euan was close behind her. His hand touched her ankle. Slowly, feeling carefully at the rock walls and the rock roof they made their way deeper into the cave. Then Beth stopped.

'This is a good place,' she said. 'We can wait here.'

'Wait for what?' Euan whispered. From the back of the cave he could hear a trickle and splash of water droplets, slipping down mossy walls and falling into a quiet pool. Even his whisper echoed. He imagined a body lying still and dead.

'Hannah and Tom will be here soon,' said Beth. 'They'll help us. Daisy says so.' Beth pulled Daisy from within her soaking coat and pressed her against Tom. 'See!' she said.

Darkness was gathering quickly outside. It was late now, maybe nine or even ten o'clock, Euan imagined, maybe later. They had been out since after lunch. They were cold and wet. They huddled close and waited as the darkness gathered and became complete. They could no longer see each other so their hands clasped in miserable, fearful dread. They shivered uncontrollably. It would not be long before the shivering would cease and the real time of danger would begin but they were fortunately unaware of that.

At that moment they heard a movement just beyond the cave. It sounded like something had suddenly stretched out a clawed limb and scraped against the cold stone. They could hear rasping breathing like some wild animal. Something was crawling into the entrance of the cave. They could hear it moving across the ground, stretching, reaching, clawing for them; they were suddenly caught in the bright beam of a torch. They clung to each other and pressed back against the wall of the cave.

They were not alone.

Chapter Twenty Nine

Alexander Finlay had booked himself a room in the Portskail Hotel. He did not want to be at home today. He left the house earlier in the afternoon, having removed the few items he needed and was now seated on the end of his hotel bed, making his preparations for the evening, and indeed the night, ahead. An open suitcase lay beside him.

First of all, he carefully removed a new shirt from its plastic packaging and removed pins and cardboard which he placed carefully on his dressing table. He unfolded the shirt and held it up to inspect it closely. He seemed pleased with it and nodded appreciatively at the soft blue hue that rescued it from whiteness. He looked closely at the slender blue threads that had been worked around the collar and cuffs, barely visible but sufficient to draw the admiration of a discerning onlooker. His taste had always been good.

He looked back at the mirror and frowned. His torso, covered only by a new, thin, sleeveless vest, revealed far more hair on arms, chest and back and more folds of fat on chin, neck, shoulder, waist and hips than was conducive to his self esteem. He averted his eyes before he was tempted to view his lower half, dressed as he was in a simple pair of shorts and dark socks. He shook his head sadly.

'What would you think of me if you saw me now?' he said, gloomily.

He carefully donned the shirt and fastened the cuffs with golden cufflinks, curiously shaped like dragons' heads. He fastened the shirt buttons as far as the collar, squeezing the last button into place, then brushed his hands over the creases. From the suitcase he then carefully withdrew a new tie and tore the cardboard wrapping from it. He fastened it carefully in a neat half windsor knot. He looked again in the mirror and seemed pleased with the result.

'How many evils can be hidden by a little sartorial elegance?' he mused. 'What secrets, unseen by anyone, unknown to anyone, can be rendered invisible by style, elegance or bonhomie? What lies and deception, treachery and deceit? What evil secrets? What lies behind the smiling masks?' he asked the face in the mirror. 'What would we find if we could penetrate the stench of affluence, the neat hair and sparkling teeth, the kindly words and the outstretched hands?' He stopped for a moment and then walked back to the wardrobe, 'Nothing but corruption and filth,' he muttered, 'decadence and decay; selfishness and hypocrisy.'

He drew out an item protected by a full length plastic cover and laid it out on the bed. He rolled back the plastic cover to reveal a blue, three piece suit of high quality. He had bought it from a gentleman's tailor in the capital. It had been made for him from materials he had selected himself. He had no need to worry about expense. Only the very best would be good enough.

'Understated but undeniably fine,' he said. 'Anyone with any judgement at all would recognise its quality. Some people can't recognise quality,' he told himself, 'but then it only reflects badly on them. They are philistines,' he muttered, 'savages! The world is full of them. It doesn't mean that I have to lower my standards to theirs. Leave that to the politicians.'

He sat down and pulled on the trousers and then carefully slipped his arms into the waistcoat and then the jacket. He stood once again before the mirror and made some fine adjustments.

'The disguise is almost complete,' he said. ''I look what I am not. No-one would know me for what I am,' He looked at one of a number of photographs laid out

on the dresser top, 'except you, my love; except you.'
He picked up the photograph and paused for a moment.
He stroked the face, young and gently flushed by the
sun, and sighed. 'Now for the final touches,' he said,
turning back to his task, 'and the illusion will be
complete.' From his bedside table he picked up a white
carnation, its stem wrapped round with silver foil. He
carefully pinned it to his jacket and checked the result.
Then he carefully set a dark trilby on his head at a
rakish angle.

'You never liked the trilby,' he smiled, 'but I am
sure you will forgive me this once. I have some tasks to
complete and then I will be yours for the rest of the
night, just as always.'

He walked over to a table where he had placed a
crystal glass decanter, brought for this particular
purpose, and poured himself a glass of wine. He poured
another for Helen.

'To us!' he said and drank.

'To the future!' he said and drank again. 'To what
might have been and what should have been!'

He drew a large overcoat from a hook behind the
door and fastened it over his shoulder by a single
button. Then he walked out of the hotel, climbed into a
four by four and set off purposefully from the car park
and through the town. He stopped briefly at his work
and vanished inside for some minutes before emerging
and setting off once again. He had only travelled a short
distance when he recognised a slim figure at the
roadside and pulled up. He leaned over and opened the
door to let him in.

'At least the rain has stopped,' he said. They drove
on without speaking until the glowing afternoon lights
of the town shops and houses were behind them. It was
already late evening.

'I don't know why we have to trail all the way out there,' the passenger grumbled. 'Why couldn't we have met at the Portskail Hotel? Why do we need to go to Inverstrach?'

Sandy laughed slowly and easily. 'My dear boy,' he said, 'I have my reputation to think of! What would people have thought if they saw me, dressed in all my finery, seated in a public bar, sipping whisky beside the infamous Simon Keller? No, it is better that we meet somewhere far more obscure. Inverstrach Mountain Hotel is only a matter of miles away and they serve an admirable range of single malts, or so I am told. Sit back. The evening is on me and at the end of it you will have a story worthy of your ghastly tabloids.'

'I'd better,' snarled Simon, 'I've already got enough on you to make ....'

'Oh, please, please!' Sandy interrupted him, 'let's not ruin the evening with unnecessary threats. They are so uncouth and common. I have told you that I will co-operate. As you said, I have no choice. If I can't give you something better, then you will expose my little fraud and the world will know all about my sad life...blah, blah, blah! No need, my boy! No need! Let us, at least, meet as civilised people in a civilised setting and conduct our sordid business in as conducive a manner as possible. We must retain the illusion of civilised behaviour, must we not?'

'If you say so,' Simon sneered.

Sandy placed a CD in the player and turned it on. 'Ah,' he said, 'I have always had a passion for opera. Listen! Mozart, Don Giovanni. I love this aria. But I love Rossini, Puccini and Strauss too. When I lived in the city I would take the train down to the capital simply to enjoy an evening of opera. Alas, now I must wait for an annual holiday break. Do you like opera?'

'No,' Simon grunted.

'What sort of music do you enjoy?' Sandy enquired, 'Or perhaps music is not your particular vice. Perhaps you are a keen film buff or an avid reader.'

'I like Reggae, horror films and books about spies and warfare.' Simon shrugged. 'It really doesn't matter. We don't need to talk.'

'Oh dear,' Sandy smiled, 'Perhaps you are right. I suspect our interests are mutually exclusive. Perhaps a healthy silence would be our best course of action – unless you would care to discuss the weather or foreign holidays or the state of the nation.'

Simon looked out of the window and did not speak. Sandy's sarcastic tone was working its way under his skin. It happened every time. Every word that emerged from the pathologist's mouth seemed to carry a barb whose sole intent was to grasp at his skin and stick there. Simon grimaced in the dull evening light and saw his own face briefly reflected in the window.

'This time you won't escape me,' he thought with satisfaction. 'It's my turn to laugh at you. When the moment comes I will make you squirm like a fish on a hook. It's my turn now, my revenge.'

They continued in silence until Sandy pulled into the rear car park of the Inverstrach Mountain Hotel. They walked into the public bar and sat down on opposite sides of a wooden table. Sandy still sported his trilby but removed it once they were seated and placed it before him on the table. The leather chair hugged round Sandy's broad flanks whilst leaving Simon sufficient space to admit the presence of a friend, if he had one. Gavin Lord beamed from behind the bar, a model of professional joviality. The smell of food emanated from the kitchen and, from the lounge bar, there emerged the rumble of several voices.

'It has been a much better day,' he said, nodding towards the outside. 'That was quite a storm last night. Perhaps that's the worst over now.'

'Ah, in my experience of life,' Sandy said, 'the worst is always ahead of you. It is an illusion, albeit a very common one, to think that it has passed.' Gavin laughed, without comprehension. 'I think I shall have a single malt.' He glanced towards the display and made his choice, 'and my colleague.....' Simon gestured to the lager pump, '....will have a large one of those.' He winced slightly as if the word offended his refined taste. It was a measured reaction, intended to elicit a response, which it did.

Gavin looked at him closely. 'You were in here a few weeks back, weren't you? I remember the trilby. They're not a common sight any more.'

'Indeed I was,' Sandy smiled, 'although on that occasion I was in rather different company.'

'Yes, I remember!' Gavin laughed. 'That friend of yours had already drunk far more than was good for him before he arrived. After a couple of whiskies here he was almost on the carpet.'

'Ah yes, a most embarrassing incident and not one I am likely to repeat. My friends and colleagues now have to take a breathalyser before I allow them into my car. I'm afraid he took us both by surprise that night. I remain eternally grateful to you for helping me pour him back into the car. I don't know how I would have managed without you.' He laughed.

'I never forget a face,' Gavin informed them as he walked back to the bar and vanished behind it, 'or a hat!' He laughed.

'Let's get down to business,' Simon snarled. 'I don't want to spend any more time here than I need to. Tell me what you are offering.'

'I heartily concur,' Sandy drawled. 'To be drawn together like this can only have an adverse effect on both our reputations. But would it not be better if you were to elucidate the precise nature of your threat before I make my bid? Would that not be rather more in keeping with your normal practice and far more enjoyable for you, at a purely personal level? Please, do explain! I will make them a counter offer which you must consider on its merits.'

Simon opened a wide mouth and allowed his lager to slide uninterrupted down a mean and greedy throat. He wiped his lips with the back of his hand.

'I know that you moved the body from the cave and sat it upright in order to terrify your junior colleagues,' he began, 'and that you then removed it when no-one was there and pretended it had vanished. I assume that was another sick joke. I know that you didn't send any forensic evidence to the city and that some other evidence was conveniently lost.'

Sandy was undisturbed. He looked at his watch. 'Oh dear,' he said, 'how very disappointing. I thought you had brought me here to reveal some infamy or some dreadful secret? Is that all? A body was moved from one place to another, I admit. I also admit that the said corpse subsequently disappeared (although, to ensure we keep our conversation on a correct footing I will never admit that fact beyond these walls). However, it would be difficult to prove conclusively that the movement of the body was in any way the result of actions of mine; equally, the body has been found and is now in the mortuary – ah, I see you were unaware of that fact. What a pity! – so it would be rather perverse to argue (and difficult to prove conclusively) that it ever disappeared at all. As for the evidence which you suggest has been misappropriated, no doubt for some nefarious purpose, all I can suggest is that a failure to arrive does not by necessity prove a failure to depart. I would suggest you phone your city contacts again tomorrow. I suspect the materials you suggest are missing will, in fact, mysteriously appear in the morning. There must have been some unfortunate delay but nothing of a criminal nature, nothing in fact that could even be ascribed to negligence.'

He smiled and sipped but his eyes never left the face of the journalist.

'Round one to me, I believe,' he smiled.

'There is a long way to go in this fight,' Simon threatened darkly. 'Let's move on.' He prepared his knockout punch. 'Let's talk about you and Helen.'

'No,' said Sandy, 'let's not.'

'I'm afraid we have to,' sneered Simon. 'Now, let me get this right. You met at University and were married in the city. You spent three or four years together and then she was diagnosed with leukaemia. She died and you were left alone. You never married again, out of grief, and have remained a bachelor ever since.'

'That is correct,' said Sandy, 'but I doubt if you can make much of a story from that.'

'No,' sneered Simon, 'but the truth is far more interesting and it leaves far more openings for insinuations and suppositions. That story could be quite interesting. The question that would offer most to my fertile imagination and creative tendencies would be this: why would you hide the truth?'

It was Sandy's turn to look uncomfortable. Simon noticed with pleasure that he had grown pale and the sarcastic smile that played perpetually around his lips had gone. He frowned and gripped the rim of the trilby tightly.

'Should I rehearse what I know?' Simon asked. 'For example, that you did not marry and your 'wife' did not die of leukaemia and that, in fact she died on the eve of your wedding? I could also prove, I believe, that you were waiting in this very hotel that evening but that she never arrived. I could, of course, add a great deal by way of insinuation. You had, after all, never had a relationship before Helen and you have not had one since. There is a great deal for me to pursue.'

Sandy gripped the trilby with both hands. He was fighting hard to retain his composure. His knuckles were white and his teeth clenched. He stood up suddenly and leaned angrily towards Simon.

'I will never speak to you about Helen!' His voice rose. 'And you will never insult her memory again by speaking her name in such a manner.' Simon flinched at the menace his voice conveyed. 'You will never write about her. There will be no slur on our relationship, no questions about its sincerity and no insinuations. I will never permit you to pervert the truth to such a degree. You must understand this or we can have no further discussion.'

Simon tried a sarcastic smile but he was anxious and disturbed. Gavin looked across at them from the bar; he was watching carefully. It was still early season. Locals would soon appear in ones and twos but at present the bar was empty but for the two men and he didn't want any trouble. He saw Sandy release the trilby, reach across the table and hold Simon tightly by the arm. He saw Simon wince and pull back. He was relieved to see Sandy sit down again. Sandy laughed and curled the hat round in his hand, his composure restored.

'What I have to offer you,' Sandy said slowly, 'is worth more than any cruel lies and perverted truths you can write about me. But write what you like about me; I don't care. Accuse me of anything you like and I won't even flinch but let it be understood, you will get nothing, nothing, if you even think of writing about my Helen. Is that understood?'

Simon nodded.

'Then let's go,' said Sandy. He stood up and finished his drink. He headed towards the door.

'Where are we going now? What about my story?' Simon asked.

'It has already started,' said Sandy. 'You are in it.'

'Tell me where are we going?'

Sandy turned back towards Simon. He saw Gavin was watching and listening.

'Aultmore House,' he said loudly. 'We are going to Aultmore.'

He closed the door behind him and walked across the wet car park to his car. Once inside, he threw the trilby on the back seat, rested his head back and breathed deeply. He closed his eyes. By the time Simon had followed him and was opening the door he appeared to have regained his composure. Simon slumped on the seat and fumbled to fasten his seat belt.

'I don't feel well,' he mumbled, 'I think I'm going to be sick.'

'Ah, that will be the effect of the substance I injected into your arm when I grabbed you so roughly,' Sandy smiled. 'That really was unforgiveable and I apologise. I do not usually indulge in such theatricals but it was important to me that our goodly landlord remembered our presence and my parting words. I think I achieved that with my little drama, don't you? Rising to my feet was perhaps a little melodramatic but its effect was notable. I really do think the foolish man thought I was about to engage in some sordid bout of fisticuffs.'

Simon struggled to escape from the car but found himself unable to move.

'Don't worry, you won't be sick. That feeling will ease off in a moment and you will just be beautifully drowsy.' He shook his head. 'You will, however, find it very difficult to speak and impossible to prevent me taping your mouth.' He drew a roll of black tape from beside him and broke off a length. He pressed it firmly into place across Simon's mouth. 'Now, where did I say we were going? Oh yes, Aultmore.'

He turned the key and the engine rumbled. He put the car in gear and drove slowly out of the car park. Within moments they left the hotel lights and the narrow heart of Inverstrach and were swallowed by the black, gaping road.

Chapter Thirty

'It does my heart good to see you so silent and
thoughtful.' Alexander Finlay glanced at the sedated
figure slouched in the seat beside him. 'I feel proud to
have, in some small way, given you this opportunity to
reflect upon your sad and meaningless existence.'

The eyes that met his were wide and frightened and
flickered constantly as if beset by needle like thoughts
that pricked them from within their sockets.

'You are so beset by the immoral urge to reveal
what you so mistakenly call the truth that you fail to see
it when it is right in front of you.'

The headlights from an approaching car briefly
illuminated his face and flickered over Simon, slumped
on the seat beside him. Sandy drove down the narrow
lanes which were progressively engulfed in the dank
gloom of the evening. He smiled a coldly benign smile
and patted Simon's knee.

'Oh dear me, my poor boy, you do look so different
this evening. I don't think I've ever seen such an honest
expression on your face before, so free of manipulation
and deceit. It is quite endearing, in a strange sort of
way. It forms a bond between us, don't you think? You
and I are sharing a few brief, fleeting moments of
complete sincerity. How rare that is!' He shook his
head and sighed. 'Poor Simon, you really don't
understand what is happening, do you? Perhaps I
should explain.

'You really must look upon these moments of
incapacity and fear not as an evil which has befallen
you but as an opportunity for self improvement. I am
offering you a few moments to reflect and repent. This
is your chance of redemption, my boy. Now, at last,
you may consider that you have something to say
which is sufficiently important to be worth expressing.

How frustrating that you are unable to do so! How desperately you must want to speak to me and to ask me questions, questions that are genuinely interesting and important. What is happening to me? Why am I here? Is my life approaching its end? Does it have to be like this? Is my life worth no more than this? Now, at last, you are reaching out to me and asking me to be you, to lie as you lie now, to fear as you fear. You want me to understand. Only then, you imagine, could I understand how important your pathetic little life is, how much you want to live, to continue, to enjoy days and days and days. In your feeble, ineffectual way, you are even driven to want to understand something about me. Of course, I am only important to you in so far as your future lies completely in my control. Nonetheless, that is a useful first step. It is a start, don't you think?'

He paused for a moment and looked along the narrow beam that now illuminated a brief section of the black tarmac ahead offering a limited perspective on his physical world. Gorse bushes and trees closed in to form a narrow tunnel.

'That's all I have to guide me,' he murmured, 'that fragile illumination of the fringes of darkness. No matter how I strive or study or dream or hope, I can see no further. Oh look!' He applied the brake suddenly and Simon slid even further down his seat. A field vole, caught in the headlights, had scurried across the road just escaping into the damp, grass verge before the terrifying rumble of tyres passed her, like a warning of destiny. 'It flits from darkness to darkness briefly revealing its secret life. How wonderful that is!'

He paused. 'Do you know,' he continued at last, 'There are times when I think the whole world should be gagged and silenced. My ears are beset by a constant gurgling and simpering of inane chatter. It never ceases. Even in my sleep I can hear the ramblings of the terminally stupid. Millions upon millions of voices are demanding to be heard and yet how few have anything to say that is worthy of indulgence? Chatter, chatter, chatter!

'You must take this opportunity to listen, Mr. Keller! Now, for the first time, actually listen! Can you not hear them? Chatter, chatter, chatter! Chatter, chatter, chatter! They phone in to radio programmes as if they have an opinion worth hearing! They upload, download, tweet, text, email, video link, phone, advertise, gossip, insult, seduce, pervert. Noise! Everywhere I am surrounded by noise! The young are made old by it, the innocent perverse, the clean sordid, the sensitive harsh, the intelligent stupid, the honest corrupt, the loving hateful. They rush onward but they go nowhere, trampling under foot whatever lies in their way. In their wake lies destruction and devastation.

'There is an asylum at my back, Simon, and the doors are opened wide. I am not sure whether the inmates are coming out or I am being drawn in.'

He fell into a gloomy silence. Then he spoke again.

'Well, here we are, Simon, you and I together, and I have such a story to tell. You would have ruined it, of course. You would have sensationalised it for mere profit. You would have made me a monster. You would have trampled on the memory of someone as superior to you as the vast universe is to a speck of bacteria. I could not allow that. You can see that, can't you? I have chosen to write and publicise my own history in a manner more suited to my life and character. I posted it this very afternoon, - to a national broadsheet, of course. It would not have been becoming for me to vomit in the tabloid gutters where you grovel. I have also ensured that the one man worthy of the name of friend will be freed from your contaminating and odious besmirching. Tonight, as you lie waiting,

(waiting for what, you must wonder?) you will be able to think of that. The story of a lifetime, the scoop of the decade, will be lost to you. No doubt it will be a very temporary setback but it gives me some perverse pleasure, nonetheless.

'But, of course, you aren't thinking about that, are you? You are still wondering about those other words, aren't you? – '*as you lie waiting*' – and you are wondering where you will be lying and what you will be waiting for? You fear that you will be lying in a ditch waiting for death.'

He laughed slowly and without mirth.

'Well, let me at least reassure you on that account. I am not a savage. I am not a wanton, rampaging killer. I have killed – yes. I suppose I must confess that to you now. It was not without reason and they were, after all, no more than cancerous cells requiring eradiation.

'I have merely eliminated harmful tumours. I like to think I have acted to improve the health of the world on which they grow but that is a lie and I will not lie to you, Simon, not now. It was simply that their death mattered more to me than their lives mattered to the world. They were nothing. They had achieved nothing, made nothing, created nothing. They had wasted their lives as we all waste our lives. Chatter, chatter, chatter! Noise, noise, noise! They are the mad men at my back, Simon! Besides, no-one will miss them, not in the long term. There will be a few unimportant tears added to an ocean of grief and that is all. That is all our passing amounts to. Even Helen, even she is fading from all memories but my own……..but enough of that. I will not waste my words or pollute my grief by sharing such things with you. Ah, here we are at last. I am about to answer the questions that most concern you.'

He slowed down as Aultmore House came into view. There were lights in several windows and a police car was parked outside. He slowed down and then reversed a few yards. He opened the door and clambered out, breathing heavily. He seemed to struggle round the front of the car, leaning against the bonnet as he walked. Having opened the passenger door he grabbed Simon by the shoulder and, with some effort, dragged him from the seat and onto the road side.

'Now, my dear Mr. Keller, the moment has come for us to part,' he panted. 'You have your ditch to grovel in and I ……..' He glanced momentarily towards the sky and the mountain ridges, already nearly lost in the bitter gloom of evening, 'I have a most unpleasant journey to undertake and an important appointment to keep.'

Simon could not move. He was dizzy and sickly and his limbs flopped uselessly. He tried to move his legs but it was like lifting a sack of flour. He tried to thrash his limbs and to resist but he could barely stir them into the slightest movement. He felt himself being rolled over and a plastic tie attached round his wrists. Sandy rolled him back and fastened his ankles in a similar manner. Simon could hear him breathing painfully under the effort and was aware of warm breath against his face and neck.

'Now,' he heard Sandy's voice pant in his ear, 'we have to position you carefully so bear with me for a moment whilst I roll you down the bank.'

Simon's eyes widened in sudden panic and he struggled to move and to fight against the arms that were gripping him and rolling him towards the road edge and a banking which, to his horror, he realised led down to a ditch half hidden by birch trees. He emitted a strangled cry as he slid and rolled down. His shoulders and arms banged against jutting rocks before he landed heavily on his back in water. His head was submerged for a moment and he struggled to raise it above the flood water that was flowing over him. He tried to scream from behind the black tape and to stir his heavy limbs into a semblance of resistance but it was futile. He felt his head falling backwards into the water and the current flowing over his mouth and nose and he held his breath as much as his bruised lungs could manage. A surge of horror and panic rushed through him as he realised that in a matter of seconds he would have to breathe but that all he would inhale would be dark, peaty water. He would die.

Two hands grabbed at his shoulders and lifted his head clear of the water. He felt a rock being placed beneath his head and he looked down and saw water covering much of his lower body. Then he looked up and saw Sandy staring down at him. He tried to struggle again.

'A young, healthy man like you should survive a few hours of cold,' his tormentor murmured. 'Slowly you will regain some control over your limbs but you will still be faced by a rather uncomfortable distance to the house and safety. You will have time to wonder, perhaps, if this cruelty – as you no doubt perceive it – is worse than the cruelty you inflict as a matter of course in your daily work. No doubt you will conclude that this is worse. After all, this is criminal, isn't it? No doubt you will derive comfort from knowing that your work is in the public interest. Isn't that so?

'I wonder,' he mused, momentarily affecting abstraction, 'whether I might argue the same in my own defence? It was in the public interest, your honour, that I prevented that insignificant little worm from insinuating itself into the memory of someone so superior to him that he would not dare raise his eyes in her presence. It was in the public interest, your honour, I assert, to stop him at whatever cost. Look at his history of malice and lies, Milord! Look at what he is. There he lies, crawling on his belly in a ditch.'

He turned contemptuously away and allowed the sound of the breeze to fill the vacancy left by his angry words.

Simon watched in horror as he climbed back into the car and it moved slowly forward to pass Aultmore. Only as it moved on down the lane did the car headlights come on and pick out the road ahead. The sound of the engine and the wheels on the tarmac gradually diminished until Simon could only imagine it in the empty distance. The sound of the water, the damp penetrating his clothes and skin and an awful sense of loneliness and isolation, more fearful and complete than anything he had ever known before, surrounded him in a gathering darkness.

Sandy drove on for some miles. The road curved gradually round before passing down the deserted street of Laurimore. A solitary cat loped from the side of a house, dashed silently across the road and jumped on the stone wall of a cottage garden. It watched him pass. Beyond the village his headlights caught the eyes of a small group of sheep by the side of the road, watching blankly. He was out into the open moorland again. Soon he passed by the side of a tiny lochan. He pulled up by a narrow path which led to a secluded boathouse by the water's edge. It was overhung by branches of birch and sallow and had a narrow slipway over which a few waves broke.

It was not, however, to the slipway that Sandy directed his steps but towards the rear of the boathouse where double doors faced the pathway and the road. He unlocked the doors and pulled them back to where he could wedge them with large stones set aside for that purpose.

It was perhaps not untypical of Sandy nor was it something that should have been unexpected that the boathouse contained no boat. In its place, washed, polished and cleaned to a pre sale condition, stood a large quad bike with a small trailer. Even the tyre treads had been cleaned and the black rubber had the pristine look of showroom cleanliness. Sandy tapped it affectionately. He took a pair of large, walking boots from the trailer and was about to exchange them for his polished black shoes when he seemed to think better of it. He shook his head. No need. He returned them to the trailer. He revisited his car and removed from it a torch, a bottle of expensive champagne, two glasses and a small plastic container of the sort one might use for a picnic lunch. These he padded carefully and packed into a rucksack before lifting it onto his back. Thus incongruously clad, with polished shoes, his suit trousers tucked neatly inside his socks and a rucksack over his suit jacket and coat, he unhooked the trailer, bestrode the bike and started the engine. Having removed the bike and closed the boat house door he carefully drove his car off the road. He then turned back to the bike and drove with evident purpose out and along the road away from Laurimore.

He had proceeded some miles before he turned off the road and onto a farm track which led out onto the moorland and rose gradually higher, initially through small fields and grassland and then over heather moor. Occasionally, as the track surface, initially stony, became grass and mud and then curved through heather, he stopped to check his route. The presence of tyre tracks ahead of him, caught in the lights of the bike, were sufficient indication that he was on the correct route and he moved carefully forward. It was now completely dark.

The track grew steadily less distinct as it rose higher and higher above the valley. Sandy gripped tightly. Despite the chill air he was sweating profusely and his breath came in short, heavy bursts. It was taking much of his remaining strength to hold the bike as it bounced over rougher terrain and now wound through boggy areas of spagnum and peat. He came to a small bridge of level concrete slabs set over a small burn after which the track turned even more sharply and headed steeply uphill, following the stream. Sandy had to stand now to maintain the stability of the machine as it bounced along a small, stony path and then, at last, onto a pathless tract of rising grass and peat.

Sandy grimaced at the pains in his arms and legs. His breath came in short gasps. But he was determined to reach his destination. His eyes showed that. Despite the buffeting of the wind and the damp clawing of a thickening mist he gripped the bike with hands and knees and revved it on and up. He was wrapped in a tiny bubble of light, moving irregularly and erratically up towards the watershed. He was aware of nothing beyond it and yet of everything beyond it. He kept his mind on the small illuminated area ahead. It would not do to think of the darkness, not now. It was too awful to think beyond that light. Yet it hung there, a ghastly presence of which he could not help but be aware.

The bike suddenly lurched forward and down and stopped. The engine spluttered and died and the lights went out. Sandy, who had been flung heavily against the steering, grunted with pain and lay for a moment leaning forward, struggling to breathe.

After a few moments he was sufficiently recovered to clamber heavily away from the bike. The fog was now so deep and the darkness so complete that he could barely discern the bike to which his words were addressed.

'Thank you for your service,' he said. 'You have performed well. For the second time you have brought me much closer to my goal than I had any right to expect. The rest I must manage without your assistance.' He patted the seat from which he had been flung almost affectionately and then turned and looked ahead. The mist was like a wall and the night black enough to touch but it mattered little to Sandy. His goal was directly ahead, at the foot of a small limestone outcrop. He could not see it but he knew it would be there. It was waiting for him. It was from here that Helen, having concluded her research and collected her samples, had returned to the road near Aultmore where she had met her untimely death and it was to this place that he had driven with the unconscious body of her killer only a few short weeks before.

He stumbled forward increasingly aware of the tight knot pulling painfully in his chest. He reached the rock face and stumbled along it until the cave entrance opened beneath his hand. He staggered inside and unhitched his rucksack. Then he sat on the ground in the darkness and listened to the catastrophic pounding of his heart.

Then, from the silence, he heard strange whimpering sounds. He struggled to open the rucksack and fumbled for his torch. He switched it on.

Trapped in its bewildered beam, like two tiny elves, he saw a boy and a girl of seven or eight years of age. He drew his breath in sharply and stared.

Chapter Thirty One

For Jack, the day after the storm was intensely frustrating. He arose that morning feeling somewhat better than the night before and prepared for the grim tasks that lay ahead.

Unfortunately he was to be thwarted at every turn. The day began badly and got progressively worse. Phone lines were disrupted and the internet signal, poor at best, was completely down. It was after midday before he managed to get a line to the city and to make the enquiries he needed and considerably longer before he could confirm from various unwilling and uncooperative sources that his suspicions were correct and had a ghastly logic of their own.

Eventually the first phone call came through in the early afternoon. Jack grabbed the receiver. A colleague in the city had spent a begrudging hour retrieving details of the events Kate had unfolded about the death of Helen.

'Hello,' he said, 'Yes?' He listened and nodded. He snapped a few sharp questions and listened closely to the response, demanding frequent repetitions 'Names! Can you give me the names?' He listened again and jotted something on a piece of paper. 'Can you find out the whereabouts of this Russell Dean?' he asked. 'I know! I know! You have work of your own to do but this really is important. It's not pretend-important, not form filling important, not target achieving important, but real life and death important. Humour your country cousin just this once, eh?'

He put the phone down and sat back on his chair, his hands supporting his head. His eyes were moist. He sniffed and wiped his face in embarrassment and turned his back to his bewildered and concerned colleagues.

Half an hour later the phone call came through. Jack listened.

'Yes,' he said and he sighed deeply, 'yes, it is what I expected. You say he's been missing for four weeks? I think I may have found him. I'll get back to you.'

It took a few moments for Jack to compose himself and assume a professional air. He walked across to his colleagues.

'I've found the link that connects our dead men to each other,' he said slowly, 'and I know the hideous truth that connects them to their murderer. I also know who that murderer is and, God knows, I wish I didn't.'

They looked round, open mouthed, as expectant as baby birds. He stroked back his hair, nervously, and then spoke again, quickly, sharply, business like. His words were flat and meaningless and hollow. It was as if someone else was speaking. It wasn't him. It wasn't real. He wasn't even here, in this room, with these people. He was numb, without warmth, without feeling.

'I need you to check a few details for me,' he said bleakly. 'You will need to be discreet and I don't want any of this getting back to our visiting city colleagues. The Chief will be sitting in front of his computer screen at the moment waiting for service to be resumed. He may have a long wait but that is all to our advantage. Without his internet he is paralysed. Until it is restored he is incapable of 'progressing matters' – I think that was the phrase.'

Jack tried to assume his normal cutting tone but it didn't work. Julie and Phil attempted smiles which faded like shadows in fog. He briefly told them what he knew.

'But it couldn't be!' said Phil. 'I mean, it's just not credible. Why would he? What....?'

'God knows,' said Jack, 'I wish it wasn't true; but it is, it is.'

Jack explained patiently and painfully. His voice was heavy and it cracked and faded at times as he unfolded the tale. Occasionally, despite his efforts, he could barely restrain the emotions he felt, which were forcing their way through all his defences and broke on his surface like a wave. He suddenly stopped as if assailed by a sudden vision from which he could not escape. This wasn't some puzzle, some game to play. It couldn't be thrust to a cynical distance by the ironic play of words or the hardening of a heart. This was him and Kate, Sandy and Helen; it was love and life and death. It was grief and parting, regret and sorrow. It was a tragedy through which they had walked together as through a tunnel. It was only now that they had emerged from the tunnel and Jack was suddenly and utterly exposed to the devastation and waste through which they had moved. The world lay barren and empty around him, a derelict, decomposing, stagnating mire. People stood like corpses amid apocalyptic ruins and rubble. In his vision he clung to Kate and she to him and their children walked towards them from the shattered horizon. Sandy stood there alone. He stared outwards and Jack shuddered as he saw the look of utter isolation, utter loneliness and despair in his eyes.

He was rescued by an unlikely source. There was a nervous knock at the door. He blinked his eyes and drew himself back from the precipice over which he leaned and looked to see who was entering. He had been interrupted by the arrival of Sandy's twin assistants who, unable and unwilling to communicate by phone and unable to remain where they were, had made the courageous decision to leave their place of work and search for Jack at the Police Station. Rebecca pushed Duncan forward and then closed the door carefully behind her and slunk into the shadow of his angular form.

'You'll need to come back with us,' Duncan told him, his brow furrowed like a dry tuber.

'Straight away,' Rebecca nodded, peering from her place of concealment, 'You'll have to come straight away. We don't want to say anything here,' she added mysteriously, 'because we don't know what it means and we don't want to make a mistake or do anything wrong.' She looked anxiously at Duncan who nodded supportively.

'It won't wait,' he said and then, fearing that such a degree of insistence was beyond his lowly status, added meekly, 'if you don't mind.'

Jack donned an outdoor coat and, with a grimace towards Julie and Phil, conveyed instructions that did not require the medium of words. At the door he stopped momentarily and turned back.

'If Detective Chief Inspector Cool arrives or phones, tell him to go to hell. I'm sure you will think up your own careful and diplomatic phrasing. I want to see this business through without that interfering twerp getting involved. These are our crimes,' He paused and looked suddenly older and more troubled, 'and this is our tragedy.'

He followed the mortuary assistants back to the laboratory where he was forewarned about what lay within by an overpowering stench of decay that emanated from behind the doors. He accepted a carefully proffered mask but still held his hand over his nose and mouth as he pushed back the door and was assailed by the full force of the nauseous smell inside.

Laid out on the table, as if ready for autopsy lay the purple and putrid, decaying remains of a barely recognisable figure, - barely recognisable but nonetheless identified by Jack with scarcely a glance.

'This, my dears, is the very late Russell Dean,' he said. 'He has been missing from his home for several weeks but no-one thought sufficiently highly of him to consider sharing that information with us. Russell here is our corpse from the cave,' he added quietly by way of clarification. 'I believe he had been hidden away in one of the unused and locked compartments that Sandy may have told you about. It would appear that the normal refrigeration procedures were not consistently applied.'

He said no more, although he privately wondered if these compartments had been locked all those years ago precisely because they might be needed for such a grotesque eventuality. The plan for these murders had been a long time brewing. Probably not, he told himself, probably not. He didn't want to think about it.

Russell Dean, he now knew, was also the driver of the car which had ploughed at speed into Helen and had left her to die alone in a ditch by the roadside. The phone calls had conformed that.

He left the assistants to secure the rotting cadaver and, having made a brief phone call to his office, walked across the town to the quiet street where Sandy lived in a small, detached house neatly gardened and half hidden behind shrubs and bushes. The house was dark and deserted. He walked around and peered in the different windows. Everything inside was meticulously tidy and clean. It looked as if it were inhabited by someone who shared none of the traits of normal, untidy, chaotic humanity. It had the look of a house that was only superficially inhabited, as if walked through by a ghost which left no trace of its passing.

It was the anniversary of Helen's death. Sandy would be at home alone. It was what he always did. He would have taken the photographs from the drawer and caressed them, one by one, and floundered in grief. It was a service he attended annually and at which he officiated as mourner and priest.

Jack looked at the blank upper windows. No light, no sign of movement or life was betrayed within. He would have to return with a warrant. It was not what he wanted to do. He wanted to resolve this alone, just him and Sandy, friend to friend. Warrants and the harsh formalities of cold, professional practice were not for him, here, now. Leave that to Captain Cool and the other Computer Age Super Heroes.

But where would he find Sandy? Where could he be?

The answer cam to him immediately and simply and with a certainty that defied all logic. He turned and walked through the lonely streets to his office.

It was much later before Jack heard about the two children missing on the moor. A mountain rescue team from Portskail would be setting out to search for them within the hour. Unfortunately, the weather, which had been relatively calm all day, was becoming rather fractious and difficult again. It blew petulant clouds and dropped surly mists and stamped occasional showers on the darkening roads. The day was heading begrudgingly towards mid evening. Jack worried that the children might not be found before dark. If the weather came in as it threatened to do they would have little chance of survival out there on the high moor. He hoped their fathers would find them and not fall victim to the same menace.

He remained in his office awaiting news. He phone Alice to offer what reassurance he could. It was not much. He spoke of his confidence, his knowledge of the rescue team, their skills and determination. He told Alice and Meg to be patient, to expect the best. They would all be found and found soon. The children would be with their fathers and they would have found shelter for the night. It would all be well. He spoke with quiet confidence but it was much more than he felt. If the weather worsened, even the rescue team might be forced to retire for what was left of the night.

They still hadn't been found when he returned home late that evening. Kate heard his familiar step and the door opening slowly but it was much later before his agitation and distress could be expressed even to her.

He spoke about the missing children first; then, in a dull and broken voice, he told her what he had discovered about the murders. 'It was Sandy,' he said and he held his head in his hands as if overwhelmed by the anguish that dwelt there. 'It was Sandy all the time.'

'What? What do you mean?'

'Sandy is our murderer. Sandy killed the men in the graveyard and by the war memorial and he killed the man in the cave as well.'

Kate's face flushed with shock. She sat beside him and held his hand and he slowly unfolded the details of his sad and gruesome discoveries.

'You see,' he explained, 'the police always suspected that the driver of the car that killed Helen had been drinking. The tyre marks and other factors also led them to suspect the car was travelling at a reckless speed. They also believed that the car actually stopped some distance beyond the body and the driver ran back. Helen was rolled into the side of the road and left there. Worst of all, she was probably still alive when they left her and died alone in that ditch hours later.'

'….and Sandy knew all this?'

'Oh yes, Sandy knew. It has haunted him ever since.'

'….and the other two men, who were they?'

'They were in the car. I would guess that Malcolm McColm was in the front passenger seat. He saw what happened but would not say what he saw. The eyes were our clue. He said he didn't see; he was blind to what had happened. William McPhee was in the back. He heard the other two, he knew what they had said but he would not say what he heard; hence the removal of the tongue. They conspired together to hide what they knew. They escaped prosecution and punishment and went on with their lives, successfully in two cases and rather less so in the case of our Russell Dean. He had drifted from alcohol to drugs and petty crime and from relationship to relationship, like a destructive nomad. He had no criminal convictions but the evidence of his lifestyle was clear enough.'

'I would hazard a guess that Sandy met Dean quite fortuitously, probably at some court hearing where Russell was appearing for some reason. I doubt Dean even recognised him but Sandy knew Dean alright. He would have arranged a meeting, probably with the promise of a potential financial advantage or some other precept which appealed to Russell's sense of greed. How the murder was committed I don't as yet know and how Sandy could have transported him to the cave is beyond me, but that is certainly what happened.'

'But why was he left naked? What did the presence of the children's clothes signify?' She stopped and went deathly pale. She sat down heavily on a chair and stared. 'Oh, no Jack!' she said, 'Oh please, no!' She looked up. 'Helen was pregnant, wasn't she?'

Jack nodded.

'But they were a child's clothes; they weren't baby clothes. I still don't understand.'

'Let's keep to the things we do understand,' Jack sighed. 'It's easier. Sandy knew about the cave. It was where Helen had been working on the day she was killed. Why naked? Until we ascertain the cause of death everything is speculation but, for what it's worth,

I think Sandy somehow managed to disable Russell Dean. He was a big lout of a man; he would have been more than a match for poor Sandy who, after all, hardly has the build of a street fighter. I think, having drugged and disabled Russell, he transported him to the cave, removed his clothes and left him there to die of exposure.'

'And your witness from Aultmore......'

'.......ah, that was pure, unfortunate coincidence. Having disposed of Russell, Sandy knew he would need to complete his task before the body was found and identified. He must have imagined he had plenty of time. No-one would be likely to discover a body in such a remote location. It must have come as something of a shock to find it being trundled into the mortuary so very soon after.'

'So it was Sandy who moved the body in the mortuary and who then hid it?'

'Of course,' Jack said. 'He only needed a few days to complete his work and that was easily bought. Since he was also in charge of the autopsies he was also uniquely positioned to hide any details that he didn't want exposed. He had also provided himself with a very useful insurance policy – the empty, sealed off compartments, remember? I still don't know whether that was by accident or design. They had been empty for years. Who would think of looking in them now? Certainly not the two anxious beings he has working for him!'

'And what better place could you think of to hide a body than in a mortuary,' Kate concluded. 'But he must have known he would be caught?'

'Yes, of that I am sure. He had no desire to escape justice. He said so himself. He is one of the damned. The next two murders were planned very carefully and the locations of the bodies were intended to convey their significance - a memorial to despair and a memorial to futile, arbitrary death. That's how Sandy would have seen it. The deaths were sacrificial. Of course, they would both have been dead before the unpleasant wounds were administered. Sandy is no sadistic butcher. He was also uniquely placed both by nature and opportunity to ensure the crime scenes betrayed little or no evidence. Who but Sandy would have carried a wheelbarrow to transport a body? Who would have carried a garden rake to straighten grass and remove any trace of footsteps and tyre marks from the gravel path? He was also on the scene very early – even before I got there – and so had the opportunity to remove any lingering trace that the darkness of the previous night had obscured.'

'He went into the church?' Kate asked.

'He took his shoes off at the door and walked in. He placed them by his feet and he sat and he contemplated what he had done. Would it be too much to imagine that he spoke to Helen? I don't think so. Who else could possibly understand?'

'Where is he now?' Kate asked.

'He's at the cave!' he told Kate. 'I knew immediately. Don't ask me how! He has gone to the cave. It was where Helen had been working on that last day; it was where he took the body of Russell Dean. It is where he will have headed this evening and it is where we shall find him when the weather clears.'

'Will he be alright?'

'I don't know. I don't know. I just know that there are so many things I want to say to him, to ask him. I want to tell him I'm sorry. I'm scared that I may never have the chance.'

'But what have you to be sorry for?'

Jack shrugged helplessly and gestured around him and finally at the window, the empty street, the desolate hills and the vast unending sky.

The phone rang as the first dull light of morning dropped dismally over the town. The helicopter was on its way to take him to the cave. From there it would join the search for the missing people. It was time to go. He turned and hugged Kate then gathered together the few items he needed and clothed himself for the journey. A few moments later he was on his way to the landing pad and, within an hour, as the sun opened a bleary eye on the finite world, he found himself whisked out, over the town and away over the lanes and rivers to the moor. He was surprised with what certainty he travelled and with what faith that he knew – absolutely knew – he would find the cave. He was less certain that it would answer all his questions.

Even when the helicopter slowed and sank and eventually settled on a level area of lichen, heather and stone, the sun had barely touched the wet ground. Jack clambered out. A hundred yards away to his left he could see the familiar, pale escarpment. In the distance a group of patient figures were moving across the hillside; Mountain Rescue, he thought. Without waiting for the pilot, he walked towards the cave.

Chapter Thirty Two

The children cowered back and clung together. They could see nothing beyond the beam of torchlight in which they were trapped like butterflies at a window. Bethany whimpered and Euan cried, 'Please don't hurt us?'

The torch was turned off. 'Don't be frightened,' the voice told them. 'I mean you no harm. I expected no company and I wanted no company, but I'm glad of it now, very glad. Come; you look cold. Come and sit over here.'

The torch flashed again for a moment and indicated a patch of sandy soil. The bulky figure, half glimpsed in the shadow, struggled to his feet. The children didn't move. They clung even closer together and cried. They watched him stumble round the cave edge, selecting items from the ground, as they were caught in the faint beam. He returned after several minutes and dropped a number of dry heather roots, branches and sticks onto the floor. They heard a crack and noticed a strange smell, rather like petrol. He had broken a cigarette lighter and spilt the fluid on the sticks. A moment later a match struck and the small bundle of dry tinder burst into flames and illuminated the deeper corners of the cave and a small, low tunnel beyond. Ungainly shadows danced monstrously then settled back in dark corners. The fire illuminated the figure that had so terrified them a moment earlier.

'Come over here,' said the strange man, 'Sit here and share the warmth of the fire. It won't last forever; nothing does. You should gather what you can of it before the darkness and the cold return. It's still a long time until dawn.'

The children, drawn by the glow of the flames and the promise of warmth, drew carefully closer until they entered the glowing dome of light. They watched the strange man carefully. They had been warned about strangers. He might be evil and cruel; he might hurt them. He too was watching. He watched them as he might watch small, wild animals but there was a strange sense of wonder in his eyes. There were things about their movements and their fears that he knew and understood; but so much was a mystery, a secret not yet revealed even to them.

'Are you a stranger?' Bethany ventured, bravely, anxiously.

The man smiled. 'Aren't we all?' he said. Then he added reassuringly, 'But you have no need to fear me. No harm will come to you and you will be safe here until morning.'

'What will happen in the morning?' Euan asked nervously, imagining himself momentarily as the breakfast for some grey ogre.

'They will come for you,' the man sighed wearily. Then he smiled. 'All those people to whom you are so very, very precious will come for you.' He turned suddenly towards the back of the cave and the hollow tunnel. 'Did you hear that? I heard laughter again; I thought it was you but I was wrong. Listen! They are laughing and playing, even there. Can you hear the echo of their voices? They are like a memory, a strange memory of what might have been or should have been.'

Bethany and Euan tried hard but the only sound they heard was the gentle trickling of water echoing hollowly as it fell and rolled into the blackness. But Bethany knew what he had heard.

'That is Hannah and Tom,' she tried to explain. 'They are from long ago. They brought us onto the moor to play with them. Then they lead us here to the cave to be safe.....with you,' she added. 'This belonged to Hannah.' She held Daisy gently in her hands and held her for Sandy to see.

The old man, for he seemed as old as the cave to the children, was dressed in light and shadows as the fire danced. He was like a story book creature. His features, cragged and hollowed and carved with the fire glow, were like the rock around them. He took Daisy gently and looked at her and for a moment seemed lost in thought; then he handed her back.

'Who are you? Are you their father?' Euan asked, and then immediately felt foolish.

The old man didn't laugh at him. He merely smiled wearily and leaned forward over the fire. Bethany, to whom both questions seemed equally sensible, merely waited to see if the old man would answer. At last he did.

'Perhaps they are my children,' he said. He spoke to the children and to the flames. He looked towards the passage. 'I would like to meet them if they are.' He was silent a moment. 'But I shall not.' His voice was barely audible. The last words were spoken so quietly they were heard only by him. 'You are still shivering,' he suddenly said. 'The fire makes you warm on the front but your backs remain in the cold of the cave. Here,' He shuffled to his feet and removed his coat and jacket which were of sufficient size to cover both their shoulders. He wrapped them carefully round the children and then retreated back to his place by the fire.

'Why have you come here?' Bethany asked. 'Did you get trapped in the fog like us? Were you scared?'

'I came here to meet someone,' he told her. 'Look!' He took something from the edge of the darkness and dragged it into the light. It was the rucksack he had brought up the hill with him. He opened it and took out a bottle of champagne and two glasses. He then removed the modest lunch box which he had carefully packed earlier in the day. 'We are going to have a picnic. She will be here soon, although she will not come out of the darkness and join us.'

'Is she shy?' asked Euan.

'And beautiful?' asked Bethany, for whom the presence of a princess was far from unrealistic.

'She is the most beautiful and kindly person in the whole world,' Sandy told them, 'but you will have to imagine her. No-one can see her but me.' He nodded towards the back of the cave. 'I think she is down there with your lost friends. She likes children. She will look after them.' He was startled from his reverie by a trickling of stones falling, 'Here, have some of our food,' he told the children, 'You must be hungry.'

'Won't the princess mind?' asked Bethany.

'She would want you to have it. Here, I'll keep a bit of cake for her.'

'It tastes like wedding cake,' Euan said.

They had not eaten very much since lunch and Sandy watched them eat the small sandwiches and cake. It was not long before the box was empty. He did not eat anything himself. He did not need to. He reached over and took something from the pocket of his overcoat. 'Here,' he said, handing them a bar of chocolate each. 'Save these for when you wake in the morning. It will help stave off the hunger until help arrives. Now,' he sighed, 'it is time you slept.'

He took the coat from their shoulders and laid it on the cold ground. They lay down, suddenly sleepy from the heat, the exertion of the day and the food they had eaten. Sandy put his jacket carefully across them and tucked them in as if they were in a bed.

'Why are you dressed funny?' Beth asked sleepily.

'I'm getting married tomorrow,' Sandy said with a shy, sad smile.

'Is that why you've got a flower in your coat?'

'Yes, that's why I have the flower.'

'Will you marry the princess?' Beth asked.

He nodded. 'I will marry the princess, yes! Good night.'

Sandy moved away to the edge of the darkness and opened the champagne. He poured two glasses and made a silent toast. He was aware that the fire was sinking and the embers were fading fast and clambered to his feet. He needed wood, roots, anything to keep the flames alive just a few hours longer. He carefully followed the edge of the cave, searching in his torch bean, gathering what he could. There wasn't much and the land outside had nothing to offer that would be of use. He removed his shoes and smiled ruefully.

'No need for these any more,' he smiled. He lifted some sticks and placed the shoes carefully beneath them. 'The finest leather,' he commented, 'and the finest silk,' he added, as he dropped his tie onto the embers, 'A sacrifice on the dying embers of my hope of redemption.' His socks too were added to the flames.

He looked again. In a distant corner of the cave, fleetingly illuminated by the flames, he could see a small piece of fabric, a torn piece of old clothing. He crawled over and picked it up, handling it gently as he brought it into the firelight to see it more clearly. He stifled a cry and his hands shook. He crumpled it tightly in his hand.

'Perhaps it was you all along,' he murmured. He looked at the faded cloth and smiled strangely. 'This I cannot burn,' he said softly. He glanced towards the dark tunnel. His lips moved as if he was speaking but no words emerged.

There was a sound on the wind beyond the cave. He turned and listened. Was it an animal, perhaps? No, not an animal! He listened. There it came again, rising and falling as the wind rose and fell, carried to him like flotsam on the waves of air. It was a call, a name, like the cry of a bird.

'Bethany! Euan!'

'Euan! Bethany!'

A song, a bird call, a lonely voice, losing hope and losing life, kept going by what? Kept alive by what? They could not last the night out there.

He stumbled barefoot to the entrance of the cave and stared out into the fog, the rain and the darkness. The pains in his chest, never completely subdued, re-emerged with increased force. Breathing grew more and more difficult. He dragged air into his lungs and, barely used, cast it out again. He could see little but there was a faint beam from a fading torch. He knew now they were heading towards him, shouting their calls like repeated beacon cries. Euan! Bethany! Bethany, Euan!

By the time their shapes emerged from the mist, one on hands and knees, the other offering weak support, he was soaked and he shivered with cold. He smiled grimly to imagine what sort of spectre he appeared, barefoot, dressed in shirt, waistcoat and suit trousers. He did not smile for long. The chill and the damp were weapons in merciless hands. The two men, despite their protective armoury were cold and near exhaustion. He would wave his torch to lead them to the cave and to the fire and, warmest of all, to the children. Then he would disappear and be seen no more.

The children stirred and their tired eyes saw what they feared might be a dream. The old man had gone and in his place stood their fathers looking down at them and smiling. But it was no dream and soon they were enfolded in caring arms and hugged until they thought their bones would be crushed to powder and their breath driven out. Then they sat by the fire and grew slowly warmer and felt gradually safer and their conversation, which came at first like a storm blast and then light flurries, settled and grew calm. The children drowsed and the fathers, having shared a few last joyful words, fell into their own exhausted sleep.

Sandy slipped away from the circle of firelight, unseen. It was theirs now. That soft circle was for them. He had no place there. He stood by the wall of the cave beside the tunnel which fell hollow behind him. He watched and he listened as if hearing distant voices and laughter. Then he stirred himself and crept round the cave and gathered what few sticks remained and laid them quietly on the flames.

'No need now for this now,' he said, and stripped the waistcoat from his back and folded it into the embers. It too could be sacrificed on this strange altar of life. He wouldn't need it where he was going. In shirt and trousers he crept over to where the bottle and glasses lay. He gathered these and items from the bag, which then became fuel, and he crept, crawled now, to his place by the wall, by the tunnel, in the darkness. For a while he just sat there and listened. He could hear voices. The cave echoed with the sound of childish voices and childish laughter. The tunnel was full of them. He heard another voice too, rising over theirs with tones a mother might use. He heard her again, coming closer to him and closer still until he heard new and different words, addressed to him now and whispered in his ear in the tones of a lover and friend.

'Forgive me,' he cried and wept and he knew she did for she understood; she understood as no-one else could because she knew him as if she had created him as he had created her. This was not peace or redemption but it had something of both. It was not despair despite the absence of hope. He had been drawn to the heart of loneliness and was not alone. He clung by the slenderest thread of imagination and compassion to a world rejected and rejecting.

He pours the glasses with trembling hands, numb now with cold. He fumbles in the bag for syringe and tablets; coolly administered and without grief. He raises the glass, the final dregs: 'To us!' he smiles and he hears voices, far down in the black cave and they call him; she calls him. 'Coming, my love,' he whispers and he slips into the long tunnel and is swallowed by darkness.

In the early dawn the children slowly open tired eyes. 'What's that rumbling noise?' they ask drowsily and their fathers tell them, 'It's a helicopter. It's come to rescue us. It's time to go home.' They smile. 'We're safe!' they say.

'Where's the old man who saved us?' Euan asks.

Garth remembers a light, briefly glimpsed, which led them to the cave. He thinks about the fire and he sees the coats which kept the children warm. He notices for the first time the half burnt clothing on the dead fire. He turns and sees in the wisp of light from the rising sun a dark tunnel. He stumbles towards it and in its depths by torchlight he sees a hunched body lying curled and motionless. He crawls back and conveys a wordless message to Marcus; they distract the children, wake them, tell them they must head out into the cold morning, that their mothers are waiting for them and there will be breakfast and warm fires. But first they must shout. The helicopter pilot won't know they are there. They must shout, shout loud and keep shouting to tell him we're here! We're here!

They don't have time to shout much. They have barely escaped into the morning light when Garth sees a familiar wiry figure crossing towards them. Jack! Jack beams a wide smile. He shakes their hands, hugs the children. 'The helicopter will take you back,' he tells them, 'a treat to end your adventures! Sandy?' he asks Garth.

'He saved our lives. He's in the cave but……..'

Jack already knows; he knew before he set out. His smile fades and he feels lonely and old.

'Take them home.' He tells the pilot. 'There's no hurry here.'

'And you?' the pilot asks.

'I'll stay here with my friend.'

Jack walks slowly towards the cave. He pauses for a moment before bending to clamber into the small entrance and then waits again until his eyes grow accustomed to the gloom. Outside, the helicopter rotors throb into life and lift the families into the air. The sound slowly fades to a slow pulse and then nothing.

Jack shines a torch down the narrow passage. He sees the curled body of Sandy deep in the tunnel and makes his way to it. He sits down beside him and takes a cold hand in his. It is a moment before he sees, through tears, the note clasped in the other dead hand, 'to my dear, dear friends, Jack and Kate.' It takes another moment for him to see, drawn by a finger in the wet clay, one word, 'Helen'. Beside it lies a piece of old and crumpled cloth.

He shudders as if a cold breeze, whipped from the dark depths of the tunnel, has suddenly passed through him.

'Kate,' he whispers, 'Kate.'

Lightning Source UK Ltd.
Milton Keynes UK
UKOW03f1258221014

240480UK00003B/81/P